A TALE OF

LIGHT
AND
SHADOW

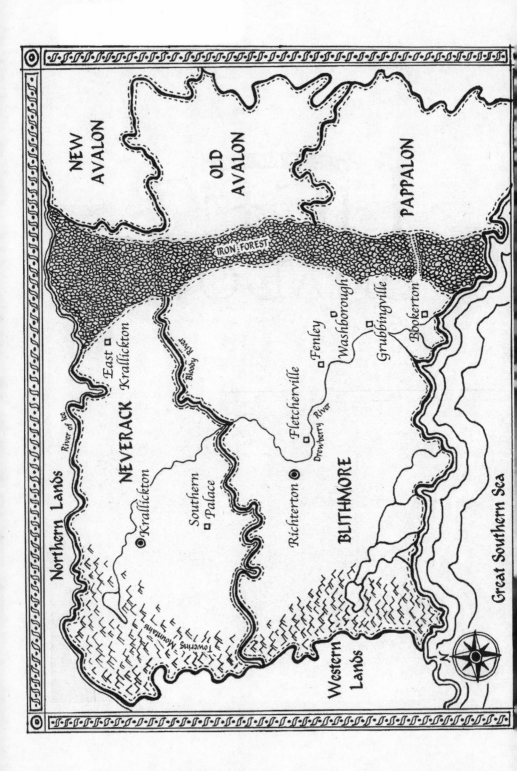

A TALE OF
LIGHT
AND
SHADOW

JACOB GOWANS

SHADOW
MOUNTAIN

Visit us at ShadowMountain.com

First printing in hardbound 2014
First printing in paperbound 2015

Library of Congress Cataloging-in-Publication Data
Gowans, Jacob, author.
  A tale of light and shadow / Jacob Gowans.
    pages cm
  ISBN 978-1-60907-872-0 (hardbound)
  ISBN 978-1-60907-981-9 (paperbound)
  [1. Love—Fiction. 2. Kings, queens, rulers, etc.—Fiction. 3. Adventure and adventurers—Fiction.] I. Title.
  PZ7.G7468Tal 2014
  [Fic]—dc23   2014000273

Printed in the United States of America
Lake Book Manufacturing, Inc., Melrose Park, IL

10 9 8 7 6 5 4 3 2 1

To Lily,
whose presence in my life
is a constant light.

Contents

CONTENTS

The Old Man

C an't your horses go any faster?" I begged the driver for the third time. My head stuck out the carriage window, and the chilled wind blew hard against my face, stinging my nose and ears enough to force me to withdraw back inside.

"I'm sorry, sir." The thick wool scarf wrapped around the driver's mouth muffled his husky voice. "These aren't the youngest horses in town, and I'm afraid they tend to stiffen up in the cold."

I glanced at the sun, low on the cloudless, violet horizon and ready to disappear at any moment. One moon already shone high and bright. The other two could hardly be seen, but I found them after a brief search of the sky.

"I can't lose this job." I'd be hard-pressed to find much more in my line of work. With the last remaining sunlight, I opened my traveling bag and checked my supplies, counting everything for the last time.

"Everything's here," I reassured myself, "and that may be the only positive thing this whole evening."

"What's that, sir?" my driver called out.

"Nothing. I was only speaking to myself." I shivered and pulled my cloak tighter around my neck.

"We're almost there, sir. Just passing onto the main road now. The inn's just ahead."

I considered asking him if he could go even slightly faster, but

decided against it. Fortunately for me, he was right. We arrived at
the inn in moments, and no sooner had the carriage stopped than
I let myself out, clutching my bags in one arm while my other hand
searched my pockets.

"I could have gotten that for you, sir," the carriage driver said. He
was a heavy man with a thick brown beard that made his red nose
appear like a small beet surrounded by dirt.

I replied with a weak smile as my searching became more frantic.
"Er, how much do I owe you?" I asked, though I knew the amount.

"Three silvers should do it, though I wouldn't say no to a gratuity!"
He guffawed at his own joke.

His answer bought me the time I needed, and there, in the deepest recess of my pocket, was the amount I had been certain I possessed. I paid him the three silvers, apologized that I couldn't pay
more, and bade him a good night.

The inn was on a crowded street lined with shops, homes, empty
market stalls, stables, and quite a few buildings I couldn't identify at
sunset. Standing outside the inn, hearing the sounds and smelling the
food, I could sense it was alive with business. My stomach gave an
angry lurch, and I went straight in.

Bodies filled nearly every chair. Mugs and plates littered the
tables. More food and drink poured out from the kitchen, served by
beautiful women whose perfume mingled with the smell of herbs and
meats to form a truly divine scent. Men played dice games in one corner and bet on ring tosses in another. The inn was a good one, better
than most I'd visited.

I spotted the man I was certain must be the owner. He stood
not far from the kitchen, speaking to a table of well-dressed men.
I made my way forward, noting his neat work clothes, the walking
stick he didn't use, and his friendly habit of greeting everyone with an
arm around the neck or a firm pat on the shoulders. When I got near
enough to hear him, I noticed that he knew every customer's name.

He caught my eye as I approached, probably identifying me as someone needing assistance, so he concluded his conversation and gave me his full attention.

"Hello, young man." His voice was warm, and he offered me his hand. "Benjamin Nugget, owner of the Silver Nugget. How can I help you?"

"Geoffrey Freeman," I said, shaking his hand with vigor. "Just traveled up from Vistaville."

"You're here for tonight's entertainment?" His knack for listening made me feel as though the whole inn were as silent as a cemetery.

"Yes, but I also need lodging."

"I have plenty available. Almost everyone here is local. Do you plan to stay for more than a night?"

I informed him that I did. Then, due to my own embarrassment, the conversation became awkward. "You see, I used the last of my money to get here—the very last. However, I'm here for work. I mean, I have work. This is my work." I opened the bag stuffed with writing supplies. "I was hoping I might pay you at the end of my stay rather than at the beginning. I won't receive pay until after—"

"So you're the scribe!" Benjamin declared. Then he pointed at the bag I carried, filled with paper and ink and pens. "I should have noticed it sooner. Yes, yes, don't worry about a thing. I'd been told you were coming, but it slipped my mind. I'm certain I even saved you a place to sit."

Without any trouble, he procured me half of one table all to myself. As I sat, I thanked him for his kindness. Outside the window, the sun had vanished. I searched in vain for a clock, though I knew it had to be nearly time for the entertainment to begin. I went about preparing the table for my task, stacking a sheaf of paper next to me and then arranging the feather pens and inkwells as I liked them. A loud shout startled me, nearly causing me to spill my ink.

"Say, when's the storyteller getting here?" a man sitting behind me called out. "Should be near that time."

"Any moment now," Benjamin responded smoothly. "Have another drink." That brought several laughs and mutters. Benjamin returned to his duties, observing the women distributing his food and ale and checking on the cooks in the kitchen.

After several minutes of waiting, my papers were perfectly arranged, my quills lay ready, and I'd set out a few candles to ensure myself enough light to see my notes. All I needed was someone to dictate.

"Is everything all right, Mr. Freeman?" Benjamin said to me as he passed by my table.

I could see sweat forming on his brow, and his eyes kept flitting to the door. I smiled sympathetically. "Perhaps I should ask you the same thing."

He forced a small chuckle and looked around the tavern. "In a few more minutes, I'll be handing out free rounds and apologizing for the absence of my distinguished guest." He took out a modest cloth from his pocket, wiped the perspiration from his forehead, and excused himself. He ran about offering apologies for the delay and trying to put off the moment of surrender as long as possible. Then several men who had been betting on dice stood and marched to the door.

"Gentlemen, please!" Nugget exclaimed.

The men stopped at the threshold as though they had walked into an invisible barrier. Most of the other patrons did not seem to notice this because the volume in the tavern was louder than ever. The men at the door parted to reveal a bent-over old man with long white hair and a clean-shaven face wearing a worn traveling cloak and magnificent riding boots. He might have been tall once, but he was so hunched over now that no one would ever guess.

The magnitude of his presence was so great that the tavern, beginning with those closest to the door and moving toward those nearest

4

to me, fell silent until the only sounds came from the cooks in the kitchen. Every eye (including mine) was fixed upon the man, yet he took little notice of the change in the crowd as he drew a long wooden cane from the folds of his cloak and struck the floor with a resonating tap. Each small step the old man took was accompanied by another tap, and the eyes of the patrons followed him. When the old man finally reached the small stage where a chair waited for him, he gently set his cane on the floor and sat. I heard his joints creak and pop as he bent. When his body finally reached the seat, a collective sigh broke through the audience and was quickly hushed.

"Water, please," the old man said to no one in particular. A mug of water was in Benjamin Nugget's hand nearly faster than the words registered in my ears. The old man received it gratefully, took a small sip, cleared his throat, and lifted his head. He had many features common to men fortunate enough to reach such a ripe age: large ears whose lobes hung down his cheeks and a grand nose, red from the same cold I'd experienced. His eyes shone so brightly that I doubted his memory had dulled a whit. His lips were heavy and thick. All this made the tufts of long white hair on his scalp appear even whiter.

With a brief glance his eyes surveyed the large crowd. For a moment they rested upon me, startling me from my entranced state. I grabbed my pen, dipped it into the ink, and let the excess drip steadily into the inkwell. The blank paper called to me to fill it with words.

"Love . . ." he began, his voice low but strong, ". . . friendship. Do these words mean anything to us anymore? We throw them around like bare chicken bones. Nothing is more precious or powerful than *true* love. Nothing is more valuable than a *real* friend. Not armies or navies, not governments or gold, not even those who walk in Light and Shadow. Some people live life without experiencing what it actually means to have either. I pity them."

A flinch rippled through the crowd as the old man surveyed them with the utmost seriousness.

"Great things are born of great loves and friendships. Such are the essence of stories. Such things bring me here today, for I shall tell you of a man who was fortunate to have both. Indeed, some might say that to love and to be a friend were his only real skills. In this world of light and shadow, his magnificent light attracted the equally terrible shadows of the world—horrific powers that tested his love and friendships to their utmost cores. The tale begins here . . . in Blithmore, although I have never told the story in this land before tonight, and I may never speak of it here again. I will tell you about a man named Henry Vestin, a woman named Isabelle Oslan, and those closest to them.

"This story begins many, many years ago, in a time when there were still nobles and kings and emperors. Atolas was a different world, almost. King Sedgwick Germaine had been sitting on the throne for . . . forty-one years. Nobles in Blithmore in that day were distinguished not by ownership of land, but by occupation and title only. After all, it was King Germaine's father who gave all Blithmorians the right to own land. So it was that Henry Vestin's father owned a wood-carving shop near the heart of the capital, Richterton, and earned the reputation of a fine master of his art.

"Behind Master Vestin's house and across a very large lawn stood Oslan Manor, owned by Lord Rogar Oslan. Only a row of tall evergreens separated the properties. Lord Oslan's gardener had planted the hedge two years before Henry's birth, the same year James Oslan was born. It was Lord Oslan's way of trying to forget the Vestins existed at all. He was among the poorest of the nobles, having made several bad investments in exotic juices, cutlery, 'healing oils,' and other things of that nature. Master Vestin, on the other hand, amassed a respectable wealth, especially for a shop owner.

"Despite the disparity in riches, the two families were alike in many ways. For example, they each had one elder boy and one younger girl, although Mr. and Mrs. Vestin also later took in a foster child, Ruther, who turned out to be quite a disaster. Both fathers were strict and both mothers wanted their children to be given every possible advantage in life. As it so happens, this was a time in Blithmore's history when education had become quite popular, even for women. So fashionable was it that Henry's mother, Mrs. Vestin, earned a certificate from the Office of Royal Educators so she could set about teaching her two children.

"Desperate to keep her own children fashionable, but unable to afford the cost of sending them to school with other young nobles, Lady Oslan made an unconventional arrangement with Mrs. Vestin and sent her two children through the evergreen hedge every morning to be taught alongside Henry and his sister, Margaret.

"On the first day of class, Henry dumped a handful of dirt into Isabelle's hair. Isabelle screamed until her brother, James, became so angry that he wrestled Henry to the ground, tearing Henry's shirt in the process. This behavior so offended Lord and Lady Oslan that if Mrs. Vestin hadn't apologized in person and assured them of an immediate change in her son's behavior, that would have been the end of it all, and there would be no story to tell today.

"On the second day, out of revenge, Isabelle pinned Henry down and put her muddy handprints all over his new white shirt. And so began the long courtship of Henry Vestin and Isabelle Oslan. All they had left to do was to grow up like the evergreen trees of the hedge that separated their parents' properties—every year a little taller, a little older, and a little closer together."

ONE

Ruther and Henry

Henry shut the washroom door behind him and shed his work clothes so quickly that he tore his shirt. He pumped water into the tub, furiously working the lever, causing it to squeak and squeal like a small pig. As soon as the tub had enough water, Henry plunged himself in and scrubbed the dust and grime off his body and out of his hair. Wasting no time, he jumped out and dried himself as he ran back to his bedroom stark naked.

"Hey, friend," a deep voice called out. It came from a very tall man with shaggy red hair that sat on his head like a mop. His large gut wobbled in front of him as he strode down the hall toward Henry, waving with his long, thin hands.

Henry yelped and covered himself. "Ruther!" he exclaimed as he shut the door between them. "What are you doing here?"

"I came to wish you good luck. And I can see how badly you'll need it."

"I'm running late! My apprentices thought it would be funny to play a prank on me and turn the clock back. Then they forgot to tell me what they'd done." As soon as Henry had put on his under-garments, he opened the door for Ruther. "How was your trip?" he asked as he turned back to the clothes his sister, Maggie, had laid out for him to wear. He noticed Ruther seemed to have gained more weight, especially in his face. Ruther's fat face was almost always jovial, but, unfortunately, being fat in Blithmore had gone out of style three years ago when King Germaine had fallen ill for six months, finally reappearing at the baptism of his eldest granddaughter clearly missing fifty pounds.

"It was a very fine excursion. I was well received in every town." From under his vest, Ruther withdrew a small leather flask—no doubt containing ale—and took a long draught. "Everyone loved me."

"Isn't it a little early for drinking, Ruther?" Henry asked as he buttoned his shirt. When he reached the top button, he realized he'd done the buttons up wrong and started over.

"Never too early for that, friend," Ruther chuckled.

Henry's fingers worked furiously at the cloth and buttons, getting them right this time. He pulled up his pants and jammed the tails of his shirt inside. The blue scarf was next. Henry picked it up, trying to remind himself the proper way to tie it around his neck.

"Isabelle has assured me several times that her father will say yes, but I can't help but worry. What will I do if he says no?"

Ruther grinned and gave a hearty laugh. "Trust me, he won't. Not in his situation. You're wealthier than a tenth of the country's nobles—"

"That's only because a tenth of the country's nobles can't hold on to their money."

"He's one of the poorest and he knows it, friend."

"But I'm desperate! I can't marry her without his permission!"

"Yes, you are desperate, but so is he—he can't afford to pay a dowry to any respectable noble family. Everyone knows that regaining his social standing is all he cares about—and that's where you come in. If you ask for Isabelle's hand, he can demand you pay a bride price, which you have the ability to pay. Everyone wins."

Henry's concerns were not assuaged. "You know how he is, Ruther. You remember how he treated us when you lived here."

"Sure I do. That stick game we played one time . . . I went through the hedge to get my stick. He grabbed me and shook me. '*You dirty little boy—good for nothing bastard child! Get away from my house!*'"

Henry choked out a laugh that sounded more like a cough. Ruther had impersonated Lord Oslan to perfection. "Oslan has hated me since I was a lad."

"Has he *loathed* you?" Ruther asked. The tone in his voice told Henry that Ruther had started one of his word games.

"Yes." Henry's answer was weary. A look in the mirror told him his attempt to tie the scarf correctly had failed. He hurried to undo the damage. "That's one."

"Despised?"

"Definitely. Two."

"Abhorred?"

"Enough." Henry sighed as he rewrapped the blue silk, this time with more success. Then he adjusted his shirt again and tried to tuck the ends of his brown hair under his collar. He decided that looked ridiculous.

"Fine then, rehearse with me what you plan to say."

"I have to go!"

"Just once. No point in going if you aren't going to do it properly."

"Good evening, sir," Henry enunciated with careful measure. He tied off the scarf and reached for his boots. "It is an honor to speak with you man to man."

"If you say it like that, he'll think you're challenging him."

"He knows I'm not challenging him."

"Do you want my help or not?" Ruther asked.

"I have to go. I should've trimmed my hair. For the love of the King, nothing is right today!" Henry rarely concerned himself with things like clothes and hair. When Maggie thought he needed new clothes, she bought them. When his hair needed cutting, she cut it.

"Calm yourself," Ruther said, lifting the lid off his flask. "Things are not that bad."

"If he refuses me, I'll fall on my sword the moment I return to the house."

"You'd probably miss the sword and hit the floor."

Henry chuckled despite himself. Their eyes met in the mirror, and Ruther grinned at him. Henry was glad his friend had come; Ruther helped him keep a proper perspective.

"Lord Oslan won't refuse you," Ruther said. "If Isabelle is certain, then you can be too."

"Bah!" Henry exclaimed as he wiped his forehead with his sleeve. It came away with a good-sized wet spot. "I wish there were some other way than speaking to that man."

"Well, friend," Ruther said, getting up and taking a small swig from his flask, "you're the one who will be calling him *Father*, not me."

Henry watched Ruther take another drink with disappointment. "I wouldn't if I were you," he said. "It's too early. You'll be sick all day."

"No, I'll only be sick until evening."

"Just in time for your story."

Ruther took another long swig from the flask. "No, the owner canceled my performance."

"Why?"

"Possibly because I was so drunk last night, I couldn't pronounce my main character's name?"

"Which story was it?"

"The Tale of Thurgerburder the Furious Sheepherder."

Had it not been such an important day for Henry, he might not have held his tongue. Instead of speaking his mind, he straightened the scarf one last time.

"It doesn't matter," Ruther continued. "I've secured myself several jobs over the next three or four weeks in other towns not too far away. I'll be quite busy."

"When do you leave?"

"The next day or two." He took another long draught from the flask. "And where is Maggie in all of this? She should be here for support or familial obligation or whatever you call it."

"She's at the market, selling her cabbages before they rot."

Ruther went to the window and looked down to the street, then up at the sky. "If you're going the long way, you'd better be on the move!"

"All right, I am!" Henry put his tan cloak around his shoulders. "I'm gone!"

As he sprinted out of the bedroom and clattered down the wooden stairs, he heard Ruther call out to him in a woman's voice: "You look so *handsome!*"

TWO

Oslan Manor

enry lived on Shop Street, the busiest area of the city. Shop
Street had the reputation of selling the finest goods in
Richterton, the capital city of the kingdom of Blithmore, one
of the most powerful nations in all of Atolas. In the late afternoon,
Shop Street often caught the shadow of Germaine Castle looming in
the north. It was clearly visible on this bright, robust day, but Henry
set his sights on a closer goal: the next street up.

Shop Street, lined with modest but lovely homes, was never quiet
from sunup to sundown. Nearly all the houses were attached to a
shop, some even two. Lots of people. Lots of customers. Lots of life.
Henry loved that about the city and the street. At the moment, tinker-
ing sounds from old Master Franklin's silver shop were background
noise to his thoughts, in which he practiced again what he would
say to Lord Oslan. None of the words in his head sounded right. He
hoped it was just nerves. In the back of his mind, he heard his father's
voice saying the same words Henry often repeated to Brandol, his
journeyman: *Don't fret; do the best you can. If you make a mistake, it
can be fixed.* Henry had gotten past his fear of botching a carpentry job
long ago, but not his fear of Lord Oslan.

As he passed by the silver shop, a blast of hot air hit him, accompanied by a whiff of molten metal sweating out its impurities. It
was a scent he'd grown up around and knew as well as the difference

between pine and oak. The heat added a fresh layer of perspiration to his forehead, which he mopped away with his handkerchief.

"The big day, Master Henry?" the croaking voice of Master Franklin called out. The old silversmith stood in the open door of his shop, wearing the same heavy, stained apron he'd worn ever since Henry had known him. Henry's earliest memories of Master Franklin were of him perched in that doorway watching the streets with a hawkish fervor, just as he was today. Being called "Master" by the old silversmith still took some getting used to. At barely twenty-one, Henry's hard-earned title was still a novelty.

"Very big, Master Franklin," he answered, squinting into the shop from under his handkerchief. "One of the biggest."

"I think you look well-dressed for the occasion."

"Thank you."

"Don't put that there, you idiot boy!" Franklin screeched as he turned to check on his apprentices. "Are you trying to burn down my shop?"

"I—no—I—" a voice inside struggled to answer.

Henry could not remember the boy's name, but sympathized with him nonetheless. Master Franklin was a good man, but his wrath came both swift and strong.

"Stop stammering and clean it up," the silversmith said. Then over his shoulder he added, "Good luck, Master Henry!"

Henry picked up his pace, hoping as he did so to outrace the traces of doubt and doom trailing after him. He passed other stores, each with their own sounds or smells he could name by heart: a tailor shop, several blacksmiths of different specialties, a masonry, and a potter's shop, where three journeymen sat pumping wheels and shaping vessels while the apprentices prepared the glazes and portioned clay. Most of them knew his name and many called out to him. He either waved or responded with a short greeting. A sharp clatter came from the wheelwright's shop, and several wagon wheels bounced out into the street followed by two apprentices trying to catch them. Henry would have stopped to help them gather up the merchandise, but time was his greatest enemy. He rounded the corner, walked one block north up Richterton Lane, the city's main street, and turned east on Noble Road.

The scenery changed at once.

Gone were the shops. Houses, stables, and gardens ruled the landscape. The homes were larger, as were the tracts of land between each. Not the finest homes in Richterton—they stood too close to the guild district for that—but finer nonetheless. Henry paid them no attention. Their luster had worn off long ago. Only the one near the end of the row concerned him. His heartbeat quickened.

"Don't be a coward," he told himself. A trickle of sweat ran down his nose, and he deftly flicked it away. He turned around and peered back at the way he had come. The road back home seemed quite welcoming.

Oslan Manor was much smaller than the other houses on the row and set farther back, as though it had been tucked away so as to not spoil the grandeur of its neighbors. In Henry's youth, its blue paint had been bright, but only a trained eye could spot any color now. Cracked latticework surrounded the lower front windows. Tall grasses and weeds sprouted everywhere, surrounding the withering trees that had once borne blossoms and budding fruit this time of year. This season, Isabelle had only been able to coax one red rose to grow from the bushes, but the rose stood out proudly among the thorns and leaves. To the left Henry saw the stables, empty but for one horse, Esmond, an old gray beast who still clung to his haughty air.

Despite his familiarity with Oslan Manor, Henry felt like a stranger—or worse, an intruder. He crossed the dry lawns on a bare cobblestone walk and came to the large oak front doors, splitting with age and neglect. Henry had offered more than once to refinish and stain them free of charge, but to no avail. Taking one of the wolf-head knockers in hand, he brought it down gently on the metal plate. Almost immediately, the door opened to reveal an ancient man in servant's attire dabbing at his long drooping nose. Moisture hung about the baggy skin around his eyes and mouth, too, but the signs of his age failed to conceal the bright hazel shine of life in his squinting eyes.

"Master Henry," the servant said in a kind, but low, breaking voice. "Lord Oslan is in his den. You may meet him there."

Henry took several deep breaths as he tried to force the terror from his bosom. "Thank you, Norbin. Where's Isabelle?"

"In her room," Norbin answered, dropping his voice to add, "but she asked me to tell you that she has every confidence in you today."

"And Lady Oslan?"

Norbin sighed and gave Henry a grave glance. "In bed. Her condition continues to worsen."

He led Henry to the den. Because Norbin's spine was bending more and more with the weight of time, his pace was roughly that of a tortoise. Henry reminded Norbin that he knew the way to the den, but Norbin explained that Lord Oslan insisted on formality. The house, unlike the grounds, was well-kept despite the out-of-style and threadbare furnishings. Henry remembered the time he and Isabelle had left a trail of greenish mud through the kitchen and dining room. Lord Oslan's reaction to the mess had been tempestuous.

Quicker than he had wanted, Henry was at the den, a room he had seen many times. The room stank of old tobacco and vinegar. The mantel at the hearth was large and ornate with four magnificent portraits hanging above. Henry guessed a swipe of a finger along the mantel's length would yield little dust, if any. The portraits were of the Oslan family: Lord and Lady Oslan both appearing stately and well-groomed, their son, James, stiff in his military uniform, and their daughter, Isabelle. Even in the portrait, her exquisiteness shone. Henry had always found it ironic that a person such as Isabelle could come from a man like Lord Oslan. He glanced again at her portrait and found strength.

The doors shut tightly behind him, leaving him alone with the master of the household. Lord Oslan sat in the best chair in the house, wearing his finest clothes, and smoking his favorite pipe. Henry had rarely seen him without his pipe. Sunlight shone through the window behind the chair, enveloping every feature of Lord Oslan's thin frame in shadow. Tendrils of pipe smoke curled and clung around his head like a crown of snakes.

"Good afternoon, Henry." Lord Oslan's voice reeked of overcooked geniality. "Please take a seat."

Henry sat carefully in the chair closest to Oslan and made sure to keep his back straight. Oslan looked on with such apathy that Henry squirmed. When Oslan saw this, he smiled and took another long drag from his pipe, puffing it out in spurts with his chuckles.

"So why are you here today, Henry?"

"What do you mean, sir?" Henry leaned forward because he was certain he had not heard properly.

Oslan puffed again. "To what do I owe the incident of your visit?"

"You don't know why I'm here?"

Lord Oslan shook his head, causing the smoke to writhe as if the snakes were now moving. The perspiration gathering under Henry's arms and around his neck was dense and hot. He cleared his throat and shifted his shoulders to create separation between his body and his clothes. Lord Oslan must be lying; how could he not know?

"*Ahem*. Well, sir, I admit I came here today under the assumption that you understood the purpose of our meeting."

"Please," Oslan said with a polite smile, "do not hesitate to tell me."

Henry cleared his throat again. The house was too quiet, and Henry had the impression that unseen ears bent to hear his next words.

His voice dropped to a near whisper, and he shattered the silence with his fumbling words. "I—I, sir, I have come to—to ask for your hand in marriage."

Oslan paused on his pipe for a long moment, holding the smoke inside his lungs as a smile grew around the stem, exposing his short yellow teeth clamped down on the bit, and making a tapping sound. His hearty laugh started strong, but ended in a wheezing cough, the smoke from his lungs escaping in bursts.

Henry closed his eyes tightly as the noise continued. "What I—" He swallowed hard and tried again. "What I mean to say is that I wish to ask you for your daughter's hand in marriage."

For some reason, when Henry said the words he originally intended, Lord Oslan's mirth grew. His dark green eyes widened as his body convulsed, coughing and laughing and wheezing. Two large veins appeared on his forehead, converging over the bridge of his nose, bulging each time he gasped for air.

"Excuse me," Oslan choked out, composing himself in a dignified manner. "I have not been so amused in quite some time."

Henry tried offering a humoring smile, but it didn't sit right, and he knew it. He quickly stopped before another fit of laughter hit Lord Oslan. He rummaged around the corners of his brain for the eloquent phrases that Ruther might have offered in his place. Nothing seemed adequate anymore. All he could hear was his father's voice telling him to stop fretting.

"I'm sorry, sir," Henry said. "My tongue slipped. As you might guess, I'm all nerves this afternoon."

Whatever traces of humor were left on Lord Oslan's face vanished with a quickness that scared Henry. Oslan took the pipe from his mouth and held it rigidly. "It's not only your stammering that amuses me, it's also your pretentiousness."

"My pretentiousness, sir?" Henry repeated the words much more softly than he meant.

"I think I've tolerated your vain imaginations long enough. Look around you, boy. This street isn't filled with markets. No shops here. This is a manor, and for far too many years I have permitted you to enter it on my goodwill." Lord Oslan's voice grew in volume as his speech continued. "I am insulted that you have even considered the possibility of entering my home and asking for my daughter's hand in marriage. It should never have even crossed your mind . . . or hers."

"Sir, she's eighteen."

"I'm not referring to her age, but her station. I care about my family—the honor of my family. If you cared about my daughter, you would relinquish her from your petty lust and allow her to marry someone of respect and regard."

Henry's face flushed at Lord Oslan's statement. He did not know whether to be angry or afraid, but he knew whichever he chose, he could not respond without emotion getting the better of him.

"Don't you understand the way things are?" Oslan's eyes searched Henry's face as he clutched his pipe. "You should, given your family's . . . history."

Henry's cheeks flushed until they burned from heat. "With all respect, Lord Oslan, and I truly mean all the respect I have, your daughter and I are deeply in love."

Lord Oslan's eyes blazed at the mention of the word *love*. He leaned closer, and the chair beneath him groaned loudly.

"And what do you think that is? Playing games as children and whispering through hedges as adolescents? If so, then we are both fools. You for believing in such frivolous fantasies, and I for allowing myself to think that giving my daughter an education from a family of rubbish would not tarnish her view of the world around her."

Family of rubbish. Henry closed his eyes to keep a level head after such an insult. Fury would not serve him here—he knew that—but what could he possibly say?

"Sir—please—sir, can we leave our station out of the conversation for now? I would speak to you man to man."

"Is that a challenge, boy?" The pipe snapped in Oslan's hands, and the stem clattered to the wood floor. His eyes narrowed and his voice dropped to a visceral growl. "You suggest we set aside our stations. What kind of preposterous talk is that? Your lesser mind thinks only of lust and greed and pride. That's why you want my daughter—to satisfy your every whim on her female flesh and my family's coffer!"

"You know that's not true!" Henry shouted, suddenly on his feet without realizing he had stood. "You've known me since I was an infant! How can you say such things?"

"Because you are in my house, asking me for my daughter when you know I would never let you have her. Come now, use your brain! Can you really imagine me giving her away to you at a wedding ceremony? Will I wear a sack over my head to hide my face from my peers—or pierce my heart with a dagger to end my shame? If you had half a brain, you'd know that this is the way things are."

"Your shame?" Henry yelled at his loudest. "No one respects you. No one! I'm here willing to do whatever I can to make an agreeable arrangement for both our families, but you prefer to insult me and my family. Who is the fool?"

"How dare you speak down to me?"

"How dare you pretend you're nothing but an old, moneyless fraud?" Henry replied. "You've destroyed your family's status with your greed, your ill temper, and your foolish pride, but none of that has changed my feelings for your daughter. I love her despite you and your efforts to keep us apart."

The whole house fell silent once more. Henry's question hung in the air, never to be answered. He suddenly felt very foolish. By losing his temper, he had lost all hope. Oslan trembled, holding the remnants of his broken pipe in his right hand.

Henry tried to shunt the anger away by apologizing, but all he could manage was, "Lord Oslan, I beg you to forgive what I—"

"You! *You!*" Lord Oslan roared, though his words had all the force of an empty soul who knew the words Henry had thrown at him were true. He jumped up from his chair and sprang to the mantel, where a large sword was suspended on large wooden pegs. Henry stood as Lord Oslan hefted the metal and brandished it menacingly. "Say those words again and I will cut open your stomach!"

Henry backed toward the door to the den. He had no words to say. His focus fixed on the weapon held by Isabelle's father.

"Norbin!" Lord Oslan shouted. "Get this filth out of my house!"

Norbin appeared at the door of the den. His eyes studied the scene warily. "Yes, my lord. Right away."

"See him straight out." The order was more like a growl than a voice. "And one more thing," Lord Oslan drawled when Henry had turned his back. They looked each other in the eyes, and Henry found himself once again more afraid than angry. "If I see you near my daughter, there will be a duel."

Henry nodded, only wanting to leave. Norbin took him firmly by the arm. In defiance of Lord Oslan, Henry attempted to shake himself free as soon as they quitted the den, but surprisingly, Norbin's grip held firm until they reached the door.

"I could have seen myself out," Henry said on the threshold.

"Isabelle will meet you when the candle is lit in the servant's chamber," the wrinkled butler hissed in Henry's ear.

This news did not, however, raise Henry's spirits as the large wooden door closed resolutely behind him.

THREE

Master Henry's Lament

Brandol helped Maggie push a small wooden cart down Shop Street; only two small, wilted heads of cabbage remained inside. The cart's front wheel wobbled ever so slightly, reminding him how he'd told her he would help her fix it. He'd made the cart, after all, but like most of his woodwork, it wasn't very good. Maggie was talking about her cabbage sales, her brown, nearly black curls bouncing with each step, but Brandol wasn't paying attention. Yes, her crops had sold well. They always did. Maggie had a gift for making things grow. Even Master Henry's livestock flourished under her care.

When they reached the corner of Shop Street and Richterton Lane, Brandol saw Master Henry walking toward them. His head hung low, and in his hand he carried a blue silk scarf. Maggie's chatter ended abruptly.

"Oh, no . . ." she sighed, doubling her pace. Brandol hurried to keep up with her. Henry looked up as they approached, but quickly looked away again. "Are you all right, Henry?"

He didn't answer. His fist clenched the scarf, his knuckles white.

"I'm so sorry," Maggie said. Brandol thought she sounded on the verge of tears.

"I lost my temper," Henry said. "Now I can think of a hundred better things to say to Lord Oslan. Why couldn't I think of them then? Why did I need to insult the man?"

"You insulted him? Why?"

"Because I'm a fool," he answered.

"But you said Isabelle was certain—"

"She was!"

"You said—"

"Maggie, please!"

Maggie fell silent. Brandol tried to think of comforting words to say to his woodcarving master of almost a year. "May—maybe if you just say you is sorry, he might forgive you. Then you can still be marrying Miss Isabelle."

"No, I've messed it all up. Everything. I've shamed my mother and father—well, their memories, at least." He held the scarf up to his chest and squeezed as if he were trying to wring out the pain that infected his heart. "I've wanted this day to come for so long, and—I—I—I botched it."

They came to the house. Master Henry opened the door to the shop so Brandol and Maggie could wheel in her cart and cabbages. Then he slammed it shut behind him. The shop was quiet. Master Henry had given Brandol and the apprentices the rest of the day off to celebrate the special occasion.

"What are you going to do now?" Maggie asked Master Henry.

He glanced around the room. "I don't know. Clean, perhaps. Anything to take my mind off of . . ."

The shop was immaculate. Brandol liked it that way, and so did Master Henry. Brandol liked knowing where everything was at all times, and thus avoided misplacing anything. In one corner of Brandol's workspace stood the vanity he had been making for one of Master Henry's customers. He hoped Master Henry wouldn't notice it. Along one wall, different woods rested in careful stacks arranged by size and cut. The apprentices' workspaces were spotless, except for Darren's, the senior apprentice, but Master Henry had given up that fight months before. Tools hung exactly as they should. The smell of oil, coal, and dust was heavy, as it had been since the day Brandol started there.

"I kissed Isabelle for the first time right there," Master Henry said, pointing to the back door. "Just under the door frame. She told me—" His voice cut off, and a look of helpless fury crossed his face, which concerned Brandol. In an instant, his master grabbed a small clay bowl filled with chalk and threw it across the room. It spun through the air, creating a thick trail of white dust until it collided with the far wall. It shattered, and chalk exploded into the air.

"Henry, I made that for Father!" Maggie rushed across the room, but it was useless. The bowl was in dozens of pieces and far beyond repair.

"Curse you, you old monster!" Master Henry's neck turned a bright shade of red as he shouted at the ceiling. "I dedicated myself to becoming Richterton's youngest master carpenter so I could earn the money and respect to win your favor! When other boys were learning to use the sword or playing fisticuffs or going to inns for drinks, I stayed home and perfected my craft. Ironic that you threatened me with the sword, I suppose."

"He—he—he threatened you with . . . his sword?" Brandol asked. He felt his lungs tighten as Maggie examined her brother for any sign of injury. "Did—did he strike you?" Each word came to Brandol with great struggle. "Did you s—s—strike him?"

"Forget it. It doesn't matter anymore." Master Henry clutched his head in his hands. Brandol had never seen him so distraught. "I should have known better." He began sweeping up the mess of chalk and broken clay. Brandol rushed to assist him. While they worked, Master Henry told what had happened at Oslan Manor, but Brandol had the impression that his master was speaking more to Maggie than to him.

Maggie's face grew red as she listened. "Oh, I hate him! This isn't right. He knows you and Isabelle are going to be together—why try and stop it?"

"I don't know," Master Henry answered in a quiet voice. "Perhaps Lord Oslan believes if he holds out, someone with money and title will notice Isabelle and save the Oslan family from shame."

"So she is his investment?"

Master Henry shrugged.

Maggie stood up as if she'd been stung by a bee. "Nothing I say is going to make you feel better, so I'll cook you the best meal I know how. Will your apprentices be here for supper?"

"I doubt it."

Maggie pursed her lips and clicked her tongue. Master Henry said it was a habit she'd picked up from her mother. "And Ruther? What about him?"

"I don't suppose so, no."

This seemed to brighten Maggie's mood. "Good. I could tell he was here earlier today by the smell. Why you still spend time with him is—"

"You're not Mother, Maggie," Master Henry reminded her.

"I'm sorry. I—I guess I'll get started on that dinner." She paused in the door frame. "What are you going to do about Isabelle?"

"Meet her tonight," Master Henry said. "What else?"

"Aren't you worried—"

"I'm more than worried." Brandol's master swept the last bits of the chalk and bowl out the door and into the street. "I'm terrified. I can't use a sword. I can't fight." He took a deep breath. "And I can't *not* meet Isabelle, either. So that's my choice. If we're caught, I'll defend myself as best as I can."

Maggie left, leaving Brandol and his master in the shop alone. Master Henry wandered around the workbenches looking for something to do. Brandol had seen his master do this before. He wished he could say or do something of use, but by and large, he was a useless person. He'd known that since he was a boy.

Master Henry looked with his bright blue eyes at Brandol. Brandol's eyes were of similar color; they also shared the same brown tint to their hair. Master Henry's friend, Ruther, often called Brandol "Little Henry" as a tease. The name had caught on among the apprentices, too, despite how much Brandol hated it. While it was true that Brandol and his master did look alike in the face, they weren't *that* much alike. Brandol was a couple inches shorter and stockier than Master Henry—and far less talented.

"You finished the vanity," Master Henry said, nodding at Brandol's work tucked into the corner.

Brandol lowered his eyes and tried to ignore the burning in his cheeks and ears. "It—it was the best I—I coulda done, Master Henry. I'll start over if that's what you be wanting."

"Why would I want you to do that?"

Crossing the shop to the vanity was like a walk of shame for Brandol. His master followed close behind. Brandol turned the vanity so that its left side was better exposed. "See there? I done scratched it."

Master Henry felt the scratch with his fingers and then ran his hand along the rest of the piece. Brandol wished he'd stop. Each place his master touched, Brandol noticed more flaws. He decided he'd smash it and burn it the moment his master told him to start over.

"It's wonderful, Brandol."

"It—it—it—no, please, Master Henry. Don't be teasing me."

Master Henry stared at Brandol with an intense focus. Brandol could still see the sadness and anger in his master's face and was grateful these emotions weren't directed at him.

"You can do anything if you are determined, Brandol. This work is almost the quality of a master. You are close. Very close. Your skill has grown by leaps and bounds in the last few months."

"But I made so many mistakes. And that scratch—"

"Will be noticed by no one. You have talent. It's time you accept it."

"Master Henry, I ain't—"

"Not just with woodworking, either. I've heard you sing when no one else is in the shop. You have a beautiful voice."

If Brandol's ears had burned before, now they felt like torches had been lit inside them. "I didn't know . . ."

"I think there's nothing you can't do once you decide to do it. Appreciate the work you've done. Appreciate what you have. You never know when it will be taken away from you." That last sentence from Master Henry's lips sounded grim. "Maybe someday you'll learn to embrace your gifts and not be so afraid of them."

FOUR

In the Dark

I sabelle pressed her ear against the door to her father's room and listened for the signs of his slumbering. Across the hall a thick, wet cough came from her mother's lungs. The coughs sounded worse every day. Isabelle lingered at the door to her mother's bedroom an extra moment before moving on. Holding her shoes in her hands, she descended the stairs; her bare feet made no noise. When she reached the bottom, she dragged her fingernail across Norbin's door, giving him the sign to light the candle in his window. With a steady breath, she crossed to the back of the house and exited through the rear door.

The grounds behind Oslan Manor sloped gently downward toward the hedge separating her yard from Henry's. Isabelle slipped on her shoes and walked the same path she'd taken as a young girl to the Vestin home for daily lessons.

She held her breath until she reached the hedge, where the branches of the evergreen trees left barely enough space for a full-grown person to squeeze through sideways. It was the same spot where she and James had crossed into the Vestins' yard in their youth. Like her father, Isabelle was tall and thin, though, thankfully, she'd inherited all her other features from her mother. She passed easily through the hedge, but her cloak billowed behind her, catching on the branches and then whipping her legs with each gust of wind. The screeching of a silver eagle high overhead startled her. She glanced up and saw the mighty bird's feathers reflecting the moonlight with the tips of its wings. It circled lazily as it hunted in the darkness.

"Henry?" she whispered. "Henry, are you here?"

The only response was leaves rustling and goats bleating in Henry's barn. The wind died down for a few seconds, and she heard a soft thumping and snorting from Henry's favorite horse, Quicken, in the stable. The horse poked his head out the stable door, chewing his food.

Isabelle headed toward Quicken to pet him while she waited for Henry to come outside. She didn't dare go to the back door for fear of her father seeing her silhouette entering the Vestin homestead. Quicken snorted again into her hand as she rubbed his long snout. She spoke soothing words to him and glanced over her shoulder.

She saw movement in the hedge and covered her mouth. Had her father followed her? Isabelle flattened herself against the wall of the stable. The shadow in the hedge became more pronounced and a figure in a dark cloak emerged.

"Henry?" she asked, recognizing the clothing instantly. She abandoned the stable and ran across the grass until her arms were around him. Henry hugged her tightly in return, and the crisp scent of fresh-cut wood filled her. She associated his scent with so many good things that it always made her feel at home.

He let out a breath of relief as he gave her an extra squeeze. "You gave me a start. What were you doing?"

"Waiting for you. What kept you?"

"I saw the light in Norbin's window only a moment ago. We must have reached the hedge at the same time and missed each other." Henry's voice was low and his eyes lacked the spark Isabelle normally saw in them. Her stomach filled with hot guilt.

"Henry, what happened today was my—"

"It was I who lost my temper, not you."

"No, please, you need to listen. My mother told me she'd made a deal with my father to convince him to accept your terms for marrying me. She gave me her blessing to encourage you to speak to him. My father changed his mind."

"*I* changed his mind. I offended him." A sudden sound made them both jump until they realized it was a bird fluttering to a nearby tree. "Now I don't know what to do." The defeat in his voice chilled Isabelle more than the gusting wind. "I fear what your father may do to me if he finds us together. I fear even more what he'd do to you. What good am I? I can't even stand up to an old man."

Isabelle cupped his face with both hands. She kissed him and fixed her light brown eyes on his blue ones. "You have proven to me more than once that while your strength isn't in the sword, you are still strong and capable of protecting me. I'm scared, too. I'm scared of not being with you." The moons reflected their light in Henry's eyes, and Isabelle thought he looked majestic.

The door behind them opened, and Maggie came out the back door to pump water. She wore a pretty market dress. Isabelle thought it made her face appear more elegant and her deep brown, almost black, curls shine more brightly. Among the local men, Maggie was considered quite a prize. Her even, white teeth and thin red lips complemented her petite face and frame well. However, she consistently rejected offers of courtship. Maggie claimed it was because she had no interest at the moment, but Isabelle believed Maggie refused to be married before Henry.

"I think she's spying on us," Henry whispered.

"Let her." Isabelle kissed Henry again.

Henry grimaced as he pulled away. "I want to say something of comfort, but I don't know the words. Part of me wants to hold you as tightly as I can before your father wrenches you away from me."

The wind carried a distant voice to Isabelle's ears. It belonged to Ruther. In her mind's eye, she could see Henry's friend strolling down the street, swaying gently to the tune he sang, drinking from his leather flask. Almost on cue, she heard him: "And if the dog bites you on the leg," he sang at the top of his voice, slurring some words together, "bite him right back, you scurvy scoundrel!"

"What was that?" Henry asked.

Isabelle sighed. "Ruther is drunk."

They both laughed softly.

"We need a plan," Henry said, speaking in his lowest voice. "We've always assumed that when we're married we'll live in my home and I'll provide for us with my shop. Suppose this isn't the case."

Isabelle pondered his words before replying. "What you mean to say is, 'What if we have to run away and I have to start over?'"

Henry nodded.

"Then we run away," Isabelle told him. "We pay someone to make us new letters of identity and start a new life. It wouldn't be too difficult."

His lips pressed against her forehead.

"It must be a last resort. My mother—" She allowed herself a moment to calm down, but she felt her cheeks flush as she fought back her emotion. "My mother's health is turning for the worse. She already needs constant care. She—she could be gone tomorrow or the next day, or perhaps not for several weeks. I need to be there for her. Norbin's getting quite old, and my father will not lift a finger to help. I know she'll want to discuss our marriage again with him as soon as she has the strength."

"What can she say to change his mind?"

"She won't tell me everything, but I know they'd reached an agreement a week ago, when I told you to approach him. He must have changed his mind before meeting you today. Perhaps—perhaps he's trying to get more out of the deal than they originally bargained."

"I'll fix this, Isabelle," Henry said. "I'll apologize to him."

"Don't you dare!" Isabelle demanded. Henry glanced over his

shoulder toward the manor, reminding her to keep her voice down. "The way he treated you is inexcusable. I heard every word. If I'd known what he planned to do, I would have warned you. I don't care if he consents."

"We need his consent to—"

"I don't care. I'll run away with you before I'll see you grovel to him, but first let me help my mother. She deserves to die with dignity." Isabelle pretended to brush a hair into place while wiping away a tear.

"Dapper! Decided! Deciduous! Defenestration! Deferentially . . . curse it!" Ruther shouted in his singsong voice, now much louder than before. His game ended as they heard him ordering a stray dog to get off his leg. The wind picked up again, and its whistling drowned out some, but not all, of Ruther's profane exclamations at the "brazen mutt."

Henry spread his cloak out on the ground so she could sit without getting her own cloak dirty. They sat side by side on the grass. The wind's direction changed, and the tall hedges blocked the worst of it. One moon climbed higher in the night sky, shrinking as it did so. The night sky was beautiful and cloudless.

"James is the only person I know who doesn't fear my father," Isabelle said, "and it took him quite a while to become that way. Things will be all right in the end, Henry."

He responded by putting an arm around her. "Do you really believe he would harm me if he were to find us together?"

"Gallant, gigantic, gratuitous, gregariously!" bellowed Ruther so loudly that Isabelle guessed he must be sitting on Henry's front stoop.

"My father knows I'll leave with you before I allow him to give me away to someone else. If we give him a few days to regain his composure, I think he'll accept an offer from my mother. If not, I'll go with you wherever you wish."

"I don't trust him."

"Henry, nothing will happen to me. I swear it. We love each other too much to let him stop us."

"My mother was a drunkard!" Ruther began crooning at the top of his voice, "My father was a corn plucker! Is it any wonder then . . ."

"Oh Ruther," Henry muttered. "Please don't sing that song."

"I turned into a lousy—"

"—Ruther!" Maggie shouted from a window. "If you don't quiet yourself right now, I will beat you with my broom!"

Ruther fell silent instantly, as did many of the animals in the barn and stable. Isabelle tried not to laugh, but her chest rose and fell spasmodically. "I love your sister."

"She means what she says."

"But I love you more."

"Good," Henry breathed back into her ear.

"I've known since I was a girl that I'm happiest when I'm with you."

She could feel Henry's smile against her cheek in response to her words. They stood up together, and Isabelle leaned forward so her tall frame could complete the distance between her lips and Henry's.

"I'll see you soon," she said over her shoulder as she passed back through the hedge. "Tomorrow, if I can manage it."

Just as they said goodbye, Ruther stumbled into the backyard, raised his flask high, and tripped onto the grass. He quickly got up and raised his hands to show that he was fine.

"So when's the big day?" he asked.

FIVE

Death at the Manor

In Isabelle's youth, Lady Oslan had been a tall, slender, majestic being whose principal endeavor had been to put her family into the center of Richterton's social circles. However, when Isabelle turned ten, her mother's health took a sharp, inexplicable turn, and over the last nine years, the elegant woman had gradually wilted into a fragile, prematurely aged invalid who slept more than twelve hours on a normal day. Most mornings, Isabelle read to her mother from a book of stories handed down through the family, spoke about her plans for the future, and brushed her mother's silver hair out of her face when a strong draft blew through a window. It was imperative that Lady Oslan have someone in the home within earshot at all times, and since Lord Oslan wouldn't answer her summons, Isabelle and Norbin bore the responsibility together.

For three days after Henry's disastrous meeting with Lord Oslan, Isabelle and Henry met in the secrecy of night. Isabelle spent the rest of the time in her mother's room trying to raise the frail woman's spirits, but her efforts were futile. Lady Oslan's condition continued to rapidly deteriorate.

On the fourth day, Isabelle simply had to get out of the manor. Hearing from Norbin that her father intended to eat lunch with one of his few friends, Isabelle sent a message to Henry telling him to expect her around noon. Norbin would ring a bell from the back door if Lord Oslan came home earlier than expected.

She and Henry focused their lunch conversation on places they wanted to visit, pretending as though they were going on a very long vacation. Isabelle was reluctant to return home, but the sky threatened a rainstorm. Their picnic lunch took well over an hour but was still much shorter than she would have liked. She left, promising Henry that she'd try to visit him again before she retired for the evening, and returned home with a smile stuck to her face. Norbin was in the kitchen scrubbing dishes and smiled as he watched her enter.

"Do you need help?" she asked him, reaching for a wet dish and a dry towel.

"I've told you before; Master Henry wouldn't like it if I let you. Your hands are too well-made, Miss Isabelle. Oh, and before I forget. A letter from Master James arrived today."

Isabelle was about to comment when she heard her mother's bell ringing upstairs.

"Excuse me, Miss—"

"No, Norbin." Isabelle put down the dish, dried her hands on the towel, and flattened her dress. "I'll see to her." The ringing became more urgent as Isabelle reached the stairs, so she quickened her pace to Lady Oslan's room.

Her mother's colorless, quaking hand clutched the bell tightly, her eyelids tightly closed, making her face appear even more sallow without the natural color of her eyes. Perspiration dampened her face and plastered her hair to her scalp and cheeks.

"Mother, what's the matter?" Isabelle rushed to the bedside. "Are you in pain?"

A little smile grew on the pale pink lips of Lady Oslan. "I'm dying, Isabelle."

"Mother, don't talk that way," Isabelle pleaded. "I'll get Norbin."

Lady Oslan reached out and took Isabelle's hand. Her eyes

opened, and she seemed happy despite her anguished state. In fact, Isabelle noticed her mother was more alert than she had been in months. "Please listen. I'm beyond Norbin's care and yours. Will you believe me?"

Isabelle sobbed twice. "No, Mother. I won't believe that. We'll do everything we can, and then you'll be—"

"You've already done everything a daughter can do for a mother. Let me help you now."

"Have faith, Mother." She tried to sound brave, but tears betrayed her. Why did this have to happen today? Life seemed too dark to face without her mother's guidance.

"You must listen to me, Isabelle, or I will not be able to help you at all." Lady Oslan's voice had a soothing effect.

Isabelle wiped her eyes and nodded. "All right, I'm listening."

"Pay attention to me. When I married your father, my parents gave me a large sum as a dowry. Your father spent most of it, but our marriage contract stated that some of it belonged solely to me for as long as I wished to keep it."

Isabelle remembered her parents fighting over the money on multiple occasions, but her mother had never caved to Lord Oslan's demands. On James's sixteenth birthday, Lord Oslan announced that James had one year to make arrangements to leave and start supporting himself. When James left at age seventeen, Lady Oslan made it a point of giving her son the money. That decision had led to one of the biggest altercations Isabelle had ever witnessed between her parents.

Her mother touched Isabelle's cheek to get her attention. "Recently, I promised your father that if he gave Henry his permission to marry you, not only could he demand from Henry a bride price, but I would also give him one thousand crowns."

Isabelle inhaled sharply, trying to grasp all this information. "That's impossible! We've been nearly penniless since James—"

"I never gave the money to James."

This news stunned Isabelle, and for several seconds the only sound in the room came from the gears of Lady Oslan's clock ticking away the time. "But I saw you give him—"

Lady Oslan could barely move her head side to side, but the effort silenced Isabelle. "I gave him a bag of coppers. We tricked your father into thinking it was gone."

"Where has it been all this time?"

"In banks earning interest for the past seven years. I had it returned to me only weeks ago when I sensed I would need proof of it to barter with your father. He had no idea until I showed him one of my receipts, but he doesn't know where the money resides or the exact amount."

"Why are you telling me this now? Please let me get you a physician."

Lady Oslan coughed several times, but gestured *no* to Isabelle. "I would have told you sooner, but I feared if your father pressed you for answers—threatened you—you might have told him."

"No, Mother, never."

"Think, Isabelle," Lady Oslan insisted. "Your father still holds great sway over you, especially with your desire to marry Henry. He can use your feelings as a powerful lever."

"I would be firm."

"That remains to be seen. There isn't a thousand crowns in the coffer now."

"How much is left? Why not leave it where he can't reach it?"

Her mother licked her lips and caught her breath before continuing. Each word took great effort. "When I die, your father receives the money without question. I have no control over the gold if it is tied up in banks. I had Norbin remove it—a sense of foreboding. Now I need you to take the gold and give it to Henry."

"Why not will it to me and James?"

Lady Oslan pointed to the water pitcher, which Isabelle hastened to get. Her mother drank two large mouthfuls from her goblet and coughed up half of it. Isabelle wiped her mother's mouth with a towel and eased her back down to the bed. She said a silent prayer, begging the Lord of All Worlds to spare her mother.

"Part of my marriage agreement states that my first heir is my spouse. Under the laws of Blithmore, it cannot be willed to anyone else unless your father agrees. I had five lawyers review this."

"Unless he opens the coffer and finds nothing there?"

Lady Oslan smiled. Her eyes dimmed. "You must do it quickly—before your father returns. If the money is gone, it will be believed that I spent it. He can do nothing about that. You will need help moving it, and Norbin is too old."

"Norbin and I can manage a thousand crowns together."

Lady Oslan coughed and shook her head. Isabelle offered more water, but her mother declined. "The coffer holds over fifteen hundred double crowns."

Isabelle reeled backward. "Mother! That's enough money—"

"To build Henry a second woodshop and furnish it. That's why he must have it. I gave your father the choice: a thousand crowns and allow you to marry Henry, or never see the money again." Lady Oslan's face paled. Isabelle finally realized her mother's death was near. "Henry has so much talent. I am sure . . . wherever you go, you'll be fine. The coffer is buried at the hedge. Only Norbin knows exactly where."

Isabelle's tears fell as she clenched her mother's hand to prevent Death's pull. Lady Oslan's face tightened into an awful grimace. Seeing her mother in such pain crumbled Isabelle's spirit.

"Isabelle." Lady Oslan had to whisper between breaths. "Isabelle, if you wish . . . to be with Henry . . . you must get the chest . . . before your father returns home. Do you understand me, Isabelle? You must—before he returns. He often looks in on me, checking to see if—if I'm—he has plans, ideas, and if you give him time, he will make your life more miserable than he's made mine."

"I will, Mother," she answered through her cries, "even if Norbin has to bar the door, but I won't leave your side right now."

Lady Oslan's face grew more wrinkled, and for a moment Isabelle felt her mother's surge of agony. "Thank you, Isabelle," she muttered softly. "I am glad your father is away, but—but I wish James were here."

"Me too." With her free hand, Isabelle put a cool cloth on her mother's head. "Are you comfortable, Mother?"

Lady Oslan squeezed her eyes shut tightly. "Tell me again how your wedding will look."

Isabelle calmed herself and then began to describe in detail her dreams for her wedding ceremony. She talked about her gown, the flowers she would put in her hair and around her wrists, and what Henry would wear. Then she explained how she wanted James to give her away, and sang to her mother the bridal song she would sing to Henry. As she finished the song, her mother's breathing quickened and the trembling in her hands lessened until they were far too still. Hope left Isabelle, and she tried to accept her mother's death. "I will miss you, Mother," she whispered. "Don't go. Don't leave."

"No, no, it's all right . . . we'll be together again." Lady Oslan's voice was barely louder than a breeze. Then her eyes lost their focus, and with her last breath, she said, "Tell James to climb the windy side."

SIX

The Coffer

Isabelle opened her mouth to ask her mother what that strange last utterance meant, but Lady Oslan's eyes softly closed and her chest rose no more. A tiny sound of surprise left Isabelle's mouth, and she gasped for air as her vision began to blur. Her anguish in that instant was tortuous. She thought she would cry for hours before being able to calm down, but she underestimated her own strength. Something inside her, a spot of warmth, sprouted deep in her chest. The warmth spread until it filled her with a burning heat that gave her the focus she needed to obey her mother's dying wish.

With tenderness, she covered her mother up to her chin so anyone looking in would think Lady Oslan was sleeping. Then she let go of her self-pity, drew in a shaky breath, and hurried downstairs.

"Norbin!" she called as she reached the back door, "Fetch a spade and meet me at the far hedge."

Norbin tried to sputter a question, but Isabelle raised a hand and repeated the order with increased urgency.

Isabelle sprinted across the lawn. The rain that had been threatening at lunch now fell lightly, making the grass on the slope glisten. As she passed the hedge, she wondered which piece of earth covered her mother's treasure. When she burst into Henry's woodshop, her breaths came in sharp pants. A cry of surprise came from the far southwest corner where Henry stood.

"Henry?" she called out.

"Isabelle?" Not Henry. Brandol. "What's it you want?"

"I need Henry now. It's urgent!"

Brandol stepped closer. It wasn't the first time she'd mistaken the two from a distance. "Boss's on delivery," he explained, taking off his work gloves. "Took his 'prentices with him."

"Can you help me?"

Brandol glanced back to his work and then back to her. "I s'pose."

She led him to the hedge. Norbin was coming down from the manor as fast as his skinny, wobbly legs would carry him with not one but two spades.

"Follow me," he wheezed to them, somehow understanding exactly what was going on. As Brandol obeyed, his face wore all the confusion Isabelle had felt only a short while ago.

The afternoon sunlight dimmed as clouds gathered rapidly above them. The air was thick with a steady breeze that made the rain fall at a mild slant. Isabelle prayed that her father would be gone long enough for them to get the gold.

Norbin stopped only a few yards over from the spot where Henry and Isabelle normally met in secret at night. Isabelle wondered if he had chosen this spot with them in mind.

"How deep is it?" she asked.

"It took the man who delivered it almost an hour to bury it," Norbin wheezed.

"Dig, Brandol," Isabelle said, thrusting a spade at him. As she made to start, Norbin stopped her.

"My lady, please allow me to—"

"Norbin, you are a dear," Isabelle said as she brushed hair out of her face, "but you're too old for this."

"No, Miss, it's not that. If your father sees you dirty . . ."

"I have no other choice," she said as she sank her spade into the dirt.

Several minutes passed in silence as Isabelle and Brandol dug. Norbin watched anxiously, his gaze flitting between the house and the digging and back. The rain continued to fall, softening the dirt they worked at. Isabelle was grateful that Brandol did not stop to ask questions. She bent her will to unearthing the coffer before her father came home. A low rumble sounded overhead, and in a matter of seconds heavier drops splattered her face.

The dirt grew sloppier until it turned to mud, slowing them down. They dug faster to compensate until, at last, they struck something solid. Isabelle threw aside her shovel and frantically pushed aside the mucky soil with her hands. Norbin raised a small yelp, but didn't attempt to stop her. Brandol entered the hole with her to help, and finally the lid could be seen.

The coffer was as long as a grown man's arm and wider than Brandol's chest, made of black oak with gilded corners. For a brief moment, the party of three stopped and stared at the large black box.

"At least we don't have to lift it," Isabelle commented.

Even Brandol must have sensed what was inside, because his eyes widened in anticipation. The sound of hooves in the distance interrupted their efforts. Isabelle recognized instantly the distinctly feeble gait of Esmond, the family horse.

"The key!" Isabelle cried. "The key, Norbin!"

The ancient servant reached into his pockets, fumbling about, trying to find where he had placed it. After too much time, he retrieved a small silver key from his vest pocket and handed it over to her.

"You must hurry back to the house, Norbin. Close all the shutters if you can."

"Miss Isabelle, if he asks me where the money is—now your mother is dead—I can no longer deny my knowledge of its location. I could be arrested if I do."

"Then do whatever you can to keep him out of my mother's room and away from the back windows!"

Without another word, Norbin turned toward the house, walking and puffing with vigor that defied his age.

Isabelle put the key in the hole and turned. It wouldn't budge. Grime and other debris clogged the keyhole. She let out a groan of frustration and dropped to her knees, using the key as a tiny shovel to scrape the dirt and pebbles out. Brandol looked on with interest, but said nothing. She tried the key again, but there was no improvement. She peered over the edge of the hole, but saw no sign of either her father or Norbin.

"Here . . . let me have a go at it." Brandol jumped in beside her and took the key. He scraped and blew sharply into the keyhole, dislodging some of the debris.

"Hurry!" she urged in a terrified voice as she thought she saw a dark shadow pass by one of the windows in the back of the house.

"I ain't taking my time!"

Rain poured down on them while lightning streaked the sky in what promised to be a terrible storm. Isabelle's eyes went back and forth from the coffer to the house, growing wider with her fear. She was no longer certain whether the shapes she thought she saw moving past the windows were real or imaginary. How long would it take for her father to discover what had happened and then seize the information from Norbin?

Brandol blew sharply into the lock and was rewarded with a soft rattling sound. He blew three more times in rapid succession, and a small pebble tumbled out. Then he slipped the key into the lock and turned it with a click. Isabelle's attention went to the coffer as Brandol opened it. Both of them gasped.

Gold coins filled the coffer to the brim, all emblazoned with a Blithmore crown on each side. The sight of so much gold had an intoxicating effect. Isabelle had to resist the urge to handle the money.

"Brandol, I need you to fetch me a sturdy sack," she ordered. "Run as fast as you can!" Brandol reluctantly looked away from the coffer. When his eyes finally met hers, he appeared dazed. "A sack!"

With a start, he jumped up and sprinted toward the house, leaving Isabelle alone and anxious. She ducked down inside the hole, peering back at her house over the edge. She tried to get the hair out of her face, but smeared dirt on her cheek and forehead instead. Mud caked most of her dress, ruining it. It covered her fingers, nails, and palms. What little skin she could see was red and raw from shoveling.

She considered trying to put the gold in her dress and carrying it into Henry's house, but the idea was far too impractical. "Hurry, Brandol, hurry!" she cried. He hadn't been gone more than two minutes, but it already seemed too long. Finally, the door to Henry's workshop reopened, and Brandol returned with not only a large potato sack but also Maggie.

"Is it true?" Maggie exclaimed, running alongside Brandol to the large hole, but her question was answered as soon as she looked down. Her hands flew to her face and covered her gaping mouth. "Oh, great heavens!"

"Brandol, what's the best way to move it?" Isabelle asked.

"Maybe—maybe you and Maggie hold the bag, and I scoop the gold in."

Brandol and Isabelle switched places, and Brandol began shoveling the gold. However, fifteen hundred double gold crowns weren't easily moved. It was clumsy work. Isabelle's trembling hands shook the bag as she kept one eye on her house, gold pieces fell off the spade into the mud, and more than once the wind slammed the lid on the coffer shut.

Isabelle crawled back into the hole to help him grab handfuls at a time while Maggie did her best to manage the bag. How much more time did they have? The absence of constant coughs and sounds of Lady Oslan's fitful tossing and turning would certainly rouse Lord Oslan's suspicion.

When the last gold piece finally fell in the bag, Isabelle slammed the lid of the coffer shut. "We have to get the gold to a safe place inside," she told Maggie.

"My house?" Maggie asked.

"Yes! Brandol, take it inside while we fill in the hole."

"I cain't carry that load with no help," he told her.

"Maggie, will you help him?"

"Me? Are you mad?"

Thundering shouts came from Oslan Manor. Both Maggie and Brandol stared in that direction.

"You must go now!" Isabelle urged. "Run!"

Together, Brandol and Maggie heaved the bag, Brandol supporting it from the bottom, and Maggie pulling from the top. Isabelle spent no time watching them, and began shoving piles of dirt into the hole. From across the lawn, she heard the back door of the house bang open.

"Hurry up, old man!" Lord Oslan yelled, his head turned toward the manor.

Frantically, Isabelle stood and stamped on the earth, then kicked leaves and grass over the spot where the coffer was buried. It was a terrible job of disguising her activity. Norbin appeared again at the back door, clutching his side and gasping for air as he chased her father down the lawn. Isabelle grabbed the spades and ran to Henry's woodshop; Maggie and Brandol were only halfway across Henry's lawn, still struggling to move the bag of gold inside the backdoor to the homestead.

Closing the shop door behind her, Isabelle leaned against it and let the spades clatter to the floor. From inside, she heard her father shouting at a distance. "Where's the spade, Norbin? My spade!"

She could not hear Norbin's response, but she knew it wouldn't be adequate.

"We *do* have a spade! I've seen it. Go to the Vestin house and borrow one from them if you have to."

Isabelle moved from the door and retreated to the darkest corner of the shop she could find. Moments later, Norbin knocked on the door. Isabelle froze. Should she risk handing Norbin the spade? She decided against it. Norbin could let himself into the shop. The spades rested on the floor next to the door, right where she'd dropped them.

Norbin knocked again. "Master Henry, are you there?" his aged voice wheezed.

"Hurry up!" her father shouted. He sounded louder than before, and Isabelle heard the beginnings of rage in his voice.

Norbin knocked a third time, his raps now hard and urgent. Isabelle doubted her decision. Her chest heaved in fear. What would her father do to Norbin if he couldn't find a spade? She made up her mind. Crossing the room, she opened the door enough to peer outside.

"It's about—" Her father stopped speaking when he saw her. "What are you doing here?"

Even at an early age, Isabelle had known she had little talent for lying. This didn't stop her from trying. "I—I'm helping—I'm watching the shop while Henry is on an errand."

"The devil you are!" her father yelled. He pushed the door hard enough that it upset her balance, and she stumbled over one of the shovels.

He pushed his way inside and appeared genuinely surprised to find that Henry was nowhere to be seen. When he saw her state—mud covering her hands, face, and dress, his own spades beneath her, and the look of guilt she wore—Lord Oslan became apoplectic.

"What have you been doing?"

"I told you, I've been watching Henry's shop." She watched his eyes as they flickered once more around the room and braced herself.

"You . . . !" He grabbed her by the hair and yanked her to her feet.

". . . lying little whore!" He swung her through the door using her hair as a rope. Isabelle cried out in pain. Her scalp burned and the pain forced tears to her eyes, but her father was relentless.

"Please let me go!" she begged as they made their way across the lawn. "Please, Father, it hurts!"

"Shut up! *Shut up!*"

She tried to keep up with him to lessen the burning in her scalp, but her father moved quickly. Her pleas turned into screams of agony and fright. She tried to look behind to see if Norbin was following, but another sharp, biting jerk of her hair forced her to give up. The back door of Oslan Manor was already open. He led her upstairs with the same forcefulness. Isabelle made sure to not trip on the steps for fear that she might rip out her hair. Through the den and up the main staircase he dragged her, past her own chambers and headed toward her mother's. The moment they were inside Lady Oslan's chamber, Lord Oslan threw Isabelle to the floor.

"Stay here," he ordered. "Mourn over your mother's dead body until I get back." He left the room and locked the door from the out-side. "Where are you going?" she heard him shouting at Norbin. "Get out there and dig up that coffer! I don't care how long it takes you!"

Isabelle knelt on the floor and rubbed her head, checking for any spots where her hair might have been pulled out. She looked around her mother's room and tried the door. It was locked. Nothing in the chamber had been touched. She felt better knowing her father hadn't put his filthy hands on anything. After calming herself, she blew out several of the candles, leaving the room in the dim, respectful light of the late afternoon. Then she washed her hands in the bowl on the bedside table and pulled back the sheets so she could tend to her mother.

The work absorbed her and cleansed her emotions. For a time, she forgot about her father and focused on her mother, letting the full impact of everything that had happened soak in. She wept unabashedly as she changed her mother out of the nightgown into her old but magnificent white wedding dress, then she brushed her mother's hair and applied a touch of color to her mother's cheeks and lips. The process took a long time. When she finished, it appeared that the last thing her mother had done before passing away was groom herself. Tears still came, but Isabelle didn't bother to brush them aside. She took a fresh white sheet from the linen closet and laid it over her mother. She had barely finished when her father's voice boomed through the manor.

"*WHERE IS THE GOLD, ISABELLE?*" It sounded so loud and deep, it was nearly inhuman. She heard him thundering up the stairs toward her and cowered against the wall.

"Henry," she whispered. "I need you right now."

SEVEN
Not a Hero

As Isabelle cowered in Henry's shop listening to her father yell at Norbin, Maggie and Brandol were making poor time getting the sack of gold into the house. Brandol didn't like their situation one bit. The world around him felt and looked darker as frightening questions filled his mind. Why was Isabelle so terrified of being seen? What would happen if Lord Oslan caught him? What if he tripped and spilled the gold all over Henry's lawn? Was he involved in a crime? Could he be arrested for stealing?

Brandol considered himself a strong man. He helped Henry move wood and furniture, loading and unloading the cart daily, but he had never tried to heft anything this heavy. He guessed the sack must weigh nearly two hundred pounds. Maggie's face was red as a tomato, and he could only imagine how his own looked. The shouts they heard from Lord Oslan grew louder, urging them to move faster.

"HEAVE!" Brandol's voice came out strained. The bag went up two steps. Four more to go. Brandol lifted again, but the steps were slick, and his foot slipped. His knee crashed down with a bang as he lost his grasp on the bag. Somehow, miraculously, Maggie held on until Brandol regained his grip. Impossible as it was with her slight frame and thin arms, she bore the weight for at least two seconds. Then, with one last great tug, they cleared the steps and the porch, closing the door behind them.

He did not bother to check if Lord Oslan had seen them go inside. The bag dropped to the floor with a heavy thud. The muscles in Brandol's back, arms, and hands burned as though branding irons poked deeply into his skin. His knee smarted where he'd smacked it against the stair.

He looked at Maggie and followed her gaze to the bag of gold. The thick coins reflected dozens of tiny points of light back at them like a pot of rich honey. Brandol had never imagined so much money. Maggie seemed to be thinking the same thing.

"Where we gonna put it?" He lay on the floor waiting for the aching in his back to subside.

Maggie tried to raise an arm, then dropped it again with a sigh. "I don't know. Let's leave it right here. I can't move my arms right now."

Brandol didn't like the idea. What if Lord Oslan barged his way into the house? He had not spent all that time in the mud digging up the gold to see it get taken right back. Plus, the thought of defending the gold from Isabelle's irate father terrified him. Before Maggie said anything else, he got up, went into the kitchen, and returned with a stack of large wooden bowls he'd helped Henry carve for Maggie to display her vegetables at the market.

"How 'bout using these?" he offered.

A double gold crown was the same circumference as a single crown but twice as thick. The emblem of the crown of Blithmore adorned each side, instead of one. It surprised Brandol how cold they were, but each handful he grabbed brought with it a new jolt of excitement. He imagined himself as King of Blithmore, unable to ever spend so much gold.

Maggie grinned as she watched him scoop it up in bowls. "It would take me all day to count this, Brandol."

Brandol had very little arithmetic skill. For all he knew, the bag contained almost a million coins. It certainly looked like a million. His mother had once told him that a million was the largest number, and that the Lord of All Worlds had not created a million of anything. Maybe she'd been wrong.

They hadn't emptied even half the bag when they heard more shouts from Lord Oslan, but these new ones came from the wood-shop. Brandol got up first and ran across the house to the side door connecting the house to the shop. He cracked it open and looked around. He saw nothing unusual except that the shop had been left open—something Henry didn't like. He went to close it and heard another cry. Through the doorway, he saw Lord Oslan dragging Isabelle up the lawn by her hair. His first impulse was to run after her, but that noble thought was immediately extinguished by an overwhelming feeling of impotence.

When he returned from the shop, Maggie stood at the window, a look of shock on her face. "Brandol, you have to do something!"

"I can't do nothing to help." His shoulders slumped as he spoke. His ears grew hot. Throughout his life, he'd been called many names: stupid, dunce, pathetic, useless, even *runt* by his own parents, but never "hero."

What did Maggie expect him to do? Chase down Lord Oslan and challenge him to fisticuffs? He joined her at the window to see Lord Oslan yank his daughter through the hedge and out of sight.

"Brandol!" Maggie yelled. "Get out there now!"

Brandol had no choice but to try to help. He'd never done anything like this. As a child, he'd been the one needing help. He ran to Henry's shop to find something useful. A slow perusal of the wood-shop gave him no ideas. In fact, Brandol didn't know if he wanted any ideas because that idea would have to be acted upon. Biting his lip, he glanced around the shop once more. Isabelle's spades lay on the floor near the door. He picked one up and held it awkwardly.

"Good as anything," he muttered to himself.

His thoughts were jumbled as he leapt from the porch onto the grass. The spade shook in his hands. What would he do if he caught

Lord Oslan? Threaten him? Bludgeon him? Brandol didn't think he could even speak properly in this state. And any violence he managed to inflict on the nobleman would likely be severely punished. Isabelle's cries had long vanished. The rain still came down steadily, although it wasn't pouring down as it had been.

As he crossed the hedge, the spade caught in the branches and threw off his balance. He gave the handle a hard tug, and the spade jerked free, but his feet slipped on the wet grass. He hit the earth, knocking his head on a sizable rock as the blade of the spade crashed down on his face, dazing him. He stayed conscious long enough to crawl back to Henry's side of the hedge and cover his face with the shovel. Then he passed out.

When Brandol opened his eyes, he had no idea if he'd been out for seconds, minutes, or hours. What he did know was that his nose, forehead, and the back of his skull ached terribly. Water and mud drenched his clothes, the forgotten key to the coffer dug into his back, and he still had a shovel covering his face. Slowly, he sat up, looked around, and remembered how he'd gotten in such a messy predicament. He wiped his nose with his hand.

"I shouldn'ta done this," he moaned when he saw blood on his palms. Blood always made him queasy. "What'm I doing?"

Getting up proved difficult on the slick ground. He looked toward Lord Oslan's manor, then down at the shovel. Everything, including the ground, started spinning, and Brandol lost all heart. He closed his eyes and clutched his leg, feigning horrendous pain. Leaving the shovel where it lay, he crawled back to the woodshop, dragging his arms and knees through the mud and slick grass. He thought he heard shouts coming from Oslan Manor behind him, but didn't dare look back. He slumped to the floor of the shop, wondering what to do next. When nothing came to mind, he simply sat in his misery and watched the blurry, colorful world spin in front of him. Would Maggie find him like this? He hoped not. Several minutes later, the street door opened and Master Henry walked in, shaking the rain off his cloak.

He saw Brandol's state and asked, "What happened to you?"

Brandol ignored Henry's question and explained as best he could in his current state of distress about Isabelle, Lord Oslan, and the gold. Words never came easily for him, but any distress made speaking much more difficult. Henry didn't listen long. As soon as he heard about Isabelle being dragged off, his expression turned furious and he ran through the side door. Brandol stayed on the floor long after Henry had gone, trying to ignore the pain in his nose, waiting for the bleeding to stop, and feeling absolutely worthless.

EIGHT

The Fury of Lord Oslan

L ord Oslan's key rattled in the lock before the door burst open. Isabelle turned to look at her father. His face was red and puffy like a huge blister. It gave his bared teeth an even yellower hue. His eyes blazed with the fires of hell. For once, he paid no mind to the muddy spots on the floor. He walked to the hearth, withdrew an iron poker, and advanced toward her.

"Where . . . is . . . the . . . gold?" He punctuated each word by tapping the poker on the floor.

Somehow Isabelle's voice remained calm. "I don't know what you're talking about."

"M—Master." Isabelle heard Norbin's exhausted voice at the stairs as he slowly climbed. "Please . . . You must come to your senses before something happens that you will regret."

"Tell me where it is, girl, or I'll beat it out of you."

He moved forward, brandishing the poker like a sword, and Isabelle knew she must either confess or die. Her father had lost his reason, and Norbin could do nothing to save her. She recoiled back, trying to sink into the wall, and closed her eyes. She remembered her mother's admonishment not to give in to her father's intimidation.

Summoning her strength, she opened her eyes, raised her head, and said, "Give me your best, Father!"

"My Lord!" Norbin cried as he appeared in the room, "Master

Vestin is at the back door. He appears intent on coming inside, and he is armed."

Lord Oslan swung the poker savagely. Isabelle closed her eyes and braced herself. The iron struck the wall right above her head, and sent pieces of stone showering into her hair. Her father marched down the stairs, screaming curses at the Lord of All Worlds and Beyond.

"I told that fool of a boy I never wanted to see him again!"

Isabelle tried to get up and stop him, but her body was drained. A groan escaped her as she slumped back down on weak legs, but all she saw was the image in her mind of her father running Henry through with a sword.

"Do you love him or not?" She stood back up, grunting through the pain and fatigue. "Then get up!"

Lord Oslan's footsteps boomed across the den. The clatter of metal on stone reverberated through the house as he dropped the poker to the floor. Then Isabelle heard the sound of her father removing his sword from its place above the hearth followed by his steps marching to the back door. Isabelle had barely made it halfway down the stairs when her father left the manor. She jumped over the railing and pain shot up her legs, nearly causing her to fall over. Ignoring it all, she grabbed the abandoned poker and chased after her father.

Henry and Lord Oslan circled each other on the grass, swords held at the ready. Henry's lips were pursed, his face pink, and his eyes wide as they darted between Lord Oslan's face, sword, and feet. What scared Isabelle wasn't Henry's horrendous footwork, but that he wasn't even holding the sword properly. Her brother, James, had taught her a little about swordplay—enough to know that Henry stood no chance.

Her father attacked as he yelled, "I warned you!"

Isabelle shouted a warning. Henry ducked as he tried to parry Lord Oslan's attack, barely saving his own life.

"Your gold is in my home!" Henry's words came in a stammering rush. "Kill me, and you won't get it."

"Oh you think so?" Lord Oslan swung his sword again, this time downward at Henry's head. Henry leapt back and slipped on the grass. Lord Oslan saw his opportunity and took it. Isabelle rushed forward and hit her father in the back of the knees with the poker, sending him crumbling to the ground in a yelp of pain. He rolled and looked up at Isabelle. Henry scrambled to his feet while Isabelle stepped on her father's wrist.

Her father had no chance with his sword pinned to the ground and Henry's blade pointed at his neck. Isabelle knew it hadn't been a fair fight but didn't care. She watched the madness leave her father's eyes, noting the rage still simmering below the surface. He glared at both of them in disgust.

"I yield! I yield!" He released his grip on the sword, allowing Henry to pick it up. The two swords in Henry's hands were almost identical. Isabelle took her foot off her father's wrist and allowed him to pick himself up very slowly. Lord Oslan refused to look them in the eye as he brushed himself off and limped past them. All he said was, "We can discuss this inside."

Henry surveyed Isabelle's disheveled, filthy state and, with only a look, asked her if she was all right. She answered him with a nervous smile, and his expression of relief touched her. They followed Lord Oslan into the den, where he picked up a pipe from the mantel and lit it. Then he sat in his favorite chair and waited for them to take their seats. Henry, wet and half-covered in mud, sat on the threadbare couch. Isabelle, even filthier, sat opposite him. Lord Oslan watched them, daring one of them to speak first. Norbin entered the room from the hall, looked in briefly, then muttered an excuse to leave them to their business.

"My condolences about your wife, Lord Oslan," Henry offered with real sincerity. "She was a good—"

"Spare me the nonsense and tell me where my gold is."

"I returned home only minutes ago from a delivery; during my absence the money passed into my possession—"

"It can't be 'in your possession,' boy." Lord Oslan tightened his grip on his pipe. "Don't you get that? It is legally mine! I can take it from you."

"I forbid you from entering my home."

Isabelle tried to speak, but her father cut her off. "I have a receipt from my wife of a thousand crowns. I have an empty coffer buried at the junction of our properties. Any magistrate looking into the matter will draw the appropriate conclusions."

"But I have witnesses who can bear record that I was gone during the time your gold went missing."

"They will search your home and find it!"

"You won't find it, Father." Isabelle's voice sounded much braver than she felt, but saying the words gave her a deep sense of satisfaction. "But it will interest you to know that Mother did not have a thousand crowns, but over three thousand. You may have it all if you give me written consent to marry Henry."

After two strong puffs, Lord Oslan pulled the pipe from his teeth. "You think you can bribe me, Isabelle? You've hated me—despised me—even though I've given you food and shelter for almost two decades. Should I feel shame for wanting to keep your honor and name intact for you and your children?"

Isabelle wanted to scream about how he cared not one whit for her or her future children, but held her tongue. Henry closed his eyes and rubbed his temples. Lord Oslan took another long puff before speaking.

"Think of me however you like, but always remember that you are ungrateful and unworthy of what I've already given you." The pipe in his mouth trembled up and down with his jaw, and the spit that had formed at the corner of his lips flew as he spoke. "You will never see the day when I allow you to bribe me with money that is legally mine!"

"Go to the city officials. Order your investigation. Henry and I will hide the gold."

"And by the time the magistrates decide anything we'll be gone," Henry added.

"And good luck finding someone who cares enough to help you," Isabelle finished.

Lord Oslan's face reddened once more. His teeth clamped down on the pipe as he sputtered twice and finally hissed, "I am through being the pauper-nobleman. I have played that role for thirty years. I've tolerated the smirks and comments from my own peers, and will not stand for it another day. Not one more day. Hear me?" He stamped his foot hard enough to shake the room. "Do you hear me? I will have that money! Now. Get. Out. *GET OUT!*"

Henry and Isabelle left through the back of the manor. The rain had lessened, but not stopped. When they crossed the hedge, Isabelle slowed her pace, unable to put up a front of strength any longer. Henry helped her to the ground, not worrying about ruining her dress now with all its stains and tears. Then he put her head against his chest and held her, stroking her hair as he did so. Listening to Henry's steady heartbeat calmed her. As he whispered to her, telling her things would turn out all right, she believed him. When she pulled away, she kissed him fiercely.

"Thank you."

Henry took her face in his hands. "I'm so sorry about your mother. Brandol told me the moment I returned home. I came as quickly as I could."

Isabelle nodded quickly to tell him she was fine. She brushed away her tears before he could do it.

"You can't go back there," he said. "He wanted to kill you."

"What choice do I have?"

"Isabelle, you are not going back!"

A sad laugh came from her. "Everything I own is there. Look at the state of me! What am I going to do?"

"We'll think of something." His hand caressed her cheek. She closed her eyes. "But it's no place for you anymore. I won't feel safe until you've left that house forever."

Her eyes opened again. "Are you suggesting what it sounds like?"

Henry nodded solemnly and pulled a long piece of grass from the lawn. "Yes. We're leaving as soon as possible."

"You can't say that, Henry. It's not that simple."

"Why not?"

"What about Brandol and your apprentices? Where will they find work? What will you tell Maggie? Will she come with us?"

"I will answer all those questions as soon as I can."

It amazed her that they had so quickly come to terms with leaving Richterton. They had discussed it on occasion, but it had always been one of those ideas she believed would never really happen.

"I have—I have so many questions—so many thoughts running through my head right now, I can hardly think clearly."

Henry kissed her. "Share them with me."

Isabelle took a breath, which helped focus her mind. "My mother's funeral—how will I plan it? Where will I sleep until we leave? What will I wear if I can't go back home? Where will we end up? What will we do when we get there? How will we be married?"

"All right, all right," Henry laughed. "Not so many at once. You'll stay in Maggie's room with her. As for your things, Maggie or Ruther may have some ideas, or we'll buy you new clothes at the market. I'm certain we can arrange your mother's funeral together. Maggie will want to help, too."

Henry pulled her in for a tight hug. They sat together in the wet grass and talked until crunching footsteps on the Oslan's side of the hedge startled them. Henry stood up and moved between Isabelle and the hedge, his sword raised, his face white and strained.

"Hello?" he called out.

"Miss Isabelle?" Norbin asked as he came through the hedge. "Is that you?"

Isabelle exhaled her relief. "Yes, Norbin, I'm here."

"Thank the heavens you weren't hurt, young lady!" her butler cried in a cracking voice. "Your father was fit to kill." He emerged from the hedge still wet, muddy, winded, and flushed from neck to ears. "He left . . . moments ago. Ordered me to pack his clothes. Then he said to prepare the carriage. When I'd finished, he left without another word to me. Never seen anything like it. I thought now would be the best time to move Lady Oslan to the cellar where it's cooler until the undertaker can come for her."

The three of them bore Lady Oslan's body from her chamber down the stairs. Isabelle's wrapping held up well, and they carried her with all the respect she deserved. As they moved past the den to the kitchen where the stairs to the cellar were located, something struck Isabelle's eye.

"Henry, look!" she cried.

On the wall above the mantel of the fireplace, instead of four handsome frames, there hung three, and only two of these frames now held canvases. Lady Oslan's portrait and frame were both gone. Isabelle recognized the remains of both in the crackling fire. Far more alarming was that the portrait of Isabelle, commissioned by her mother only a year ago, had been hastily cut out.

"Did you see him do this, Norbin?" Henry asked.

"No, Master Henry. As I said, he ordered me to pack his belongings."

They stared for a moment longer at the wall that now seemed strangely empty, then continued through the kitchen and into the cellar. The room was dark, cold, and smelled of dried fruit. As Isabelle helped set her mother's body down on a long table, her mind held so many questions. Foremost among them were these: where had her father gone, and what had he done with her portrait?

NINE

Henry's Surprise

Henry and Isabelle decided to leave Richterton immediately after the funeral of Lady Oslan. But when to hold the funeral? They both needed time to tie up loose ends before leaving town. Isabelle wanted to give her brother, James, ample opportunity to return, and Henry had to deal with finishing outstanding orders and placing his apprentices and journeyman in the hands of capable new masters. Ruther had not yet returned from his latest travels abroad telling stories, and Henry could not imagine leaving without bidding farewell to his best friend.

The undertaker said he could preserve Lady Oslan's body for two weeks past her death, and not a day more. With a date in mind, Isabelle sent letters to James and all the friends of her mother, informing them of her death and the date of her funeral ceremony. Henry wrote to all the woodworking masters he knew or had heard of through his own work and his father's contacts. He also visited several in the nearby area.

On the merit of his reputation alone, Henry had no problem placing his apprentices in training with new masters. It was Brandol who proved more difficult. As an apprentice, Brandol had made a name for himself among the trade masters as a hopeless cause with no self-confidence. Henry visited everyone he could think of, but the most promising answer he received was from a cabinetmaker on the outskirts of town: "I'll think about it."

It was evening when Henry left the cabinetmaker's shop, and he was still far from the heart of Richterton. Homes and places of business were few and far between in this area, and Henry came upon a small quiet tavern with only one horse tied to the post. As he passed the tavern, he looked a second time at the horse.

"Ghost?" he muttered as he rode closer to the animal. On a third inspection, Henry was almost certain it was Ruther's horse. He tied Quicken up next to Ghost and went inside.

The tavern was empty save for two people. One man sat at a table carving a small block of wood, his eye on the second person, across the room—a cloaked figure with a shock of red hair sticking out from under the hood, slumbering deeply, his head resting on his arms.

"Are you the owner?" Henry asked the first man.

"Aye," was the answer.

"You know this man?"

"Nay."

"How long has he been here?"

"'Bout three hours. Came in 'ere like the devil was after 'im. Asked to tie the 'orse up in back. Said 'e could as long as there weren't no problems. Drank himself to sleep about an hour ago. Brought his 'orse round front 'cause it was bothering mine. Temper-y-mental, mine is. Figured I'd throw 'im in the cot out back 'til morning if 'e don't wake up soon. Gets busy 'ere soon and I need all the space I 'ave."

Henry moved to the sleeping man and pulled the hood off his head. It was Ruther. He had a large bruise around one eye and a puffy upper lip oozing blood. "What happened to him?"

The owner shrugged. Henry shook his friend vigorously until Ruther's eyes opened.

"Hello, friend," Ruther croaked. "What time is it?"

"Time to go home," Henry said, pulling on Ruther's shoulders. As he helped Ruther up, Henry turned to the owner again. "How much is owed?"

"One silver and five coppers."

"Good heaven, Ruther. You drink like a fish." He reached into Ruther's purse and found it almost empty. He thought this odd considering Ruther was coming home from telling stories for the last several days. He reached into his own money bag and handed six coins to the owner and thanked him.

"No . . . no . . ." Ruther protested on their way out the door. "I can pay for it."

Henry helped Ruther onto his horse and they rode slowly into town side by side. Ruther came to his senses about halfway through the journey, and Henry told Ruther about all that had transpired since Ruther left.

"I wish I'd known this story days ago," Ruther commented. "I could have made a small fortune with it!"

"Thank you. That's very comforting."

Ruther swayed in his saddle a bit, then caught himself. He began whistling a low tune that Henry vaguely recognized. Then he abruptly stopped. "Where do you and Isabelle plan to go? South? I would, it's warm almost all year around."

"Probably west, but we aren't certain—"

"The funeral is when?"

"Just four more days. We need someone to forge legal documents for us first. Records of identity, certainly. Writs of passage, too, if possible."

"I know a man who can make excellent records of identity. He's among the best forgers in the business, but it'll cost you. Most won't forge writs of passage these days."

"Why am I not surprised that you know forgers?" Henry asked. "And what happened to your face?"

Ruther grinned, making his puffy, split lip more pronounced.

"Some buffoon didn't like my story's ending, so he hit me in the face. He was drunk and chased me out of there."

"What story was it this time?"

"'The Shadow Walker,'" Ruther responded.

Henry searched his memory for the details of that particular tale. "Isn't that the one where you mock those who believe in the Path?"

"The very same."

"And the woman who walks the Path of Shadow triumphs over the man who walks the Path of Light?"

"It's a comedy—I received numerous hearty laughs and a thunderous applause. It's a popular story that also happens to bring a little enlightenment to the ignorant masses."

Henry snickered. "And one ignorant man punched you because you tried to enlighten him."

"Obviously a man who believes in the Path." Ruther shot Henry an annoyed glance, chastising him for his laughter.

Henry tried to hide his smile with his hand, but it was too late. "Obviously."

"What about you, friend, do you still believe in it?"

"I do. My parents claimed that they knew the Path to be real. That was always enough for me."

"So you take their word for it."

"I thought that last time we talked about this you said you were open to belief."

Ruther stared off into the horizon where two moons shone. "I'll believe in anything if someone shows me proof. But this . . . magical force that has existed since Atolas was created? The power of the Lord of All Worlds given to man? Come now, Henry, we're not children anymore. Time to let these stories die, isn't it?"

Henry shrugged. "It doesn't matter. We don't walk the Path. No one we know walks it, either. Besides, all the stories I've heard say that those who walked it were hunted down and killed generations ago."

"If it were real, it would be widespread news. Instead, only those who love conspiracies and rustic notions cling to it."

"Some believe that the Path only reveals itself to those who seek it or those who believe in it without proof."

"Yes, well, that's all well and convenient, but you see what my attempt at rousing a good debate got me." Ruther gently probed the bruises on his face.

"An expected result from a rough crowd."

"One man does not a rough crowd make. But I'll never go back there again." Something in Ruther's voice sounded off to Henry, but he couldn't tell what it was and let it go. It brightened his spirits to have Ruther back in town. Hopefully Ruther could help him and Isabelle prepare for their departure and figure out exactly where they would make their new home.

The last few days before the funeral ticked away like seconds on a clock. Ruther was at Henry's home every day examining maps and giving Henry and Isabelle advice on the best places to consider relocating. Maggie made up her mind to stay behind and try to sell the Vestin house and shop. She would use the money to buy herself something smaller that suited her needs until she married. Isabelle anxiously awaited word from James, but none came. And perhaps most importantly, there was no sign or rumor of Lord Oslan's whereabouts.

TEN

The Funeral

A small crowd of guests arrived at the cemetery to pay their respects to the late Lady Oslan. So also did large gray clouds, which hung low over the hillside of Lady Oslan's family plot. As the proceedings began, the rain fell in a constant drizzle. On the faces of the guests, Isabelle saw the same question: where was Lord Oslan? Isabelle still did not know the answer, and she still did not care. The abbot's voice and words cast a somber mood over the crowd. Isabelle tried to listen, but her thoughts delved into her own memories.

"The most difficult aspect of death," the abbot said in his deep voice, "is the hollowness we feel as we try to fit pieces of our life into the spaces vacated by those we love. We who have seen the best and the worst of our loved ones, we who have forgiven and loved them unconditionally—we must trust in the Lord of All Worlds."

Isabelle's earliest recollections of her mother were starkly contrasted with her later ones. Lady Oslan had been a forbidding woman before her illness. As a child, Isabelle had believed her purpose was to be put on display for her mother's friends. *Now Isabelle, show off your new dress to them. Recite your poems. Sing the song I taught you. Go get your flute so you can play Father's friends a tune.* Affection only came when Isabelle had amused or astounded those in the Oslan social circle, and disapproval was quick if she missed a note or forgot or mispronounced a word.

When Lady Oslan became ill, her priorities abruptly changed. Her relationship with her children changed, too. Isabelle marveled at how a loving, nurturing relationship with her mother had grown and blossomed over the nine years since the start of her mother's illness. Isabelle never faulted her mother for treating her in the way she had; it reflected the way Isabelle's grandmother had treated Lady Oslan, and the way her great-grandmother had treated her grandmother, and so on back through generations. Isabelle saw the same behavior between many of the daughters and mothers of nobility; Lady Oslan would have continued to transform her daughter into the same mold had she not seen the error of her ways.

"We struggle with answering the questions we have," the abbot continued, "such as why loved ones are taken from us when we still need them here. The Lord of All Worlds is our greatest teacher. He teaches us that the answers will be made known through our faith . . . although the answers may come in this life or the next."

Lady Oslan had intended to send her children to Mrs. Vestin only temporarily while she raised enough money to send Isabelle and James to a reputable school. In fact, for years Lady Oslan claimed to her friends that she taught the children herself. Then, the same day that James enlisted in the Guard and left home, Lady Oslan invited Mrs. Vestin into her chamber and tearfully thanked her for all the good she had done for her son and daughter. James had received higher scores on his entrance examination than any of the school-reared nobles from Richterton. Both proud of her son and ashamed of her behavior, Lady Oslan offered to write letters of recommendation for Mrs. Vestin so she could tutor more children from noble families.

"After putting our trust in the Lord, we must lean on those around us and let them be the Lord's hands to support us in our weakness. The Lord Almighty does His greatest work through charitable men and women who are engaged in His service."

Lady Oslan initially disliked Henry and Maggie because of the influence they had on her daughter. She believed if Isabelle were to be ready for Richterton's high society, she would need to sacrifice her friendship with the Vestin children. As a budding adolescent, Isabelle believed she could live without Maggie and her habit of nagging and bossing, but Henry . . . that was another matter. Even a young woman of nobility such as herself could see that the other girls in the markets had grand ambitions of marrying Henry Vestin.

After all, Henry's father had wealth, respect, and a successful business, and Henry stood to inherit all of it. His strikingly handsome face, promising carpentry skill, and generous nature guaranteed that the girl who married him would be a lucky one. But not a girl of noble birth, Isabelle had to remind herself. Yet no matter how often she did, her spirit soared every time he smiled at her or contemplated her with his calm, blue-eyed gaze. Her mother had plans for her to marry not a carpenter, but a guardsman rising quickly through the ranks—someone with a bright future in the King's army. A man like that would be chivalrous, provide protection, and let his wife want for nothing. She constantly reminded Isabelle that Mr. Vestin hadn't taught his son to wield the sword, and swordplay remained very fashionable in Blithmore, a fact Isabelle believed until life taught her that Henry could protect her without using a sword.

When Isabelle was fourteen, she and her girlfriends were strolling through the market on an early morning. Some boys no older than ten were chasing a large stray dog away from the meat stalls. One of the boys got a little reckless and pelted the animal with a rock. Somewhere in the dog's mind, madness set in. With a feral snarl, the dog turned on the boy, who shrieked and ran for safety—behind Isabelle's dress. The dog's attention went to Isabelle, and he lunged for her with his fangs bared. From out of nowhere, a large melon struck the dog's face, knocking the beast to the ground and sending it yelping down the lane in a disoriented panic. Henry tried to convince

Isabelle that Ruther had thrown the melon, but his blue eyes gave him away. At age fourteen, it was the first time she'd wanted to kiss him.

The incident with the dog was the catalyst that changed Lady Oslan's mind about Henry. She cautioned Isabelle less often about seeing Henry outside of their morning schooling sessions. She spoke kindly of him more frequently, even occasionally asking Isabelle about his health and work. Then, late one night, after a particularly nasty altercation between Lord and Lady Oslan, Isabelle heard her mother sneak into her bedroom and kneel at Isabelle's bedside.

"Are you awake, darling?" Lady Oslan asked her daughter.

Isabelle looked up. She hadn't been able to sleep through the shouting. Silence in the room followed as Lady Oslan stroked her daughter's hair and cheek as she had when Isabelle was young. In the darkness, Isabelle heard her mother's heavy, wet breathing and understood she had been crying.

"Marry for love, Isabelle," Lady Oslan urged with a strange passion in her voice. "No matter who it is, marry him for love and nothing else. If it is strong enough, your love will see you through to the end of time."

Then her mother kissed her forehead and cheeks, and left.

Murmurings in the crowd at the cemetery tore Isabelle from her memories. The abbot faltered and stammered in his eulogy. Someone was moving among them, pushing through the crowd. Isabelle pulled back her cloak to see better. The rain masked her tears and washed them away. That was fine by her. She was weary of crying.

Her father emerged from the crowd and stood graveside. The abbot glanced at Isabelle and then continued his elegy. Isabelle glared at her father. How dare he interrupt her mother's ceremony in such a fashion? He met her gaze, but she saw no malice in his eyes. He simply looked at her, nodded, and then turned his attention to the abbot. Henry took her hand and held it tightly.

The abbot finished his last words and offered a prayer. When it was finished, Henry and Norbin stepped forward to bury Lady Oslan. Lord Oslan tapped Norbin's shoulder and asked if he might do the honors. Norbin gave him the shovel. Isabelle wanted to stop him. Her father didn't deserve the honor. However, the idea of creating an ugly scene during her mother's funeral was even more repulsive.

As the dirt fell into the grave, she placed her fingertips against her lips and gave a kiss to her mother, imagining that she could press her lips to her mother's forehead and cheeks one last time. Her mother had spent her last breath, energy, even her last moment doing everything in her power to give Isabelle a chance at lasting happiness with Henry. Her mother had not rested until she had bestowed on her daughter real hope. Gratitude flooded Isabelle, and she thanked the Lord of All Worlds for blessing her with such a mother.

After the last shovelfuls were placed on the gravesite, Lord Oslan stood next to Isabelle and thanked each person for their support and attendance. When the last person left the cemetery, Lord Oslan turned to Isabelle and Henry.

"My apologies for being late," he said. "I returned to town less than an hour ago and heard the news. I came with all haste."

"What is it you want, Father?" Isabelle asked.

"I wish to speak to you—to both of you—this evening after sunset. Now that I've had time away and calmed myself, I think we can easily reach an agreement that will be mutually beneficial."

ELEVEN

Decisions

Isabelle, Ruther, Henry, and Maggie returned to the Vestin homestead to discuss what should be done. Henry's mind raced in circles. The traveling carriage in the stable stood ready and packed with their clothes, belongings, and several small bags filled with gold double crowns to help them purchase a new life. All he had to do was hitch the horses, shake Ruther's hand, and bid farewell to Maggie. On their way out of town, they would pick up their new identities—Adam and Whitney Morrison—and vanish into a city in the far west of Blithmore: Dunkerton. Along the way they would find an abbot to marry them by their new names. Henry didn't like them much, but Isabelle had chosen them.

Maggie fixed a late lunch of lamb and potato stew, and the four friends sat around the table discussing options.

"I think I should first state that I don't trust my father," Isabelle said. "Though that probably doesn't need saying, does it?"

"He seemed very sincere at the funeral," Maggie said. "Maybe he really has had a change of heart."

"I agree with Isabelle," Henry said. "I remember perfectly the way he looked the day Isabelle's mother passed away—and the things he said before he left."

This sparked a debate that lasted several minutes regarding whether someone of Lord Oslan's nature could ever truly change.

"I don't see why it matters either way," Ruther stated as he reached to the middle of the table to refill his bowl. Maggie looked on with disapproval at Ruther's lack of table manners. "Isabelle, Henry, you need something. He needs something. Why is trust even an issue?"

"Besides finding a new master for Brandol, we're ready to leave," Henry said in between blowing on the steaming contents of his spoon. "I've written him a strong letter of recommendation to help him in his search. Isabelle and I can walk out now and be gone forever. Her father could put a big knot in our plans."

"Or not," Maggie said. "I can't believe I'm agreeing with Ruther, but he's right. Lord Oslan needs money and you want to stay here, don't you?"

"Yes, we do," Isabelle answered, "but you have no idea—"

"What can he do?" Ruther asked. "He can't have you arrested. He can't kill you without challenging you to a duel first, and if he does do that, you and Isabelle run back here, hop in the carriage, and leave. Don't you see? He wants the money. He's thought it over and realizes that agreeing is his only option."

Isabelle and Henry exchanged a glance. She wasn't convinced, and neither was he.

"Henry," Maggie said, "if there's a chance you could stay, please take it. I have tried to be supportive through all this, but if you want to hear the truth, I don't want you to go. You're the only family I have left."

"You have me, too, Maggie," Ruther offered.

Maggie pursed her lips, a sure sign she was biting back a cutting remark. "I know I've got to settle down in the next year or two, but soon after you marry you'll have a son or a daughter. I can be of help to Isabelle around the home when that time comes. Please . . . at least hear what Lord Oslan has to say. For my sake. To keep our family together if we can."

"Certainly we will," Isabelle said. Her statement surprised Henry.

Again their eyes met, and he saw her sympathy for Maggie. If they stood a chance of being able to stay here with friends and family, why not try?

"Certainly we will," he repeated.

"Then that settles it," Ruther said. "I will get to be your best man, after all!"

Henry helped Isabelle put on her cloak before they headed out. They did not speak as they crossed the lawn. Their fingers were tightly knit, making Henry's hand sweat in the warm summer air. He kept his eyes fixed on the window with the candle. An owl hooting in one of the old orchard trees broke the silence, and Isabelle's head jerked in that direction. When they realized what it was, they shared a nervous chuckle.

Candles had been lit in the den. They heard two men's voices through the window. The moons had almost fully waned, so Henry couldn't properly see Isabelle's face until they were near the house. It was white and strained. Still, she gave him a weak smile and opened the door.

The conversation stopped at their entrance, though they heard Norbin bustling around in the kitchen with at least two pots. A fog of smoke wafted over from the den where Lord Oslan puffed on yet another pipe in his chair. Above the mantel, Isabelle's portrait hung next to James's in a frame that was almost identical to the old one. Isabelle noted with sadness the blank wall where Lady Oslan's had once hung.

"My prodigal daughter has finally come home?" Henry could not remember the last time he'd heard such a friendly note in the old man's voice.

"Hello, Father." She addressed her father in the same tone she would a stack of logs. Henry released his grip on her hand, but Isabelle didn't let go. She led him to the couch, where they sat across from her father. "Where have you been these last two weeks?"

Lord Oslan's lips closed tightly around his pipe. "On a small vacation . . . for my health and sanity. I needed time away to consider what I should do—what is best for my family."

Henry saw Isabelle's eyes flicker twice to her newly repaired portrait. "You nearly missed Mother's burial. You left no note telling us how to reach you—nor have I forgotten your abuses to me and Henry before you left."

Lord Oslan nodded. "I know. Believe me, I know I haven't won myself any friends, but I haven't many to worry about." He smiled as if his attempt at a jest had been funny. "I didn't love your mother. You know that. She didn't love me. You know that, too. Our marriage was arranged by our parents—"

"What about respect for the dead?"

Lord Oslan's eyes lowered to his lap. Henry almost lost his jaw to the floor. Isabelle's father looked sad. In all Henry's years, he had never seen this. He had never even imagined it. His first reaction was to disbelieve it, but the emotion, combined with this new tone of voice, seemed genuine.

"I never respected your mother in life, why should I in death?" he asked. "I was a beast, and she was unkind. It was a terrible marriage. If I could do it once more, I would marry for love." He puffed out a large smoke ring and watched it float up to the ceiling. Then he sent up another almost as big. "It's made me think about what I'm doing to my own kin, you and James. We have our differences, Isabelle. Many of them are probably irreparable, but I can still give you what I've never had. I can give you love."

Isabelle made a sound of disbelief, and Lord Oslan looked at her.

"Not my own love. I know that will not happen—at least not soon. It will take years to earn that. I mean with you and Henry. I've—I've made up my mind to accept your offer."

Henry and Isabelle exchanged a glance, both thinking the same thing. Of all they had expected to happen tonight, this had never crossed their minds.

"Why did you take my portrait, Father?"

Her father's eyes went to his bag. "I had an idea—a terrible idea. Once I calmed myself, I repented of it instantly. I guess you could say I had an epiphany in which I saw myself for what I am: a monster. I've spent all these years gilding the saddle on the steed carrying me to eternal torment, so now it's time to change." Henry and Lord Oslan looked into each other's eyes. Henry tried to detect some sign of deceit, but saw nothing except sincerity. Norbin stood in the kitchen watching everything. Henry wished the old servant would do something to break the silence.

"What was your idea?" Isabelle asked.

Lord Oslan shrugged and took another long drag. "I don't wish to speak of it. I was beside myself with rage."

"Then you'll write your consent to let us marry?" Henry asked.

For a moment Lord Oslan's eyes flashed some of the old anger, but then it was gone. Henry caught it and knew the old man's feelings had not changed toward him. It didn't surprise him—not after the insults he'd levied at the nobleman.

"Yes, but I want one thing clear. I still want the gold. I don't want to be poor. I've learned from the mistakes I made in the past with my poor financial responsibility. I think with a sum of three thousand crowns, I could manage quite nicely. Is that so terrible? One other request I have: I'd like to spend time with you and James before you marry. If he's received your letters, James should be here in a matter of days. It would be nice to take you both to the parade, Isabelle, as I did when you and he were children. After all, it only comes once every two years. What do you say?"

Henry saw the struggle in Isabelle's face. The idea of her father experiencing some sort of reformation was almost too much to believe. However, his offer seemed genuine and safe. Could she bear to spend more time around him? Even if it meant being able to stay in

Richterton permanently? If Isabelle was at all capable of real hate, it was only because of her father's nature.

"Fine," she decided. "I'll agree to that, but I want to see your permission in writing. Right now."

Her father held up his hands. "It won't do any good. I'll need to have the letter notarized, and that will take days. I am certain the two of you have made plans to run off. I don't blame you. You hold onto the gold, come with me to the parade next week, and afterward we'll make the exchange."

She looked at Henry, silently asking his opinion. All he had to offer her was a doubtful expression. Since Isabelle knew Lord Oslan far better than he did, he figured she ought to make the decision.

"Say something," she told him.

Henry started to speak, then stopped. He looked at Lord Oslan who smoked his pipe serenely as he watched them. Had it really been only three weeks since he'd last sat in this room asking Isabelle's father for her hand in marriage? He returned his gaze to Isabelle.

"As he said, it will take a long time for me—or you—to trust him." What Henry wanted to say, however, was that he didn't think he could ever trust the old man. "All I can suggest is that I want you to choose whatever your instincts are telling you right now."

Isabelle nodded and thanked him with a smile. After glancing at her father, she stared down at her hands, which were fiddling with a stray thread on her dress. As Lord Oslan waited for an answer, he rolled the pipe between his front teeth, making a series of clicks over and over again. Norbin announced from the kitchen, "Your food is ready, my Lord."

"Hold it for me, please, Norbin."

Something in what Lord Oslan had said to Norbin helped her make a decision; Henry guessed it was the word *please*.

"All right, Father. I'll give you one last chance. After the parade, we'll make the exchange."

Lord Oslan listened without reaction. Henry saw no sign of triumph in his face.

Isabelle took Henry's hand and held it up for her father to see. "This man means everything to me. Everything. If you have any love for me at all, please do not disappoint me."

TWELVE

The Grand Parade

Parades had been in fashion for a long time, and Richterton, being the capitol of Blithmore, celebrated all major holidays with fantastic festivities. The biggest holiday in the kingdom was the birthday of the reigning king, followed closely by the birthday of the queen, but most folks considered even those parades to be trifles when compared to the Grand Parade, which celebrated the Feast of Rulers.

The Grand Parade had begun one hundred and ten years previously, after the last war between Blithmore and Neverak, Blithmore's northern neighbor, had ended. Every year since the Treaty of Richter, the two countries took turns honoring the other by sending a magnificent procession through the country's capital, and the host country would then hold the Feast of Rulers. This feast served one purpose: it forced the leaders of both countries to meet and discuss foreign relations. The length of the feast often reflected the strength of the friendship between the sovereigns. The master of the parade this year was Ivan Krallick, sovereign Emperor of Neverak, and the feast was not expected to make it to dessert.

Henry wasn't a fan of these spectacles, especially the Grand Parade. Every two years the streets of Richterton filled with both Blithmore locals and citizens from the farthest reaches of the country. Parties and festivals abounded. Shops stayed open late into the night to accommodate the influx of visitors. Inns all around the city had to turn away those who had been foolish enough not to write for reservations months in advance. Though Henry had enjoyed the parade in his younger years—mostly for the sweets and toys thrown to the crowd— he now found it to be a nuisance. While business did pick up a little, especially among people who needed emergency carriage repairs, for Henry and Maggie the parade mostly meant kicking people off the front stoop the morning after the festivities had ended.

Regardless of his feelings, anticipation filled the city as carriages, carts, and riders arrived in town throughout the day. Henry had a difficult time keeping his apprentices focused on their work. Even Brandol appeared affected by the town's mood, and he rarely got excited about anything. While Henry's workers were distracted by the parade, his own mind constantly slipped to thinking about his meeting with Lord Oslan later that night.

Isabelle surprised him by showing up unannounced at the workshop mid-afternoon. "Is everything all right?" he asked. "Is he doing anything unusual?"

"I don't think so. He's been at home all day reading in his study."

Henry pulled her close to him, and she sighed deeply, as though being with him unloaded a great burden from her. Darren looked over at them and whistled lewdly. Henry responded with an angry look that told Darren to get back to work.

"It's like I've told you already," Isabelle said. "He's done nothing to make me suspicious. He leaves me alone to do as I please."

"How does he talk to you?"

"We only speak when we must, but it's pleasant enough."

"Any word yet from James?"

Isabelle shook her head. "Not even a note. I don't understand it. It's been almost three weeks. I wish he were here, though. My father wouldn't try anything foolish with James around."

Henry stroked her hair. He wished they had left when they had the opportunity, and he blamed himself that they hadn't. Now they depended not on themselves to make their own destiny, but on the honesty of her father.

"Everyone put your work down!" he called over the noise in the shop. "I need to speak." The sounds of carving and sawing stopped at once. "I'm going to need your assistance tonight, all of you."

"You said we could have the night off!" they complained. "It's a holiday."

"I know you have plans, and I don't intend to take you away from the festivities—and I'll pay you double wages for the evening."

No one raised any objections.

"I want all of you watching out for Isabelle, and I'm very serious about this. Understand? I'll give you specific instructions, and I want them obeyed."

He spent several minutes explaining what he wanted each boy to do. They weren't happy about what was required, but they cheered up when Isabelle thanked them all with a kiss on the cheek.

"Do you think you'll feel safe tonight?" Henry asked her after his boys went back to work.

"I do, thank you." She gave Henry a much longer kiss than those she'd given his apprentices. "I'm going home now. I can't wear this dress to a parade. What will you be doing until it all starts?"

"I'll track down Ruther to solicit his help, too."

She flashed a brave smile. "We'll get through this. Nothing is going to stop us."

As evening came, Shop Street and the surrounding blocks filled to the brim until there was barely enough room for the floats of the procession to pass down Richterton Lane. Isabelle sent Norbin to the Vestin house to inform Henry and the boys what she would be wearing to help them follow her. Ruther convinced the owner of the tailor shop on the corner of Shop Street and Richterton Lane to let him and Henry climb onto the roof so they would have a better view.

"Trust me," Ruther insisted to Henry, "you'll be able to see everything better from up here, and the boys won't have to look so hard to find you for directions."

Maggie decided to join them, but sat away from Ruther, who had brought his largest flask to accompany him through the festivities. Pandemonium reigned below them. Musicians and minstrels played their instruments on the stoops while crowds around them danced and sang along. Vendors pushed their carts selling dried meats and fresh fruits, cakes and breads, and small parade candles.

On the horizon the sun slowly set, but the thousands of candles and torches lining the streets gave the illusion that the sun had not disappeared at all. As night arrived and the fervor in the crowd reached its peak, Isabelle appeared with her father. She wore a light blue dress with brilliant white gloves, her hair decorated in almost a dozen large, pink bows. The bows made her easy to spot from the rooftop.

The roars of crowds farther north in the city carried a long way. Henry heard the cheers of approval and screams for candies and trinkets from the float masters. Horns and drums announced the gradual advancement of the parade with occasional fireworks bursting in the sky and outlining the few, faint clouds high above. Henry found it difficult to not be distracted by the flashing lights and patterns off on the horizon.

"Look!" Ruther shouted with youthful enthusiasm, pointing to the north. "See them?"

Henry followed his friend's finger to see the first float appear over a mile down the street. Even from a distance, it looked magnificent. As it drew closer, Henry saw it carried a great bird of prey with silver-tipped feathers, a white beak, and black eyes. The eagle stood taller than a man, and the only thing keeping it from flying away from the float was its collar and ropes fastening it to several iron rings.

"A captured silver eagle," Henry said. "It's sort of sad to see."

The crowd gasped and screamed in excitement when the eagle screeched at them and flapped its wings. Henry's eyes immediately went back to Isabelle. She stood about thirty yards away, completely surrounded by the throng. It took Henry another minute to find her father, but he eventually spotted him a few feet away from her. Lord Oslan, in his tall, bright green hat, seemed uninterested in the festivities. In fact, he appeared to be searching for something in the masses. Henry followed the direction of Lord Oslan's gaze but saw nothing of interest.

The floats that followed fell short of the standard set by the first, but not by much. Some featured live animals, others displayed dancers and fire-jugglers, one had a giant drum that needed four men to beat out its booming, hypnotic rhythm. The procession was occasionally interrupted by lines of musicians and twirlers wearing all black, making it difficult to see anything more than their faces and instruments. Those in attendance, particularly the younger ones, hunted and begged for the gifts and food thrown from the floats.

With the combined efforts of Ruther, Maggie, and Henry, Isabelle was never lost from sight, but this didn't satisfy Henry. It took very little to distract his apprentices from their duties. Between the gifts, the music, and the dancing girls, they often left Isabelle completely alone for minutes at a time. Henry constantly had to whistle and yell over the crowd to be heard by them, and even when they saw him, their responses were typically exasperated or reluctant.

Then the last float came. Henry had not seen anything so grand. The float was drawn by over a dozen fire-breathing dragonoxen, their scaly horns like massive curved spears. Henry shuddered as he remembered his own experience with a dragonox. It had nearly burned and gored him.

"Hey, Henry," Ruther said with a nudge, "Why don't you go dance on one of those?"

Maggie shook her head. "Not funny, Ruther."

The crowd quieted momentarily as they stared at the spectacle. On the float, Henry recognized the corpse of an enormous scorpion roughly twenty feet tall. Its abnormally thick legs supported a bloated black body and a large head with glittering red pincers swinging out from the sides. In the back, arching high over the body, was the pointed tail, and at the top of the tail sat the Emperor himself, Ivan Krallick.

Henry remembered as a young man seeing the royal leader of Neverak, but none of these memories adequately reminded him of the Emperor's unique appearance. The word that came to mind was one Ruther had taught him during one of his word games: *angular*. Beginning with the widow's peak at the top of his forehead, to his sharp nose and jaw, to his muscularly lean body, everything about Krallick seemed pointed, and his scorpion steed only enhanced that image.

The crowd announced its approval with a roar. Without warning, another burst of fire shot forth, this time from the scorpion's tail, a bright green and blue, bigger and brighter than anything the crowd had witnessed thus far. After the float passed, Henry found he couldn't see anything because of the bright spots in his vision.

The shock of losing his sight caused his heart to race. "I can't see Isabelle! Ruther, Maggie, keep her in your sight!"

"Friend, I am as blind as you," Ruther responded in a slight slur.

"I—I can barely see the crowd," Maggie said. "Everything's a shade of blue, but let me try and find her."

Henry rubbed at his eyes and opened them as wide as he could. Slowly images of the crowd rushing to the float came to him. "I can't find her." He stood and cupped his hands around his mouth. "Brandol!" The frenzy of the throngs drowned his shouts. He spotted his three apprentices in the clamor of people begging for gifts from the great float.

"Useless," he muttered to himself. He found Lord Oslan because of the green hat, but he was behaving peculiarly. He stood on a stump of wood, his head a foot above the crowd, and gestured wildly to someone far away. Henry thought it might be Isabelle, but still couldn't find her. Then he noticed a man worming his way through a river of people fighting for the Emperor's attention. This strange man's face was painted half ivory and half ebony, contrasting symmetrically down the center of his face with opposing colors around each eye and on his lips. The hairs on Henry's arm stood up. Lord Oslan caught the man's attention and pointed. The painted man nodded, and his hand went behind his back as though he concealed something there. Henry tried to see what it was, but his eyes were still too dim from the blinding fire.

"There's Isabelle!" Maggie shouted.

Isabelle stood almost exactly halfway between Lord Oslan and the strangely painted man. All but three of the pink bows in her hair had fallen out, making her much more difficult to locate. Only twenty yards separated her and this mysterious man, but with the mob the way it was, twenty yards was more like a hundred.

Henry's instincts told him this man meant to harm her. He yelled for Brandol and his apprentices. He tried whistling, waving—anything to catch the attention of his boys, but the noise of the parade made his efforts futile. Ruther and Maggie shouted with him, but still . . . nothing. And the man with the painted face continued to close the distance between himself and Isabelle.

Henry couldn't stand by and watch. On an impulse, he went to the edge of the roof and sprang, but as his feet left the ground, Ruther pulled him back. "Honestly, friend, do you want a broken leg? Will you be able to help her then? Use the ladder!"

Henry clambered halfway down the ladder and then, still impatient, jumped. In a flash he was around the house and into the street, but a wall of people obstructed him. The crowd hadn't seemed this impervious from the rooftop. He let Ruther and Maggie direct his movement from the roof, but it took him too long to navigate through the crowd. Their desperate gestures told him he had little, if any, time. Finally, he took a deep breath, dropped his shoulder, and plowed through the crowd. People shouted and protested, but he ignored them. From a distance that he did not have enough time to cross, he saw the man with the painted face grab Isabelle by the shoulder.

Isabelle, eyes wide with confusion, turned to meet him. Henry pushed forward as he watched the painted man bring his arm out from behind him. He held something . . . but all Henry could see through the crowd was that the object was black and thin—certainly dangerous from his perspective. Then the man bent forward as though he had something to say. Isabelle's head dropped as the man's hand moved in further. Henry shouted and shoved as he ran, but he couldn't reach Isabelle in time.

The man bowed deeply and snapped up as straight as a taut rope. Then, noticing the commotion that Henry was causing, turned in the opposite direction and disappeared into the swarm of people.

When Henry reached Isabelle, he saw she was holding the object in her hands. "Are you all right?" he gasped at her. "What is that? What happened?"

Isabelle handed Henry a heavy envelope made from black paper. The front appeared blank.

"Let's go home," he said, panting. "I don't need any more excitement tonight."

They pushed their way back to Shop Street, then to Henry's front door. Once inside, Henry held the envelope near a candle. There on the front, as if the light had some magical effect, in thick shining letters as white as bone was written:

To Miss Isabelle Oslan

THIRTEEN
The Black Envelope

Isabelle turned the envelope over in her hands. The candlelight reflected sharply off the richly drawn white letters, giving them a pale but fiery appearance.

"Who—who would send me such a ghastly thing?"

Henry handed her a letter knife. "Open it and find out."

"I don't think I want to," Isabelle said as she slit the envelope open and removed its contents: a matching heavy black parchment with the same shining white ink. In the top corner was an imprinted seal, its meaning foreign to Henry. Tilting the letter to the light, Isabelle read aloud:

> To the beautiful Miss Isabelle,
>
> When two kindred souls exist in the world, it is always fated that they should meet in order that love may blossom between them in fertile soil. It is in my power to arrange such a meeting between yourself and myself that perhaps we may become "ourselves." Therefore it is my most ardent desire that you will join me for supper tomorrow night so that we may together ponder on the blossoming of such a growth. I only ask that you keep our meeting an utter secret from everyone except your father, that I may remain a humble "gardener" in the eyes of your people. I will be wearing clothes to match the colors of this letter that you may

better recognize me. I will expect you at sunset in your finest at the Glimmering Fountain.

Very truly hopeful,

Emperor Ivan Richter Krallick III

"I don't believe this," Isabelle hissed. "This—I can't—"

"Do you think your father knew this would happen?" Henry was incredulous.

"My father receiving an audience with Emperor Krallick? It doesn't seem possible."

"Yet you're holding the blackest letter I've ever seen."

"And it's from the Emperor."

The front door opened, and Ruther came in smiling and swaying. "Well, we had a great adventure, didn't we? I think my eyes are still—"

"Get out, Ruther," Isabelle and Henry said together.

Ruther turned and left.

Henry read the letter twice more. "Now we know where he took your portrait and why."

"The Emperor intends to court me?" Isabelle asked over Henry's shoulder. "It makes no sense."

Henry put the letter back into the envelope. "I think we should ignore it—unless, of course, your greatest ambition includes being an empress."

Isabelle smiled and answered, "It does, actually. Only I counted on being *your* empress."

The door opened a second time, but this time it wasn't Ruther. Lord Oslan entered the Henry Vestin home for the first time ever—and without an invitation. He was an imposing figure in Henry's den, wearing his dark gray cloak, that ridiculous bright green hat, and a victorious smile brighter than any light Henry could have put in the room.

"I see you've received your post," Oslan said.

Henry had never seen such hate on Isabelle's face when she looked at her father. "You're mad if you think I'll meet him."

"You're mad if you think you have a choice." Triumph laced his voice and his lips wore a nasty grin.

"Certainly I have a choice," Isabelle snapped. "I don't have to submit to your whims, nor do I have to make pretenses of following your wishes. Henry and I are marrying with or without your blessing!"

"It would be best if you left now," Henry told him.

"Believe me, boy, it brings me no pleasure to stand in your hovel. Before I go, let me remind you of one thing, Isabelle. What you hold is a royal invitation which you officially accepted when you took it from the hand of Emperor Krallick's herald. Therefore, you are bound by law to fulfill your obligation to his summons."

Henry stepped in between Isabelle and her father. He spoke more forcefully this time. "The Emperor's royalty has no bearing on foreign soil, so I'll ask you again—"

"Except when on foreign soil by invitation of the King . . ." Oslan bared his yellow teeth fully, ". . . as during the Feast of Rulers." He uttered these last words with all the drama of a gambler playing his trump card. "I'll accept your invitation to leave now, and remember, girl, should you choose to break the law, I will be more than happy to help the King's Guard find you."

Henry grabbed Lord Oslan by the lapels of his cloak. "Leave us alone! Leave us *alone!*"

"Unhand me!" Oslan growled at Henry.

"Gladly!" Henry shouted, then kicked back the door and heaved Isabelle's father into the street. Lord Oslan landed in a puddle of muck with a wet thump and struggled to get up, his cloak tangled around him and his feet covered in slick manure. His face was scratched, soiled, and bleeding.

"How dare—"

"You forgot your sword this time, old man!" Breathing heavily,

Henry stepped forward and jammed a finger into Lord Oslan's chest. "If you trespass onto my property again, I will use every means I have to protect it."

When the door shut, Isabelle slumped into a chair with her face in her hands. "Why did I take that letter? I'm an idiot! A complete idiot!"

"This isn't your fault," Henry told her. "Don't let him do this to you."

"Besides, the solution is simple," Ruther added with only a slight slur, entering the main room from the kitchen. He was eating an apple.

"When did you come in?" Henry asked his friend.

"I went around to the back of the house when you so rudely told me to leave. I was listening to your conversation, waiting to see if you needed help. You know . . ." Ruther drew a finger across his neck.

"Why didn't you come out sooner?"

"Because I didn't think you needed help."

"How can the solution be simple?" Isabelle asked.

Ruther crunched loudly into his apple. "All you need to do to fulfill the requirement of the law is meet the Emperor for dinner, tell him you enjoyed the meal, and say, 'Thank you, but no.'"

"It can't be that easy," Henry said. "Her father is up to something."

"I don't care what my father says," Isabelle said. "I want to leave. You and Maggie can come with us if you wish."

"Leave?" Ruther repeated with a barking laugh. "Who said anything about leaving?"

"It doesn't matter." Henry felt an unusual heaviness in his chest. His voice sounded tired and flat. "I agree with Isabelle. I want to get out of here. I am through dealing with that—that—that—"

"Do you need me to supply you with some good words, friend? I know plenty."

Maggie walked into the room behind Ruther. "Leaving? Henry, why are you talking about leaving again?"

"Henry and Isabelle are letting the wicked Lord Oslan force them into his nefarious trap so he can have them arrested!" Ruther informed her through a mouthful of apple. "It's sad, really."

"I'm not letting him force me into anything!" Henry exclaimed. "We're choosing this. We're walking away with our heads high. You can come with us, Maggie, if that's your preference. We want you in our life. It's him we don't want."

"Maggie," Isabelle said. "I don't feel good about this."

"Neither do I," Maggie answered, "but I'd feel worse about you going to prison."

Henry didn't believe for one second that Isabelle would go to prison, but before he could say so, she spoke.

"My father has done something. I don't know what." She shook the black envelope at Ruther and Maggie. "This is more than just an invitation."

"What if it's not?" Maggie pressed. "What if this is his last attempt to make a profit from his daughter?"

"She's right," Ruther cut in. "Please don't take offense to me agreeing with you," he said, winking at Maggie. "Isabelle, Lord Oslan thinks if you meet the Emperor, you'll forget Henry, and before the day is done, he will suddenly be rich and powerful."

"You'd be a criminal! Henry, you can't let her do this." Maggie looked to her brother, pleading with him. "You both deserve a better life. Her father knows you don't trust him. What if running away is what he *wants* you to do? Then he'd have the final laugh as he ruins both your lives. Isabelle gets arrested—possibly you, too—*and* he gets his gold back."

"This is the drawback of falling in love with the most beautiful woman in all of Atolas," Henry said with a wink to Isabelle. "Emperors take notice and try to steal her away. I've seen it happen time after time."

Isabelle smiled at him. Ruther made a gagging sound, and when the others looked at him with annoyance, he held up his apple. "Almost choked to death."

A distant roar from the crowds in the streets told Henry the parade had moved far enough south that the excitement was over in their part of the city. Maggie stared at the floor and chewed her lip. Ruther munched nonchalantly on his apple.

Henry didn't know what to say. He knew Ruther and Maggie would never agree with him. "I'm sorry, both of you. I think Isabelle—"

"Don't tell me that, Henry!" Maggie turned to Isabelle. "You are both being too dramatic. This is easily fixed. Ruther's right. For once in his life, he's right! All you have to do is meet the Emperor, fulfill your obligation to the law, then leave town and get married where Lord Oslan—or the Emperor—can't bother you. You're already packed. Don't you see how much easier that is than living the rest of your lives on the run?"

"She's right, friend," Ruther added, ". . . about me being right."

"Please be quiet, Ruther," Maggie said with a heavy voice.

Henry stared at the floor. He didn't want Isabelle to see his indecision. What was the best choice? Run away with Isabelle and change their identities? Would that keep them safe? He couldn't imagine the King making much fuss over a woman who turned down the Emperor's dinner invitation. What if he was wrong?

"Henry," Maggie pressed, "you'll be making a mistake if you choose to ignore the invitation. How will you know when you've run far enough from Lord Oslan's reach? What kind of life is that?"

Isabelle's hand rested on Henry's shoulder. He saw sadness and hope in her eyes. "Let's listen to Maggie," she said. "I've been afraid for a long time. I shouldn't—*we* shouldn't be making such rash decisions based on our worst fears."

"I'm not going to let you meet him alone," Henry said. He looked to his friend for help and asked, "What do you suggest?"

"Where is the meeting taking place?" Ruther asked as he sat

himself into a chair and crossed his legs importantly. "Did I hear the Glimmering Fountain?"

"Yes," Isabelle answered.

Ruther took another large bite from the apple and chewed several times before speaking again. "If I were an emperor meeting an unknown woman in an unfamiliar inn for the finest dining in a foreign city, a woman who my spies—or even the father of the woman—have told me has a lover . . ."

". . . betrothed," Henry corrected.

"Often the same thing." Ruther gave Henry a dismissive wave and crunched his apple again. "I would be wary of repercussions from said lov—*betrothed*—and would therefore make arrangements with the owner of the inn to secure the entrances from any suspect personage, and certainly would have all patrons checked for arms. Wouldn't you?"

Henry and Isabelle exchanged a weary, and wary, glance. When the moment passed, Henry turned back to Ruther and said, "All right then, what do I need to do?"

FOURTEEN

Dining with an Emperor

Isabelle stood before her mirror wearing her best evening gown. Henry had given it to her as a gift almost a year ago (though Maggie had picked it out for him). The gown was resplendent, but the bedroom reflected in the glass was bare—devoid of the possessions a typical young woman of nobility would see surrounding her. She had a bed in one corner: a lumpy feather mattress resting on the floor with two blankets—one nearly thick enough to be called a quilt. Her only pieces of furniture were the mirror she'd received for her twelfth birthday and an empty wardrobe that might have once been handsome. The wood was cracked in several places so that the doors didn't quite close, and it leaned to the left. Henry could have fixed it for her, but Isabelle had always been too embarrassed about it to tell him.

Her hands shook as she finished buttoning her dress. She wished her mother were still alive. About three years before, on the night of her first official outing with Henry (her father had known nothing about it), Isabelle had stood before the same mirror while her mother sat on a chair behind her, rocking slowly and talking to Isabelle about the repercussions of a union between a noblewoman and a common laborer. Isabelle had listened politely, and her mother had known that her words would have little effect, but she felt it her duty to speak her mind. A smile would play on her mother's mouth whenever Isabelle's naiveté came out in the form of a question she could never ask in front of James or Norbin. Her mother's answers were both witty and truthful, and they had laughed together, helping Isabelle overcome her embarrassment.

The dress fitted her well, accentuating her sleek, tall figure and creamy skin, and gave her light brown hair a lighter tint. The Emperor would be pleased, and (hopefully) too enamored with her curves and fairness to focus on what was happening around him. Satisfied she had done her best, she blew out the candlestick in her window and wondered what Henry was doing at that very moment.

She wore no jewelry. Her few pieces had been packed away days ago, and she had no desire to search for them. She extinguished the last three candles illuminating her room, and with two and a half moons as her only light, looked herself over one last time. She locked her gaze onto her reflected eyes in the mirror and said, "Everything is going to be fine." Then she donned her best cloak and left the room. Norbin waited for her at the bottom of the stairs.

"Are you ready, Miss Isabelle?" he croaked. Lowering his voice, he asked, "You are packed, aren't you?"

"Yes, Norbin, thank you. The bag is in my room. You'll see it gets delivered?"

Norbin nodded as he put on a small black cap and his gloves.

"Where is my father?" she asked.

From the back of the house, Isabelle heard him call out. "Goodbye, Isabelle. Fare thee well!"

The tone of finality in his voice chilled the back of her neck, but she did not respond. Norbin led her to the stable where Esmond, the old horse, stood harnessed to the small covered wagon. The night air was perfect, her cloak worn more for fashion than protection from the elements.

Richterton's finest inn and restaurant, the Glimmering Fountain, sat not far from Germaine Castle. The ride was lengthy, as Oslan

Manor was one of the farthest of the noble houses from the castle. The cart was by no means elegant or comfortable, but Norbin did his best to direct Esmond over the smoothest parts of the dirt roads. In Isabelle's younger years, the Oslan family rode in a wonderful cart, but that possession, like many others, had been sold. As the cart traveled closer to the inn, the activity in the streets grew. It reminded Isabelle how she used to long for the time when she could spend her evenings among the city's elite, only to discover as a young woman that her father's reputation and poverty had already made her an outcast in many social circles.

As the journey wore on, the weight of the impending meeting pressed on her mind. Norbin attempted to discuss the plans she had agreed upon with Henry and Ruther the previous night, but she had memorized every contingency. The worry in Norbin's voice unsettled her. To distract herself, she peeked through one of the holes in the wagon cover to search the sky for familiar constellations.

The wagon approached an elaborate bridge which crossed a branch of the Drewberry River. On the other side of the bridge stood Castle Germaine and the homes of the wealthiest nobles in Richterton. A sharp but familiar smell stung Isabelle's nose as they crossed the river. Soon after, the carriage turned a corner and abruptly stopped.

"Are we—" Isabelle asked Norbin, but another voice cut her off.

"That'll do right there, old man." Only the voice of a member of the King's Guard carried so much authority. Isabelle knew because James was a guardsman and spoke the same way. They must have reached a blockade. "What have you got in your cart?"

"Only a passenger," Norbin responded through a dry throat.

The guardsman laughed. "In that tiny old thing? Of course you do. Derbin, get off your lazy rear end and search this wagon!"

Isabelle heard the faint sounds of a groan and a curse followed by footsteps in her direction. Then the heavily bearded face of an unhappy soldier appeared around the flap of the cover. The man, apparently named Derbin, held a lantern into the cart. When he saw its cargo, his eyes got very wide.

"Aye, sir," he stammered, still staring straight at Isabelle. "I'll say there is a passenger, indeed. Looks dangerous, this one." With greedy eyes, he added, "May have to search her."

The guardsman swore. "An old woman would be dangerous for you."

Isabelle heard the guardsman approach, then he yanked back the flap from Derbin and looked inside for himself. He, too, seemed to have the need to look more than once at Isabelle. When he was certain of what he saw, Derbin caught a backhand to the face.

"You filthy mongrel! 'Dangerous!' You better pray I don't make you a eunuch in the next five minutes." He looked back to Isabelle one last time, bowing his head gallantly. "Miss, how are you this evening?"

"I'm fine," Isabelle answered in a rather flattered voice.

"That's well," he told her. "Based on Derbin here, you may think chivalry has left the world, but I assure you it hasn't."

"Thank you, sir."

"What's your destination?"

"The Glimmering Fountain."

The man's face fell slightly. "Oh, I see. If that's true, then you will have to be searched. Order comes from King Germaine himself. Can't take chances."

Isabelle reached into her cloak pocket and removed the invitation. "But I was invited."

The man picked Derbin's lantern from off the ground and held it up. "Let me see that." He extended his hand and took the black paper. From the expression on his face, Isabelle could tell he had a hard time believing the parchment was anything more than a joke.

"If you let the candlelight hit it just right . . ." she suggested.

The man did so, and then his eyes widened larger than Derbin's had moments ago. "Forgive me, Miss," he hurried to say. "It's not my place to hold you up." He disappeared from view, but Isabelle heard him ordering other soldiers. "Clear the way for this one. You and you, escort her to the Fountain. No one stops her."

Sounds of hurrying and scurrying accompanied the commands. The blockades were dragged away, and Norbin urged the old horse forward. As she passed through, Isabelle saw several lantern-lit faces peering to catch a glimpse of her.

The distance from the blockade to the entrance of the Glimmering Fountain was measured in seconds. The wagon came to a sudden stop again, but Isabelle maintained her balance and allowed Norbin to help her to the ground. As she lighted, a man in a finely tailored coat and pants stood ready to receive her. He wore a large, round hairstyle and a matching black mustache. His arms and hands moved with quick precision as though he had been born for this exact duty, and in a flash his arm was out to receive her.

"Welcome to the Glimmering Fountain, beautiful Miss," he said in a strange and smooth accent. "I will be most happy to escort you inside, for no one walks into this fine establishment alone."

Isabelle smiled warmly at Norbin as this new stranger led her away, and the old servant returned the gesture, but with less enthusiasm. The escort opened the door and gave Isabelle her first glimpse of the interior of the Glimmering Fountain. For a moment Isabelle forgot her fears as she gazed at the grandeur of the inn. She had not been in any place so fine for several years. When Henry was younger, his father had made a small fortune on the work he'd been hired to do inside this building. Most of the ornate woodworking on the doors, frames, chairs, and tables had been done by the late Master Vestin's own hands, and, according to Henry, old Master Franklin, his neighboring silversmith, had done the fine metalwork.

"Are you meeting someone here, beautiful Miss, or dining by yourself?"

"I am meeting someone."

"Do you see your fellow diner?" her escort asked, but Isabelle didn't hear. What her eyes saw occupied so much of her thoughts that her ears had stopped working. It made sense now that Henry's father had been paid so handsomely—every wooden surface in the inn was carved with rich and detailed images of roses, sunsets, and, more than anything else, water spraying up and out in myriad fountains.

In the middle of the inn stood a great stone fountain. The bottom of the pool was gilded in gold and silver. Isabelle had seen nothing like it and marveled at the feat of engineering to make such a thing possible. The sound of its splashing waters was quite merry when accompanied by the smell of exotic dishes, the chattering of dining guests, and women dressed in lovely costumes serving food and flirting with the men. Everywhere she looked some new sensation captured her attention.

"Miss, please." Her escort gently stroked her hand to get her attention. "Have you found your fellow guest?"

Isabelle broke her gaze away from the fountain and searched the room. "A humble gardener . . ." she muttered to herself. Her eyes stopped at a table in the middle of the room.

"Excuse me, Miss?"

It was not a humble gardener that caught the eye of Isabelle, rather a man wearing a spotless white shirt with black pants and a red scarf around his neck.

"I believe that's him," she said, pointing to the man's back.

The escort paled slightly and his accent faltered. "The Emperor?"

"Then that's him for certain."

"Allow me, if you will," he said more graciously than ever. He took Isabelle's cloak and led her to the Emperor's table, already laden with food, though nothing had been touched.

"Your Majesty," the escort said at the Emperor's side. Several men sitting at nearby tables watched them closely. "Your guest has arrived punctually."

"Thank you," Emperor Krallick said. Isabelle was surprised that his voice, though drenched in a heavy Neverak accent, was pleasant in its unique blend of softness and well-polished articulation. "Please seat her."

"As you wish, your Majesty," the escort said as he helped Isabelle into her chair across from the Emperor. "Is there any other way in which we may enhance your dining experience?"

"No, you have done wonders already." The escort bowed himself away, leaving Isabelle feeling very alone. "How was your journey, Miss Oslan? Or may I call you Isabelle?"

"Isabelle is fine, your Majesty." Not having any prior experience around royalty, she wasn't certain how to behave or respond. She settled on answering in her most proper manners. "The journey was uneventful and as short as I could ask for. I thank you for asking."

She inspected him as discreetly as possible. His pupils were as black as his pants, and the outer corners of his eyes pointed at downward angles. His hair, a mixture of black with a dash of natural reddish orange was cut short, a widow's peak pointing to his angular nose, which aligned perfectly with his strong chin. Even as he smiled at her, his white teeth appeared square and angular. Isabelle could not help but wonder if the effect was intentional or if his mother had swallowed something with adverse effects while carrying him in the womb. His face had very few age lines. He couldn't be more than ten years her senior.

"Come now, you must have had some trouble getting here because of the blockades, for which I apologize. I thought it would be possible to move about inconspicuously while in Blithmore, but it has proved impossible."

"Did it really surprise you, your Majesty?" Even as she asked the question, it surprised her to find that she felt no intimidation from this man—something she had not expected.

Emperor Krallick smiled as though he had been caught. "No. No, of course, it did not surprise me, but one can always hope."

He reached into a small bag at his side which Isabelle hadn't noticed. From within its depths, he retrieved a large napkin, a steel knife, and a fork. After examining each of them, he began cutting his food into uniformly sized pieces. Isabelle didn't comment on the strangeness of what she was witnessing. Instead, she set her own napkin on her lap. From the corner of her eye, she noticed a table of three men, all watching her. The food on their plates was untouched and they hardly spoke to each other. Then she spotted two other tables with more men doing the same thing. Other patrons at the inn seemed genuinely enthralled by the Emperor's presence, though a few displayed an obvious dislike for him. Isabelle wondered if the Emperor could be in any danger.

The people around her were distractions. Henry had asked her to focus on discerning the intentions of her host. Occasionally she caught glimpses of patrons entering, sometimes in groups and sometimes alone, like the monk who limped in slowly, aided by Isabelle's same escort to a small table not far from where she sat. Seating for him must have cost extra, because when the old monk sat down, his trembling hand pressed a small number of double crowns into the escort's waiting palm.

"You must be thrilled beyond words for this meal," Emperor Krallick said, pulling Isabelle back to the conversation. At first, she thought she hadn't heard him correctly. Then he continued, "Let me assure you that the real thrill belongs to me. I consider myself fortunate to meet you."

Isabelle tried to smile at the Emperor's words and was ultimately successful. "May I ask a frank question, your Majesty?"

"Yes, of course you may."

She realized that when he looked at her, his gaze focused more on her lips than her eyes. Was that a normal custom in Neverak?

"Thank you. How did you come to know about me? Was it my father?"

Emperor Krallick chuckled, put a slice of bread on his plate, and topped it with blueberry jam. "Berries don't grow as well in the north, of course. I do enjoy Blithmore blueberries. Please help yourself to anything you see. I insist on it."

He held the bread while wearing his gloves. It was against the custom of Blithmore to eat while gloved, but he took a large bite of his food anyway. He chewed slowly, as if to demonstrate to her how delicious the bread tasted.

"Now to your question. The answer is yes. Your father came to my country and sought an audience with me. When I granted his request, he came to my throne with only your portrait and your story."

As he spoke, Isabelle gave in to the temptation of the food and chose carefully among the selections the dishes she most preferred. The Emperor watched as she made her selections and seemed pleased with her decision to sample the roasted duck.

"My story?" she repeated.

"Yes, of course." He put a small morsel of lamb into his mouth and savored its flavor. "I'll admit, I was moved. He told me of your family's financial state, the tragedy of your mother's early death, and your inevitable marriage to a wealthy craftsman who is trying to take advantage of your father's poverty. May I inquire as to the taste of the duck?"

Isabelle took her first bite and swallowed. "Delicious," she replied. It was the truth. In fact, she had never tasted better.

The Emperor sampled a piece for himself. "Yes, it is, isn't it? I prefer the lamb, of course. We raise hundreds of thousands of them in the colder climate of Neverak, but all the meats here are very tender."

"Your Majesty," Isabelle began, "I'm afraid—I am sorry to tell you my father may have . . . misrepresented many facts to you."

"I think you are being modest," the Emperor said as he tried the green beans, "and there is no need."

"No, I am telling you—"

"Do you mean to deny that your father is all but a pauper nobleman?"

"No, not—"

"Or that your mother recently passed on?"

"What I'm saying—"

"Or that you are not about to announce your engagement to a man beneath your title?"

"Yes!" Isabelle cried a little louder than she meant. "I do intend to marry a man, but out of love, not compulsory means."

Emperor Krallick was truly surprised at her statement, and his eyes narrowed on her as he chewed another bean. "A man you . . . love?"

"Dearly."

"Certainly not enough to refuse the offer of an emperor." He gave her a small grin, as though they shared a private joke.

"Yes," Isabelle replied, her eyes on her food. "Even that."

"You don't even know me yet."

When she finally looked up, she thought he appeared very disappointed at her confession of affection. "I have no doubt you're a wonderful person, your Majesty, and I know most women would think me utterly mad for doing this, but I can't accept your offer."

Emperor Krallick sat up straight with a small sigh and put his fork down. "I had hoped this wouldn't happen. There is no way you would willingly go with me? Live in my enormous palace for the rest of your life? Have your every need met in an instant?" He snapped his fingers loudly, as if to show her exactly what he meant.

Isabelle smiled, flattered by his offer. "The man I love is worth giving all that away. To him, I already am an empress."

"An empress?" Emperor Krallick repeated with his eyes fixed on hers. His voice was soothingly soft, almost entrancing. "Isabelle, you are beautiful. One of the most beautiful women I have ever seen . . ."

"Thank you, your Majesty."

"But an empress?"

"Yes, it's much to pass by, I know." She gave him a nervous smile and wiped her lips with the cloth napkin.

"You could never pass it by," he told her, his accent thicker than ever. "I have not offered it to you."

Isabelle stopped chewing her small piece of bread and swallowed a large gulp of water. It tasted bitter after the sweetness of the bread. "I don't understand. Your letter to me spoke of love and implied marriage."

The Emperor nodded, his eyes again on her lips. "I imagine it did. I hired a writer to compose it. Was it effective?"

The comment surprised Isabelle, but hearing it emboldened her. "No, the letter was awful."

Emperor Krallick's smile disappeared. Isabelle thought it almost laughable that he was upset over the contents of a letter he hadn't bothered to write himself. "That will have to be mended. Regardless, my offer to you was not of marriage."

"What was your offer?"

"Simply put that you live in my castle and be there to serve me when you are wanted."

"A hired servant?" Isabelle repeated with disgust.

"No." Emperor Krallick's expression betrayed his surprise at Isabelle's lack of understanding. "Not a hired servant . . . a concubine."

"I refuse." She took her napkin from her lap and wiped herself again with it. "And I wish to leave immediately."

Emperor Krallick's hand immediately rested on hers. The swiftness and gentleness of his touch amazed her. "Isabelle," he said in that same soft tone, and quieter than ever, "I have already bought and paid for you."

It could not be true. Slavery had been outlawed in Blithmore—and almost everywhere else in Atolas—for almost two centuries. Slaves could not be purchased, sold, or kept. Isabelle pulled her hand away and made to stand, but her legs did not respond. She tried again with the same result. She looked around at the other patrons, but everyone was oblivious to her plight. Only those men who had been watching all along knew what was happening. They seemed amused at her horror.

"Let me go!" she meant to cry, but sound did not accompany her mouth's movements.

The Emperor's smile remained as gentle as ever with his square teeth glistening whitely behind his lips. It broadened only when he saw her lips move without sound. He spoke to her in a near-whisper. "It's beginning to take effect, the poison." Then he let out a slow sigh. "I sincerely hoped you would be flattered by my offer. Of course, I'm not an unhandsome man. I know that. Your father warned me you might react this way to my proposal." He watched her obsessively as her head dropped, giving her the appearance of being deep in thought. "Don't fear, Isabelle, and don't panic. Getting upset only makes it work more effectively."

Isabelle's heart raced, and she tried to scream, but nothing would respond. She tried getting up again, even pushing herself up, but her mind now felt disconnected from her legs and arms.

"You will appear very sick—as though you've fainted. I'll carry you out in my arms, take you into my carriage, and in a few days you will be with me in my kingdom. I wish I had you there already, but these things take time to arrange."

Isabelle's last attempt was to move the small finger on her left hand. Though her muscles were sluggish, she moved it with great effort against the handle of her thin steel goblet. It shook mightily as she felt the cold metal against her skin. Finally, she hooked it. The goblet toppled down onto her plate in a crash, spilling water onto the table.

Several people looked in their direction. Out of the corner of her eye, she saw the old monk get up slowly, trembling even more than before. The Emperor made to get out of his seat, probably to carry out his farce of helping her to his carriage. Before he could stand, there was a flash of light at the top of Isabelle's vision. Emperor Krallick froze.

Isabelle was barely able to see what was happening as her sight dimmed. She saw the monk's robe behind the Emperor's chair, and realized that the flash of light was the reflection of the candles on a sword—a sword pressed against the Emperor's neck.

"Move an inch, and I'll slit your throat," Henry's voice ordered from beneath the hood.

FIFTEEN

An Unlikely Rescue

Though the Emperor stayed quite still, several men around the room drew swords or crossbows. Other patrons cried out in fright. Those with swords moved forward, and those with crossbows leveled them at Henry. In response, Henry's trembling hands pressed the blade tighter still against the Emperor's neck, causing the Emperor to gasp.

"Order them to stand down," Henry told Emperor Krallick.

"Stand down!" the Emperor announced.

A loud *twang* rang out in the silence. An arrow flew within two inches of Henry's face. His startled jerk drew a line of blood from Emperor Krallick's skin.

"Stand down!" the Emperor hissed again, his head remained stiff but his eyes darted to see who had fired the shot. This time the order was followed by the clanking of swords dropped on the wooden floor and the careful placement of crossbows at feet.

"Henry Vestin," the Emperor's voice sounded much calmer than Henry had imagined it would be, "you will not make it out of here alive."

Another patron stood up. This second man had a very large blond mop of hair and an unruly mustache. Henry didn't react as the blond man began collecting the swords and disabling the crossbows, but the roguish grin on his face helped Henry think clearly.

"Who is that?" the Emperor asked, watching this man out of the corner of his eye.

"No one of your concern," was all Henry dared answer.

"You've killed him, too—I hope you know that," came the reply in the same soft, confident voice that Henry found so unsettling.

"I said it's none of your concern."

"His death should be your concern. The penalty in your country for an assault on royalty is death."

"I am fully aware of the laws I am breaking," Henry answered as he watched the man in the wig remove all weapons from the vicinity.

"Then you haven't thought of your family, your employees, or your friends. All of them will suffer prison or death if they have aided you."

It stunned Henry that an emperor could know so much about him and speak with such control while a blade was pressed to his throat. Ruther finished with the weapons, and Henry gestured to Isabelle's limp form now motionless at the table. Ruther quickly scooped her into his arms, and for the first time, Henry sensed an aura of real displeasure from the Emperor.

"Stand up," he told the Emperor.

The Emperor slowly complied. "Be ready to leave the moment I am released," he commanded his own men. Then to Henry he said, "I will watch you die. I swear it."

Ruther led the way with Isabelle in his arms, while Henry backed out with his sword still pressed against Emperor Krallick. Henry's fastest carriage stood ready outside the inn with Maggie holding the reins of the horses. Getting the carriage through the blockade had not been cheap. Getting back out would be a completely different story.

"What happened to her?" Maggie asked when she saw Isabelle's state, but Ruther didn't answer. He gently placed Isabelle in the carriage, climbed in behind, and let Henry know he was ready. Henry gave Emperor Krallick a sound kick to the backside. The Emperor fell to his knees, and Henry sheathed his sword as he jumped into the carriage behind Ruther.

"Drive!" he yelled to Maggie. "Just drive!"

Though Henry and Ruther, both in their disguises, had been required to submit to a search by the blockade to enter this area of the city, no such examination was necessary to leave. Shouts came from the inn as they passed the guardsmen. The Emperor's soldiers yelled at the King's Guard to stop the carriage. Maggie urged the horses forward at full speed while Henry and Ruther attended to Isabelle. Henry did all he could to revive Isabelle short of harming her, but nothing invoked a response. He called her name several times, but it was like speaking to a corpse.

"The King's Guard are getting on their horses!" Maggie reported. "They're giving chase!"

"Did you hear what he was saying to her?" Henry asked Ruther.

"No, he spoke too quietly."

Henry nodded. He, too, had been unable to hear, and only the signal of the tipped goblet had told him something was wrong. Now he hoped that his ineptitude had not cost Isabelle her life. "Is she—I don't know how to help her. How do I know if she's even alive?"

"They're not far behind!" Maggie shouted. "The bridge! The bridge!"

Ruther grabbed the lantern hanging from the ceiling of the carriage and threw open the door. The stench of the staining oil that he and Henry had dumped on the bridge in copious quantities a few hours ago assailed his nose. He slammed the lantern onto the bridge, shattering the glass. Flames erupted and spread across the wooden planks, traveling in all directions much faster than Ruther had expected.

"Faster, Maggie!" Ruther yelled. "Or we're going to roast!"

He leaned out the door and saw the guardsmen pull back on the reins of their steeds and turn to find a different route. He choked back a laugh, mostly because the smoke had gotten into his lungs.

"It worked!" he wheezed as he closed the door and sat back down.

"Ruther, look at her," Henry begged. "I need to know if she's all right. Is she even alive?"

Ruther pulled open Isabelle's eye for a moment and stared. What he did looked painful, and Henry moved to stop him. "She's alive, friend. I learned a trick from an innkeeper out west. You check the eyes to see if the hole in the center changes in the light. If it does, she's alive."

"What if she's dying? If she's been poisoned?"

"I don't think this poison, or whatever it is, will permanently harm her," Ruther said. "I think she's asleep."

"Why?"

"Think, Henry. Why would the Emperor want to harm her?"

"I don't know. How long do you think she will sleep?"

Ruther frowned at him. "I'm a storyteller. What do I know? It could be minutes—or years."

Henry took the monk's robe off. Beneath, he wore his own clothes. He stuck his head out of the canvas and checked for anyone behind them.

"We're clear so far." His words sounded tight. "Thank you both for all your help. Ruther, I think your disguise fooled them. You should be safe. Just destroy that wig."

"Heavens, no, friend." Ruther folded the robe back into a neat roll. "This is too much fun. I'm going with you."

Henry saw the determination in his friend's eyes. "You owe me nothing."

"I know. You think if you leave me, I'll drink myself to death. While that could be true, if I don't go with you, who will defend Maggie and Isabelle?"

"I fared well tonight," Henry pointed out.

"All you did was hold a sword against his throat. You have no skill at swordplay."

"This coming from a storyteller!"

"Another good reason for me to join you. This adventure will give me the greatest stories to tell."

"If we survive."

"The storyteller always survives, friend."

The carriage pressed on swiftly. Henry tried to grasp exactly what path lay before them. The clopping of the horses' hooves came at a steady rhythm. Fortunately, Henry heard only his own horses.

"You're giving up much," Ruther reminded him, "and risking everything."

"I gain everything." Henry's eyes were on Isabelle as he said this. Then he shook his head and rubbed his temples. "I can't believe it came to this."

"It's not your fault."

"We should have left with the money when we had the chance."

"Only storytellers know the sequence of events from beginning to end." Ruther grinned as if impressed by his own brilliance.

"You're really coming with me?"

Ruther nodded, his grin not so bright now.

"I really am humbled. Thank you."

"What will be done with your home and shop?"

"Master Franklin, the silversmith, will sell it all and hold the money in trust, though I doubt I'll ever return to claim it." Henry's heart hammered in his chest. "We've got enough gold in hand to build a good homestead and a better woodshop, assuming I can find people who'll want my services . . . and assuming I can get us out of this country."

The carriage slowed as it turned onto Shop Street. Henry and Ruther readied themselves to act. The moment the carriage stopped in front of the house, they sprang out and rushed inside. The plan was simple and rigidly fixed: go to the homestead, harness the horses to the other carriage, load the remaining packs, and leave. While the men grabbed the packs, Maggie harnessed the horses to the larger but slower traveling carriage, as the lighter one was not sturdy enough to carry all their supplies over a great distance.

Ruther went to the pantry where their packs waited. Meanwhile, Henry crossed through the den and went upstairs into what had been his parents' bedroom. After closing the door quietly behind him, Henry went to his father's old desk, where he kept his records of his ever-growing quantity of orders. Henry opened a drawer and reached to the back of the bottom panel, activating a secret spring. The panel lifted up. Henry took it out and removed a small brown leather pouch connected to a long chain that had been concealed beneath it. A thump from the next room made him jump. He quickly put the chain around his neck, tucked the pouch under his shirt, and tiptoed over to the door.

"Ruther?" he called out, but heard no reply.

He left his parents' room and crept down the hall to the room where the apprentices slept, holding the lantern out in front of him. "Brandol?" he asked when he saw his journeyman standing in the dark room. "What are you doing here?"

"I—I had forgot something," Brandol mumbled in an embarrassed tone.

"The house isn't safe anymore. You'd better go now."

Brandol nodded. Henry hurried downstairs ahead of him and went out to the carriages. As he approached, he heard Maggie and Ruther conversing:

"We have to get it, Ruther! Aren't you listening?"

"We have no time!"

"I don't care. It's Isabelle's pack, and we aren't traveling with a coffer that won't open."

Henry stepped into the stable. "What's the matter?"

Maggie stepped away from Ruther. "Isabelle's pack is missing. Norbin was supposed to bring it and leave it on the back steps. It has the key to the coffer inside."

"I thought the money was in bags," Henry said.

"It was until Isabelle asked me to put the bags inside the coffer and lock it."

"Don't you have the key?"

"I did," Maggie explained, "but I gave it back to her earlier today so Norbin could watch it while we were gone."

Henry looked from Ruther to Maggie. "I'll go fetch the pack. You both finish getting ready."

"You do realize who'll be there, don't you?" Ruther called after him. Henry ignored Ruther's comment and left through the back of the stables. "You're not even taking a weapon?"

"What good would it do me?" Henry shouted back as he left.

He knew as he jogged to Oslan Manor that he should feel some measure of fear, but he didn't. After holding a blade to the neck of the Emperor of Neverak, Lord Oslan no longer seemed such an imposing figure.

He did not bother knocking before entering. He went straight for the stairs. About halfway there, Oslan walked out of his den with a large book in one hand and a pipe in the other. "Who is that?" he asked.

Norbin's head poked out from the servant's quarters. "Miss Isabelle?"

Oslan smiled when he saw Henry's face. "She's gone now, boy. There's nothing you can do about it."

Henry ignored him and ran up the stairs.

"Where are you going? Get out of here!"

Isabelle's pack rested on the floor in her darkened room. Through the floor, he heard the movement and voices of both Lord Oslan and Norbin. After a few seconds of searching through the bag, Henry found the key. He hefted the bag over his shoulder. The sound of footsteps reached him. Lord Oslan pushed open the door. Henry recognized the Oslan family sword gleaming brightly in his hand.

"You threw me out of your house for trespassing. Now I will kill you for entering mine."

"Believe me, I am leaving with all speed," Henry said. He made to go around Lord Oslan, but found his path blocked.

"Put down the bag," Lord Oslan said and gripped the sword tighter.

Henry took a deep breath. His eyes focused on nothing but the sword, hoping he hadn't run out of courage for the day. "No, I won't do that."

Lord Oslan moved forward with careful steps, the tip of his sword level with Henry's heart. The manic glow in his eyes made his intentions clear. "Isabelle is gone. Put down that bag."

Henry's blood pounded a war beat in his head as his reason melted in the face of rage. "You are a fool. You always have been. Did you think I would send her alone? Isabelle is at my home right now. I'll be glad to tell her that you sent us off with your best wishes."

Lord Oslan's face fell and his hand twitched. "You will not leave with her!"

"You are too late," Henry shouted back, his whole frame filled with a defiant energy ready to be unleashed.

"*You will not leave with her!*" As Lord Oslan screamed these words, he rushed at Henry.

Henry narrowly avoided the point of the blade as he threw himself aside, but the sharpened edge nicked his ribs, splitting a seam in his shirt and drawing a thin line of blood. Lord Oslan's weight carried him forward, catching the bag, and sending them both to the ground. Henry heard the sword fall with a clatter to the ground and lunged in that direction.

Lord Oslan was not slow to recover from his tumble. A taller but much thinner man, he threw himself on Henry. Henry's hand stopped mere inches from the sword's hilt. Lord Oslan scrambled to get it, but Henry used his free hand to prevent Lord Oslan from gaining the advantage. Both men grunted as they grappled on the floor, rolling back and forth, nearer and then farther from the sword.

Oslan's bony elbow caught Henry in the eye, and Henry saw nothing from it but white and black spots for several seconds. The telltale sound of metal scraping on wood told him Lord Oslan had retrieved his sword. Henry got to his feet. He swallowed hard, but his throat was dry. At that moment, the front door to the house opened loudly.

"Hello?" The announcement came from someone Henry had not seen in many months.

"James!" Henry yelled while keeping his one good eye on the sword. "Up here! Now!"

Lord Oslan's stance faltered only a little before he thrust again. Henry leapt backwards into the wall to keep his distance. James's footsteps thundered through the house until his silhouette appeared in the door and, with all the training of a soldier, he tackled the mysterious man with the sword pointed at his friend.

"Get off me, James!" Lord Oslan shouted. "He's trespassing in our house and has stolen Isabelle."

James jumped off of his father as if the old man was on fire. "Father? I didn't recognize you in the dark. What is going on here?"

Lord Oslan hollered orders at his son, but Henry, knowing he could not waste another moment, spoke loudest. "Your father has made a secret arrangement with Emperor Krallick. Isabelle's been injured, and I am taking her away, but I must leave now!"

"No!" Lord Oslan countered. "Stop him, James. He—he lies!"

James looked back and forth between the two panting men, one his own father and the other nearly a brother. Henry had forgotten what a large man James had become. He was taller than Henry and more sturdily built. Years of military training had turned his face into a stony fortress that kept almost all emotion locked inside.

"James, come with me and I will prove to you the truth," Henry pleaded.

Something settled James's mind. With a withering stare at his father, he said, "I may return here, Father. If what Henry says is true, that will be a dark and terrible day for you." Then he followed Henry, who picked up Isabelle's pack and left her room.

Norbin was in the den when Henry and James entered the room. At the sound, he looked up. His cheeks were red and wet. "Master Henry, are you all right?"

Henry nodded and came to the old man's side. He felt an overwhelming surge of gratitude for the good-hearted servant who'd done so much for him and Isabelle, even at personal risk.

"How is Miss Isabelle?" Norbin asked.

"She—she's fine, too."

"The pack, Master Henry, he wouldn't let me leave the house. I'm so sorry. He wouldn't let me leave the house!"

James clasped Henry around the arm. His hands were large, even by Henry's standard. "Where will you go with my sister?"

"We intend to leave by a route which I won't speak of here."

"Then I'll go with you and see you safely there."

Fortune was smiling on Henry. There was no greater asset he could have than James. "Grab your things," he said. "We must go now." Then he turned to Norbin. "Do you wish to come with us?"

Norbin smiled, his bright eyes filled to the brim with new tears. "I will be fine here, but thank you for your concern."

"Be safe, old friend," Henry said as James reentered the room with his travel bag.

"Hello and good-bye, Norbin," James added. "I hope you're well when we meet again."

Three full moons beamed overhead as the two men hurried onto the lawn in the cool, quiet night. Henry heard the sounds of wagons tumbling at a fast pace along nearby roads.

"Those sound like guardsmen's wagons," James told him. "Are they coming this way?"

"Probably," Henry said as he increased his pace to a jog. His legs were tired after all the running he had done tonight.

"Are they headed for your house?" James asked as he followed Henry's lead again.

"Probably," came the reply, Henry now at a run.

"Are they coming for you?"

"Probably."

"Henry," James said as he adjusted his bag, "what have you gotten me into?"

SIXTEEN

A Cut on the Nose

Henry and James reached the house at a sprint, both toting large traveling bags. Ruther waited for them inside the stable.

"Where in the—" Ruther started to ask, but then he saw James. "And what's he—?"

"We have to go now. Take this!" Henry said, shoving Isabelle's bag into Ruther's arms.

"I know we have to go now," Ruther replied, still eyeing James's large frame, "but how are we traveling with five people?"

"Is Isabelle in the carriage?" Henry asked.

"Yes."

"Maggie drives. The three of us ride horseback."

"I need to get Sissy," James said.

"Who?"

"My horse."

"No," Henry said. "I have two for the carriage and three to spare."

"Including mine," Ruther added.

"That's fine," James said, "but I'm not leaving my horse." He gave his bag to Ruther. "Pack this, too. I'll meet you on the street."

Henry knew better than to argue with James. "We need to saddle the other horses," he told Ruther. "Has Brandol left yet?"

Ruther nodded back over his shoulder. Henry's eyes followed.

There, cowering in the shadows like a scared puppy, was his journey-man.

"Brandol, can you help us saddle the horses?"

"Master Henry, I ain't wanting no trouble," Brandol said in a small voice.

"I'm the only one in trouble," Henry explained, "but not for having done wrong. Your help . . . please. No one will have to know you saddled the horses unless you tell them."

Brandol got up slowly and came to help. Ruther mumbled to himself as he struggled with the bags. Henry led Brandol to the horse stalls. The horses stamped and whinnied as though they sensed the tension of their owner. Henry found his fingers were unsteady as he tightened the saddle and bridle straps to his horse, Quicken, but Brandol fumbled his straps even worse. Maggie, who had been keeping a look out from the driver's seat of the carriage, ran back into the stable.

"They're coming, Henry!" she cried. "We need to leave!"

"Is everything in the carriage?"

"Yes."

"Go, then. Take the roundabout way to the pond."

He looked around and saw Ruther trying to help Brandol fasten the bridle. In seconds, Maggie had remounted the carriage and ordered the horses forward. As she passed the stable door, she called out, "I see them, Henry! Go quickly!"

"Brandol, get that bridle on!"

Henry's yell spooked the horse Brandol had been preparing. The horse trotted out to the street half-dragging Brandol, whose hand was caught under the strap he had finished securing only moments before. Brandol gave a cry of both fear and pain. Ruther chased after them. Maggie hadn't exaggerated. The sound of hooves and carts was too close.

A patrol of six guardsmen had arrived.

Brandol struggled with Ruther to free his hand, but the horse, confused by the loud noises both nearby and approaching, stamped its feet in a circle.

"Get on the horse, Brandol!" Henry urged.

As Brandol yanked his hand free of the strap, he stared up at Henry. The guardsmen were only a stone's throw away.

"Me?" Brandol asked.

"Yes! They've seen you," Ruther said. "Get on that horse!"

With Ruther's help, Brandol managed to mount the horse.

"Ride!" Henry cried out to his friends.

With the King's guardsmen only yards behind, they took off, Henry on Quicken, Ruther on his own horse, Ghost, and Brandol riding a third. James joined them at the end of the street riding Sissy. Dozens of hoofbeats echoed from houses and shops all the way down the street, as if a thunderstorm was on their heels. Brandol, not a skillful rider at best, had already fallen a step behind the group.

Henry leaned to Ruther and said, "Take Brandol on the shortest route. I'll lead James on a longer one. You can't be followed."

"Halt! In the name of the King!" a guardsman shouted behind them.

"I've been waiting for them to say that," Ruther said. "You'd think if they wanted us to halt in the King's name, they'd at least say *please*."

When they reached the end of the street, the guardsmen's distance behind them could be measured in feet. "This way!" Henry called to James. They turned left while Ruther and Brandol went right. Henry looked back over his shoulder.

The lead guardsman did not stop, but signaled to his soldiers. It relieved Henry to see the guardsman ordered more men to follow him and James than Brandol and Ruther. James and Henry increased their pace; the guardsmen did likewise. A sense of giddy recklessness rushed through Henry as he pushed Quicken to a faster gallop. He felt like the hero of one of Ruther's stories. When they reached a tight alley between two houses, Henry steered his horse sharply right.

James followed. A dog yelped in the darkness, scrambling to get out of the way of the stampede. The guardsmen reached the cramped street only three or four seconds behind James.

After a left turn out of the alley, arrows flew at them, and Henry's exhilaration changed into sheer panic. Of the four guardsmen chasing, two were shooting, but those two gradually fell behind. The first arrows passed wildly left or right, but the men were well trained, and each shot flew by closer than the last.

Houses became sparse, and Henry searched for a specific gap in the trees, one he'd often taken in his youth. When he spotted it, he took a sharp right, turning onto a narrow trail that cut through the forest. The darkness prevented him from seeing the path properly, so he navigated the trail with nothing but instinct to guide him. Low branches whipped his face and hair as he leaned down and squinted to see a landmark that should be rapidly approaching. Henry frowned when he couldn't find it. Had he led himself and James into death?

He closed his eyes to allow the memories of walking and riding this trail a thousand times tell him what to do. His need to survive helped him recall them vividly. The moment came, and Henry knew it was now or never.

"When I tell you to jump, do it," he said to James, loud enough that only they could hear. "Ready . . . wait . . . now!" Just as he ordered his horse to jump, he finally saw the oversized log crossing their path. James did as Henry commanded, and both men and their horses cleared the obstacle. The lead guardsman did not.

Behind him, Henry heard the cries of pain as their pursuers crashed to the ground.

"Stop! Stop!" the lead guardsman ordered his men. Henry turned his head to look, but could see nothing. A whistle through the air caught his attention, and Henry felt something brush his nose immediately followed by a sharp sting. An arrow sank into the trunk of a tree ahead of him with a loud *thwock*. Henry realized what had happened: the final guardsman, unable to follow, had shot his last arrow and nicked the bridge of Henry's nose. A stream of warm blood trailed down his face. He and James rode on, taking the trail deep into the forest and around a large pond where Henry, Maggie, and Ruther had often swum and skipped rocks together in their youth.

Henry made a low birdlike chirp. In the darkness, Ruther answered with a long high call. All was safe. And there, to Henry's relief, sat Maggie on the driver's seat of the carriage. Beside the carriage, at the edge of the pond, Brandol watered the horses. He tensed as Henry and James arrived.

"It's all right. It's us," Henry told the journeyman as he dismounted and led his horse to the others. "Is everyone all right?"

Maggie came closer to her brother, peering at him. "What's all over your face?"

Henry pawed at his nose and wiped away most of the blood from the cut. "Blood. I'm fine."

"Let me see it," she pressed, putting her lantern up to see the wound. Her touch had a soothing effect, and the stinging lessened.

"Is Isabelle still in the carriage?" James asked. "I want to see her."

"Yes," Maggie and Ruther both answered.

"Has there been any change?" Henry asked.

Maggie shook her head. "I've seen her eyes move, but nothing else."

James looked in on his sister. "She's sleeping," he reported, but there was no mistaking the deep concern in his voice. Henry put a hand on his arm, but James did not react. "I'm going to go back to Oslan Manor to duel my father. I will need a second."

"We don't have time for that!" Ruther said.

James looked to Henry. "He injured my sister, his own daughter. I cannot let that pass."

"I understand, James. I do," Henry said. "At any other moment I would be behind you, but not now. We need to flee, not fight."

James took Henry by the shoulders and faced him squarely. "Swear to me that if you ever cross his path again, you will avenge Isabelle if I cannot."

Henry had no qualms with answering, "I swear it to you."

Ruther spoke up next. "Well, part one of our plan went nearly as wrong as it could, and we still have one great problem. What are we going to do with *him*?" He jerked his thumb at Brandol, whose gaze was fixed on the drinking horses.

"I don't want no trouble," Brandol mumbled, glancing back at his master. Hearing the fright in his journeyman's voice made Henry's guts twist up inside. "And . . . and I don't want ta leave neither. Can't I stay here and . . . and find a new master?"

"I don't know." Henry lied out of pity. "Ruther? James?"

A gust of wind howled through the woods, rustling trees and leaves. The sudden sound spooked Henry. Maggie and Brandol started, too. Henry felt cold for the first time since early spring, and was reminded how late the hour was getting. Several seconds passed before the wind died down.

"Why can't we turn ourselves in?" Maggie asked. "There were witnesses at the Glimmering Fountain. They must have seen Isabelle slump over. If we show her like this, tell them about her father, about the Emperor—we'll tell them everything. How could they not believe us?"

Brandol nodded his head at this idea, but James shook his fiercely. "Even if we had ironclad proof that you are innocent, do you really believe anyone would take your word over that of the Emperor? And even if the King or his guards were to believe you, then what? Risk starting a war over an impoverished nobleman's daughter? No, put the idea out of your head. If we are arrested before we leave these borders, our heads will roll."

"So . . . so . . . so there ain't nothing else for me?" Brandol asked, his panic growing.

"Can you accept that like a man?" James's question almost sounded like a demand.

"Relax, James, the kid's almost ten years younger than you," Ruther said. "And Little Henry, no matter what James says, you don't have to salute him. Understand?"

"Please," Brandol begged. "Please, Master Henry. It's nothing against you and yours, but I want to—"

"Go back? Take up where you left off?" James said before Henry could respond. His tone softened, but not enough to mask the years of military service. "I know what will happen better than anyone here. There will be an investigation. It will begin with Henry and spread to his family. Neighbors will give a detailed description of Maggie, and that description will match any from those who saw her driving this carriage tonight. Next the search will spread to Henry's employees— you. If you return, you will be brought in to answer the King's agents. If the horse hadn't dragged you into the street, things might be different, but now the guardsmen who chased us may recognize you. And even if they don't, they *will* interrogate you. And, no offense to you, I don't think you could fool anyone."

Brandol simply stared back at James.

"I know you didn't mean to let yourself be seen, but that's the way things are. Now be a man about it. Remember, if you're caught, and they discover who you are, you'll either be put to death immediately— or you'll spend your youth in prison wishing you had been."

Brandol's face turned white and his eyes widened. Everyone else watched him with pity.

"Hit him again, James," Ruther said, winking at Brandol. "I don't think you quite made your point."

"It's only the truth."

"No matter," Maggie cut in. "How long should we wait before moving on?"

"We don't wait," Henry told her. "We go now."

James straightened at this. "I agree. The worst thing to do would be to give them time to regroup and search. I trust you want to take back roads?"

"Yes," Henry said. He put a hand on Brandol's shoulder. His heart ached with pity for him. "Brandol, you've been a fine journeyman. I've trusted you from the day I brought you into my home. You didn't deserve to be caught up in my mess. If you'll give me the same loyalty you've always given me, I'll do everything I can to fix things for you. Is that a deal?"

Brandol hesitated, but finally nodded his head.

"He should ride in the carriage with Isabelle," James suggested. "Then we'll have a fresh horse at all times."

James, Henry, and Ruther remounted their horses; Maggie climbed back into the carriage driver's seat and took the reins. Brandol squeezed inside with the luggage and Isabelle, who was still asleep. They started at a hardy pace. Henry led the way, carrying the group's lone lantern. The winds had calmed again. The night air felt cool, and all was quiet as they traveled. Ruther made an occasional comment to try to lighten the mood, but Henry couldn't stop himself from looking over his shoulder every few minutes—or jumping at any unexpected noise.

His life as he'd known it had ended. He wasn't certain what waited ahead. His thoughts rested on Isabelle. He should have insisted on leaving after Lady Oslan's funeral. If not then, he should have ignored the Emperor's letter and left the day after the Grand Parade. It would have been better to have committed that small crime than this great one. Two poor choices. He hoped the consequences would not be too great. It gave him much hope that both Ruther and James had, against their better interest, decided to come along. Brandol's inadvertent involvement, on the other hand, made him feel guilty. Brandol deserved better. Henry promised himself that he would make it up to his journeyman somehow. For the moment, however, he tucked his fears away and pressed on deeper into the night.

SEVENTEEN

Emperor and King

Emperor Ivan Krallick had never been in a fouler mood as he rode in his imperial carriage to Germaine Castle the day after being attacked at the Glimmering Fountain. His neck still stung from the wound he'd received from "the Carpenter," as he had taken to calling his assailant. Though the Emperor's physician had applied a poultice of herbs soaked in water to alleviate pain and aid healing, Emperor Krallick ordered it removed when he appeared before King Sedgwick Germaine. A wound might be a badge of honor, but a bandage represented weakness.

Impenetrable Germaine Castle towered over the heart of Richterton as an impressive symbol of might. Three circular walls of stone and cement spaced one hundred yards apart surrounded the royal home. Guard towers had been built every five hundred feet atop each ring. The walls stood over forty feet high and two guards could walk abreast from tower to tower. From a bird's view, the castle sat at the center of a bull's eye. Each wall had one gate, constructed of heavy wood and iron, allowing entrance into the next ring. When the Emperor's carriage drew close to the gate of the first wall, a loud trumpet blew twice and the doors of all three walls opened in perfect unison.

The Emperor closed his eyes to think clearly. His temples throbbed from lack of sleep, and his neck began to burn more intensely. He resisted the growing urge to touch the pulsing cut. Pushing past his distractions, he forced his mind to a higher level. This turn of events could fit into his long-term ambitions, but the riddle was how to control King Germaine's reaction to the incident. He pondered the solution as the carriage reached the front gardens and steps of Germaine Castle.

Ten of the King's servants appeared at the castle's main gate to receive the Emperor, each of them dressed in the same uniform: white shirts, green vests with the crest of a lion on the breast, and blue trousers. They stood as still as stones. One of them waited to open the Emperor's door the moment the carriage came to a stop. Another issued the formal greeting:

"Good morning, your Majesty. His Royal Highness, King Germaine, awaits you in his tea room."

Four servants lined up on the Emperor's right, four on his left, one in front, and one behind as Emperor Krallick allowed himself to be escorted to the King. He had long grown accustomed to King Germaine's lavish decorum, even if it was devoid of any real personality or taste. Sometimes he enjoyed imagining how he would redecorate the castle and grounds if he were to become its occupant during the winter months.

The King was sitting partially reclined on his couch when his page announced the Emperor. He wasted no time in standing up and assuming a dignified air. The King was, per his custom, resplendent in dress and demeanor. Indeed, King Germaine had gained fame throughout many lands for the curious patterns his valets regularly shaved into his gray beard. Today bore the same pattern as the day previous: a chain of rings stretching from ear to ear, a goatee linking the two chains. The King had retained a youthful appearance several years past what might have been thought reasonable, but his age was starting to show in his face, his skin, and his hair. Though he once had

had an imposing appearance, it had been years since the Emperor felt any sort of deference for this man.

"Ivan!" the King said with a sad smile so perfectly executed that the Emperor could not doubt its sincerity. "Please sit. I am grateful to be your host once more despite the unpleasant reason."

"Thank you, Sedgwick."

"May I offer you refreshment? Anything you like."

The Emperor kept his hands carefully together and touched as little as possible. A pair of clean gloves waited in a pocket of his coat, but he preferred to avoid using them if he could.

"No, but I thank you for the hospitality."

At this polite refusal, the King glanced down at the Emperor's hands and gave a small but knowing smile. Both men took their seats and faced each other. King Germaine seemed to be resisting the urge to recline again.

"Let's not mince words, Ivan. What happened to you yesterday was terrible, and I am already doing everything I can to bring swift justice to the offender. Now, we already have the names of three persons believed to be involved in this matter—"

"I have five," the Emperor said.

King Germaine appeared slightly dismantled at this statement. "F-five? I have heard of only three."

The Emperor held up his hand and put his fingers down one by one. "Henry Vestin, a young master carpenter. His sister, Margaret. Isabelle Oslan, the renegade daughter of a local nobleman. It is she whom I met at the inn. Her brother, James . . . I should add that he is a member of your Guard—"

"One of my guardsmen?"

It pleased the Emperor to note the King's reaction to this bit of news. "Correct, and the last is a journeyman carpenter named Brandol. No surname. He is a tall young man with blond hair. My spies say the journeyman assisted Henry at the inn."

"Yes . . ." King Germaine agreed, though rather reluctantly. "Now that is a matter where I must be perfectly forthright. Rumors have reached me that this—this Isabelle—"

"Let me finish for you. I believe the same rumors have already reached me. That she was sold to me as a slave? That she was held at the inn against her will?"

King Germaine nodded, but his face gave him away. Emperor Krallick liked seeing the King flustered. "How—?" The King cleared his throat. "You have a good explanation for these rumors, I trust?"

The Emperor waved off the question.

"Ivan, I must insist that you answer to them."

Emperor Krallick used his softest tone as he replied. "Sedgwick, I did not break a single one of your laws in this entire affair. I would never do something so fiendish, and I am on the verge of being offended by your insinuations."

"This girl—er—Isabelle . . . Oslan, she accepted your invitation?"

"I have witnesses to prove it. Citizens of your city."

The King cast a long look at his cup of tea. "What of the other rumors? It is a fact that many of your ancestors held slaves, concubines, whatever you call them. Your father was the first in a long line of emperors who refused to continue such a practice."

"I did not purchase her. You have my word of honor on that."

"It is not your word of honor that worries me, Ivan," the King hurried to say, "but that of Lord Oslan, her father. His reputation is one of the worst in the country, but because of his ancestry I cannot strike him from the nobility for two more generations."

"I have little trouble believing reports of his dishonesty," the Emperor continued in his same articulate manner. "I met him when he arrived at my palace and spun me a long tale about the necessity of saving his daughter's woeful existence. I'll be truthful, of course; what caught my eye was the portrait he showed me. When I arrived here for the parade, I sent messengers to confirm the portrait's accuracy of her likeness. At their word, I gave her an invitation to meet."

The King's mustache twitched back and forth as he fixed his gaze at the floor. Finally he looked up and cast his next question. "Yet why would this young man—who, according to my sources, has one of the finest reputations of all our master craftsmen—do something so rash? Certainly he knew death would be the result."

The Emperor leaned forward, tired of answering the King's questions. He sat so the wound on his neck was visible. "Lesser blood breeds lesser men. I want him found."

The King held up his hands as though he was a prisoner. "So do I, and as I told you, we are doing everything—"

The Emperor held up one of his own hands. "Allow me to disagree with you, Sedgwick." Before the King could profess offense, he continued. "You have not done everything."

The King's hands went down to his tea. "Name but one thing I have not done, and I will do it, if it is in my power."

"Allow my soldiers to assist yours."

These words, said with perfection on the part of the Emperor, had the effect of a gong echoing through the room. Emperor Krallick watched the King closely as he struggled to respond.

"That—that is a very strong request, Ivan. You understand what that means in terms of our kingdoms' histories and the position it puts me in."

"I do," the Emperor acknowledged with a slight bow of the head, "yet I am in your country. I dined at your inn, and one of your citizens put a sword to my throat. Must I go back to my country with a bleeding wound on my neck and look like a weakling in front of my people in order to not put you in a 'position'?"

The King's mustache quivered. "Ivan, think of it! Allowing your troops in my land. The nobility would be in an uproar."

Emperor Krallick's pointed features became much sharper. "Of course, I am prepared to share several compromises with you. One of them will no doubt satisfy you—and the nobility."

The King shook his head, and the Emperor grew sharper still.

"Sedgwick, I will not stand for inaction."

"*Inaction*," the King stammered to repeat, "I—I—"

"Had this heinous crime been done to you in my country, I would tear down every barrier stopping me from apprehending the man. Have you thought of that? Or of the consequences should this party *not* be caught?"

The Emperor spoke with such passion that the King was momentarily speechless. "What do you propose?" he finally asked.

"Allow me to send my Elite Guard," Emperor Krallick stated, and before King Germaine could interrupt, he pressed forward with his proposal. "I will send you a list of every guardsman in your borders, their assignments, even their descriptions should you require it. They will be under orders to in no way interfere with your soldiers, your citizens, or break your laws, and should they apprehend anyone from the band of suspects, the criminals will be turned over to you. In short, you need not even know they are there."

"Absolutely not!" The King's teacup clattered against the serving tray and spilled drops about the table. At the noise, several footmen came forward and began to silently clean up. "Now, Ivan, I am equally determined to see these people receive justice—"

"Not if you are unwilling to accept my help," the Emperor responded with increasing menace in his voice. "In fact, it would be a serious blow to the relations we and our fathers have struggled to build all these years."

"I have no intention of undoing the understanding between our countries, but I cannot allow your best soldiers in my land. That would be madness."

"Would you rather make enemies among your nobles or with your northern neighbor?"

"Let's not jump to those kinds of words. Blithmore has enjoyed peace all through my reign, and through yours and your father's. I see no need to let this incident cause an escalation beyond a misunderstanding that we can remedy by catching and executing this carpenter."

Emperor Krallick crossed his arms. "I am not my father, Sedgwick. Each day that passes in which that man still lives, my wrath grows. I will be watching you."

Minutes later, the Emperor left the castle in a much better mood. King Germaine had shown exactly the amount of spine expected, bending but not breaking—yet. The small plan that had hatched in his mind was now a soaring silver eagle with talons outstretched, thirsty for blood, hungry for meat. One part of the plan, perhaps the most important of all, was not yet in his grasp: Attikus. The Emperor believed that would change. The loss of Isabelle would be rectified. He would have her for himself. The five thousand crowns paid to Lord Oslan represented a significant interest and investment, and would not be wasted. The Carpenter would be caught, but certainly not returned to the King. No, he would be tortured—in front of Isabelle, if possible. And finally, when every other piece of the plan fell into place, the eagle would strike.

EIGHTEEN

The First Stop

J ust when I think I've seen every last fascinating specimen of tree and bush, I find out I'm wrong. See! Here, coming up on the left, are more trees and more bushes. They certainly are green, and they certainly are fascinating!"

James stirred in his saddle, partly from annoyance and partly from restlessness. He disliked long treks. Ruther seemed intent on making their journey infinitely longer. With his eyes, he swept the forest scene, noting the light filtering through the trees, searching for possible ambush points, and detecting signs of recent travel through the area. Seeing nothing of concern, he allowed himself a long sigh.

"I can't imagine why you gave up being a storyteller, Ruther, because we all find you *so* entertaining," Maggie said on cue. James noticed that each time Ruther made an obnoxious comment, Maggie felt compelled to respond.

Ruther let out a long laugh. "I haven't heard such intelligent insults since I told stories at Widow Esther's Home for Orphaned Children."

Henry snorted softly.

James shook his head with disdain. "Can we end the childishness, Ruther?"

"Well, pardon me," Ruther responded with mock offense. "What about Maggie? Just because I don't have breasts . . ."

"I wouldn't be so certain," Maggie cut in.

Ruther made a rude noise. "*You're* taking the side of the man who named his horse Sissy."

"It's pronounced *Seesee*," James reminded him. "Don't you mock my horse."

"I wouldn't if you'd tell me where her name comes from."

James suddenly had to squint in order to see. "Stop for a moment," he said to those behind him.

They had been following an old wagon road through the woods for the past three days. Judging by the shadows, James guessed it wasn't quite noon. The forest floor of fallen sticks, overgrown weeds, and thick scraggly bushes ended where a long pale green prairie began. Tall grasses and sparse wildflowers grew along the flat ground. A lighter, fresher scent reached James's nose, and he found it pleasant compared to the musty air of the woods. Even Sissy liked the new setting better, and she lowered her head at once to sample the grass.

"I expected to be in the forest until nightfall," he told Henry.

"We've traveled faster than planned." They both stared out into the open, afraid of what might find them once they left the shelter of the trees.

"I thought the trails would be more cluttered. We only stopped three times to clear our path—much better than other delays we might have faced." James turned and examined Henry's face. He saw the same concern in Henry that he felt in his own heart. "What are we going to do about Isabelle?"

Henry glanced back; James did the same. Ruther and Maggie were still bickering as they approached.

"Ruther doesn't want to stop," Henry told James. "He thinks it's more dangerous to go into town for a physician than to let her body heal itself. He also believes the Emperor wouldn't harm her if he wanted her for a concubine. It makes sense. Maggie won't say so, but she's afraid to stop, too."

James turned his eyes to the fields in front of them. All he saw was open space and no cover. Lots of potential danger. "What do *you* think?" he asked Henry.

"She's had only water for three days—water we've poured down her throat. She hasn't moved. She needs to be examined by a physician."

"I agree. Has Brandol said anything to you?"

"No. He doesn't say much at all."

"Would you like my advice?"

"*Yes.*"

James heard the desperate tone in Henry's voice. He stared into the distance, focusing on nothing in particular. "When I began training for the King's Guard, they made the first few weeks hell for us. We were up all hours of the night, running, riding, sword-playing . . . then, when we thought we might die of exhaustion, they made us shoot arrows. If we weren't accurate, we had to dig holes and fill them. About a third of the men couldn't handle it and went home or asked to join the infantry. It broke them down.

"You have to be careful not to break down anyone in your party. The others need to feel as safe as possible. They need a sense of self-determination. If you have a decision to make that may endanger someone's life, speak to the group first. Someone like Brandol— maybe even Maggie—could run at the first sign of trouble. We can't have anyone broken. That person will have nowhere to go."

Henry rode back to Maggie and Ruther and announced they'd be stopping for lunch. They ate at the edge of the forest, still under the cover of trees. James couldn't relax during meals. He wanted to be ready to move in a moment's notice.

The meal seemed quieter than normal, but it may just have been James's perception. Ruther and Maggie had stopped bickering. Brandol said nothing, as usual. James ate quickly and then took out one of his hunting knives, sharpening it over and over again to a hair-splitting taper. Normally, he enjoyed practicing his knife-throwing after meals—it cleared his mind—but he stayed near the group to participate in Henry's discussion. Also, he'd grown tired of Ruther's comments about wounding defenseless trees.

"Well . . ." Henry began. He cleared his throat before going on. Then he glanced at James with a look in his eye that seemed to ask for help. James gave Henry an imperceptible shake of the head. Henry had to do it himself. "Well, there is something—"

"Yes, we'll go into Fletchersville with you," Ruther said.

"Ruther and I already discussed it, Henry," Maggie explained as she helped Brandol put food and dishes back into the packs. "We don't fight *all* the time."

"I'm more than willing to do anything heroic with enough ale in me."

"What about you, Brandol?" Henry asked.

Brandol glanced back at the group as he and Maggie tidied up the camp. Most of his focus went to James's knife. "I ain't got no choice, do I?"

"Yes, you do," Henry said, "but I need you to choose now because what I intend to do requires planning. We need to take Isabelle to a physician and find out if she needs medicine."

"To do that, we need to know where the nearest physician is," James added.

As Brandol thought about his decision, James watched his eyes. Brandol reminded him of a few of the greenest soldiers he'd commanded in the King's army just before a skirmish. What could cause someone to grow to manhood with so much fear?

"I—I guess," Brandol said, "but please don't put me in no danger."

The group spent most of the afternoon making plans. James wanted to be prepared for any possible scenario; Ruther reminded him several times such a thing was impossible.

"While we're having this discussion, we should decide something else right now," Ruther said. "How many of these stops are we going to make before we leave the borders of Blithmore? Would it kill us to have a general plan?"

James went to the carriage and got his map, unrolling it for everyone to see. "The distance from here to the Iron Pass is . . ." he drew his finger from their current location to their destination, "a little over one thousand miles. If we keep our current pace, we'll reach the Iron Pass with only four more stops in a town. Eight weeks. That's our goal, isn't it, Henry? The Iron Pass in eight weeks?"

Henry nodded.

James traced his finger along the map again, adding up numbers inside his head. "That is possible, maybe even probable with good weather and no misfortune. Timing will be crucial." He tapped his finger three times to make his point. "The more time passes, the more we eat. The more we eat, the more stops we have to make."

Maggie's eyes flickered to Ruther's large stomach. Ruther grunted with annoyance.

"The more stops we make, the greater the danger," Henry added.

"I doubt the armies of the King think we'll leave the country," James said. "Most likely, they believe we'll relocate somewhere else and hide out. However, if they do think we're going to run for a border, we have another advantage. The Iron Pass is rarely traveled because of the old wives' tales about it. They'll assume we intend to make for the southern coast and hire a ship or try the dangerous western mountain passes."

After a hearty draught from his flask, Ruther leaned over James's shoulder for a better look at the map. "Where are these other four stops?"

"We're right here." James pointed to the forest edge on the map, then to the Drewberry River not far away, and traced it southeast through Blithmore. "We'll follow the river more or less, but not too close because they might anticipate it. We'll make a stop in Fenley.

We'll have to make a second one in the small towns in the hills, either Washborough or Hasting, depending on how early the snows come."

"Fenley's a good place." Ruther put his finger on the map until James brushed it away. "I've been there several times."

"It gets tricky planning exactly where the third stop will be, but we will have to stop twice after Fenley. No matter what, our fourth and last stop before we head for the Iron Pass will have to be at Bookerton. I see no other choice."

"*Bookerton?*" Ruther repeated. "Are you mad? It's huge. It'll have its own legion of soldiers, plus a full regiment of guardsmen."

"I know that better than anyone," James replied.

Ruther murmured something dark under his breath.

"It's nearly evening," Henry said. "We should be getting ready."

• • •

A half hour later, Ruther had donned his best costume: a dapper Richterton nobleman. Brandol was dressed as his squire. "See, friend," Ruther told Henry with ale-aided exuberance, "I told you these costumes would come in handy."

"I never said they wouldn't." Henry examined the costumes with a scrutinizing eye. "But I admit, I'm convinced."

"They weren't cheap," Ruther added with a large smile.

"Henry!" Maggie's voice called from inside the carriage. "Henry, come quickly!"

Even before Ruther reached Isabelle, he knew something was wrong. The carriage shook on its axles with a frightening violence. Though Henry, Maggie, and James crowded the carriage, Ruther saw Isabelle's body convulsing in a never-ending fit.

"Isabelle!" Henry exclaimed in terror. "What happened?"

"She gave a gasp for air—and I thought she'd woken," Maggie explained as she tried to hold Isabelle steady, "but she began to quake, and—"

"Ruther," Henry cried. "Go now!"

Ruther needed no further urging. He jumped on his horse, Ghost, and whistled to Brandol.

As they rode off, Ruther heard James call out, "Take care of her, Henry!" He turned back to see James following them armed with Ruther's bow and quiver.

Sundown approached as Ruther pushed Ghost as fast as he could go, letting up only when reaching the outskirts of Fletchersville, a town renowned for making the finest bows and arrows in Blithmore. He'd visited the town twice previously on storytelling ventures, both of which he wished he'd forgotten. Both occasions had been so poorly received, he hoped no one would remember him, especially in a costume. Brandol, riding on the back of the horse, clutched him tightly around the chest, and as they drew further into town, his grip became so forceful that Ruther had to wheeze out a plea for Brandol to release him.

They passed farms, homes, and shops. The few people who saw them ride by stared at them with curiosity. A small inn, a curl of smoke rising from the chimney, appeared ahead, and Ruther urged Ghost toward it. The inn was a bit too small of a place for the kind of storytelling jobs Ruther normally took. The quaint building stood between a stable large enough to service several nearby establishments and a bow shop. He dismounted and gave the reins to Brandol. Brandol returned them with an insolent stare.

"Mind yourself, squire," Ruther warned, "or I'll whip you."

The young man's eyes went wide, and he bowed, then began securing Ghost. Ruther entered the inn with the same haughty air he had observed so often among Richterton's nobles. Several heads turned in his direction, and the stares lingered on his clothes. Enjoying the attention, Ruther posed in the doorway and allowed the guests to examine as much as they wanted. The owner of the inn came out from the kitchen in a hurry as Brandol entered behind his master.

"Hello," the owner said with a large smile that revealed toothless gums. "Would you care for a seat?"

"I may, perhaps, in a moment," Ruther replied, slipping into a voice matching his mannerisms.

He scanned the inn for the first time and found it to be fairly clean. However, as it was still early in the evening, he suspended judgment on the inn's true quality until later.

"I am traveling eastward and my squire requires a physician. Is there one in town?"

"What ails him?" the owner asked with mild interest.

"He has a terrible cough." Ruther patted Brandol so hard on the back that the journeyman lost his wind. "It sometimes prevents him breathing at all. I've thought about putting him away, but he cooks such a savory lamb."

The innkeeper watched Brandol struggle for air with a concerned expression. "Yes, we have a physician. His name is Winmore, and he lives not very far from here."

Ruther listened with care as the innkeeper informed them how to find the physician.

"Is he quite skilled?" Ruther asked.

"You will not find a better one for many miles."

Ruther turned sharply to Brandol and asked, "Did you understand the man's instructions?"

Brandol nodded.

"Well then, be gone and fetch me here when you are well again."

He placed a hand on Brandol's collar and forced him rather than guided him out the door. Within a minute, he saw Brandol galloping away at a hearty pace, not in the direction of the physician, but in the direction where he would find James and later Henry waiting with Isabelle. Then, with a very smug expression, he looked back to the innkeeper. "*Now* I will sit . . . if you will bring me a mug of your finest ale."

NINETEEN

Winmore's Roof

B randol rode as though the devil chased him until he came to the small market where he expected to find James buying food and supplies. During his ride, he tried not to think too much about any one thing. His life had become nothing but terror, like some of the nightmares he had as a child. In those dreams, he was a terrified runty dog, and his older brothers threw rocks, kicked at him, and poked him with firebrands when they got bored.

His father had been right all those years ago. Brandol was too weak to survive in this world. Why had he been so foolish to go back to Henry's house that night after being warned to stay away? He could have fetched his tools any other hour of the day or night, but instead, after getting his tools, he had tried to get one last peek at the mountain of gold he and Isabelle had uncovered. He had made the worst possible decision at the worst possible moment. Tears blinded his eyes, and the rolling hills of Fletchersville became dark, reddish-black blurs.

Fortunately, Ruther's horse, Ghost, had a sharp mind and strong muscles; he scarcely needed any direction from his rider. To Brandol's great relief, he found James exactly where they had agreed to meet. Doing his best not to stammer, Brandol told James how to find the physician, took the supplies that James had purchased, and then continued onward until he found Master Henry waiting with Maggie and Isabelle, who was draped limply over the back of Maggie's horse. Isabelle's paroxysms seemed to have ended. Still, her face was paler than before and a slick sheet of sweat covered her brow.

"Were you successful?" Master Henry asked.

Brandol nodded. A feeling of breathless elation overcame him at having done something right in such a tense situation. All of a sudden, the world looked less dark; a little bit of warmth spread through him. He couldn't recall ever accomplishing something so important.

Master Henry helped him give the supplies to Maggie.

"I can take Isabelle from here," Master Henry told his sister. "Wait for us back at camp." Then to Brandol he ordered, "Lead the way."

Brandol continued at the same pace, forcing his brain to remember the instructions over and over again until they ran circles around his mind in a sort of song. Their route took them off the main roads and onto a cart-broken trail that wound over several hills with orchards of walnut and peach trees and a small lake reflecting the sinking sun. Apparently only one home occupied the north side of the lake, which is where the innkeeper had said they would find the physician.

Brandol squinted his eyes into the blinding horizon as the sun began to abandon them. Relief swept over him when he saw flickering lights in the windows of a cottage on the lake's northern shore. A cold breeze from the water teased his face, and his heart took courage. Master Henry called out to him from behind.

"Is that the place?"

"Yes," Brandol answered. "Name's Winmore."

"I will go from here," his master said, pushing on even faster. "Go back to Ruther."

"I'd rather go on with you, Master Henry."

"Thank you, but the fewer of us he sees, the better."

"Please. I'd rather go on."

Master Henry relented. By the time they had covered the distance to the cottage, the sun had nearly set. The moons shone low and bright on the lake. Two owls hooted to each other as the horses passed. The lake winds carried the rich scents of earth mixed with end-of-summer leaves on damp soil.

As Quicken's hooves stamped the ground near the home, Brandol heard wood creaking and at least two voices conversing inside in muffled tones.

"Who is there?" shouted someone from inside.

"A man in desperate need!" Master Henry answered.

"Harris, if that's you," the man inside continued, "you'd better have ten crowns."

Master Henry dismounted and caught Isabelle securely in his arms as she slid off the horse. Brandol took Quicken's reins and tied up both horses.

"I am no one named Harris."

"Well, in that case, you're still not welcome. No sun, no service. I am busy."

"Sir, I entreat you to let me come inside. I—I'm a humble traveler who can pay you handsomely for whatever service you can render me."

Brandol heard footsteps coming to the window, and a middle-aged man's head poked out. Like Henry and Brandol, this man was clean-shaven but his black hair had more gray than a man his age should have. His expression was one of intense concentration.

"Humble people can rarely pay handsomely," the strange man remarked. "Who are you to defy such a paradox?"

"Is your name Winmore?" Master Henry asked.

The man's face relaxed, and he answered jovially, "More than anyone!"

"You're not funny!" came a second voice. It was also a man's and very similar to the first.

"You wish you were!" replied the Winmore whose head was still out the window.

"Sirs, please!" Master Henry shouted.

Brandol watched his master raise Isabelle in his arms, in case the strange man hadn't noticed her already.

"This woman is my betrothed, and we are traveling south for the winter. She has been poisoned, I believe."

Winmore withdrew his head and spoke to the other. "Double, do you think?"

A response Brandol couldn't hear came back. Winmore reemerged and asked, "Are you willing to pay double our fees?"

"Yes," came the answer at once.

Winmore gestured for them to come into the cottage. As Master Henry carried Isabelle inside, Brandol heard the sound of furniture being dragged across wooden floors and as he entered the room, the same man pointed to a long table covered in sheepskins. "Put her right there."

"Thank you. Both of you."

"Certainly, Mister . . . ?"

"Jack, and this is my Susan. Also, my servant Brand—Brandon."

In an instant, the two men began a thorough investigation of Isabelle. One felt her neck, the other examining her eyes as Ruther had done days ago. One pinched the skin on her arms while the other put his ear up to her nose.

"Her heart is still beating," one of them said, nudging Henry out of his way.

"But her eyes aren't responding," replied the other.

"Comatose?"

"Possible, but not likely if it's poisoning."

The first brother's hand hovered over Isabelle's face, then moved down to her chest. "It's almost certainly poison. A particularly vile one, no doubt. Its shadow taints her aura."

"The preparer?"

While they spoke, Brandol took the opportunity to glance around the moderately sized room these men used to heal people. The table that held Isabelle was in the center of a large room filled with chemicals, plants, colorful vials, burners, fumes, and a smell that reminded him of fresh horse droppings.

He then noticed how the two men were nearly identical: both of average height and slender frame, both weak-chinned and short-fingered. Even the hair on their heads was cut alike and their manner of dress was the same. In fact, Brandol couldn't tell which had been at the window when he and Henry arrived.

"How long has she been this way?" asked the one who'd been examining her neck, now uncorking a vial of purple liquid.

"Are you the physician?" Master Henry asked him.

"Yes," Winmore responded, waving the vial under her nose.

The other pulled his hands away from Isabelle's eyes and scowled at Master Henry. "Not true."

"Quite true," the first Winmore cut in. To his brother he said, "Don't forget who sat through the lectures day in and day out."

In the midst of their bantering, Master Henry frowned at Brandol. "Maybe this was a mistake."

One of them—Brandol could not tell which was which—hurried to address them. "The Germaine College of Physicians is expensive, so he enrolled and went to classes and taught me everything he learned. Only one of us had to pay the cost."

"And only one of us received a certificate of medicine. Me!"

"I'm still the better physician," the second Winmore whispered to Master Henry. "My gifts far exceed his."

"I heard that!" the other remarked as he inspected Isabelle's mouth. "You never answered my question, young man."

"I'm sorry," Master Henry said. "It's been nearly four days now."

"Give us a description of what happened."

Master Henry told them everything that had occurred at the Glimmering Fountain, only changing the name of the inn and the position from which he'd observed the scene, describing it as though he had been seated with Isabelle. As he spoke, the Winmore brothers sometimes interrupted him to discuss things under their breath.

"You say these recent convulsions lasted how long?" one of them prodded.

"Two minutes is my best estimate."

The physicians spoke together again. They were less careful now about keeping their conversation so private, and Brandol heard snippets of their words, though he understood little.

". . . symptoms would cause—"

"—Yes, it does!"

Each brother grew both angry and calm at the other faster than the waves of the tide. Sometimes one would stamp his foot and the other would poke him in the chest or stomach.

". . . strong pulse . . ."

"—but an epileptic reaction?"

"Who is it, again, who walks—"

"—I hate when you remind me of that!"

"Jack," one of the brothers addressed Henry, "it is our conclusion—"

"Our *non-mutual* conclusion," interrupted the other Winmore.

"It is the educated conclusion of *the physician* that she has been poisoned with Devil's Delight."

"Tell him the rest!" the other brother demanded.

"I'm getting to it!" A deep sigh followed this exclamation. "Half of us believe that there may be more than poison involved."

"It's not a 'belief.' I know it!" The brother turned to Henry. "Jack, that poison was prepared by someone who walks in the path of shadow."

"In the path of shadow?" Master Henry repeated. "You mean—?"

"Yes. All the signs are there."

Master Henry turned white, his eyes fixed on Isabelle with grave concern. "Are you certain? How can you tell?"

The two brothers exchanged a dark glance, but did not answer. Apparently this did not satisfy Brandol's master. "Many believe the path is a myth," Master Henry whispered. "Are you telling me that it is not? That magic is involved here?"

"Yes."

"How do you know?"

"To walk the path . . . in light or shadow," Winmore said, "is punishable by death under Blithmore law. Normally I dare not even speak of it. I certainly won't tell you how I know what I know."

"I have never heard of such a law."

"That's because you're not a physician," came the other brother's response.

"How are you aware of such evil being used upon—upon Susan?" Master Henry asked. "I know nothing of these things."

"Let's just say I recognize the signs." At this, the other Winmore brother snorted, and Brandol sensed this was not the whole truth. "Let that be enough for you."

"We both agree to give you Essence of Angel Herbs. It should speed up her body's attempts to rid itself of the poison, and it should help soothe the disagreeable reaction." A cough from the second Winmore reminded the physician to add, "And if, after a week, that does not work, find another physician and have him let her blood."

"Thank you!" the brother cried, as though he'd been waiting to give this prescription.

"But only as a last resort," the first Winmore continued. To his brother he added, "There, Mr. Barbarian. Happy?"

"You will make this . . . herb—essence of angels for Isa—for Susan?" Master Henry asked.

"Yes, immediately."

Brandol listened and watched as they concocted and stirred and added and argued, but the physicians spoke too fast and low for him to follow what they were saying. At one point, he caught a glimpse of a brother with his back turned collecting his own tears in a glass vial. He thought about saying something—a word of warning—to Master Henry, but didn't want to make a scene. Eventually he gave up spying on them and returned to the window, looking for any sign of help. Master Henry stood by Isabelle, holding her hand while he waited.

"Would you like a demonstration of how to administer this?" one of the brothers asked, handing Master Henry a misty glass vial with a wooden stopper.

"Yes, please."

"Grab some of that excess," the twin told his brother. "Now, pay attention, Jack. You must put ten drops in her mouth, one in each nostril, and one in each ear. This will ensure the medicine reaches her belly, but also her blood from the ears, and the brain through the nose. The three Bs, if you like."

"Just a thought, Jack," the other brother added. "Why didn't you take Sharon to one of the physicians in Richterton?"

Master Henry's voice tightened as he answered, "Er—urgent business. I have urgent business."

Brandol had never been a good liar, but even he could feel the atmosphere in the room change after Master Henry's terrible excuse. What began as a casual question was now an awkward situation.

Master Henry tried to recover. "And—and I thought she was . . . tired."

The physician's brother moved a fraction closer to the door. "I thought you said her name was Susan?"

"I did. Why do you mention it?"

"Didn't *you* call her Sharon just now?" the Winmore closest to the door asked his brother.

"Oh, did he?" Master Henry asked. "Yes, her name is Susan."

One Winmore seemed oblivious to his brother's suspicions, and once again prattled on about how to administer the essence of herbs properly. Brandol felt the eyes of the other brother watching both him and Master Henry with an unraveling stare.

"I prefer to start with the nose and finish with the ears," the brother said.

"What was the name of that inn again?" came the next question from the physician. This time he directed his words to Brandol. "The one where she fell ill?"

Brandol's eyes went to Master Henry as lightning struck his brain, leaving it blank as fresh snow. What inn had Master Henry told them? He could not remember. He tried to conjure a name, but his mind had gone blank.

"I—he—I can't remember." He knew he'd paused too long before answering. "What—what'd he say before?"

"I find it hard to believe you've already forgotten the inn where your master's betrothed became ill."

Brandol was on the verge of vomiting. His face felt cold, like it had the last time a pretty girl had spoken to him. Maggie had been there and said he'd gone horribly pale. This Winmore's tone was so filled with accusation that his brother even took notice.

"Shall I pay you then?" Master Henry asked. Brandol noticed his master's face had turned gray.

"One hundred crowns should cover the expense," was the physician's response.

"One hundred crowns!" both the other brother and Master Henry exclaimed, but Master Henry added, "That's outrageous!"

"You're the man who is being hunted by the King's Guard, aren't you? Rumors of you and your journeyman have already reached our town."

Master Henry reeled back, clutching Isabelle's hand with one of his own. "Journeyman? No—no, it's me and—and—and Susan."

Brandol gasped when he heard the word *journeyman*. Ruther had been the one to accompany Master Henry. Ruther had been at the inn when all this started! He should be here now! He was the better actor, the better liar, the better everything. Why had James and Master Henry trusted any piece of the plan to a worthless runt? Brandol struggled for air and fought the urge to vomit while Master Henry somehow maintained his calm.

"You're referring to—to the man who quarreled with the Emperor," Master Henry answered. "I am not that man."

"Why are you raising such alarms, brother?" one Winmore asked the other. "We have no quarrel with them."

"Your story is already known here," the physician told Henry, "and if you wish it to remain here, it will cost you one hundred crowns."

Brandol glanced out the window. He saw Master Henry do the same. "I don't have that much gold with me."

"Then leave the vial and give us what you have."

"No," Master Henry said with such force that the Winmores looked at each other in alarm. Brandol had never heard this tone of menace in his master's voice. "I'll make you a better offer. I will pay you the amount I originally agreed, which is double your standard price, and you will accept it. Refuse me and the cost to you will be even greater."

"You mean to kill us?" the physician asked as his hand flew to cover his mouth. Both Winmores stared at Master Henry in awe. Then the brother said, "I heard the journeyman is even more dangerous."

"What do you know of the journeyman?" Master Henry asked.

The brother swallowed hard, but wouldn't answer.

"I would never harm either of you, especially after the service you've rendered me. However, if you look out that window, you'll see a flame hovering in the air seventy yards away. That is the burning tip of an arrow held at the ready by this woman's brother, an expert marksman. Three such arrows will be shot into your roof at three different points, rendering it impossible for you to quench the fire before losing your fine home."

Both brothers rushed to the window and jostled for position to see the sight Master Henry had described. Although Brandol knew they could not distinguish the figure of James in the darkness or at such a distance, he saw the effect it had as they murmured to each other. As they stared, Master Henry removed from his purse the price for their services and laid it on the table in the place of Isabelle, whom he picked up and cradled in his arms.

"We accept your proposal," one of the Winmores said, turning back to see that Master Henry and Brandol were already on their way out the door.

"Thank you," Master Henry called back. "That man will remain there through the night, and should either of you attempt to leave the house . . ." The words hung in the air like a dark cloud. "Tomorrow, should you feel so inclined, you may alert whomever you wish. Until that time, I'm deeply grateful for your help. Please spread the word that the Emperor poisoned my Isabelle, and had it not been for our intervention, he would have carried her away as a slave to his palace, to be used according to his pleasures. I had no choice to do what I did."

Brandol again rode Ghost and helped Henry steady Isabelle as he mounted Quicken. Master Henry gave a low whistle, not for the horse, but for James. In response, James took the burning torch he held and balanced it on two forked sticks jammed into the ground so that the torch rested at the height of a man's chest. Then he rejoined them, and the three men with Isabelle rode together in silence. New fears vexed Brandol as he rode Ghost in the darkness. The King's Guard was searching for five criminals for the assault on the Emperor: Master Henry and Maggie, James and Isabelle Oslan, and Henry's murderous accomplice in the Glimmering Fountain—Brandol the journeyman. The guardsmen knew nothing of Ruther.

TWENTY

The Eyes of the Seer

The day after the Emperor's meeting with King Germaine, he began his journey home. He had intended to spend the fall and winter in his palace, but with so much unfinished business involving the Carpenter, his southern mansion near the Blithmore border seemed a more ideal location, providing an advantage in being closer to the lines of communication coming in from his soldiers and spies stationed near or in Blithmore.

His servants sent messages ahead for the mansion's preparation. Only the top servants received orders to relocate to the south, as well as seven of his concubines. A deep cleaning of the entire mansion was at the top of the list, though this order came so frequently it hardly needed to be requested. Leaving Blithmore gave the Emperor great pleasure. He missed the scent of the abundant conifer trees in his kingdom, he disliked the flat accents of the Blithmorians, and the busyness of ruling Neverak brought him a profound peace of mind. He needed that peace of mind now. Thanks to the speed of his steeds, he arrived at his mansion quickly.

It had been two weeks since he'd been assaulted at the inn, and still there was no news of the Carpenter or Isabelle. The Emperor extended his patience by focusing his energies on matters of the kingdom. When his time was less filled, he amused himself with rides in the countryside and allowing his beautiful concubines to entertain him. He had also requested that several of the dozens of amusing diversions he owned be sent down with his servants and slaves. He had a pair of wings that enabled him to glide down the Northern Cliffs in the summers. He had a tube-like breathing apparatus that let him stay underwater as long as he wished. Lately, however, the toys that most kept his interest were unique weapons.

While he attended the parade in Blithmore, his engineers had designed and installed a spring-powered weapon into the arm of his palace throne. By sliding a small panel forward, he could activate a concealed spring that would shoot a small poisoned spike. A trivial thing, but he looked forward to trying it when he returned north. Another recent acquisition had been thick leather boots with small blades extending from the toes.

True to his daily routine, the Emperor woke up an hour after sunrise, exercised, and took a light breakfast in the dining hall. For his morning meals, he preferred small portions of vegetables and cheeses. After breakfast he was bathed by two of his servants in water much hotter than most people could stand, but which he had grown to enjoy. Baths were one of the Emperor's true pleasures and were never rushed or taken lightly.

"What appointments do I have today?"

His chamberlain read from a piece of parchment. "The Seer is first on the schedule, per your Majesty's request. Two noblemen have requested an audience in the late morning—a dispute over land. Your Majesty also agreed to take lunch with that woman who begged for a position as a concubine—Cecilia. After lunch, your Majesty is to receive Sir Grellek to discuss the planning of a new town in the far eastern corner and after which—"

"Tell me the name of the town again."

"Eastern Krallickton."

"I hate that name," replied the Emperor. "Do not let the meeting end without reminding me how much I hate that name."

"Yes, your Majesty."

The Emperor sighed. He also hated land disputes. However, they occurred more frequently than almost any other item of business. City planning didn't offer much excitement, either. "Continue."

"After Sir Grellek leaves, your Majesty requested to see Jackson Roving—"

"Who is that?"

"The writer you employed to write the formal invitation to Miss Isabelle Oslan."

"The invitation . . . yes, yes, of course, I almost forgot. Keep my schedule as I have arranged it except for the last appointment. Postpone it for half an hour. Do not inform the writer about the change, and do not serve him any refreshment as he waits."

"Yes, your Majesty."

Not long after his servants dressed him, a doorman entered and announced the arrival of the Seer. Emperor Krallick ordered an attendant to escort the guest to the reception hall, a much smaller version of the throne room in his northern palace. The Emperor found the throne in his mansion to be much more comfortable than his larger and more ornate palace throne. Despite all he had done to counter the problem, his palace throne often gave him aches and pains when he sat too long. Several times, he'd considered removing the throne altogether, but it had seated Neverak sovereignty for the last five hundred years. A sense of nostalgia always forced him to reconsider. After all, if they could handle it, so could he.

When the Seer entered the room, the atmosphere changed. The light in the room dimmed, as though the torches gave off less light, and the air around him cooled. A chill ran up the Emperor's spine, not out of fear, but as an involuntary reflex from being in the presence of such malevolence. Tattered black robes adorned the Seer and a hood covered his face. Rumors said that to witness the Seer's face was to witness Death itself. All the Emperor had ever seen were two small, cold, pale lights that changed color depending on the Seer's mood. It was all he wanted to see.

"Good morning, my Emperor," the Seer said. His voice fell and rose to great heights and depths of pitch within a single sentence, like a singsong tone from the grave. "For what purpose have you summoned me this morning?"

"Do you not know, Seer?" Emperor Krallick asked. "Do you stumble down the path of shadow which you walk? Or do you feign ignorance?"

"I know this visit is not about the poison I prepared for you. I have full confidence in my preparations." Though the hood of the robe shrouded the face of the Seer, the Emperor sensed a triumphant smile beneath the cloth in the darkness. "There it is . . . I see it . . . You have been busy, Emperor. You have set plans in motion. To what ends, only you and I know." The Seer withdrew a lone hand from his robes and pointed it at the Emperor's heart. Despite the skin's youthfulness, the hand appeared aged hundreds of years, the fingernails long, twisted, and poisonous green. "You wish to know whether these plans will bear fruit, either sweet or bitter."

"As always, you live up to your name."

"The wisdom you seek carries a cost."

The Emperor narrowed his eyes upon the Seer. "As your Emperor, I could take your life, drive you from this land, or strip you of every possession. What price do you wish to impose upon me, Seer?"

"A trifle only, my Emperor. A trifle." He said the last word at such a high pitch it barely registered in the Emperor's ears. "A few hairs from your head is all. Perhaps twelve."

"What sort of devilry do you intend to practice with that? Some spell, perhaps?" The Emperor nearly shouted his second question. "Who are you to request such a thing from your Emperor? The hairs of my head are not trifles!"

"Soothe yourself, Emperor," the Seer said. "The torches in the room flickered again, dimming even more, and at once the Emperor's anger quelled. "It was not my place to request such a thing, but for you to offer it should you choose."

"You shall not receive such a gift nor be paid such a sum. If this is what you require, then remove yourself from my hall before you experience my wrath."

The foul hand of the Seer receded back into his robe. "Emperor, let me adjust my request. An emerald, small and simple, will suffice. For a gem of such insignificance to you, I will tell you what you wish."

The Emperor stared at the Seer for many seconds, watching those tiny points of red light gaze back at him. A distinct voice in his head told him that he should release this man at once from his presence, but it sounded so much like his father's that he was inclined to ignore it. The light from the Seer's eyes shifted slightly, taking on a yellow then a green tint before changing back to red.

"Very well." He turned to his servant and said, "Inform the treasurer that the Seer shall receive one small emerald from the treasury."

The Seer gave a small nod. His hand again appeared, this time grasping hold of a white stone no larger than a seashell pinched between his finger and thumb, which hung around his neck on a chain. The Emperor had not even noticed it until now. Had it been there all along? He couldn't say. The Seer placed it against his forehead, and it began to hiss and smoke at the touch. As the scent of burning flesh reached the Emperor's nose, a faint purple came from under the hood, outlining the features of the Seer's face slightly. What little the Emperor saw made him grimace. The Seer's voice transformed into an inhuman muttering like something from Beyond. His eyes grew bright like two stars.

"The Ancients of Atolas speak to me. Your goal is within your reach, but not yet within your grasp. Two obstacles stand in your path. Only one must be removed to guarantee your success. The first is the woman who travels with him whom you seek to punish. Separate them and the first obstacle shall be removed. The second obstacle is your own blood. He who was lost must be found and vanquished. Accomplish either of these two things and nothing shall stand in your way. Fail at both and the future grows clouded."

The Seer removed the stone from his head and his eyes dimmed. He bowed his head. "Does my Emperor require anything more?"

"You gave me enough. I intend to separate the two as soon as possible. And the second has been a goal of mine for over a decade. In fact, I have plans later today which shall take a step toward such ends. Your counsel was hardly needed."

The eyes of the Seer shone bright purple once again, and he pointed a finger at the Emperor's forehead. The torches in the room grew more brilliant than ever before.

"Do not underestimate the difficulty of these two obstacles, my Emperor. To do so may prove perilous."

"Good day, Seer. Your service and loyalty do not go unnoticed."

With a second small bow, the Seer left the hall. As he did so, the lights returned to their previous luster, and the Emperor breathed easier, as though a great weight had lifted off his shoulders.

The day's events moved along as planned. The land dispute was tedious and grated on the Emperor's nerves. Cecilia, on the other hand, proved to be not only beautiful (though not as magnificent as Isabelle), but also charming and interesting. The Emperor made a point of dining with every potential concubine before he decided whether or not to acquire her as a slave. He'd discovered that watching someone eat revealed volumes about that person's behavior, personality, upbringing, and cleanliness. During their luncheon, he told her what expectations he had of her, and what she might expect from him. The meal ended amicably, and he ordered his servants to escort her to his northern palace at once.

The meeting with Sir Grellek went as expected: it was both interesting and dull. While the Emperor considered this new town highly important for his future strategies, how the town would be laid out was less vital to him than to Sir Grellek, a young noble with considerable political influence for his age who hailed from far northern Neverak. Unfortunately, the Emperor's stratagem backfired. His servant dutifully reminded his Majesty how much he hated the name Eastern Krallickton just before Sir Grellek was to leave, which forced them to spend another half-hour discussing appropriate names for the town. In the end, they agreed upon nothing, and another meeting was set.

Reluctantly, the Emperor ordered his page to escort the writer into the reception hall. Seeing him sparked the Emperor's memory of their last meeting. It had occurred when a local nobleman, brought before the Emperor on a charge of philandering, let slip that he had employed the writer to compose a poem for his mistress and passed it off as his own work. After pardoning the nobleman, the Emperor summoned the writer, who, when answering the summons, had appeared at the palace dressed in a dramatic fashion and donning a confident, almost arrogant air.

Today was no different.

The writer's audacity was in full bloom. He strolled into the reception hall wearing a long cape over his white shirt and green trousers. On his head, he sported a flamboyant orange cap ornamented with a shockingly pink feather. His handlebar mustache appeared to have been carefully trimmed and waxed.

The Emperor's page leaned close and whispered, "His name is Jackson Roving."

Emperor Krallick nodded, having forgotten the name. Jackson stopped a comfortable distance from the Emperor's seat and bowed so briefly it looked more like an involuntary tic. The Emperor chose not to speak while he gazed with mild astonishment at the writer's appearance. However impetuous Roving might be, he was at least aware that he should not speak to the Emperor before being addressed.

A minute or two passed before Emperor Krallick began speaking softly. "Can you guess why I have summoned you?"

"Your Imperial Highness," Jackson Roving answered with another bow that looked like a neck spasm, "my best guess would be that you wish to employ my services again, in which case I am *most* humbled."

Roving sounded anything but humbled, and the ruler of Neverak bristled. Why hadn't he ordered a spring-panel installed in *this* throne, and not just in the northern palace?

"You could not be more wrong, Mr. Roving." Emperor Krallick made his voice sound even more welcoming. "On the contrary—I am *displeased* with the service you rendered me a few weeks ago."

Jackson's face fell so low even his mustache and feather seemed to droop. "My—my Lord, forgive me . . . and allow me an opportunity to rectify my mistake."

"Can I trust you?" The Emperor sent a piercing stare directed at the writer's widened eyes. "You have proven yourself unworthy of my commissioning once. I would appreciate hearing a sample of what you wrote to the woman who was the object of my invitation."

Taking courage at this proposal, the writer began to recite his lines in the tone of a poet on a balcony bathed in the soft moonlight of a midsummer's night. When he finished, Jackson looked to the Emperor for a sign of satisfaction, but the Emperor sat unmoving and expressionless.

"She's right, of course," he said in his quietest voice.

"What did you say, your Majesty?"

"The woman was right. *Awful* is the word she used to describe your prose, and I agree. What gave you the idea I would wish to be compared to a gardener? Or a plant?"

"It is a rich symbolism used by some of the greatest poets—"

"Have you ever heard of your Emperor *gardening*?"

"No, my—"

The dulcet tones of the Emperor's voice underscored his growing wrath. "You should have consulted me before sending off such repugnant words in my name. No wonder she rejected my offer to join me. You have tarnished my name, my family's name, indeed, all of Neverak. Your insufficient pen has opened a gaping wound in our country's immaculate body!"

The writer recoiled in horror, sputtering excuses and pleas for forgiveness. As quickly as the Emperor's wrath poured forth from his tongue, it was gone. Rigid control of his emotions was one of the first techniques he had been taught by his tutors.

"Of course you must repair the damage you have done."

"I will do whatever my Lord commands," the writer cried as he removed his cap and bowed to the ground in true supplication. "I believe I can do it, and would not think of charging a fee for any other writing your Majesty would have me do until I have mended my errors."

"How honorable of you."

"Thank you, your Majesty."

"Come now and stand," the Emperor said. "Forgiveness is not so hard to come by as you might think."

"Thank you, your Majesty. Oh, how I thank you!"

A placating smile from Emperor Krallick eased the writer's tension, though in his mind's eye, the Emperor imagined blood gushing from wounds in the writer's head and neck. The small smile grew until it seemed to reach out and embrace Jackson Roving in a warm, comfortable blanket. Jackson's face relaxed until it showed no fear.

"Do you use the bow, Mr. Roving?"

"No, my Lord. I am a man of peace and love. Not war."

"A pity. It is an art, archery. Let me demonstrate it." The Emperor nodded to a servant, who stepped briefly from the hall and returned with a bow and a quiver of arrows. Emperor Krallick took both, strapping the quiver securely across his chest, and nocked an arrow in the bow. Immediately he raised the sharpened arrow point at Mr. Roving.

"I draw back the bowstring, thus, release the arrow, and it pierces the target."

"My—my—my Lord, please! Please let me—"

"Run, Mr. Roving. Run from this hall as fast as you can. If the gods of Atolas look favorably upon you, perhaps you will survive."

Jackson Roving shrieked, spun, and ran for his life. The Emperor let the arrow fly just over the fleeing writer's shoulder, close enough that the writer could not have failed to hear it whistling past his arrogant ear. The Emperor, with a half-smile, nocked a second arrow and adjusted his aim.

TWENTY-ONE
Essence of Angel Herbs

Henry faithfully applied fourteen drops of medicine into Isabelle's mouth, nose, and ears. James observed Henry carefully the first few times Isabelle received the medicine so that he could take a turn caring for her, but Henry never gave him the opportunity. Henry stated firmly that it was his responsibility and no one else's. The only other person Henry let help him was Maggie, yet each time she did, she came away sickly and exhausted.

The group's mood had visibly lifted when Henry, Brandol, and James had brought back medicine for Isabelle. It had been their first small victory since their escape. But when a week passed with no change in her condition, morale plummeted to a new low.

With the East Richterton Forest long behind them, the small party stuck to their plan of traveling along the hills east of the Drewberry River. James was careful to keep them as concealed as possible in the hills. They lit fires only in the early hours of the morning, cooking all they needed for the day. James organized the party into watches so that, day or night, they were alert and on guard for searchers. Using his military training, he always kept an eye out for possible ambush points and safer routes he and his friends might use.

He and Henry checked on Isabelle after every meal. The group wanted to see signs of improvement so badly that James feared they might start imagining changes. Yet Isabelle showed none. To make matters worse, autumn had arrived. The tall grasses grew brown and brittle, wildflowers wilted away, and strong winds and rain assaulted them almost daily. While James realized this made the party's trail through the meadows harder to follow, the morning gusts grew colder, and Isabelle's condition seemed to deteriorate.

"Looks like an early winter," James mentioned during lunch one day. He stared at the dark clouds that reflected his mood. "That doesn't bode well for us."

"Any day now, she'll wake up and be absolutely fine," Ruther answered. He'd said the same thing many times, but James heard a lack of conviction in the storyteller's voice.

They journeyed on, though the rain and wind slowed them. Isabelle's already slender frame grew thinner and frailer without food, and her skin began to take on a waxy appearance. Next, a paleness set in that reminded James of a deep, midwinter morning frost. Henry asked Brandol to ride the spare horse so he could spend his days by her side in the carriage. James quickly missed Henry's company at the head of the group. Brandol spoke hardly a word, which meant that the only conversation came from Ruther, whose random thoughts and jokes often became unbearable. It took only a few days of this for James to ask Ruther and Brandol to lead the party while he rode alongside the carriage. From there, he could hear Henry speaking to Isabelle in pleasant conversational tones. Henry would spend long stretches describing the scenery to her, telling her about what Ruther said to Maggie, and what Maggie retorted to Ruther, and revealing the dreams he had previously concealed in his heart about their life together. James felt like an intruder during some of these moments, but they also reminded him of the secrets he kept buried from all but himself.

On one occasion, James heard muffled sobs coming from the carriage. He slowed Sissy deliberately on the pretext of moving to the other side of the road. As Sissy crossed behind the carriage, he peered in silently and saw Henry holding Isabelle tightly, cradling her in his arms, whispering to the Lord of All Worlds to somehow transfer his life force into hers. Witnessing Henry's devotion to his sister touched James and made him wonder how the Lord Almighty could allow such good people to suffer.

"I thought I loved you before," he heard Henry tell her in that dark hour, "but I didn't. I didn't know what the word meant then. Now I know. I do truly love you, my Isabelle."

After that moment, James decided to ride a bit farther from the carriage. The next morning, the same day the Emperor arrived at his summer mansion, James calculated that the party's pace was far too slow. With the constant rain, their prevailing sour mood, and James's poor decision to let Ruther set the pace alongside Brandol, they had already fallen four or five days behind on their schedule. Their next planned stop in Fenley to purchase food and supplies was a week away at best. James privately advised Maggie to limit their rations, and he borrowed Ruther's bow to shoot game if it wandered near the company.

As he and Henry rode to the river that day to fill their waterskins, Henry voiced new concerns. "We need to take her to another physician as soon as we can."

James did not know what to say.

"She won't last much longer," Henry pressed. "The water and honey mixture isn't sustaining her."

"The medicine still isn't gone," James pointed out.

"I don't care anymore."

"You should, because all another physician will do is bleed her. I will not stand for such a barbaric practice on my sister. You've seen how pale she is already."

"But—"

"Ruther has reminded you several times the Emperor wouldn't give a deadly poison to Isabelle if he intended to take her to Neverak.

I don't see eye to eye with Ruther often, but on this I do. There is still medicine in the vial."

"Look at her, James! She's melting away. Her skin is tight, her hair brittle; she has no color. What good is it to let her die of starvation?"

James answered Henry with silence. His eyes, gray as the clouds hovering above them, stared off into the distance, searching the horizon for answers. "When the drops run out, we'll find a physician. Is that agreeable?"

Henry's agreement came at length.

The next morning marked a fortnight since Isabelle's supper with the Emperor. The sun had not yet risen, and the air was unusually chilly. Henry finished his breakfast first and went to the carriage to give Isabelle her medicine. James walked with him to check on her. Very little medicine remained in the vial, so little that James doubted they had enough to last through the day. With all the care he possessed, Henry poured ten drops into Isabelle's open mouth. After so much practice administering Isabelle's medicine and giving her water several times a day, Henry could complete the tasks without spilling a drop.

James watched Isabelle's tongue absorb the drops and prayed silently that they would take effect. Next were the ears and the nose; as the last drop disappeared down Isabelle's ear canal, her chest rose sharply and from her throat came a rattling gasp so frightening that James thought she was inhaling Death itself.

"Oh, no," Henry moaned. "Isabelle, no . . ."

Her chest heaved violently but her eyes stayed closed.

"Henry?" Maggie asked. Her faint voice drew nearer. "Is everything all right?"

Henry continued to hold Isabelle. James had to lean in to see what was happening. Her chest rose and fell faster and more powerfully, though this time without convulsions. The carriage door on the opposite side opened, and Maggie appeared with Brandol. Ruther tried to look on from behind them. Henry glanced at them all with wild, desperate eyes.

He pressed his cheek against Isabelle's and whispered in her ear, "You'll be all right! You're going to live, Isabelle!"

Ruther asked anxious questions similar to Maggie's. Brandol stayed silent, horror etching his face. They listened to Henry tell Isabelle over and over that he would not let her die. These statements were both pleas and commands that rose in urgency until Henry's anguish was so great that he overwhelmed the others with his tone of voice. Brandol clutched at his own chest while Maggie covered her tears and Ruther turned away. James finally squeezed into the carriage, trying to help Henry with Isabelle.

A scared whisper interrupted Henry's cries. "Henry?" the delicate voice said. "Henry, I'm right here."

Henry brought his face away from Isabelle's ear and muttered, "Thank you, Maggie."

Maggie, however, had not spoken—her body still shook with sobs. Henry turned back to Isabelle. James watched his sister's eyes open to small slits, and he brought a shaking hand to his own open mouth. A rosy hue crept up her neck and cheeks. The beating heart inside James's chest felt only gratitude, and Henry, like his sister, broke down in tears.

"Henry," Isabelle said, almost laughing, "don't cry."

James took one of Isabelle's hands in his. They were still cold, but not to the same degree as in recent days.

"I can't help it," Henry explained. "I'm—I'm overcome."

"Don't be overcome," Isabelle responded. "You have to get me something to eat. I'm famished."

Laughter broke through the group. Only James did not join in.

"Then I'll make you some food right away." Henry left, calling on Brandol and Maggie to assist. To James he said, "Keep an eye on her."

James went inside the carriage and sat by his sister.

"James, what are you doing here?" She smiled weakly at him and then closed her eyes as though she was in pain. "I'm confused. So many bad dreams . . . and some good dreams. My mind is like a brick. I can't seem to answer any of my own questions."

"What do you want to know?" James asked as she slipped her hand into his.

"Am I well?" she asked without pause. Her eyes were wide and focused on his. The expression reminded him of when they were children, and he told her stories of demons and monsters late at night. It surprised him how quickly she'd grown into a younger version of his mother. Her tone of voice was similar, and her hair color was exactly the same as Lady Oslan's before she'd fallen ill. James had seen Isabelle so little after joining the King's Guard that she had become a woman—and he'd missed it.

He squeezed her hand tightly to reassure her. "Yes. You are well now." The touch between them felt both awkward and familiar. James had never shown this kind of tenderness to anyone, and the thought saddened him. "You will recover."

Tears trickled down from Isabelle's eyes as she breathed deeply in relief. The longer James stared at her, the more he saw why Henry had been so worried. Her skin was so tight, so pale and shiny, that she could pass as a specter.

"I was terrified, James. At times I didn't know if I was alive or dead. I heard voices, but thought they were angels calling me. Or dreams . . ."

"You heard Henry's voice. Not exactly an angel, but he stayed at your side for days."

This statement brought another smile to Isabelle's lips, and she kissed her brother's hand. Again, the contact made him uncomfortable. "How many days have I been asleep?"

"Two weeks."

Isabelle mouthed the words to herself. "It felt like a very long nap."

She looked at James. Her face hadn't changed that much, he noticed; she still looked like the young girl he'd left behind when he enlisted. "I missed you so much. Especially with everything that has happened. It was like living in a nightmare with Father those last months. When did you receive my last letter?"

"I—I received no letters. I arrived home in the middle of a duel between Henry and our father. I should teach Henry to use a sword. He couldn't even defend himself against that old man. Do you have the strength to tell me about Mother's death?"

Isabelle slowly recited the events of the day their mother died. Hearing her tale left James with deep regret. He had wanted to be with his mother during her last hours, and he had written her a letter not long before telling her how she had been on his mind. For the first time in a long while, he had even penned the words *I love you.*

When Isabelle told him of the strange utterance Mother gave regarding him, he asked, "What does that mean? 'Climb the windy side?'"

Isabelle shook her head. Her gaze was far away as she remembered these things. James wished he could have seen his mother one last time. He could no longer remember the little things about her: the smell of her room, the touch of her hand, the sound of her weak laugh as she teased him for his stoic manner.

Isabelle spoke again. "Everything happened so fast . . . there was so much to do. Her eyes were not normal when she said it. I don't think she could see anymore. Perhaps she saw past the world of Atolas, and looked into Beyond—into something we can't understand."

"Or it might have all been a dream."

"Now you must tell me of everything that's happened since I was poisoned." Isabelle shuddered, and her face went pale again. "Tell me how you and Brandol and Ruther came to be traveling with us."

James related to Isabelle all that the group had done over the past two weeks. During his tale, Henry returned with a large dish of the best food that remained. Isabelle pounced on it, voraciously consuming all the food on the plate, all thought of manners forgotten. James watched her eat with morbid interest.

Ruther, standing behind Henry, remarked, "I don't believe I'll be eating anytime soon."

"Yes, you will," Maggie said. "How else will you stay so fat?"

The more Isabelle ate, the more her cheeks regained their normal color. "Water," she said through a mouthful of her second helping of dried pork. Maggie brought a large mug filled to the brim. Isabelle accepted it with the same greediness.

"Maybe we should get her more food," Ruther suggested to Henry. "Do you think she'll put away as much as she's missed the past two weeks?"

James stared at Isabelle as he whispered back, "I hope not."

"She ain't gonna, you know, split or something, will she?" Brandol asked.

"Should I say something?" Maggie offered.

"Not yet," was Ruther's reply. "I once ate a whole chicken with carrots, potatoes, and all the trimmings. And a blackberry pie for dessert. It was both the best and the worst experience of my life."

"You didn't split, did you?" Henry asked.

Ruther tried to suppress a snicker, but failed. "No . . . but I exploded." He slapped his knee as if he'd told a great joke.

James looked away from Ruther in disgust. Sometimes he saw why Maggie loathed Henry's friend as much as she did. Not an instant had passed after Isabelle took her last bite of food when she vomited most of it back up, leaning over the carriage door and spilling it onto the grass. James jumped out of the way to avoid getting his boots soiled. As she finished, she sat up, a bemused expression on her face. Then her eyes rolled into the back of her head and the plate slipped from her hand. Maggie caught the plate as the rest of the group rushed to grab her. James reached her first and supported her head as he laid her back down.

"She's only sleeping," he said after a short examination, hiding the relief he felt.

"You're certain?" Henry continued to examine her eyes and face.

"Yes."

Four bodies relaxed at once. "You'd think she could have at least warned us," Ruther complained. "After everything we've been through, would a simple, 'I'm feeling tired now and I'd like a nap' be too much to ask?"

A cold gust of wind blew through the camp, reminding James they needed to be moving. "Brandol," he said, "will you take Henry's place in the carriage again? Ruther, you're on watch until nightfall."

"I was on watch two nights ago," Ruther said as he mounted Ghost. "It should be Little Henry's turn."

"Brandol is riding inside the carriage."

"He can have my horse," Ruther argued back. "Or Henry can have a turn. He's always next after Brandol."

James looked over his shoulder at Maggie and sighed. Henry smiled.

"You're right, Ruther," James said, "but I need to speak with Henry."

"Speak with me and let Henry watch. Or let Maggie. I have no preference as long as it's not me doing the watching."

"It's so refreshing to see a man willing to pass his work off to a woman," Maggie said from behind. "I suppose in your world, chivalry is dead and laziness runs rampant."

James watched as Ruther jerked the reins of his horse in Maggie's direction so he could properly glare at her. "It's not *laziness, indolence,* or *lassitude*—did you hear all those words?" he called out, "—or *lethargy* or *idleness* or—"

"Ruther, why don't you save your energy for keeping a good

lookout?" Maggie suggested as she urged the horses on, leaving Ruther behind to mutter under his breath.

It was still morning. Henry and James trotted side by side in silence and watched the sun peek out over the crest of the hills. Its light would soon reflect off the wet blades of grass, making it difficult for them to see ahead without squinting. Miles behind, dark rain clouds threatened to overtake them at some point during the day. Sissy stepped lightly; James recognized this as a sign of her good mood.

James had always been fond of the Blithmore prairies. During his time in the Guard, he'd seen a large portion of the country: its far western mountains, numerous rivers, a large southwestern desert. But none of it compared to the beauty of the bright green meadows full of wildflowers breaking the sun's rays into thousands of points of light.

"You're a good man, Henry." James kept his eyes on the horizon and buried the emotion he felt. "You treat my sister the way she deserves."

Henry did not respond right away. James wondered if he had caught him off guard. As children, Henry, Maggie, and Ruther had called him "General James" because he'd fit the role so well. No one had been surprised when he announced his intention to join the King's Guard the very day he met the age requirement. He had the perfect temperament for a soldier, and now, it seemed, he would forever miss that life.

"Thank you," Henry finally said. A quiet fell between them again. James had the feeling Henry wanted to say more, so he waited patiently. "I feel as though I'm being punished."

"By whom?" James asked.

"By fate or the Almighty . . . by something."

"Why?"

"Hey!" Ruther called from way behind. "I want to be part of your conversation."

"For my negligence of Isabelle's safety. For yielding to your father's wishes when I knew I should flee with Isabelle. For allowing my cowardice to prevent our escape until the situation turned so grave I had no choice if I wanted to protect her."

"I agree with whatever Henry is saying!" Ruther shouted before James responded.

Henry drew himself up in his saddle. James saw a resolve on Henry's face that he hadn't seen in many of the guardsmen who served the King. "So I've made a solemn oath to never be guilty of inaction again. Whenever we have a moment, I want you to teach me to fight."

James had never cared as much about class and nobility as his father had. Such things mattered little on a field of battle. Enemies would not shoot fewer arrows at a man because he was a noble. And here was Henry, a man who thought himself a coward, but was, in his own way, one of the bravest men James knew. He had the courage to recognize his mistakes and change.

"You're not alone in your guilt, Henry. Now that I know what a state of disorder my family was in, I realize I was remiss in my duties."

"No—"

"Yes," James insisted. "My father's actions have blotted out the once-great name of Oslan. If I'd known all that had happened when I arrived at my house, his blood would have stained the floor the moment I saw him. And yet, through everything, you've stood by my sister. My father believes our family's inherent worth is greater than yours, yet I believe the opposite is the truth. *Vestin* is the most honorable name I have known. When we reach the border, I will take my leave of you, but should you ever need me, all you need do is send word."

"Thank you, James, but I don't understand. Why not come with us? You are implicated as much as we are, especially since I told the physicians that you held the flaming arrow aimed at their house. What is so important in Blithmore that you're willing to risk your life for it?"

James's gaze broke from the horizon and went to the ground a foot in front of him. He stroked Sissy's mane as he wrestled with his thoughts. Some emotions were harder to bury than others. "I have unfinished business here. That's all I will say."

Henry did not press for more information. He chuckled and asked, "Do you remember when we caught that skunk and put Maggie's book inside the trap?"

James allowed himself a small smile. "When your mother gave us our next reading lesson, and Maggie opened her book, she burst into tears."

"*My book died, Mommy! My book died!*" Henry laughed so hard it startled Quicken. "I've never smelled anything so terrible."

James looked back at Maggie, who had clearly overheard them. She, too, smiled at the memory. Her well-formed lips and brilliant white teeth gave her smile a radiant quality that lit up her whole face, making her brown-green eyes shine even brighter.

"It was awful!" she mused. "Even now, I can remember the stench perfectly."

"Your mother caught us—" James began.

"By smelling your fingers," Maggie finished, "that's right."

"She canceled the lesson," Henry added. "She was so mad."

"Your father gave *you* quite a lashing, if I remember."

Henry laughed even louder, and the smile on James's face grew. From far behind, Ruther laughed, too, though it was obvious he did it only to force himself into the conversation.

James spurred Sissy faster. Henry followed suit with Quicken. The sun broke over the top of the far hills, and James had to shield his eyes to see a hundred yards ahead. They made small talk about the possibility of the storm coming toward them. Henry mentioned his desire to try his hand at hunting if they spotted some game. James liked the idea. Henry needed to learn. In James's mind, hunting was one of life's great joys. A loud curse came from the back of the group.

Ruther's voice. He had Ghost turned around and was staring into the distance. Henry and James stopped to see what the matter was.

The carriage came to a stop, and Maggie asked, "What do you see?"

"Soldiers," Ruther answered, his hand shielding his eyes. "I'm certain of it. They're headed in our direction."

TWENTY-TWO

Hiding in the Hills

J ames rode up behind Ruther. A mile or so away, lower in the hills, a long train of about fifty soldiers rode along on horseback. Ruther didn't think he'd ever seen people ride with such formal posture, except James—not even a corpse could ride a horse as stiffly as James.

"What do you think?" Ruther asked.

"They haven't found a trail yet," James said. "That formation, loosely bunched," he pointed to the line of riders, but Ruther saw nothing he could identify as a formation, "that's for traveling. They're headed south, and at that speed we'll never cross paths. We should be safe. My guess is they are headed for Fenley or Creighton."

"Do you recognize them, James?" Ruther asked.

"Those aren't guardsmen. They're regular cavalry."

Henry and Brandol joined them. Ruther noted his friend's eyes blinking rapidly and the way Brandol bit his bottom lip as it trembled. Maggie brushed her dark locks out of her face and tucked them behind her ears, which were red from the brisk morning air. Ruther had memorized the nervous habits of his friends a long time ago, but he always found them fascinating and remembered them to use as details in his stories.

"They are going to see our trail any moment," Henry said.

"They'll probably think nothing of it. That's heavy frost, and it has been down most of the night, so we could have traveled through at any point during—"

"They're turning," Henry said, "and that soldier in front is signaling."

"What formation is that?" Ruther asked as the soldiers tightened their ranks, paired up, and fell in line.

James stared into the distance. Steam billowed from his nose as he exhaled angrily. "Search—a search formation."

"We need to move," Henry said. "What do we do?"

"We can't fly like mindless cattle," James replied. "We should split into three groups. It will be harder for them to catch us. Maggie and Isabelle should go straight south until they come to the river. I will go with Brandol farther east, you and Ruther go north and west and loop back."

"That's not what we—" Ruther began.

"Where we gonna meet?" Brandol asked. "How we gonna know if someone got caught?"

"We're only a day or so from Fenley," James continued. "We should meet at the easternmost edge of town."

"I don't know where to go," Maggie said. "I don't have a map!"

Henry raised his hands. "Wait. If we keep moving, they may give up before they spot us. They don't know how far our trail goes."

James seemed ready to disagree, but Maggie cut him off. "I agree with Henry," she said.

Ruther found it interesting that Maggie's statement ended James's will to argue.

Henry and James set the pace, leading the party through the winding valleys of the hilly landscape. They moved as fast as the carriage could manage on the grassy terrain. No one spoke. Ruther doubled back regularly to calculate the distance between the two parties. He thought of Isabelle sleeping inside the carriage and decided her falling back asleep so soon might have been a blessing after all. The stress of their predicament might have put a heavy strain on her fragile health. He glanced often at Maggie, only to be impressed each time by the presence of mind she showed while driving the carriage.

After over a half-hour of traveling, the frost had still not disappeared. Ruther could see why. The dark clouds they'd observed in the early morning had moved eastward, blocking the sun's light and chilling the air. To add to this sinister atmosphere, a cold wind howled as it sped along the valley floor in violent gusts. Each blast of air pierced Ruther's clothes and filled his ears with its low moans.

"I'd guess they're several hundred yards away," Ruther reported, "around the valley bend. At that rate, they'll know we're here within a quarter of an hour."

Henry stopped and dismounted. Maggie halted as he ran to the carriage.

"What are you doing?" James asked.

"We're not going to make it," Henry replied. "Let's try something else."

"Get back on your horse, friend!" Ruther shouted with the first real anger he'd felt toward Henry in some time. He looked to the horizon in front of them, wondering how far he might get before the soldiers caught up to Henry and the others if he were to flee now . . .

"Help me make a fire," Henry said. "James, get some food out— enough for a small brunch. Brandol, we'll need your help, too. While I start a fire, you can block the wind so the flames won't blow out."

Ruther grasped Henry's idea. It was reckless, loony—and he liked it.

"What are you doing, Henry?" Maggie asked as she climbed down from the driver's chair. "They're still following us."

"Ask James what help he'll need."

They worked efficiently. Ruther used the best and driest wood he could find as kindling. Henry attacked it at once with his flint and steel. With Brandol using his cloak as a shield against the wind, they soon had a modest fire crackling.

"Put some of the green wood on it now," Henry told Ruther.

"They're already on our trail," James protested as he stirred their little pot of food. "Are you sure you want to announce our presence?"

"That's exactly what we want to do," Ruther said. "I'll keep an eye out and tell you when they're close."

"I know what you're thinking, Henry," Ruther heard James say as he climbed the hill to peek over the ridge. "This is a much greater chance to take than splitting the group."

"Just keep your full attention on your task, James," Ruther muttered to himself as he watched the soldiers follow the trail. "You don't know everything."

"What—what's your plan about, Master Henry?" Brandol asked, still holding his cloak out like a giant bat's wings.

"Have you ever seen a three-horned gormont, Brandol?" Henry asked.

"No. Never heard of it."

"It's a rare lizard that can squeeze blood out of its skin when a predator gets near. Then it stops breathing and the blood dries over it very quickly. The predator thinks it's already dead and continues to search for live prey. A clever disguise, don't you think?"

Brandol's face paled. "You mean, we're gonna pretend dead?"

Ruther caught Henry trying to hide a smile. "We're going to disguise ourselves as something the soldiers don't want."

"They see our smoke!" Ruther announced as he peeked over the hilltop. "I hope your hunch is right, friend."

"Listen to me," Henry said, "we have to make up a story that these men will believe. We have to pretend to be a—a—"

"A traveling acting troupe!" Ruther declared, scampering back down the hill to rejoin the group around the fire.

"They'd never believe such a tale," James said.

"If we're convincing, they will."

James looked around for someone to agree with him. "You know me, Henry. I am not an actor."

"He's right," Ruther said, throwing his hands up in mock exasperation. "My wigs can act better than James. Let's all give up hope and die. I think I'll choose beheading as my preferred form of punishment. Less mess to clean."

"Has anyone got a better idea?" Maggie asked. "If so, let's hear it fast."

Ruther did not think the idea was so horrible. Acting and storytelling were not too different, and, truth be told, he considered himself to be a terrific liar.

The smoke from the fire rose up at a slant as the wind pushed it south. Brandol still valiantly guarded the flames even though his services were no longer needed. Ruther noticed that the journeyman's face had gone white and that his lip still trembled. It was understandable.

"Ruther," Henry asked. "What are some common names for actors and actresses?"

Ruther tapped one of his long fingers against his chin. "You can be Bradley," Ruther told Henry, "Brandol is Ian. I will be Robert. Maggie will be Jennifer."

"What about Isabelle?"

"Also a Jennifer—or maybe a Kate. No, two Jennifers is more catchy, and you can never have too many. We'll say that Isabelle's Jennifer is sick with consumption."

"And James?"

"He will be a mute named Jimmy who makes costumes and props, a stagehand."

"I will *not* be a mute," James said.

"You will if you don't want to give us away," Ruther told him. "If you can't pretend to have a personality, don't talk."

James held his tongue. Watching him fume gave Ruther a bit of vengeful pleasure for all the times James had taken Maggie's side in an argument. Moments later, the sound of dozens and dozens of galloping hooves announced the arrival of the troops. Brandol's breaths deepened until finally he covered his head with his cloak's hood. Ruther saw Henry glance over his shoulder toward Maggie with a look of doubt on his face. When he turned back, Ruther gave his friend a reassuring grin.

Henry nodded. "Let Ruther do the talking, everyone."

"When doesn't he do the talking?" Maggie asked.

Ruther ignored Maggie's comment and rode out to meet the small army. Other than excessive sweat forming between his hand and Ghost's reins, he showed no sign of fear.

You've been in worse situations before, he told himself.

By the sheer size of the company, Ruther guessed two full regiments of soldiers had followed them, or one brigade. Drawing closer, he could distinguish rank and insignia on the individual uniforms.

The brigadier rode in front. He had a mane of pure white hair and bright green eyes that seemed to pierce Ruther's soul. A matching large green feather poked out of his hat, waving in the wind. The captains of the two regiments flanked him. The captain to the brigadier's right was much older than the captain to his left. The brigadier raised his hand to hail Ruther. Ruther returned the gesture and brought Ghost to a halt. When the captain dropped his hand, Ruther urged Ghost forward again.

The eyes of all the soldiers were on him, most filled with suspicion. The brigadier spoke first. "Young man, are you the owner of these tracks we've been following?"

"I am, sir." Ruther maintained a humble tone and demeanor as he spoke. "We thought these hills were deserted for miles. If I may ask, why are you following us?"

"We received orders to search this area for a band of criminals. Perhaps you have heard of them?"

As the brigadier asked this question, he fixed a scrutinizing eye on Ruther. His captains' stares were almost as formidable. Fortunately, Ruther had plenty of experience with tight spots and pointing fingers. He recalled the rhyme of his uncle. "Never waver eye to eye, and they'll never catch you in a lie."

"Certainly I've heard of them," Ruther said. He smiled at the right moment, letting his face tell the men he would help them in any way he could. "I'd like to find a man who hasn't. Why do you think we travel in these windy hills? People are frightened all over, including us, but you and your men are the first search party we've seen in these parts. And I'll tell you, it's a welcome sight."

The brigadier sat as stiff in his seat as ever. "Where did you come by your information?"

The large smile that grew on Ruther's face came too easy. "Oh, people like us—we're all over, and we hear all the rumors!"

"People like *us*?"

"*Actors!*" Ruther said with a dramatic gesture that made him resemble at once both the king and a peasant. "Performers! Artists!"

The two captains exchanged an exasperated look, which Ruther knew he had to capitalize on at once.

"What?" he asked in mock offense. "Do your men lack the refinement that brings appreciation of the world's most noble art form?"

The brigadier continued to watch Ruther. "How many travel with you?"

"There is myself and five others."

"Six total," the brigadier said to his captains. "Take us to them."

"Certainly," Ruther replied, still assuming the air of a man offended but determined to be proud, "we're over and down those hills. Will all of your men be coming?"

The brigadier turned to his captains. "Pick five men each and follow me."

Ruther accepted this as his invitation to lead the brigadier to camp. Behind him, the captains shouted orders to their men. Ruther set a fast pace, expecting the brigadier to stay with the safety of his men. He arrived at the group several seconds before the soldiers.

"Remember your names!" he hissed to the group.

More than a dozen soldiers circled the small camp. All kept their hands near the hilts of their swords. Despite his cool demeanor, Ruther had never felt in greater danger in his life. At a word from the brigadier, these men could fall on them, and all six lives would end in seconds. Fortunately, an ignominious death in the hills of rural Blithmore had never been a part of Ruther's grand plan for his life.

"Gentlemen," he called out, his arms outstretched in placating friendliness. "Gentlemen, why the hostility? I have offered to show you my small troupe. If you don't like performers, you should have said so."

"What are your names?" growled the brigadier. It was more an order than a question.

"I am Robert," Ruther began, "this is Brad, Ian, Jennifer, and Jennifer is sick in the carriage . . . poor thing. Consumption."

"Then who is she?" the seasoned soldier asked, pointing a black-gloved hand at Maggie.

"That is Jennifer."

The permafrost-green eyes of the brigadier watched Ruther with the utmost scrutiny. "You said Jennifer was sick."

"She is," Ruther responded in his least confrontational voice, "but this is also Jennifer. There are two."

"What about that man?" came the question with a finger pointing to James.

Ruther followed the finger to James's face and back to the brigadier. He gave him a confident smile and dismissing gesture of the hand. "That's our Jimmy. A deaf mute so empty-headed that he is only capable of communicating through the crudest of gestures. He is our workman. He sews and cooks for us."

"A pleasure to meet you," Henry said with a wave so enthusiastic, Ruther cringed.

The brigadier surveyed the camp, but Ruther knew everything appeared normal. The breakfast plates and mugs were dirty from earlier. "The women do not do your cooking and knitting?"

"My dear sir," Ruther explained, "our Jennifers are skilled artists capable of the most precise, soul-piercing gestures and articulations. To put their feminine hands through the arduous, monotonous tasks of sewing and cooking . . . What if a needle pierced a finger? Or the cookfire singed an eyebrow? I couldn't have that! What's more, I have no doubt a performance from any of these artists, be it solo or ensemble, could extract every last tear stored in the collective eyes of your soldiers."

Many of the soldiers in the circle relaxed their hands during Ruther's speech, but the brigadier was not impressed. "When is your next performance?" he asked.

Ruther shook his head sadly. "That's the trouble. We spent several weeks in the northern cities, and now our sights are set on the south. I'm certain you've noticed the change in the season. Most troupes have trouble drawing crowds in the northern snow. We intend to seek audiences again as soon as we are south of Ramus."

"Why are you traveling so far out in the hills, and not closer to the river?"

"As I said, we fear the criminals, but also," Ruther assumed a melancholy air, "to avoid being accosted so frequently. It grows heavy on the mind after a time, and we prefer to try and have some level of anonymity. Certainly someone of your status in the military can understand the burden of fame?"

Ruther could see the brigadier was trying hard not to be flattered.

If such was the case, it could be dangerous to push it any farther. Some men smelled sycophancy better than others, another fact his uncle had taught him.

"So you intentionally stay below the visibility line of these hills?"

"Jennifer is very ill. Her consumption is compounded by the cold weather, and the sunlight irritates her awfully in the mornings and evenings."

"Of course," the brigadier said, "but since I've never seen you perform nor heard of you, I remain unconvinced until I see proof of your claims."

Henry made some small movement which Ruther did not dare risk further investigating; this was the critical moment where the brigadier would either decide for or against him. Unbroken eye contact was essential.

"What proof would you require of us, sir?" Ruther asked. "We have no writ of passage, nor letters of identification. As you know, the law does not demand proof of occupation for performers."

"You are correct," came the sharp answer, "but since we are hunting for a party of criminals roughly your size, unless you can produce satisfactory evidence, I am placing you under arrest."

"But, sir!" Henry protested. Maggie gasped and sputtered, and Brandol looked on the verge of fainting. James even flinched mildly, though by and large he maintained his illusion of deafness.

Ruther ignored the exclamations of his peers and kept smiling. "If that's your wish, go ahead and arrest us. Or, perhaps to save both parties a lot of time and distance, we can present you with the simplest proof of all. A show for your men?"

The brigadier seemed undecided, and that was when Ruther became nervous. Whether from curiosity or boredom—or simply a love of theater—the older of the two captains asked, "How long is your *shortest* performance?"

The brigadier wheeled his horse abruptly and exchanged a short word (which Ruther could not hear) with his second-in-command. The captain hurried to explain his sudden outburst. Then the brigadier turned back to Ruther and asked, "How long will this take?"

"One half-hour," came the proud announcement. "The greatest half-hour of your lives."

The brigadier raised his eyes heavenward. "You have fifteen minutes to prepare." Then to his captains he ordered, "Go gather the rest of your men."

TWENTY-THREE
A Soldier and His Lady

The easy part was over. With the soldiers' interest piqued and even the brigadier's curiosity aroused, now came the true challenge. How could he get his friends to perform a short play? Ruther keenly sensed the hopelessness among them. Maintaining his composure took every bit of self-awareness he possessed. Up in the sky, the dark clouds were moving farther west, and the sun cast its warming rays on the hills. Ruther hoped this signaled good things to come for them.

"We will require the use of our carriage to prepare," he said to the brigadier. "In the meantime, make yourselves as comfortable as you can." His attention turned to Henry and the others, who followed him out of the soldiers' sight.

"I don't know how to act!" Maggie hissed at him as soon as they were behind the carriage. "You are mad—*mad* if you think this can work!"

"It can," he explained quietly as he handed her one of Isabelle's dresses. "It has to. Go inside and put this on as quickly as you can. You've seen plays done by the local guilds, so why—"

"Yes," Henry said, "seen, but not performed in."

"Where's the difference?" Ruther asked. "Pretend you're an actor pretending to be someone else."

"I can't—I can't—I—I—can't do it," Brandol finally managed to say.

Ruther ignored him.

"What are we going to do?" Henry asked. "What will the story be?"

"One that everyone has seen: *The Soldier and His Lady*."

"I haven't seen that!" Maggie protested.

"It doesn't matter," Ruther said, "because all you have to do is pretend that you love me and kiss—"

"No. Absolutely not."

"Maggie," Henry said, "we don't have many choices here."

Loathing filled her eyes as she crossed her arms. "I would rather die than kiss Ruther."

"Fine," Ruther responded. He knew he should have expected such a reaction from her. "Brandol, you're the soldier. Get in James's uniform. I'll play the villain. James will be my mute servant. I will kidnap Maggie and perform long monologues about my villainy and infamy. Brandol, try not to mumble or stutter as you deliver your lines."

"But—but—but I can't do it! I ain't never done nothing like—" Brandol's face turned a blotchy mixture of white and red as he fumbled with James's uniform. "I get nervous when I—"

"Don't we all?" Ruther replied with an insincere smile and three patronizing taps on Brandol's head.

"Please, Ruther," Brandol begged, but Ruther did not have time to coddle him.

"What will I do?" Henry asked.

Ruther surveyed Henry for a moment. His smile turned into a look of pity. "Sorry, friend, soldiers don't have servants, but ladies do. Unless you want to kiss your sister, you'll have to be her maidservant."

"I am *not* playing a woman."

Maggie shot a sideways look at her brother. "Henry, we don't have many choices here."

"Please don't make me be no soldier," Brandol's face had become so white he looked as though he was wearing thick makeup. "I—I—"

Ruther stamped his foot. "Will you all just cooperate? I am *trying* to save your lives. For all your complaints about not being able to act, you're all playing the part of spoiled children astoundingly well." He sighed as he peeked around the carriage at the skeptical soldiers arranging themselves so everyone could see the performance. This was going to be a spectacular failure—no, an absolute disaster.

Ruther explained as much as he could in the allotted time what he expected each person to do, stressing the need to never stop performing. No one looked confident or prepared, but what else could he do? After they changed into their costumes, he took a long swig from his flask, then went out and stood in front of the crowd of soldiers that had grown from a dozen to more than one hundred. They regarded him with a blend of mild interest and incredulity.

In his black cape and trousers, Ruther was an impressive figure. His size made him a perfect villain. The attention of so many people nourished his soul and filled him with boundless energy. Ruther the man was loud, fat, and annoying, but Ruther the performer was nearly a god. True, he was not a trained actor, he was a storyteller, but in the end, performing was performing.

"Soldiers of the noble and great King Germaine of Blithmore!" he cried. Only a few cheers rose from the audience. "We welcome you to a special and private performance of *The Soldier and His Lady*. Due to the unexpected nature of the show, we will not be in makeup or full costumes, but do not worry! You will not leave disappointed! Without further adieu, I give you: *The Soldier and His Lady!*"

No applause came as Ruther left the grassy area which would be their stage. Nor did it come when Maggie walked out, dressed as much like a noble as anyone could ask of her. Ruther had been to dozens of performances in his lifetime and could not remember a single instance where a beautiful woman like Maggie had not been applauded, whistled, or catcalled upon entrance. However, when Henry arrived seconds later wearing a peasant dress, Ruther heard several stifled snickers.

"Lady Withem," Henry said in the grating falsetto voice Ruther had instructed him to use, "you look like the best—best . . . picture of beauty. I have no doubt that you will be the ball of the belle!"

"Do you really think so, Rosemetta?" Maggie asked, the fear in her voice thick—almost too much to pass as nervousness for an approaching ball. "Oh, I do hope my soldier will be there!"

"I have no doubt he will be there, milady. For—for you are too beautiful for him to not see you. And he will certainly arrive on the most punctual of times."

Oh dear heavens, Ruther thought, pressing his face into his palms, *I should have made Henry the mute. Now we're all going to die.*

"Thank you, Rosemetta," was Maggie's reply, "but what shall I wear as jewelry?"

"Only the gold necklace would dress you in your lovely suit. Er, suit you in your lovely dress. Milady."

"Will you fetch it for me?"

"Yes, milady!" Henry shouted, far too eager to sound like a genuine maidservant.

In a second, Henry came around the carriage where Ruther waited with the rest of the acting troupe. Meanwhile, Maggie continued to speak in a soliloquy about her love for her soldier. The longer she spoke, the more convincing she sounded, and Ruther was forced to conclude that with a little practice, she could probably pass as a respectable performer.

"This is not going to work!" Henry hissed. "What was going on in your head when you came up with this idea?"

"If this idea fails, the fault will be *yours*, friend." Ruther poked Henry hard in the chest, using the same tone as Henry. "You do know how to speak like an intelligent human, don't you? Because if you can, try doing it!"

"Not in front of a hundred soldiers hunting for me, and not as a woman!"

"It doesn't matter what *you* think, because you are not you. You are not Henry. You are *Bradley*, and Bradley is an actor. Bradley *likes* acting as a woman. Even in front of a hundred soldiers, who are certainly not hunting for *him*, because he is *Bradley*, not Henry."

Henry wasn't done protesting, but Ruther headed him off. "Go out there and give the lady her golden necklace," he whispered, shoving Maggie's gold necklace in Henry's hand.

Henry took it and left.

"Here is your golden necklace, milady," his high voice screeched as he walked out. "Allow me to put it around your pearl neck."

"Thank you, Rosemetta. I think I am nearly ready. Will you please summon the driver?"

"Yes, milady."

Ruther chuckled at Henry's pale face and agitated expression. It reminded him a bit too much of Brandol. Then Ruther drew his cloak around his face and straightened his flat hat. His most wicked grin crept across his lips. When he came around the carriage's rear, he pantomimed climbing in through a window and entered behind Maggie, unseen.

"Lady Witham!" Ruther cried in a booming, sinister voice.

Maggie yelped and clutched her face. "Who are you? Why are you in my room? Do you intend me harm?"

"I intend you no harm . . . unless you do not come with me, lady."

"Are you that wicked man, Bartholomew Evilute, who sneaks into fair ladies' rooms and abducts them for your own wicked purposes?"

"Perhaps I am," Ruther responded as impiously as ever. He could sense the interest in the crowd growing, their eyes resting on him, waiting to see what he would do next. "Or perhaps I am a misunderstood traveler who enjoys the company of a beautiful woman. Perhaps I am not truly as wicked as rumors would imply. Does Deity glare malignantly at a man whose history is as scarred and warped as mine?"

Ruther continued in this vein for a few minutes while Maggie watched him with an entranced interest. He spoke of the sins of his father, of his mother, and of their parents. By the time he was finished, no one could be truly certain of his guilt. Then he lunged for Maggie.

"No!" she pleaded, "Let me go! Help me, Rosemetta!"

"Quiet, wench!" Ruther roared nastily, "or I shall be forced to use bodily harm against you." Then he grabbed her behind the head and forced a kiss on Maggie's soft lips. Maggie instantly broke away and laid a solid slap across Ruther's face.

Despite the sting, Ruther stayed in character and laughed derisively. Still there was no vocal response from the audience. Maggie responded by struggling one last time, but all she managed to do was break her necklace in Ruther's hand. When the necklace broke, Maggie gasped loudly and became compliant as they exited the stage.

"You broke my necklace!" she whimpered.

"You've got to go on *now*," Henry told Brandol on the far side of the carriage. Brandol's pale face and trembling hands, along with James's too-large uniform draped over his smaller build, gave him the look of a terrified child. Ruther cringed. If anything would offend the soldiers, it would be the sight of Brandol in a guardsman's uniform.

"I can't do it, Master Henry. Ruther, please, tell him!"

For a moment, Ruther thought he was going to have to watch Brandol cry. He looked to Henry for help.

"Get out there, Brandol," Henry said. "It's your time. If I can play a woman, well, you can play a soldier."

"Please!" Brandol begged so pathetically that Ruther almost

relented. Before Ruther's sense of sympathy won out, he put his hands manfully on Brandol's shoulders and gave him a moderate push.

"Get on that stage and talk for a few minutes about how much you love Mag—I mean, Lady Witham."

"I *don't* love Maggie," Brandol said. The pitch of his voice was much higher than normal, almost as high as Henry's Rosemetta.

"Then talk about her as though she was your mother." With one final shove, Brandol stood alone in front of more than one hundred soldiers. Ruther heard a few scattered, derisive laughs from the otherwise silent troops. "Dear Lord Almighty, please don't let Brandol screw this up."

Then Brandol began speaking.

He spoke in short spurts, as though he were gasping for air and trying to vomit his words in between breaths. His voice continued to grow higher and higher until it was so unnatural it sounded like mouse squeaks. "I love me mother. She is me—my Lady Weth—Wetmum— Witham. My mother is my mother. And I love my lady. She's so beautiful. She is so . . . beautiful—very beautiful. I want ta dance with her. The dance will be—be shiny like the moons and stars. We—we—we will moon as we dance."

"Thanks for nothing!" Ruther hissed to the heavens.

Several more laughs joined the small chorus.

"She ain't—is not here," Brandol continued. "Methinks she was napped—kidnapped. By Bartho . . . lotho . . . new—the evil wicked bad man. I have to save my lady!"

The mirth of the crowd leapt another level. Ruther could not tell if this was good or bad. Was the performance so awful that the soldiers thought it was funny? Then all of a sudden, the soldiers erupted into howls of laughter. Ruther couldn't hear Brandol, so he peeked under the carriage to see what was happening.

Brandol's pants were pooled around his quaking ankles, and he was fumbling furiously to pick them up. The few faces Ruther could see in the crowd were red with laughter. Even the brigadier wept as he chortled. Brandol could not seem to keep his hands steady enough to pull his pants back up, and so they continued to slip back down, causing the soldiers to laugh harder and harder. Finally he secured them back around his waist and squeaked something about a rescue that was so high it almost didn't register in Ruther's ears.

After Brandol's first scene, the cast of *The Soldier and His Lady* could do no wrong. Every bobbled line, every miscue, every wardrobe failure was hilarious. When the climactic battle between the evil Bartholomew Evilute and the gentle soldier finally came, it ended up being quite ridiculous. Brandol and Ruther fought with swords, but Brandol's hands shook so badly that he couldn't make an offensive move. In the end, Ruther simply ran into Brandol's sword and gave a long-winded monologue denouncing his evil ways as he died.

The soldiers gave a long, roaring applause before, during, and after the bows. Coins small and large flew from the audience at the actors.

"Well done," the brigadier said, shaking Ruther's and Brandol's hands vigorously. "I stand corrected in my suspicions. I've never seen a better interpretation of a guardsman! The higher they rank, the more full they are of their own—"

"Thank you, sir," Ruther said, bowing low again. "It is enough for us that we have had an opportunity to perform for the King's bravest men."

"Oh, no," the brigadier insisted, "we owe you some form of recompense for such an entertaining show."

"Well, I can't imagine what—"

James tapped on Ruther's shoulder, gesturing wildly with his fingers and palms.

"Excuse him, sir," Ruther said, "I can't imagine what my dimwitted friend must want."

James was adamant in his gesticulations. He wrote on his hand with his finger, then channeled his hands together, then repeated the whole pattern again.

"What is he trying to say?" the brigadier asked.

"He probably wants food," Ruther said with a dismissing wave. "Eats more than he's worth, that one does."

"No," the brigadier said, "I think he wants me to write something."

"He probably wants you to sign a bit of parchment for him. He has always adored the King's soldiers."

James shook his head emphatically and continued his same hand signal.

The brigadier turned to James and spoke loudly and slowly. "DO. YOU. WANT. SOMETHING. FROM. ME?"

James nodded his head. Finally Ruther realized it. "A writ of passage!" he declared. "We would like a writ of passage! Someone stole ours while we stayed in Dairyton."

The brigadier smiled. "Oh, of course. An acting troupe would usually apply to a town's registrar for one, but that won't be a problem at all. I'll have my scribe write one for you. That will save you from any more trouble in your travels."

"Your generosity is overwhelming, sir," Ruther said with all the sincerity he possessed. "It was a blessing that we met you."

The brigadier nodded and mounted his horse. After delivering orders to his captains, he gave a call and rode off with everyone but the scribe. In moments, ink and paper were in the hand of the soldier, and he scribbled several lines down, then gave it to the brigadier for his signature and seal.

Ruther accepted it a little too gratefully, and as he watched the brigadier's backside grow smaller, his own smile grew larger.

"You are a genius!" he said, turning to James. "A true genius."

Henry clapped James on the back. "Yeah, not bad for a dim-witted mute."

Ruther threw back his head and laughed. "Not bad at all."

TWENTY-FOUR

The Throwing Match

I sabelle and the rest of the company had several reasons to be optimistic. They were only forty miles from the next town, Fenley,
where they would refill supplies, Isabelle was awake and felt herself growing healthier every day, the rain clouds were finally fleeing to
the west, and they now possessed a writ of passage. The writ meant
that anyone stopping them on suspicion of being criminals could not
arrest them without a direct counterorder from the King. James said
that small piece of parchment was more valuable than all the gold
they carried.

Maggie and James had grumbled for a few days about being forced
to perform a play in front of strangers, but Brandol took the longest to
recover from the embarrassment. Isabelle could understand why. She
had heard all about it, and while the play sounded wonderfully hilarious, the journeyman had accidentally exposed himself to a whole brigade of the King's cavalry. Despite his badly damaged pride, Isabelle
noticed the infectious optimism spreading even to Brandol.

Ruther, on the other hand, was a bottomless fount of praise for
his own flawless performance and didn't let an hour pass without
mentioning kissing Maggie or Brandol's blunders or Henry's ridiculous voice. On the evenings when he drank too much (Isabelle wasn't
quite certain where Ruther's flask kept finding more ale), he'd speak
in nothing but a perfect re-creation of Henry's ladyservant falsetto.

Brandol continued to ride Quicken so Henry could spend more time in the carriage with Isabelle. She and Henry talked for hours. During mealtimes, they took opportunities to spend time alone and reconnect. Most often, he escorted her on short walks around camp. This helped her build back her strength and gave her a chance to see the beautiful countryside of Blithmore. She was grateful to feel her health returning a little every day.

On this particular day, Henry and Isabelle took their walk before lunch. When they returned, they found Brandol sitting close to Maggie, staring into the flames and cradling his bowl of stew. James stood apart from the group, throwing his knives at the widest tree in the small grove near the camp. Every few seconds, a loud *thwock* echoed back to the group until James ran out of knives. A long pause followed while he collected his blades, and then the *thwocks* began again.

"This stew is amazing, Mags," Ruther said after he had swallowed a hearty mouthful. "What did you do differently this time?"

"Nothing."

Thwock.

"Really? I can't remember it tasting this good. What do you think, Little Henry?"

The journeyman shrugged and mumbled something under his breath.

"I don't think so," Ruther continued. "There's something different."

"Maybe I spat in your bowl," she offered, then winked at Brandol, who looked away, blushing.

Thwock.

"No," Ruther answered. "I remember your unique taste from that kiss—"

"Which I slapped you for," Maggie reminded him.

"—and this isn't it."

Isabelle patted Ruther on the back as a friendly way of telling him to go easy on Maggie. Only Ruther could get under Henry's sister's skin so quickly. He knew—or should—that kissing her during the play had gone over the line.

"It must have been a magical moment for you, Ruther," Henry said. "I remember my first kiss. It's just too bad this was probably also your last."

Isabelle laughed, and so did Ruther. She admired Henry's way of breaking the tension among his friends. Ruther took another sip of his hot soup, then asked, "In all seriousness, though, Mags, are you angry with me for breaking your necklace?"

Thwock.

Isabelle waited for Maggie's response, but she remained silent, her lips pressed together and her brow furrowed. Isabelle knew Maggie well enough to know that she was finding it difficult to hold her tongue.

Thwock.

"Do you have to do that right now, James?" Ruther said in a raised voice. "That tree isn't going anywhere anytime soon." Then, turning his attention back to Maggie, he said, "So you're not angry?"

Maggie's eyes flashed. "No, I don't get angry when a clumsy buffoon breaks a valuable family heirloom passed down through several generations of matriarchs."

"Really? For some reason I find that hard to believe."

Thwock.

"The problem with you, Ruther, isn't that you're a fat lousy drunk. It's that you don't bother looking outside yourself to consider other people's feelings."

"Do I have to? It sounds painful."

Thwock.

Ruther looked as though he might say something else, but stopped himself when Maggie got up and began cleaning. Isabelle and Brandol stood to help, and Henry left to collect more firewood. Ruther watched them with his hands behind his head, his back resting on a log.

When Isabelle and Maggie had a moment alone near the carriage, Isabelle put a hand on Maggie's shoulder. "I think that may have been his way of saying he's sorry."

Maggie shook her curls, her eyes still holding that dangerous, cold glint. "I've never been a clever person, but the choicest words fall from my lips when he starts to tease me."

"I've noticed."

"That necklace is the only thing I have from my mother. He doesn't care."

"Are you certain?"

"If I told him how much that necklace means to me, he'd only tease me more. That's what Ruther does."

"How long have you had it?"

"A few days before her death, my mother gave it to me . . . along with her last motherly advice."

"What was her advice?"

"Don't marry someone like Ruther."

Isabelle snickered into her hand. "That's very funny. What did she really say?"

Maggie's frown didn't change into a smile as Isabelle had expected it to. "I'm serious. Those were her last words of advice to me. When we were children I had a crush on Ruther, but my mother hated him. That's why he was kicked out of the house when he turned sixteen."

Isabelle turned to look at Ruther. "Oh, I see. I thought it was because he told your father that carpentry was a silly trade and a waste of time."

"Well, that helped—"

"At whom do you intend to throw knives, James?" Ruther asked from across the camp, loud enough to interrupt Maggie. "Are you expecting to ward off an army of the King's best men by knifing them, one by one, from the same distance?"

"You never know, Ruther." James spared him only a half-glance. "Luck smiles on the prepared."

"That is *not* how the expression goes."

"So? You're an actor now. Pretend I said it correctly."

Thwock.

Isabelle saw Ruther get that twinkle in his eye. She'd seen it countless times before, and it had often ended in him or Henry or both getting into trouble back when Ruther had lived at the Vestin home.

"Do you drink, James?" he asked. "I don't think I've ever seen you drink."

"On occasion."

"I'll wager you a bottomless mug in the first inn we find in Fenley that I can beat you in a throwing game."

James's next throw went wide right and landed with a soft swish in the leaves and grass. He looked at Ruther with a mixture of humor and doubt. "Are you toying with me?"

"I never jest." Ruther batted his eyes at James.

Maggie snorted so Ruther could hear it, and Brandol smirked with her.

"Well, never with a soldier, that is," Ruther added.

"I've never seen you *hold* a knife, let alone throw one." James collected his knives from the tree and ground. "How many throws do we get apiece?"

"What's a fair number?"

"Twenty should do it. I don't want you to say I won from luck."

Ruther grabbed his stomach and gave a hearty mock laugh. "Carve a circle the size of your fist in that tree, Little Henry," he ordered Brandol. "The tip of the blade has to be completely inside the mark.

Maggie will be our impartial—no—*Little Henry* will be the impartial judge. Is it agreed?"

"Agreed."

Isabelle watched as James drew a line in the dirt with his boot. Ruther accepted the distance. In Blithmore, only one ritual sealed a bet: a brief shake and a spit on the ground. James spat first, and then Ruther ejected a line that landed directly on top of James's spittle. Isabelle wrinkled her nose at them. The men decided who would throw first by scratching an X on a flat rock and tossing it. Ruther, who made the toss, asked James to call a side. James chose X side up and won.

Isabelle lost all interest in cleaning and chose to watch the duel. She wanted to see her brother beat Ruther. James used the same technique she had observed him use at least a hundred times: a throw starting at the height of his ear, releasing at the level of his chest. His first toss stuck just outside the circle's border, and Brandol pronounced a miss.

James and Brandol looked on with skepticism as Ruther stepped up to the line. He held the knife near his ear as James had done, though he didn't seem comfortable holding it this way. The knife missed the trunk of the tree entirely.

James shook his head as he watched the knife sail into the dirt. Maggie and Isabelle laughed out loud, and Brandol used his hand to cover a chuckle.

"Looks like I might be in a bit over my head, eh?" Ruther said with a good-natured chuckle to Brandol. "No scores after the first round. Nineteen throws to go."

James's next throw also hit the tree, but landed outside the mark. Ruther held the knife to his ear once more and threw, but this one went far right. Brandol grinned again, and Isabelle shook her head. Ruther didn't stand a chance. On his third throw, after James had put his knife right in the center of the circle, Ruther switched his throwing style to a hip flick. Isabelle had never seen anything like it in all her years of watching James. The knife zipped through the air and smacked the tree with a nice clunk. From where Isabelle stood, it appeared that the blade had stuck well inside the carving.

Ruther gave them all a cocky grin. "Oh . . . didn't think I could throw, did you?"

"One to one," Brandol said. "Seventeen throws left."

If James felt any measure of surprise, he didn't show it. He stepped up to the line and delivered another solid throw to the dead center of the carving. Ruther succeeded him with a hip throw that ended up barely over the line.

"Two to one."

The match continued, drawing Isabelle's interest more with each throw. When Henry walked back into camp, firewood in his arms, Brandol announced, "Thirteen to twelve, James leads."

"What's going on?" he asked.

"Shhh!" both Ruther and James hissed.

Isabelle beckoned him to her so she could fill him in on the details. James stood stiffer than normal, and Ruther's round face was ruddy and sweaty from concentrating, the ends of his red hair pasted to his forehead. He didn't blink at all as he stared at the tree.

"What are the stakes?" Henry asked her.

"Bottomless drinks at Fenley."

"Ah, yes." Henry had a knowing look. "That would explain it. He's probably been waiting for something like this."

Isabelle clapped for Ruther as he put his next knife right in the center of the circle. "How did Ruther learn to throw like that?"

"His uncle. He's decent with a sword, but with knives and bows . . . Ruther's an expert. You see, James uses the gentleman's toss, the most common type, quite accurate with practice. Ruther, however, was taught the assassin's flick. His long fingers are ideal for the technique. The throw is underhanded and subtle, useful when caught in a tight place. Extremely hard to master but deadly."

"Assassin's flick? Underhanded? Why am I not surprised?" Maggie said.

"I can't believe Ruther has matched James. James throws knives every day."

"Thirteen to thirteen," Brandol announced. "Last throw."

James, steady as ever, took his place at the line and eyed the target for about five seconds. His throw was a masterpiece of perfect form, and so was the hit. Dead center. Henry and Isabelle applauded him, and Brandol and Maggie joined in.

"Tell me something, Ruther," James began. "Do you throw well when it matters?"

A slight gust of wind blew Ruther's wet hair around his smiling face as he spun the knife's hilt on his palm. He kept his gaze locked with James, flipped the knife into the air, caught it, flicked his wrist, and a second later, there was a *thwock*. Dead center. "I don't know," came the reply. "What would you say?"

Henry and Isabelle clapped again, but Brandol and Maggie did not.

"Fourteen to fourteen," Brandol said. "Is we calling it a tie?"

"No," the competitors answered.

"Before you throw, James," Ruther cut in, "would you like to raise the stakes?"

"I should probably say something," Henry whispered to Isabelle. "This won't end well for James."

"No," Isabelle said. "I want to see what Ruther wants. James can handle himself."

"What's your proposal?" James said. Isabelle heard wariness in his voice.

"I haven't any ideas," Ruther said. "I thought you might."

"None whatsoever."

"How about the winner gets a kiss from you, Maggie?" Ruther offered with a grin.

"I beg your pardon?" Maggie said as she whirled to face him. Her neck and face turned the color of roses.

"Why not?" he asked. "It's for fun. Since I've already had the opportunity, perhaps James would like to earn the chance."

Henry chuckled with Isabelle, but Maggie glared at them. "Absolutely not!" she exclaimed.

"That's because she knows I'll win," Ruther told everyone.

"No!" Maggie protested. " I don't think it proper to—to—" Maggie shot a glance at James during her pause in speech. "Oh, fine. *Fine!* But a kiss on the cheek only."

Ruther grinned at Maggie, but James gave no reaction other than to ask, "That's your idea of raising the stakes?"

Ruther shrugged carelessly. "It makes the game more fun, doesn't it?"

"You really agree to that, Maggie?" James asked.

Maggie looked like she wanted to bury herself while Isabelle wondered how her own brother could be so oblivious to a woman's feelings. "It's just for fun."

James accepted her decision. He walked confidently to the line, whipped his hand up to the level of his ear, only to have the knife slip from his grasp. It flew straight at Maggie's face. Isabelle yelled out in warning, but Maggie froze. Just before the knife hit her, it dropped to the ground, as though slapped down by an invisible hand.

James whirled around. "Sorry—Maggie, are you all right?"

Maggie took two deep breaths, one hand resting on her chest while the other rubbed her shoulder. "Yes. I think so. It missed me, thank goodness."

James retrieved his knife from the dirt and turned back to his game. Isabelle continued to watch Maggie with a curious eye. James aimed carefully, practicing his motion several times. Finally, he threw the knife. The blade sank into the tree a little over the carving. Maggie's face fell and she started to bite on her thumbnail.

Henry, Maggie, Isabelle, and Brandol all moaned in disappointment. James, for once, seemed upset at himself. Isabelle saw Ruther glance at Henry. Henry answered Ruther with an almost imperceptible shake of the head. Ruther's face transformed into one of obstinacy. Henry's head moved back and forth with less subtlety than before, but Ruther no longer seemed to care. He went to the line, doing a bad job of hiding his grin, flicked the knife, and gave Henry a wink without even checking to see where it had marked the tree.

"Ruther wins fifteen to fourteen," Brandol said sullenly. Without missing a beat, Ruther strutted over to Maggie and presented his cheek.

"Absolutely not." Maggie's answer came as she harnessed the horses to the carriage. Isabelle noticed that she favored her right arm.

"Why not?" Ruther cried in a hurt voice. "I won a kiss."

"I don't care."

"Henry," he pleaded, "tell your sister to honor her agreement."

Henry and Isabelle laughed as they helped load the carriage. "Do you honestly expect her to kiss you?" Isabelle asked.

"James?"

James was collecting his knives and stowing them away with care. "I'm the wrong man to ask." There was a bitter tone in his voice, but Isabelle couldn't tell if it was because he'd lost the match or the kiss.

"This is *entirely* dishonorable and no one cares," Ruther said, now addressing no one but himself as he trudged to where his horse waited. "No one cares, Ghost."

His horse responded with a gentle snort.

"Don't worry yourself too much, Ruther," Maggie told him. "I'm certain there will be plenty of girls in Fenley you can pay to kiss you."

"An excellent point, Mags!" Ruther said. "And I also get free drinks."

As the six prepared to move onward, Isabelle pulled Maggie aside to speak in private. "How did you do that, Maggie?"

"How did I do what?"

Isabelle lowered the volume of her voice. "Maggie, I saw what happened. I saw the knife."

"It missed me."

"It dropped like a stone in a pond. You saw it as well as I."

Maggie's cheeks turned red, and she glared at Isabelle. "What are you implying?"

Isabelle grabbed Maggie's right wrist and lifted Maggie's arm. Maggie tried to pull it away, but didn't have the strength despite Isabelle's loose grip. "Ow! Let go!"

As Isabelle released Maggie, she pulled Maggie into an embrace to show that she'd meant no harm. A question burned in her mind, a question that needed to be asked. Before she could talk herself out of it, Isabelle breathed the words into Maggie's ear. "Do you walk the path?"

Maggie yanked herself from Isabelle's grasp. Her pale face stared in shock and disgust. "How dare you . . . how *dare* you!" She whispered the words, but her fury was still evident.

"I'm only asking, Maggie," Isabelle insisted. "Calm down and talk to me. I can't deny what I saw!"

"Yes, you can, because you're the only one who saw it."

"Your arm—the sign—"

"I scrub pots after every meal. My arm gets tired. For all I know, you could have done something to that knife!"

Ruther's voice came from the other side of the carriage. "Let's go, Mags. You don't need Isabelle's advice on how to kiss. I'll teach you everything you need to know."

Maggie raised a finger to Isabelle. "I will not hear another word about this. Understand?"

Isabelle reluctantly agreed. As soon as she did so, Maggie climbed to the driver's seat of the carriage and urged the horses forward.

TWENTY-FIVE

The Friendly Fenley

T wo days after the throwing match, as the afternoon threatened to give way to another cloudless evening, James rode at the head of the party into Fenley. He stayed alert for any sign of soldiers. Despite having the writ of passage, he knew from experience that things could go wrong at any time and therefore refused to be complacent.

Isabelle and Maggie made for the market straightway to build up the group's supplies. As they left, Henry watched them ride away with a worried expression.

"Isabelle looks much better than she did a week ago," James told him. "She'll be fine."

Henry only grunted.

"She does, Henry. She has more energy, more color in her face. I'd say she's nearly back to normal. Much of that is because of you." He looked at Henry, trying to get a response, but Henry stared glumly ahead. The previous night, before retiring, Henry had voiced his concerns that Isabelle might not be ready to go into town. His worry hadn't gone over well. Isabelle had insisted she felt healthy and refused to hear anyone—even Henry—tell her she couldn't go to the market with Maggie.

"Well, Ruther," James said without looking back, "it's time I made good on our bet. Where do you want to go?"

When Ruther didn't respond, James turned around. All he saw was Brandol.

"Ruther?"

The storyteller was nowhere to be seen.

"Where has he gone?" James asked the journeyman.

Brandol glanced over his shoulder and then back at James with an apathetic shrug.

"He'll turn up," Henry said as he urged Quicken forward. They found the town's taverns grouped together on the high street near the town square. James spotted two next to each other and another across the street.

"Ruther's probably visited all of these," he told Henry. "Probably even has a favorite. Would it be best to let him decide where our gold should be spent?"

"Since you're buying the drinks, and Ruther isn't here, why don't you pick?"

James surveyed the signs hanging from the taverns: the Furry Fern, the Friendly Fenley, and the Fenley Falcon. From the outside, all three seemed to be in about the same condition with their patched wooden frames, shuttered windows, and open doors.

"Why not the Friendly Fenley?" James scanned the street ahead and behind them once more for a sign of Ruther. "Where could he have gone so quickly?"

"Ruther mentioned he's visited this town several times," Henry reminded James. "Probably saw someone he knows."

The Friendly Fenley was busy for a late afternoon. It had all the appearances of a well-kept establishment; several knots of customers were scattered about inside. The noise level dropped when they walked in. Many customers gave Henry, James, and Brandol more than one passing glance, but James saw no trace of suspicion or malice. The owner made his way over to them. He had very little hair on his head, but he had a full beard. His apron bore ale and food stains.

In a slow, husky voice, the owner said, "Welcome to the Friendly Fenley." One of his eyes remained permanently fixed to his left while the other roamed over Henry, James, and Brandol's faces and clothes. "Name's Gertrude. Can I show you to your seats?"

"Yes, please," James answered. "We expect a fourth, if it suits you."

"Certainly it suits me!" Gertrude smiled widely and showed his yellow teeth. "This way." He led them to a corner table where only a few feet away sat a group of farmers discussing the sale of wheat and corn.

"We'll wait for our friend to start the drinks," James said. "I owe him one . . . well, several."

"As you have it," Gertrude said and left them.

"That *is* a man, right?" Henry whispered.

James shrugged.

They waited five or ten minutes before Ruther entered the tavern. He looked harried as he paused at the entrance. Two older men, recognizing him, raised their hands at him in salute. Ruther nodded to them while searching the room for James, Henry, and Brandol. When he finally caught sight of them, he walked quickly to the table, unusual for the laziest man in the camp.

"Everything well, Ruther?" Henry asked.

"Fine, fine, absolutely fine," came the reply, but Ruther looked a little off.

"Where did you disappear to?" James asked.

"I made a friend the last time I visited here and promised him I'd drop by. He owns a shop across the street. Where are the drinks?"

"We were waiting for you."

Henry leaned forward. "Say, have you met the owner here?"

"Gertrude?" Ruther asked.

"Yes."

"Yeah, he's nice enough—he'll tell you all about how he built this place with his own hands if you talk to him long enough. And don't *ever* let him hear you make fun of his name." Ruther drew a finger slowly across his throat and then, with his hand, mimicked blood flowing copiously from the wound.

"Gertrude?" James called across the tavern. "We're ready for our drinks."

"Remember," Henry said to everyone, but looked specifically at Ruther, "we don't want to attract attention to ourselves."

Two hours passed, during which time the four men's faces grew redder and their voices louder as the empty mugs on the table accumulated.

"Perturbing," Ruther said.

"Fourteen," counted the men who had crowded around their table.

"Disrupting," Ruther continued.

"Fifteen," came the reply.

"Pestering!"

"Sixteen."

"Four more, Ruther!" Henry shouted. "Four more, you can do it!"

"Distracting!"

"Seventeen!"

Ruther paused to think before speaking his next word. "*Exasperating!*"

"Eighteen!"

"By Germaine, he'll do it," shouted a man holding two mugs in each hand.

"Grrrr . . . ating!" Ruther slurred gleefully.

"Nineteen."

"IRKSOME!" Ruther shouted as he slammed his mug down on the table. Ale sloshed out from all sides.

"Twenty!" the men around them cried as copper, silver, and gold coins fell on the table. "He did it!"

"Ruther the word wizard!" one old man cried. "Ruther the . . ." Before he could finish his next declaration, he passed out on the floor.

"To Ruther the knife-tosser!" James roared in a thunderous voice.

"To Ruther the—the—to . . . Ruther!" Brandol added.

"To writs of . . . passssssages!" Henry said.

The four men raised their mugs into the air and clanked them together. Several more mugs joined them held by unknown hands. More gold changed hands in the crowd as bets on Ruther's word-chain were settled.

James sat back in his chair. Ruther's eyes closed as he sat up straight, singing out in a clear baritone, "A woman who bathed in the nude . . ."

Most of the voices died down when they heard Ruther's first line, and the rest quieted soon after until a hush fell over the Friendly Fenley.

"Saw the wind blow her clothing a-strewed. Then a man walked along, and unless I'm quite wrong—you're expecting this song to be lewd!"

Guffaws of laughter and praise erupted around the table. "More! More!" they roared.

Ruther opened one eye at Henry and James to signal them. They both knew the verses well. Back when they'd been in Mrs. Vestin's school together, they'd helped Ruther invent them. Henry began singing. His voice was deeper than Ruther's, but not as crisp.

"I knew a man named Giles. His stench was smelt for miles. He'd bathe and wash in tomato sauce, but he always smelled like bile."

The crowd approved of this one as much as the first. "More! *More!* MORE!"

"Give them what they want!" Ruther shouted over the noise to James.

"I stumbled into my friend Kurt. A man who couldn't pay for dirt.

He tried to sell honey, to make a little money, but he was still so broke it hurt!"

Roars and cheers followed the verse. Ruther opened his mouth to start the next limerick when four men dressed all in black entered the public house. Each man looked surlier than the one previous, and the last one to enter had a grizzled face that reminded Henry of a shrewd tomcat. All four men were dusty and haggard. Gertrude greeted them by name in a very delicate manner and escorted them to a table near James. The atmosphere changed immediately and the crowd around James's table dissipated.

"Eight days wasted," one of the men muttered to the other three when they sat down.

"Not wasted when we collect the booty," the one with the tomcat-like face returned with a growl. "And we will. They're around."

James sobered quickly, and he called Gertrude over to the table.

"Who are those men?" he asked the owner quietly.

"Local bounty hunters. Been out for days searching for them who attacked the Emperor of Ne'erak when he was here a few weeks back."

Brandol spluttered into his mug and coughed up ale through his nose. Ruther patted him on the back several times.

"What's the bounty?" James asked.

"Two hundred gold crowns for the man Henry. Same for his woman. Hundred fifty for the journeyman with him. Hundred each for the siblings."

James noticed Brandol's face drain of color. He exchanged a meaningful look with Henry and said, "Thank you, Gertrude."

The man with the tomcat face leaned back in his chair so he could see James and his company. "You heard well from Gertrude, young man, but more importantly, who are you?"

"Who am I?" James asked. "Or who are we?"

"Both. Only one outta you I recognize is the drunk-awful story-teller."

"Speak for yourself, Kelric," Ruther drawled into his mug. "Caught any bounty lately?"

"I wouldn't put it past you to keep company with criminals, story-teller. Ain't you from Richterton?"

"A cause of concern coming from anyone but you, *bounty hunter*." Ruther's words seemed to come with great effort through his drunken state. He turned to his friends and jerked his thumb back at the bounty hunters. "When was the last time you actually caught some-one?"

Alarms clamored like church bells in James's foggy head. Who knew what Ruther might say in this state?

"I could gut you right now, vermin." Kelric stood, holding some-thing at his hip. James glanced down and saw a knife so large it made his throwing knives look like toothpicks. The menacing tomcat expression in his face was more pronounced than ever as the hairs on his beard and head bristled in anger.

"*Vermin?*" Ruther said, gasping with laughter. "Rodent, pest, flea. I could find these criminals faster than you."

"Why don't we pay our bill and leave?" Henry interrupted. "Actors aren't much for fighting, after all."

Two of the men sitting with Kelric howled mightily at Henry's comment, but Kelric and another hunter scowled even deeper. Kelric's eyes stared murderously into Ruther, increasing James's sense of urgency. Henry and Brandol stood, but Ruther waved a hand for them to sit.

"I'll prove how fast I can catch these criminals," Ruther slurred. "Watch this—you watching me?" Then he grabbed Henry's wrist and shouted, "Got one right here!"

Brandol's face lost every drop of blood remaining in it, and James smacked Ruther in the back of the head hard enough that Ruther's forehead clipped his mug and started to bleed.

"Ouch!" Ruther cried through his laughter. "Kidding! I was kidding! This man whose wrist I have . . . his name is—his name . . . is . . ."

"Ruther!" Henry yelled, but Ruther would not listen. James and Brandol grabbed Ruther's arms and lifted him from the table. Meanwhile, Ruther continued his babbling.

"I can't remember his name, but he could play the part of the . . . Henry . . . very well. Guess what else, Kelric? We have a writ of passage!" He howled even harder at this as he pulled the parchment from his shirt pocket and waved it like a flag.

Kelric's lips curled nastily at Ruther, baring his yellow and brown teeth. "Get this trash out of here!"

Henry paid the owner while James and Brandol dragged out Ruther, whose mumblings grew more and more incoherent. By the time they reached Maggie and Isabelle at the carriage outside of the town's center, he was sound asleep. James and Brandol were both too upset to speak about the incident despite Maggie's insistence that they explain what had happened. When Henry finally told her, she refused to move on with Ruther, and demanded that he be left behind. Brandol agreed with her, and James offered no opposition to the idea.

"No," Isabelle told them, "Ruther was at the inn when the Emperor tried to take me. He made a mistake, but I'm not leaving him."

"No—no—no skin offa *his* back!" Brandol said in a rare display of anger. "You ain't heard 'im at the tavern! And remember, it ain't Ruther being sought, it's—it's the journeyman! They thinks it was me what helped you at the inn. Ruther's a free man!"

Isabelle remained adamant, and eventually they tossed Ruther unceremoniously into the carriage across from her. No one spoke much that night. Maggie seemed determined to hit every bump on the path.

James led the group even though his head felt ready to topple off his shoulders. He chided himself for making such a stupid choice. It had not been his first time around Ruther in such a state; he should have anticipated the storyteller would misbehave.

"I could have—should have—prevented it," Henry said. "I put everyone's life in danger."

James's and Henry's eyes met as they realized they both blamed themselves.

"I'm not a leader." Henry pointed to the heavens. It took James a moment to see where Henry meant him to look. Then he spotted the South Star casting its first light into the evening sky. It was the only star he could see. "I made poor choices before we left Richterton and ever since. I haven't even started learning swordplay!"

"You've spent time with Isabelle, and she's making a quick recovery because of it. I don't think that's time wasted."

"I look at that star and I think of a constant light—no matter the conditions, always constant. It guides sailors, wanderers, and criminals alike. The path ahead of us—the uncertainty of it scares me because I know I'm not prepared. I can't lead if I'm not prepared. I can't be that constant guide."

"Some good has happened," James reminded him. His eyes left the heavens and searched the landscape around them, always looking for signs of followers or better paths to travel. "The writ of passage. Isabelle's recovery. We've traveled a quarter of our journey in safety. Our pace hasn't been great, but that's not your fault. We also have all that gold."

"But it's not enough, James. I'm failing."

"In the meantime, I can teach you swordplay during our meals if that's what you want."

"I also worry about keeping everyone's spirits up," Henry said. "Brandol's in particular."

"Maggie is going to tear into Ruther tomorrow."

"She nurses a stronger dislike for him than you realize, and has for years." Henry shook his head angrily. "Look at us! We weren't meant to travel together."

"Yet here we are."

"Here we are," Henry repeated. "Winter is coming fast, James. How will our little band manage in such miserable conditions?"

James pondered on the question. As the company veered toward a forest ten miles east of the Drewberry River, a white fog settled over the countryside. The evening turned into night, and the fog stayed, blocking out the firmament and chilling James's skin.

TWENTY-SIX

The Cost of Attikus

T he Emperor of Neverak had a splendid training room. It was
large and well stocked with scores of weapons and armor.
He used it at least once a day, but the timing varied. If his
morning was busy, he trained in the evenings. Otherwise, he preferred
to start his day with a vigorous routine. On occasions when morning meetings became so unbearable that his stress was tangible, the
Emperor ordered the room to be readied in the afternoon, during his
lunch.

Today was an "after-lunch" training day.

A second consultation with Sir Grellek, the ridiculous nobleman
planning the northeastern city, had occupied his whole morning. The
Emperor knew he could have ended his torture at any time and re-
scheduled, but the thought of a third helping of Grellek's stubborn
demeanor made him want to commit random murder. As the meeting
entered its third hour, the collection of bows hanging on the west wall
between the windows called to him—begged of him—to put an arrow
between Grellek's shoulder blades, to watch him run down the hall
screaming for help only to be silenced by a sudden sting.

Fortunately for Grellek, the Emperor possessed a healthy appreciation for history. He knew he could not simply kill anyone he wanted—especially a noble with a pedigree like Grellek's.
Those sorts of emperors found themselves quickly deposed, as his

sixth-great-grandfather had been, the man responsible for losing Neverak to the King of Blithmore for two generations.

Several of the Emperor's servants were well trained in swordplay, a sport the Emperor had learned at a very young age and had cultivated into a passion throughout his life. He loved it enough that, when bored, he slipped into thinking about technique, body balance, and footwork. Nothing in his experience possessed more subtlety, passion, and intricacy than the Dance of Death, as his teacher had called swordplay.

Five of his servants stood in the training room, two off to the side: one held towels, the other waited to wipe spots of sweat off the floor. Swordplay could be both invigorating and messy. The other three servants wielded weapons. Emperor Krallick fought with them, savoring the movement, the sound of steel on steel, the rushing of blood from his heart to his arms and legs. He rarely took time for rest. Experience had taught him that in order to make the most of these afternoon sessions, he had to push himself relentlessly.

"How long has it been since you have been truly challenged in swordplay, my Emperor?" a voice asked.

The words belonged to a man standing at the door with his hands clasped behind his back imperiously, wearing a fully complemented uniform of the Neverakan military. Every medal and honor Neverak made available to its soldiers could be found somewhere on the man's clothing. His smooth-shaven face and cropped gray hair embellished his unblemished tan skin. His most distinguishing feature, however, was the depth of his light brown eyes. Emperor Krallick, in all his life, had never looked into a pair more intelligent.

The Emperor raised a hand and his servants lowered their weapons. The servant carrying towels stepped forward to pass them around. The other servant began scrubbing the floor with a pail of hot water.

"Of course I should have known you would be early," Emperor Krallick replied.

The man at the door frowned as he inspected the Emperor's state. "Only proof of how long it's been."

"It's a pleasure to have you here, Attikus."

Attikus bent his head in a bow. "I am at the service of the Emperor. Let me venture a guess. You did not summon me here to improve your swordplay."

Emperor Krallick's smile was genuine. Attikus's eyes averted at the gesture. "We have not crossed swords for many years, but I'm certain you would still easily beat me."

"Perhaps not so easily as you think, Emperor, but the statement still brings a question to my mind."

"Please ask."

"If you truly wish to improve your skill, as I have always known you do, why don't you find more skilled competitors?"

"I think you know the answer."

"I do, Emperor. You fear for your safety. That's common sense, but so is the solution."

The Emperor of Neverak did not miss how easily a belittlement fell from the lips of his former trainer and teacher. He would have been gravely insulted had it come from any other man, but he knew from experience how great minds often overlooked the failings of lesser minds. Though he did not consider his own mind much the lesser.

"What is your solution, Attikus?"

"Dip into your treasury, your Majesty. Hire men to fight you, and only—" he paused with a finger in the air, so quickly assuming his familiar role as teacher, "—pay them when they strike you."

Emperor Krallick laughed and handed over the hilt of his sword to his servant for cleaning. "Shall I execute the man who mortally wounds me?"

"That depends, Emperor, on your motive. Do you train for personal merit or for fear of an impending attack?"

"Both are appropriate reasons."

"But one is a much stronger motivator."

"And wear armor, of course?"

"Not every accident can be prevented, my Lord, but luck favors the man who protects his own skin."

"I was never blessed with the genius you possess for the sport, Swordmaster," the Emperor remarked.

"Yes, you were," Attikus responded with alarming intensity, "but you never pushed yourself to it. My skills were honed in battle, which you, thankfully, have never had to enter. Mark my words, Ivan. One day your life will be threatened, and you will see your own genius, naked and bare, and you will remember this conversation."

The Emperor held back a laugh, knowing how unlikely such a situation would be. Attikus seemed able to discern the Emperor's thoughts, and disappointment etched itself into the smooth lines on his face. His eyes roamed the weapon room. "You've made many changes since our training days."

"It is always a joy to revisit the past," the Emperor commented as he led Attikus out of the weapon room. "I've missed you, old man, and I've certainly never forgotten your lessons."

They came to the Emperor's bath. Servants entered with hot water and poured it into the large porcelain tub with exotic soaps.

"Revisiting the past isn't *always* a joy, my Emperor."

"I refuse to be philosophical today." The servants placed a screen in front of the bath, and Emperor Krallick stepped behind it to undress. Once he was submerged into the cloudy water, the screen was removed. "We have other things to discuss, General."

The use of that title had a strong effect on Attikus, and he looked gravely upon the Emperor. "Please . . . call me by something other than that name."

"Leave me," the Emperor told the servant who washed his arms. Then to Attikus he asked, "Why do you despise the title?"

"I do not despise it. I've put it aside."

"Of course—I remember the occasion perfectly."

"As you should, my Emperor. It was one of your finest days."

"Perhaps. Are you willing to wear the title again?"

Attikus fixed his gaze on the wooden floor. To Emperor Krallick, the depths of Attikus's eyes had never seemed so bottomless. He slid deeper into his bath and enjoyed the rich smells emanating from the swirling water, the cleanliness that flowed about every inch of him. During moments like this, he had no concerns at all.

"I enjoy my retirement. I believe my years of unimpeachable service to the previous emperor earned me this."

"My father trusted you more than almost anyone. More than me—or my mother," Emperor Krallick added with a boyish smile that softened his normally sharp features. He couldn't help the nostalgia that overcame him around Attikus.

"That's because your father saw more of himself in you than he liked."

"My father was a better man than I."

Attikus's gaze returned to the Emperor's with that same unabashed brilliance. "Your father had his secrets," he paused, measuring the Emperor, then added, "and his black patches."

"Yet you won't tell me what they were, will you Attikus? *Or where they are?*"

"I know to what you are referring, my Emperor." Attikus almost smiled, but the Emperor knew in the end it would turn into a frown. It always did. In all his years of learning swordplay and military tactics from Attikus, he had never once seen the man smile. Even at a young age, he'd known his teacher was incapable of it. "You don't even know if such a thing exists."

"Secrets always have that uncanny way of being found, don't they?"

"If you are right, time will prove it."

"What about *your* secrets?" The Emperor pushed Attikus with more of that boyishness he had already displayed. "Will I someday learn yours?"

"My secrets?"

"You know to what I refer."

"There's a difference between secrets and fables passed around by bored soldiers."

The Emperor knew he had Attikus. No matter how great Attikus's reluctance was to take up the old mantle, loyalty triumphed over comfort. Or perhaps discomfort. Could there also be restlessness in the old warrior? The Emperor didn't know.

"Of course, you taught me that every rumor, every fable has some grain of truth. Did you not, Swordmaster?"

"I did teach you that." He remained as straight-backed and militaristic as ever. The Emperor then realized that Attikus's decision had nothing to do with their old teacher/pupil relationship. It was the old emperor, Ivan's father, to whom the old general felt duty-bound. That fealty carried over to the throne—and the son.

The Emperor drew himself up in the water, though he knew he could not intimidate Attikus. "Will you reenter my service, General?" He marveled at the way his direct question had no visible effect on the older man. It reminded him of what his father told him once after a long council meeting: *The general is made from the oldest mountains in all of Atolas.*

"My Emperor, you require of me the one thing I am reluctant to give."

"You knew this was what I would ask you when you received my summons."

"What threat to the crown can there possibly be that only I can solve?" Attikus asked. "I hear no rumors of war."

"Yet you've heard, of course, of my personal insult and injury in Blithmore?"

"Nothing unpreventable, especially by a man of your prowess, my Emperor. Has your title become a blinder for personal attacks?"

"I will not have a lesson. King Germaine denied my request of allowing my soldiers or my Elite Guard to enter Blithmore. I only wished to assist the King and his forces in their search for the criminals who attacked me."

"No doubt you would have done the same had the situation been reversed."

"Nonetheless," Emperor Krallick now signaled for his servant to return and wash him before the water became too cool, "I want my Elite Guard in Blithmore."

"It would require a most unusual agreement."

"I imagine so. It is also unusual for an emperor to be attacked on foreign soil during a holiday designed to celebrate the friendship of kingdoms. The King's search does not go well. It has been a month now. His forces are spread too thin, and they do not take my affront seriously. What motivation do they have to find the would-be assassin of another nation's royalty?"

"What is your proposal, Emperor?"

"The proposal will be yours, Attikus, not mine. You will deliver it to King Germaine in my name. Two hundred Elite Guard under your control and two hundred under General Derkop. They will assist in the search for the criminals."

"Am I to be relieved of duty when the criminals are found?"

The Emperor was uncertain of whether Attikus would be able to see through a lie after so many years. So he answered, "That remains to be seen."

Attikus's face remained as unreadable as ever. "May I make one request of the Emperor?"

A satisfied smile grew on the Emperor's lips. "You may."

"If I am to lead your men, grant me control over all your forces in Blithmore. That way I can more efficiently accomplish the task."

The answer came at once. "Approved." He motioned to a servant waiting by the door who nodded and left the room. Another took his place. "I'll have General Derkop relocated to the northern armies at once. I don't want any struggle for power. He'll be pleased with the decision. Is that your only request?"

"I also ask that you remember my desires to return to retirement when this campaign has ended."

"I will remember."

Attikus fixed his gaze upon the Emperor. "Will my sons—"

"They will remain in Neverak unless you request otherwise."

"I wish for them to remain."

The Emperor sighed and relaxed in the water. He knew if he could somehow peel back that rocky layer of skin covering Attikus's emotion he would find a face of relief. "I will arrange for a meeting between yourself and General Derkop. Would you prefer it here or at another location?"

"Here, my Emperor. I will make arrangements to leave immediately."

With these last words, Attikus did something he had not done since the day of Ivan Krallick's coronation as Emperor. He saluted Emperor Krallick in the manner of a soldier, crossing his wrists and then raising his right fist level with his temple, saying, "For the glory of Neverak."

"For the glory of Neverak," the Emperor repeated.

Attikus left and the Emperor watched him go. He could not help but wonder if he was beginning to see his own genius blossom already. Everything was moving along as planned. The most important piece of the plot was now in place. The silver eagle climbed higher and higher into the sky, and once it reached its zenith, it would drop.

TWENTY-SEVEN

Following the Leader

M y fingers are stiff," Ruther grumbled as he stoked the flames in the camp's fire pit. "Look at this." He held up his hands and held them completely still. "I'm trying as hard as I can to move them, but they won't obey me. We've traveled this far south, and it's like living in northern Neverak."

"Ruther," James said.

"What?"

"Catch." James threw an apple at Ruther, who caught it easily. Isabelle grinned at her brother. Henry, his mouth full of food, chuckled into his hand. Even Brandol smiled.

"Seems like your hands are in working order after all," Henry told Ruther.

"It's autumn," Maggie said slowly, in a sugared voice. She sat nearest to the fire between James and Brandol. "At this time of the year, the weather turns colder, as it is now. We may even see snow—you know, small white flakes of ice that fall from the sky."

"And yet, miraculously," Ruther said, "those frozen flakes will never be quite as frigid as your cold, black heart."

Isabelle leaned over to Henry and quietly asked, "Will you come with me to gather wood?"

Henry nodded and took another bite of stew. The way he closed his eyes told Isabelle that he was savoring its warmth.

She fixed him with an urgent look. "Can we please go now?"

They excused themselves and left the camp, listening to Maggie and Ruther's conversation as they walked away. The small party had traveled over a fortnight from Fenley, making six weeks since they'd left Richterton. They had crossed through an ever-thinning patch of forest only seven miles east of the Drewberry River in unseasonably cold weather. The leaves had all but abandoned the trees and would soon become soaked and rotted if the dark snow clouds decided to unleash an early winter storm.

Isabelle stomped on a dead branch, snapped it in half, and collected the pieces. It was so nice to get away from the others and be alone with Henry. "Can't you do something about them?" she asked him in a hushed voice. "Their bickering brings everyone's spirits down."

Henry gazed again in the direction of camp, so Isabelle looked to see what he was watching. Ruther sat alone, munching on the apple James had thrown, huddled in a blanket. "What should I say? It's one thing to give correction to my apprentices when they misbehave, but Maggie and Ruther are adults."

"They snap at each other like stray dogs," Isabelle said a little bit louder. "Tell them to stop it—to treat each other civilly. She's your sister, and he's your best friend."

Henry brought his boot down on a long stick and cracked it. Another stomp finished the job. "I don't know." He tucked the pieces of wood under his arm and moved on in search for more.

Isabelle followed after him. She chose her words carefully to avoid sounding like a nag. "Henry, you know how it is between them. It's been like this for years. Why expect it to change now? Is it some kind of twisted love-hate relationship? Do they have feelings—?"

"No. No, trust me." He smiled until he saw her disappointed expression. "No, it's not like that. There's no love—nothing—between them."

"Well, it's becoming a problem. James and Brandol have nothing positive to say about Ruther, and Maggie keeps saying she wants to leave him tied to a tree." Henry tried to say something, but Isabelle pressed on. She needed Henry to understand the urgency she felt regarding the problem. "She's serious about it, and it's hard to not be understanding after what he did in Fenley."

"I talked with him privately about it, and he assured me it was only to get a rise out of the bounty hunter, Kerprik, or whatever his name was. Ruther would never—"

"But he nearly did!"

"What do you want me to do?" His voice was soft. His words came out in visible puffs of air, lasting long enough to reach her nose.

She took his hands and held them. Hers were much warmer than his, but her heartbeat sped up. "I don't like what Maggie suggests," she said, giving him her best reassuring smile, "because Ruther's more faithful to you than she'll ever admit. Far more loyal than Brandol or even James."

"I don't like this."

"What?"

"Being the leader of this group. Why must I make the decisions? No one appointed me. No one voted. If there had been a vote, I would have picked James. It's one thing to tell people how to carve wood, where to put hinges and pegs. Those orders are simple—one plank is just like another! It can be replaced if something goes wrong."

"I used to hear you tell Brandol that he needed to stop being so afraid and just do his work. When are *you* going to stop being afraid of leading people?"

"My mistakes can lead people to their deaths. Shouldn't I be afraid?"

"Cautious, yes. Afraid, no."

A small red leaf drifted into Isabelle's hair and tangled itself there. Henry reached up to remove it. Isabelle caught his hand and pulled him to her. When they came into contact, she kissed him firmly. Her lips were also warmer than his. When he began to pull away, she slipped her hand around his neck and pulled his face back into hers, kissing him even harder. Several moments passed with no sounds save the occasional bickering of their four friends at the fire.

"Wow . . ." Henry grinned when she finally released him from her clutches. She loved the foolish, giddy expressions he wore after she kissed him. "Thank you."

"No." Her eyes blazed back at him. "Thank you. I feel wonderful—better than I've felt in a long time—because of you. It's not only the medicine that's healed me. It's you. When I was younger, I thought your love was all I'd need to survive. Then recently, because of my father, I started believing that maybe such a notion was naive. I don't know anymore. *Is* it naive?"

"Ruther would say you're being supernaturalistic."

Isabelle's eyes darted to camp, then back to Henry. "But I am the one healed." She placed his hand over her heart, letting him feel its rhythm against his fingers and palm.

"Thank you," Henry whispered into her ear as he embraced her.

"Just remember I'll always love you more," she said with a teasing smile.

Henry kissed her again.

"Henry! Isabelle!" Ruther cried in his falsetto tone, the one he used to mock Henry's performance in *The Soldier and His Lady*. "When are you going to bring that wood?"

They laughed as their kiss broke. Henry shouldered their piles of firewood and headed back to camp, ignoring Isabelle's demands to let her help carry the load. Brandol and Maggie were huddled around the coals of the fire facing Ruther, who seemed unperturbed by his isolation. James, as he had every day since losing to Ruther, practiced his knife throwing. Ruther had offered to teach him the assassin's method he'd learned from his uncle, but James declined. According to Henry, James had fallen for one of Ruther's most successful ruses. Henry looked at Isabelle with a face that told her he still didn't want to address her concerns with the group. Isabelle returned this with a brave smile and raised eyebrows, but she knew he wasn't going to do it. Instead, he helped Ruther build up the fire until it was snapping and cracking. Isabelle joined Maggie to warm herself at the coals.

"We'll be leaving this bit of forest tomorrow," Ruther commented. "Probably in the morning."

"Will we reach cover again by nightfall?" Henry asked.

"If we make good time, friend," Ruther replied. "The gap in the forest is only twenty miles wide."

"I disagree with Ruther," James said, sitting down next to Henry. "We're only covering twelve to fifteen miles in a day. Sixteen to twenty, if we're on a good trail. If the storm is as bad as it looks, we should make camp here until it passes. If it turns into a blizzard, we could be lost for days. Stay here, and we can keep a fire going to keep warm and relatively dry."

"We know the way," Ruther told James. "If we start early and take shorter meals, we can easily cover the distance needed."

"I'm not suggesting you don't know your way," James responded, "but it could turn dangerously cold. If the snow deepens enough, it will be hard to build a fire. We could get snow sickness. Long stretches of snow can do strange things to people."

"Like what?"

"Like make them go blind and mad."

Ruther snorted.

"Come on, Ruther," Henry said, "his concerns are worth considering."

"The last thing we want is to be wandering around following nothing but Ruther's advice," Maggie said. "Next thing we know, we'll be in the hands of the King's Guard, or worse, his bounty hunter friends."

Ruther's playful mood disappeared. His tone turned defensive. "As you might recall, Maggie, I've been with Henry at every stage in this journey. All you've done is drive a carriage."

"Everything you did was undone at the Friendly Fenley. You nearly had us killed."

Ruther stirred the fire in silence. Isabelle felt a surge of sympathy for him and an equal amount of resentment toward Henry's sister. She had never understood why Maggie hated Ruther so much. This cruelty was unwarranted and had lasted too long. Henry only looked at the clouds. Isabelle knew what he wanted to say, and she wished he'd take her advice and say it.

"What will it be, Henry?" James asked. "Leave in the morning, or stay?"

A dark silence filled the camp. Brandol appeared satisfied with Maggie's response. James, as always, was unreadable, but watched Henry expectantly. Henry finally met Isabelle's gaze, and she silently reassured him that whatever he decided, everyone would follow.

She knew how much he hated being in charge, but he still had to choose. A feeling in her gut told her that the more important issue at hand was to repair the camaraderie within the group, not when to move on to the next forest.

"Let's—let's go with Ruther's plan," he offered, "but we should gather more wood in case the snowfall is heavy."

Maggie, James, and Brandol did not complain, though they seemed disappointed. Ruther gave Henry a grateful smile.

"I'll gather a little more wood in case we need it," he said. It was his first time volunteering for the duty; usually he feigned injury to explain why he couldn't help.

"Right behind you," Henry said, getting up. Isabelle squeezed Henry's hand as he walked past her. His touch reminded her of their recent kiss, and again she felt that warmth they'd shared. Next to her, Maggie mumbled instructions to Brandol to begin cleaning up dinner. James and Isabelle began conversing together in low tones.

Isabelle watched Ruther put a hand on Henry's shoulder as they walked away. "Thanks, friend."

TWENTY-EIGHT

A Deep Frost

Henry and Ruther collected firewood for almost an hour before returning to the campsite. Isabelle and Maggie were asleep in the carriage, out of the elements, while Brandol and James were bedding down near the fire under heavy blankets and skins. After several minutes, everyone but Henry had fallen asleep. His mind wrestled with many questions as he watched the first flakes of snow fall into the camp. Then without knowing it, he too slipped into slumber. Had he stayed awake just a while longer, he might have become alarmed at the size and number of the flakes; he might even have decided to awaken his friends and urge them to move on immediately. Instead, he slept soundly.

Hours later, he awoke first. Almost four inches of snow had accumulated on the ground, but the wind was milder and the air slightly warmer than the night before. It was only a lull in the snowfall, but as far as Henry could tell, the storm had ended. He woke the others and hurried them through breakfast. Within an hour's time, they were packed and moving.

For the first part of the morning, the group's mood remained pleasant, and they made good time traveling out of the woods and into the long clearing. A ray of sunlight even warmed the back of Henry's neck, and no sooner had he thought the snow might begin melting than an enormous black cloud rolled in and blocked out the sun.

Next came cold winds from the north, followed shortly by thick flakes coming down at a long angle. James, who always sat high in Sissy's saddle, soon rode huddled over, his head close to her mane. The patch of skin on Henry's neck that had tasted the sun's gift had to be covered to protect it from the wind's bite. Maggie, who enjoyed driving the carriage with her black curls bouncing and blowing, drew her cloak tightly around her face so only her eyes and nose were visible. And Ruther's incessant talking had devolved into occasional mutters.

To make better time, the group decided to forgo lunch. For the next few hours the carriage pushed through the clearing, following the three men on horseback. Their pace slowed significantly as the carriage struggled through the deepening snow. When Henry, Ruther or James had to speak, they yelled to hear each other over the whistling of the wind in their ears. As snow continued to pour from the sky, conversations between James and Ruther lasted longer and became more heated.

Eventually, the snow swirled so badly that Henry could hardly see or hear Ruther and James, though they rode only twenty or thirty feet ahead. The carriage looked like a brown box floating on a cloud behind him. As he removed his gloves to breathe needed warmth on his frozen hands, Henry realized he'd made the wrong choice. He cursed himself for not listening to James. With all of his military and traveling experience, James's opinion should have had a much greater sway on Henry's decision than his friendship with Ruther. Why had he let sympathy for his friend put everyone in danger?

"We're lost, Henry," James said, suddenly at Henry's side. Snow hung onto his eyebrows and cloak. His skin, normally a light tan, was now a blotchy red. His breaths came out in great puffs. "I have no way of knowing if we're headed for the forest or not."

Ruther appeared next out of the thick white fog. "Don't listen to

James. He has snow sickness. If we keep going straight, we'll hit the forest. It's too wide to miss."

Henry had never seen James so close to losing control over his tongue. He sent angry glances at Ruther every few seconds. "We may have veered too far west. We may be heading back north for all I can tell! This was foolish of us to leave under such conditions."

"Don't blame Henry—"

"I don't blame Henry," James said to Ruther. "I blame you."

Ruther appealed to Henry. "If we keep going in this direction, we'll find the forest."

"We should have reached it by now."

Ruther leaned forward on his horse as though he wanted to block James from Henry's view. "It's taking longer because we're moving slower!"

James wanted to say more, but Henry cut him off. "Let's try moving in Ruther's direction for another half hour. If we don't reach the forest by then, we'll—we'll reassess our position."

Rather than voicing a rebuttal, James shook his head free of snow and growled at Sissy to trot on through the slush. Henry and Ruther exchanged a glance. Ruther looked more worried than anyone, which Henry thought was strange.

"I know we're headed the right way, friend. I do."

Even though Henry nodded back to show his trust, it took all his faith to follow Ruther. He measured the passage of time not by the sun's descent to the horizon but by how much colder his fingers grew. The more the muscles in his hands stiffened, the more he doubted himself. In fact, he was focused so intently on keeping his hands warm, he didn't see the first tree until he had nearly ridden Quicken into it. They had crossed the clearing as Ruther promised they would. Thankfully, Ruther had the sense not to brag, because not far into the woods, the snowstorm transformed into a full-blown blizzard.

"We've got to stop and make camp," James said. "The horses are exhausted. Maggie's been on that carriage all day."

"It would be folly to set up camp now!" Ruther called out. "We couldn't get a fire going unless hell unleashed itself into the firewood."

"What happens when we're stuck, frozen, and still have no camp?"

Henry led Quicken back to the carriage, trundling through what was now over a foot of snow. He was grateful he'd built the carriage as sturdily as he had. The two horses pulling it moved sluggishly. He glanced up to the sky. Were the clouds more gray now than black? He couldn't be certain, but he wanted to believe it.

"How are you doing?" he shouted up to Maggie.

Snow covered her hair and cloak. Her nose and cheeks were bright pink, but she answered, "I'm fine." She gave him a pleasant smile so he could see she was trying to be brave.

"Really?"

"Yes. I can go a while longer if we must."

Henry checked on Isabelle and Brandol, too, before riding back to James and Ruther.

"Everyone is doing as well as we can hope. Let's move on."

They kept their horses pointed south as best as they could manage, but with no point of reference it was impossible to be certain. Henry found breathing to be painful as the moisture in his nose froze. Snow leaked into his cloak and chilled his back. Even Quicken seemed miserable. His horse's pace slowed as each step plowed through a foot of snow. The thick clouds created the illusion that it was nearing nightfall.

Ahead of the group, James called for Henry and Ruther to halt.

"Are we lost?" Maggie called out as the carriage reached the group.

"Yes." James practically spat the words at Ruther.

"No," Ruther said. "Henry, I know we're headed south."

"How could you possibly know that?" James said with his smoldering, quiet voice. "If you hadn't suggested that we leave—"

"We did what was best!"

"It was foolish," James said.

"Which of your ideas have turned provident, James?" Ruther returned. "If Henry had listened to you when we were being chased in the hills, we'd have lost our heads by now."

"Don't accuse me of folly after what you did in Fenley. I got us the writ of passage."

Henry climbed down from his horse and went to the carriage as Maggie joined in the argument. Isabelle and Brandol were peering out the windows from behind the thick wool coverings.

"What are you doing, Henry?" Isabelle asked.

"I can't say anything to stop them."

"Yes, you can. They'll listen to you."

"No, you don't understand," he said, gesturing stiffly with his trembling limbs. "They hate Ruther. They would—they would feed him to fire-eating dragons."

Isabelle grinned at Henry. Her nose, cheeks, and chin all had red spots from the cold, but she was still happy. "Don't you mean fire-*breathing* dragons?"

"I do."

"Well, that only proves they care about him, because it's so cold that they would be doing him a service. Now go talk to them."

She gave him a wink. Henry felt only slightly cheered as he walked back to the group where James, Ruther, and Maggie were all shouting at each other.

"Stop it, please," he said forcefully, but no one listened. "Stop it!" He filled his lungs with frigid air and shouted above everyone, "STOP THIS NONSENSE AT ONCE!"

Maggie squinted through the snow, aghast at Henry. Her astonishment left a foolish expression on her face.

"Maggie, you haven't offered any solutions, so what pleasure does it give you to endlessly attack Ruther? Do you think it entertains us when you behave like that? James, I appreciate your help, but I felt inclined to go with Ruther's advice. That's my prerogative, but Ruther . . . you—you need to stop annoying people on purpose and act like a grown man!"

Maggie shifted in her seat, angry but silent. Henry's chest heaved from yelling in the cold. No one moved except Brandol, who had poked his head out of the carriage window again to watch the scene.

Ruther fiddled awkwardly with his horse's reins. "I apologize," he said.

James shifted his weight in his saddle. "As do I." He spoke the words stiffly, and did not look at anyone. Maggie still would not speak.

The wind had died off and Henry hadn't even noticed. It got so quiet he thought he could hear the snowfall. Despite the apologies, he still sensed tension among his friends. He was about to say more when a heavy crunching sound came from the east. It was accompanied by the snapping of twigs and magnified as it echoed through the white-coated trees. James was instantly alert, reaching to unsheath the sword from his back. Ruther brought his horse around to face the noise. Henry's cold breath made a small gurgling sound in his throat that only he could hear. Finally, a booming voice called out:

"Henry Vestin!"

TWENTY-NINE
Roasted Venison

Henry did not recognize the voice, which scared him. He, James, and Ruther squinted in the direction of the sound, but the thick snowfall acted as a curtain between them and the source of the voice. James drew his sword fully. Henry watched as years of training transformed James into a different man: a man keenly aware of his surroundings and hardened from years of rigid discipline.

"Who goes there?" James shouted into the eastern woods. "Friend or foe?"

"Friend, and lucky for your lot," the voice returned, deep and merry.

"How may we be certain?"

"Because you ain't dead!"

"Dead?" James repeated to Henry.

Three boys, each taller than the last, emerged from behind trees on both sides, arrows on taut bowstrings pointed at James, Ruther, and Henry.

"You see? Could have killed you!" Henry still couldn't see the source of the voice. "Now how may I know if *your* party is friend or foe?"

Henry examined the boys. They were all young men with coarse, bark-colored hair and wood-brown eyes covered in thick white wool bodysuits. "What's your name, young man?" he asked the tallest of them, the one whose arrow pointed at his heart.

"Wilson," the boy answered with a voice similar to the unseen man's, though not as matured or rough.

"James, give Wilson your sword," Henry said.

Wilson let his bow go slack and returned the arrow to its quiver, then reached out his hand expectantly. James cast a long stern look at him. "Do you know what it means in the King's Guard to offer someone the hilt of your sword?"

Wilson shook his head.

"It means defeat. It means surrender." James glanced angrily at Henry. "Here." Instead of the hilt, he offered the sword by the blade to Wilson, who accepted it with gloved hands. The youngest boy whistled a strange bird call.

"Bring them up to the house, boys," the faceless man called from his hidden place.

Wilson offered the sword back to James, who instantly returned it to his sheath. "Follow me," the oldest boy said.

Ruther turned to Henry. "Is this wise? We don't know these people from our second cousins."

"You'd be sorry not to come with us," Wilson said and turned to walk. "You'll likely freeze to death."

"Henry . . ." Ruther said in a cautioning tone, but Henry believed he could trust these people. The numbness spreading to his legs and arms from his toes and fingers made the decision easy.

"How far is the house?" Henry asked as they began to move.

"Not far," Wilson replied, pointing vaguely to his right.

"And how does your father know my name?"

Wilson shrugged. "He didn't say."

The youngest boy looked back at Henry. "But he was glad when we saw you."

"What do you mean?" James asked. "How did you see us?"

"It wasn't seeing at first, it was hearing," Wilson said. "We was hunting over the hill following a rhinelk's tracks when we heard you. Father said it ain't natural for folk to be around our parts, 'specially in this weather. Took us around the south bend so we could catch you. We was supposed to shoot you when he gave us the word, but then he changed his mind and said to surround you."

"What's your father's name?" Henry asked him.

"Wilson," said Wilson.

"So you're Wilson the second?"

"No," the young man answered Henry with a big smile and thumped his puffed-out chest, "I'm the ninth."

"What are your brothers' names?"

"He's Blake." Wilson pointed to the middle boy who, thus far, had not said a word. "And this is—"

"Let me guess," Ruther said with a tease, "Muskrat."

"No!" The little boy giggled into his gloves. "Lafe."

The youngest boy smiled to reveal several missing front teeth and bright brown eyes much lighter than Wilson's. He maneuvered himself well through the snow even though it went up past his knees. Normally the carriage had troubles moving through the wooded areas, which was why James, Ruther, or Henry had ridden ahead to pick the path. However, with the boys leading they were soon on a route that offered no resistance. Henry realized they were on a very narrow road winding through the forest over the slope of the hillside.

He tried to think of how someone named Wilson could possibly know him so far south. He had never taken carpentry orders from anyone in these parts, nor traveled anywhere near here, and while he knew several men named Wilson in Richterton, none of them had three boys. He dropped back, letting James and Ruther ride behind the three brothers, so he could inform Maggie, Isabelle, and Brandol of the situation.

Minutes later, a comfortable home constructed from logs

appeared through the shroud of snow and trees. Beside it stood a large stable and shop. Henry guessed that in such an isolated location, the shop housed equipment for many trades. This pleased him, as he'd longed for a place where he could make some repairs on the carriage. The thought of doing any kind of work with wood again, even if only a small project, excited him. For several weeks, all he'd been able to do was whittle small pieces of wood that were too green to burn.

Wilson and Blake hurried forward to open the stable for Henry's party. Meanwhile, Lafe went into the house to inform the elder Wilson of their return. The stable provided suitable shelter for several horses, cows, and sheep, and a wooden partition separated the shop that held a blacksmith's furnace and three woodworking tables. A modest but adequate collection of tools adorned the walls. After the boys cleared a space for the carriage, the horses pulled it into the shop. Henry and the other men hurried to get the animals into the stables and covered with blankets.

Warmth enveloped Henry's body when they crossed the threshold of Wilson's log home. His body, desensitized after many hours in the wind and snow, revived as heat traveled to the ends of his fingers and toes.

Wilson the elder came with his wife to receive them in the main room. He looked exactly as Henry thought he should: wild brown hair with a coarse complexion and the same brown eyes as his boys. He was thicker and taller than his oldest, but not by much. The only difference that Henry found between his imagination and reality was that he had expected him to have a thick bushy beard covering his jutting chin, but Wilson had none.

His wife had green eyes and dark auburn hair. She was much lovelier than one might expect in a woodsman's wife. Her pink dress, though not ostentatious, compared well with many of the dresses Maggie wore.

"Well, ain't this a ragged bunch of criminals?" Wilson asked no one in particular. "I wondered if you was going to pass through my part o' the country. Are you hungry?"

All answered in the affirmative. Wilson turned to his wife and gave her a kiss on the cheek. "Becca, can you ready some food for us while I answer their many questions?"

His wife nodded and waved to Henry as if they were old friends.

"Come sit," Wilson the elder said. Just then, his boys came in, stamping their feet and breathing in warm air. "Boys, come take our guests' wet cloaks!"

After Henry helped Isabelle and Maggie unburden themselves of their heavy cloaks, the party sat around a glowing fire in a room furnished with good sitting chairs softened with animal skins.

"Where are you bunch headed?" Wilson asked as he nestled into his own cushioned seat. His eyes rested on Henry, smiling at him like they were already acquainted. Henry couldn't understand why this family acted as though they already knew him.

James, who sat between Isabelle and Brandol, spoke first. "To say we appreciate your hospitality would be an understatement. We are grateful. However—"

"—you won't be telling me where you're headed," Wilson finished for him. "That's fine for now, but you'll change your minds."

"Again," James said to Wilson, "we mean you no disrespect by this. It appears that you already understand our position, perhaps more so than we do."

"I'll admit, I ain't too surprised to find you in my territory," he said, looking at Ruther now, "but I'll take a guess that we'll all be learned somewhat before you go."

Henry couldn't hold back his question any longer. "How do you know me? And why are you taking us into your home if you know we're—well, we're not criminals—but certainly we're wanted by the King. We know there's a price on our heads, and if you intend to collect it—"

"That's not his intention," James said. "It would be near impossible in the weather to reach the nearest outpost, and he'd have made us surrender our arms when the boys had their bows trained on us."

"You must be the man in the King's Guard," Wilson said.

"Something like that," James answered darkly.

To Henry, Wilson added, "Smart."

"You mean James is smart, or I made a smart decision bringing him with me?"

"I think I mean both," Wilson answered. "To answer your other question, Henry, the whole barking kingdom knows some version of what happened at the Richterton inn."

"How many versions are there?" Ruther asked.

"Enough to satisfy the needs of an entire country. I'll be honest, I didn't think you'd make it this far, as famous as you've become. Your surviving is probably the closest thing to a miracle I've ever seen."

Henry thought again of the writ of passage and Ruther's cleverness in getting them out of that situation with the soldiers.

"What are people saying?" Isabelle asked.

Wilson scratched his face and then ran his fingers through his hair. "I'd say you got two main stories going 'round, and everything else is a branch off those. One says you're a bunch of vicious assassins who was hired by King Germaine or someone from a neighboring country to do in the Emperor, but botched the job. Other story says— and this is from them who are the smarter breed of humankind, mind you—they say you, Henry, tried to save your lady from the clutches of a greedy tyrant."

"Which do more people believe?" James asked.

"The more sensational of the two, naturally," was Wilson's answer. "It ain't helped that you threatened to burn down a physician's house and poison his well."

"We never threatened to poison his well!" Maggie protested.

Wilson shrugged. "Half the rumors out there probably ain't true, but you gotta remember, the smarter people I've talked to, they'd be as willing to help you as I am. And if not help, at least turn a blind eye."

"But how do *you* know me?" Henry asked. "And how much help are you willing to give us? Our presence here could put you in danger."

Wilson smiled, making his large chin even more pronounced. He held out his arms widely. "You are welcome to whatever you need: food, lodging, supplies. I have it all here, and I'm a ways off the beaten path."

"That's far outside the range of normal brotherly kindness," James pointed out. "What's the cost? What's in it for you?"

Wilson's smile neither faded nor grew. Henry could tell Wilson had some secret inside bursting to escape; whether it was for good or ill remained to be seen. "Nothing—nothing. Let's just say I have a personal interest in you lot surviving. If we got time, how about you give me your full story? That way, maybe I can set a few heads straight on some necks when I'm in town next. I reckon Ruther will want to do the talking."

For once, Ruther looked like he wanted to do anything but talk. Then it occurred to Henry that Wilson knew Ruther's name before it had been introduced to him. Had he seen Ruther perform in one of the towns nearby?

Ruther bowed to his host's request. Before long, his natural instinct as a storyteller took over, and he became as engrossed in telling the tale as Wilson's family was in hearing it. Even the delicious odor of the roast wafting in from the kitchen distracted no one. Becca, Wilson's wife, announced dinner ready before Ruther had finished even half the story, so Wilson asked him to finish once they'd resettled in the dining room.

Upon entering the dining room, Henry needed only a glance to answer the question of how Wilson had known him. Plates of roasted venison, dried fruit, bread and jam, and a large wedge of cheese littered the table with jugs of milk and ale set among them. Everything looked delicious, but Henry recognized the table supporting the small feast at once.

"My father made this," he announced, "and these chairs, too!"

"Doesn't miss a tick, does he, Wilson?" Becca said.

"That carriage in my stable," Wilson said. "You made it. That's my guess."

Wilson's wife smiled brightly at her husband and Henry as they took their seats around the magnificent table.

"I did," Henry said. "It was the piece I crafted to be made a master in the guild."

Wilson asked Ruther to give the Lord of All Worlds thanks for the food.

"I heard you hollering before I saw you, Henry," Wilson said once Ruther had finished. "Your voice sounded familiar, but it was the striking resemblance your work bears to your father's—and your infamous reputation—that gave you away. I known it was you at once. In my head, I said, *That's an original Vestin if I've ever seen a scrap a wood in my life.* And so's you know, any son of William Vestin is a friend of mine."

"When did Mr. Vestin make this table for you?" Isabelle asked.

Wilson glanced wistfully at Becca. "That was her," he said, gesturing to his wife.

"When Wilson asked me to marry him, I made one request he couldn't refuse." Becca took her husband's hand and squeezed it.

Henry silently prayed that Ruther wouldn't make a gagging sound.

"I wanted a beautiful table with chairs to match it. So, we looked all over."

"And I mean all over!" Wilson confirmed.

"I couldn't find anything I liked," Becca said. "Finally we heard about this young man in Richterton who was—what was it they said, Wilson?"

"'Curiously brilliant,'" he said.

"Yes!" Becca said. "That was it. Even though we'd already been up to Richterton once, I insisted we go again. We loved everything we saw the moment we set foot in your father's shop."

"How long ago was this?" Henry asked.

Wilson answered while scooping a large helping of venison onto his plate. "I'd say you was a wee boy, no more than two or three."

"My father became a master just before I turned three. You may have been one of his first customers."

"He was very glad to have us in his shop," Becca said. "I feared he might shake Wilson's hand clean off."

Wilson laughed at her comment, and Henry had no doubt that what she said was the truth. In fact, he could not stop himself from laughing as well. They talked more of Henry's father, but the conversation soon returned to Ruther's tale. Henry watched Wilson while Ruther spoke, wondering why his host, who almost always smiled, seemed less than pleased whenever he looked at Ruther.

The tale and dinner finished about the same time. Wilson set his boys to the task of cleaning so the adults could finish their conversation around the fire. After another hour of talking, Maggie and Brandol were both nodding off, and Ruther couldn't seem to stop yawning. Isabelle had already fallen asleep on Henry's shoulder.

"Looks like it's time for bed," Wilson suggested. "I'll have the boys bring you out some more blankets and such so you can bunk here in the great room."

"I'll check on the horses," Henry told his friends since he guessed no one else would want to go back into the cold.

He wrapped himself back in his cloak, now much drier, and stepped outside the house. The snowfall had lessened, but with the conditions they'd already endured, that didn't mean much. Icy wind battered his skin, and he quickened his step until he reached the shelter of Wilson's barn.

The first thing he checked was not the horses, but the gold. To lighten the load, they had long since abandoned Lady Oslan's coffer and put the bags of gold underneath packs of clothes and supplies in a secret storage compartment of the carriage. Everything inside looked untouched. As he went to check on the horses, he heard a creak from the same door he'd used to enter the barn.

"Hello?" he called, holding his lantern out in front to cast more light in that direction. A black shape moved from the doorway toward him. "Who's there?"

Wilson's face came into the light. "Henry," he spoke in a quiet voice, "I'm glad I caught you here alone." His expression had changed, now much more serious. His eyes looked to the door and then back to Henry. "We need to have a word about Ruther."

THIRTY
Enemies of King and Country

The same day that Wilson received Henry and company into his home, the King of Blithmore welcomed General Attikus at the steps of Germaine Castle with great fanfare. The reinstated general had sent advance word to King Germaine, and in transit to the castle received a reply expressing the King's eagerness to get reacquainted. Attikus's reception at the doors was far superior to what the Emperor had received at the Feast of Rulers. Besides the King himself being present, a full complement of servants and soldiers lined the way. The castle had been scrubbed to the darkest corner, and Richterton's best cooks had prepared a fine meal, finer than any the Emperor had ever received in Blithmore.

The cavalryman driving the general's carriage stopped so the door lined up perfectly with the middle of the procession, and before Attikus could even think about opening his door, his footman opened it for him. The general found it very droll how even after eight years of retirement, his subordinates continued to venerate him.

King Germaine made a great sign of respect by descending halfway down the stairs to meet Attikus. They clasped hands, and the King smiled. "Attikus! You have no idea what it means to me that you are here. Your stay will be long and happy, I hope."

"As do I, your Majesty," Attikus said with a similar enthusiasm, though his posture remained as formal as ever. They made small talk about family as they entered the castle doors. Attikus asked about the health of Queen Katherine and the royal couple's two daughters and two sons, then answered the King's inquiries regarding his own three sons.

They had their fill of lunch. Though he'd never admit it to anyone, Attikus preferred Blithmore cuisine to anything found in Neverak. When they finished, the King ordered away his servants and turned their attention to the serious matter which he knew brought Attikus to Blithmore.

"All right, let's get this part over with." He pushed his plate away and pulled his wine goblet closer. "I can't remember the last time something has both troubled me and pleased me as much as hearing of your reinstatement. For that reason alone, I was overjoyed when I received your letter asking for an audience with me. Now I have to ask: *Why?* Why has Ivan brought you into this?"

Attikus did not answer immediately because he truly didn't know, or, rather, he wasn't certain if his instincts were correct. And to divulge to the King what his instincts were telling him would be a cataclysmic mistake. King Germaine picked at the gristles of meat in his teeth while waiting for Attikus to respond. After a nice swig of the King's best wine, Attikus felt he had chosen the right words. "The last time you spoke with the Emperor was the day after his assault, correct?"

"Yes."

"Since then, the Emperor has grown . . ." Attikus again stalled to search for the most diplomatic word ". . . *impatient* at the lack of results from your soldiers."

"And also his spies, I presume?"

Attikus nodded. "And also his spies. He knows there is a lack of motivation, possibly even from the top down, to catch the criminals who have been sighted at least once, and as many as four times, since their escape."

"Why is that his belief?"

Attikus wondered if the King really didn't know the answer, or if he was feigning ignorance so he could measure Attikus. King Germaine was rarely subtle, but he was certainly more cunning than he let on.

"For example, the bounty."

King Germaine lifted his finger in protest. "The bounty is the standard amount the law dictates for such an offense."

"Upon a nobleman," Attikus added gravely. "Imagine, your Highness . . ."

"Attikus, please."

The general relented for the sake of argument. "Very well. Imagine, *Sedgwick*, if you will, that the offense had been upon a member of the Blithmore royal family."

"The Lord Almighty forbid it."

"Yes, but where would you have set the bounty to catch someone who assaulted your son? Or your daughter? Or the Queen?"

King Germaine began chewing the pieces of gristle more thoughtfully.

"You see now where the Emperor of Neverak finds fault?" Attikus asked in a calm tone that held no trace of accusation.

The King spat the gristle out onto his plate. "You're right, Attikus. Now, please, look at the situation from where I sit. Half my kingdom—or nearly half from what the reports say—believes the Emperor bought the young woman—who is, I might add, from a noble family—as a concubine, and then her lover rescued her."

"Have you addressed these concerns with the Emperor?"

"I tried, but you know Ivan. He's nothing like his father, nothing at all, and that's the real problem. Emperor Peter Ivan Krallick would never have taken concubines, though his father and grandfather did. He would never have tried to make an arrangement to bivouac his soldiers within my borders, but your young Emperor demands and demands and demands . . ."

"You don't like the son?"

The King gave Attikus a look that told the general he should know better than to ask such a thing. "A bold question from the man who requested his retirement on the day of the new Emperor's coronation."

"What everyone seems to forget is that my eldest son turned of age to enter the service on the same day," Attikus replied. "A soldier has no right to command his son. War is bloody enough without nepotism."

King Germaine smiled in a way Attikus recognized as an attempt to get him to smile back, but he did not indulge the King, not ever. His brown eyes dropped to his goblet where the last of the fine wine waited for him.

"I don't trust Ivan; you know that." The King's face told Attikus he felt ashamed of admitting his feelings. "I do believe he purchased the daughter of Lord Oslan, and I don't blame the carpenter for doing what he did. I think the carpenter was beyond foolish for handling the situation in the way he did, but I'm not going to put Blithmore into an uproar over this matter. I'm not encouraging the army to search every nook and cranny of my kingdom! Would you?" The old King looked as if he was about to confess his greatest sin. "And yet I'm afraid of what Ivan will do if I don't help him with this situation—and I'm afraid of what your involvement means in all this."

Attikus listened to all of this with a level eye and an unchanging expression.

"I am not like Ivan," the King sighed. "I'm past the age of ambition—and I never had the amount of it that he has. During his father's reign, Neverak and Blithmore dismantled much of our militaries so our countries could enjoy greater prosperity. We trusted each other!"

"That trust carries over to me, doesn't it?"

"Certainly it does and without equivocation—but only personally, not as this Emperor's general."

"That trust will be needed now more than ever, Sedgwick." Attikus fixed his eyes on the King. "I've been sent to you with a propos—rather, a demand. It was an understatement for me to say that Ivan is impatient for the capture of his assailants. His wrath only grows. He has asked me to strike a deal with you."

King Germaine appeared neither surprised nor happy. He folded his hands together and waited for Attikus to continue.

"It goes as follows: you formally declare Henry and Maggie Vestin, Isabelle and James Oslan, and Brandol the journeyman to be Enemies of King and Country, with a bounty of one thousand crowns per head; place copies of the decree and sketches of the criminals in every town and village; demand writs of passage of all travelers; and allow the Emperor to send five hundred of his Elite Guard into your borders to aid in the search. In return, he permits three hundred of your Guard to patrol his palace. In return, he will reduce the tariff on lumber, sheep, and wool for five years. The percentage is negotiable."

King Germaine shook his head angrily. "This is an example of what I mean. Peter and I never made demands of each other. We worked together. I can't—this is unacceptable. Neverak forces—his Elite Guard, no less—free to roam my lands? I can't help but wonder if Ivan has other motives."

Attikus knew the role his Emperor wished him to take, but he earnestly hoped it was not for the end the King feared. "Sedgwick, why else would Ivan reappoint me? For no other reason that I know of than to set your mind at ease. Not only will I oversee these five hundred Elite, but I have assumed this role by my own will and not by royal decree. What more can I say to satisfy you?"

King Germaine spat another piece of gristle onto his plate and surveyed it with disgust. When he looked up at Attikus, his face had lost only a portion of his anger.

"Tell me this: what if I refuse the Emperor's demands and choose to continue my present course?"

Attikus displayed his empty hands. "I am only performing my duty."

"Do you think I've forgotten the reason why a man of your background became general over all the armies of Neverak?"

"Did Emperor Peter Ivan tell you the reason?" Attikus asked. The last of his wine sat in the bottom of his goblet like a small pool of blood.

The King's face fell. "No, he didn't tell me. The rumor was—"

"There will always be rumors."

"Are they true, Attikus?" King Germaine asked with such exposed curiosity that Attikus was ashamed for him.

The general raised his goblet as if he was poised to drink, making sure it covered part of his face as he spoke. "No, it is not true." Then he drank the final measure of wine from his goblet. It tasted as bitter as guilt.

King Germaine breathed deeply as though he had unloaded a great burden. He smiled again at Attikus, though briefly this time, remembering finally that the smile would not be returned. Attikus didn't smile. He had never learned how. He wished the King would not place so much trust in him, yet he couldn't tell him this. The future was too shrouded, but there were signs he didn't like. King Germaine gripped the table with both hands, not in anger or in fear, but a steady grip nonetheless.

"I don't want war, Attikus." His voice was suddenly very tired, even more than the old emperor's had been when he lay on his deathbed. "What is wrong with peace? I'm no fool—at least I hope I'm not. It's not a perfect world we've built, but there's no reason for our countries to not enjoy decades more of prosperity and peace."

Attikus spoke only truth now. "I know nothing of designs for war or subterfuge, I can assure you that. When I appeared before the

Emperor to receive this appointment I saw a man who wanted justice. No doubt he chases it too far and too hard, but it is still justice he is after."

King Germaine's gaze pierced Attikus in a way the old general was very familiar with. The tired face changed again to the face of a noble king whose experience was long, tried, and tested. He surveyed the food on the table, the room in which they sat, and perhaps even all of Atolas with that piercing gaze. At long last he spoke. "Very well. I may be roasted for it by my council, but I give you my permission to bring your Elite Guard."

THIRTY-ONE

A Cold Conversation

Henry held the light closer to Wilson's face. "What about Ruther?"

"We'd best get comfortable. Take that over there and bring it 'round." Wilson pointed to a rickety old chair in the far corner of the shop. Henry retrieved it and sat directly across from Wilson. "You certain you'll be all right in this cold? I won't be faulted for your catching somethin'."

"I slept under the stars last night, Wilson."

Wilson pulled up a wooden bucket for himself to sit upon. "How'd someone like yourself get to be traveling with that Ruther?"

"Ruther's my best friend. He has been for years."

Wilson's eyes widened at Henry's answer. "That complicates things, don't it?" He put his hands under his arms and rubbed his legs together. "Brrrr! I think even the world Beyond ours is freezing over right now. Look, Henry, I feel a certain allegiance to you."

"I'm not comfortable talking about Ruther without him present." Henry voice was weary with emotional and physical fatigue.

"You're referring to gossip, which is indeed an ugly thing as you'll probably come to know better on your journey, what with all the talk about you and yours going 'round. This ain't gossip, Henry. This is a warning based on things I've witnessed with my own eyes. You may think you wouldn't be Ruther's friend if'n you listen to me, but I wouldn't be a friend if'n I didn't warn you."

Henry put his face in his hands. He didn't want to hear what Wilson had to say, but at the same time, he did. For a moment, he opened his mouth to decline, but something made him hold his tongue. Wilson took this as an invitation to continue.

"You know what town's only ten miles west of this house, don't you?" Wilson asked.

Henry had to think about the answer. "Washborough?"

Wilson nodded with a grim face. "Ruther's a very popular man in Washborough."

"He's a storyteller. He's popular all over the country."

"Ain't that the truth. When was the last time you heard him tell a story?"

"In public? Not since he first started in his profession—unless you count tonight," Henry added, smiling.

"He's darn near the best anyone 'round here's heard. If he makes the amount it's rumored he makes, well, he oughter be made of gold by now. Now, why do you think I bring this to your attention?"

Henry knew what Wilson was getting at—something he had always wondered about himself. "Ruther never has any money."

"Yes. Fact is, Henry, your friend has less than no money. He's in it up to his ears with lenders north and south, east and west. He's havin' to be real choosy when it comes to where he works. If he weren't choosy, he'd be losin' a pound of flesh in near any town he happened into. If you're wondering whether any of this is true, I'd be more than happy to take you to a good friend of mine in Washborough who Ruther owes seventy-five crowns."

"Where would that kind of debt come from?" Henry asked. "There's not an inn I've heard of that would extend such credit."

"It ain't sleeping and eating, Henry, it's drinking and gambling and women. Your friend has a taste for—but no real skill in—dice games, and evertime he's drinkin', he's bettin' on the games. Rumor also tells me he's been caught cheating more than once. Even I go into town sometimes. Where else could I have seen him? And you can be certain he's seen me too and prob'ly in the company of my friend what he owes, from the way he ain't said more than three words to me other than that story. I've knowed men like Ruther before, and he's probably thinking one of a couple things or three."

"What's that?"

"He wants to get you all outta my house before I send for my friend, tellin' him he's here, or before I pull you aside and tell you what I'm saying now. Either that, or he's thinking of how and when he can sneak out and settle his debt with my friend before I say somethin'. Then he can pretend I've gone mad—which is exactly what you're thinking now."

"I don't think you've gone mad, but Ruther *is* a common name."

Wilson gave Henry a petulant stare. "I told you I seen him in town. How many fat, red-haired, storyteller Ruthers are there that cheat at dice?"

"I've never seen him gamble, nor have I heard him say anything about dice or debts or creditors."

"I don't doubt ya, Henry. As I've said, I'm on your side, but think about it like this: do you tell Ruther everthing?"

"Absolutely," Henry said without even a thought to his answer.

"That so? Then I suppose Ruther knows all about the sword you carry and where it comes from?"

Henry glanced at the carriage where his sword was stored and then back to Wilson. "That was my father's blade."

Wilson gave a short laugh and rubbed his hands against his knees before putting them back under his arms. "And your grandfather's 'fore that. I know all about your sword and where it comes from."

"How do you know about it?" Henry asked.

"Because I have one similar. Got it from my father's father. Master

Vestin didn't think much of his sword until I mentioned a thing or two about it, seein' it in his shop. He took it down from its display and hid it the very minute I finished talking. Now, I'll ask again: does Ruther know about that sword?"

The story behind the sword wasn't what Henry thought about, but rather the secret compartment he'd built into his carriage. He shifted nervously in his rickety chair. Wilson had a good point, but it made him uncomfortable. In fact, between the cold, the chair, and the conversation, everything seemed uncomfortable.

"Maybe you see it now?" Wilson asked. "You two don't tell each other *everthing*."

"You're right that I don't—or didn't—know everything there is to know about him, but it doesn't change things. The worst of what we do doesn't reflect the best of who we are. I trust Ruther with my life."

"You do *now*," Wilson said, "but it won't always be that way. He's a drinker of the worst kind: he stops thinking when he drinks. His mouth shoots off ever which way, and all he wants is to make someone laugh. Does whatever it takes. Mark my words, you let him near ale or gambling and before you know it he'll be singing a tune called 'Henry and Isabelle Lose Their Heads.'"

Henry tried not to think of what had happened at the Friendly Fenley or how Ruther had disappeared before that incident. Or the bruises he'd seen on Ruther weeks before in that tavern in Richterton. Had he been paying off a debtor in Fenley? With what money? Ruther hadn't gone near the gold. Henry's mind seized onto that thought. Ruther hadn't touched the money they'd received from Isabelle's mother.

He answered Wilson, "I'd worry about your information if I had not already experienced Ruther's loyalty."

"Yep, he's loyal. I heard your story, but when a man's brain is muddled from ale and women and music and dice, loyalty ain't his highest priority. I know lots of men in this town who are loyal to their woman—up until the third pint. Hear me? Ruther ain't a man you want with you. Otherwise all of his vices are your problem."

"Why?"

"You got ta realize Ruther's going to get noticed at some point. Maybe the next town you visit. Anything drawing attention to him draws attention to you."

Henry watched the steam rise from his face as he sighed in frustration. "I don't—I don't know what you want me to say to all this, Wilson. I'm not a leader or a soldier. That's probably obvious. I'm a friend, and that means I can't drop someone who has shown me the kind of dedication that Ruther has."

"You're a good friend, I'll say that, but you got more to think about now than friendship. You got your woman and her brother. You got your sister and that quiet one, named . . . uh . . ."

"Brandol," Henry said quietly.

"Yeah, him. Now, you don't think I know Ruther as well as you, but you watch and see if old Wilson can't teach you something. Tonight or tomorrow, he'll leave. You stay awake a little while and you'll hear him."

"Why would he leave?"

Wilson stamped his feet several times on the stable floor and made another *brrrr* noise with his lips. "Self-preservation. Ruther's the same as any man in most ways, and he ain't wanted like the rest of you. Should he ever decide to part ways with you all, he'll need work. Most places won't hire a man what owes them money or has been caught cheating. A reputation as a good storyteller only takes a man so far—only covers so many sins, and Ruther has many sins to cover."

Henry tried to smile, but found himself unable. Either the cold had frozen his lips or his emotions wouldn't allow him. "I trust him, Wilson. I can't make it any clearer than that."

"That's fine, just fine, but you remember that it ain't a betrayal to stay up a little later for the next few nights. If I'm wrong, alls you've lost is sleep. If I'm right, I've done you a great service."

The conversation ended. Wilson led Henry back to the house, where everyone else had already fallen asleep, Ruther included. The room was quiet but for the flames crackling in the brick fireplace. Too many thoughts prevented Henry from sleeping, so he lay still on a soft pillow under a thick blanket, mulling things over. Many minutes passed, perhaps an hour, before he finally slumbered, but one thing he knew: Ruther did not leave the house.

The next morning, for the first time in weeks, Henry woke on his own, not from the cold or from James shaking him awake. It was a wonderful feeling, a joy he had almost forgotten. Wilson's youngest son stood at the edge of the room, watching Henry with a large smile that showed off his missing teeth.

"You sleep loud," Lafe said, grinning and giggling. "There's breakfast for you in the kitchen, and Father says you can use the shop when you're done eating. He's there now."

Sounds of Becca's and Isabelle's voices carried from somewhere not too far away. Henry closed his eyes again and listened for a few moments. They were talking about nothing in particular, but Henry enjoyed hearing the happy tone in Isabelle's voice.

He spent most of the day in Wilson's shop with brief interruptions for lunch and an afternoon nap. Wilson was thrilled to be able to work with a master carpenter, and he peppered Henry with questions about woodworking and carving all day. He happily shared his materials and tools, so long as Henry always explained what he was doing. James and Maggie helped examine the carriage and discussed repairs and improvements. Maggie's input proved most useful as she was usually the one driving it. James, on the other hand, was more of a nuisance, thinking he knew what to do but not understanding even the most basic principles of woodworking. Henry enjoyed the company but gave James tasks that kept him out of the way. Ruther and

Maggie were always nearby, helping when asked, but keeping plenty of distance between themselves.

The work refreshed Henry more than naps and food. It was the old adage his parents had impressed deeply upon him and Maggie: work brings happiness. It was true, even though it had taken Henry years to realize it. On that long, wonderful day spent in Wilson's woodshop, everything would have been perfect if not for one thing: whenever he found himself absorbed in his labors, his conversation with Wilson from the previous night would spring to mind, begging to be remembered. And as much as Henry wanted to trust Ruther, he couldn't help but wonder if Wilson was right.

THIRTY-TWO
Tales of the Pass

D inner was not as extravagant the second night as it had been the night before, but it was still a fine meal. Afterward, they spent the evening in conversation around the great room. Henry, with Isabelle's blessing, decided to disclose the secret of their intended destination to Wilson, despite Ruther's protests.

"The Iron Pass?" Wilson repeated when they told him. He rubbed his hands together and stared into the fire. "Not a bad choice if you're hopin' to fool your pursuers. You're betting they'll assume you're headed to the southern shore, right?"

"Precisely," Henry said, "if they think we intend to leave at all."

"Settle down in Pappalon?"

"Perhaps, or we may move on eastward."

"You'll need to pass through Bookerton if you're serious about it." Wilson glanced meaningfully at Henry. "But a word of warning: things might be bad enough by then that you could well be walking straight to your deaths."

"Do you have any other suggestions?" James asked. "Your knowledge of the area is far superior to ours."

"There ain't much you can do about Bookerton. It's the only place for the supplies you'll need to cross the pass. You'll need at least, what, a week or two to reach it from Bookerton? Another two weeks to cross it, so three to four in total? That'll be a chore going four to five weeks without a market to shop." Wilson regarded them all shrewdly. "Assuming, 'course, you make it through the pass at all."

Ruther snorted at the comment. James looked skeptical. Henry lowered his eyes as though he were embarrassed. Isabelle had no idea why he should be. Before this all began, they had discussed all their options in case they had to flee the country, and they had settled on crossing the pass.

"You're not scared, neither, Miss Maggie?" Wilson asked her.

"I didn't know I should be," Maggie answered.

Henry cleared his throat. "I've not told any stories about the pass because I don't think they're true."

"Don't buy into the rumors, eh?" Wilson asked. "That's because you're northerners. Southerners think different."

"It's not that," Ruther said. "It's that none of us are superstitious."

"Superstitious?" Maggie repeated. "What do you mean? What's wrong with traveling through the pass?"

Brandol's face had grown a shade paler as his lips formed a small O. Ruther and Henry both quickly answered, "Nothing," but Maggie waited for Wilson to give more information.

Wilson noted her interest and looked pleased at the chance to tell his tale to a fresh listener. "It's like I said, Miss Maggie, they're rumors, really, but when you hear similar rumors years and years on end . . ."

"There's no proof," Ruther said. "Even *I* know the difference between fiction and truth."

"I know much more about truth than you do," Wilson said with a directness that surprised Isabelle. "Contrary to what these fine men say, Miss Maggie, there's plenty of facts to support my claims." He ignored the several disbelieving expressions and pressed on. "The stories of the Iron Forest and the pass that cuts through it go back some— oh, I don't know, as long as I've been 'round. That's near fifty years, so certainly longer than that. People claim they've seen spirits, heard voices, things of that nature."

"'Seen spirits'?" James repeated. "What do spirits look like? I've been told all my life that spirits are invisible."

"I'm only telling you what I've heard," Wilson responded. "I used to feel the same way. Heard a saying once that goes, 'The greatest skeptics become the strongest believers.' I believe there is something happening in the Iron Forest."

James chuckled cynically at Wilson. "I have a saying that goes, 'I'll believe something when I see it.' That goes for spirits, angels, ghosts, and anything to do with the Path."

Isabelle glanced at Maggie, who immediately averted her eyes to the fireplace.

"So evil spirits walk the Iron Forest?" Isabelle asked. "How do you know they're wicked? Maybe they're just misunderstood?"

Henry let out a short burst of laughter. Isabelle squeezed his hand and gave him a wink. She believed that nothing Wilson might say could scare her or change her mind.

"Good spirits don't kill," Wilson said this seriously enough that Henry stopped laughing.

"There have been deaths?" Maggie asked.

Brandol sat up straighter in his seat and fixed his eyes on Wilson.

"Why haven't I heard about them?" was Ruther's question.

"Like I told you already," Wilson said, "you're northerners. There've been deaths, yes. Never bodies. Never blood."

"How convenient," James muttered to Ruther.

"The first person I met who said he'd seen the inhabitants of the Iron Forest was old Barney Dentin," Wilson continued. "He was a stick-thin man who'd done lots of trading in Pappalon—lived in a tiny village right on the edge of the Iron Forest for most those years. He came up here to Washborough when his farm failed. I was a lad then and found employment at an inn—the same inn where Barney

Dentin spent most his time. The owner back then, he must've paid old Dentin in grub and ale just for coming inside and sitting down. Half the people who drank at the inn were only there to hear Dentin's tall tales.

"On my first day, there sat Dentin, surrounded by half a dozen men pokin' him with questions. I was too busy to listen to what they was saying. Just trying to do my chores right. After some weeks, I'd got to know him a little better. He knew my name and whatnot, but that were the extent of it. Wasn't until I was clearing his plate one day that I caught a bit of what he was telling people. I heard words like 'floating' and 'evil.' I stayed for a few seconds to listen, but my boss swatted my head with a broom and then gave me a tongue-lashing for standing 'round.

"I woulda come to the inn on my own time, but my father wouldn't hear nothing about it. I told him I weren't going to drink, I wanted to listen to old Barney Dentin, but my old man was opposed to that, too. The old feller thought Barney Dentin was a loon, getting free meals for telling lies—according to my father, he'd made a deal with the owner to keep each other in business.

"But I was a lad, and my father's words didn't make no sense. All them little bits of things I'd heard old Dentin say kept me up at night trying to put them together. What could that old loon be telling people that they all found so interesting? One day, I'd had enough of guessing. After telling my folks I was turning in early, I went out the window. I'd acted sick all day so they'd believe I weren't feeling well. We lived closer to town those days, so it wasn't too far a walk for me. I went in the inn the same as I always did, only this time I didn't let my boss know I was in for work. No, I went straight for Barney Dentin. I don't know if I'd found him on a good day or if the inn was less busy on my days off, but his eyes brightened up like small suns when he saw me.

"'Wilson, why am I not surprised to see you?' he says.

"His voice reminded me of the wooden stairs in our old house: creaky and thin. 'You want to hear my story, then?' His bone-thin hand pointed at the chair across from him. I sat, and he leaned in toward me. What had been a nice dinner rested on a plate in front of the old-timer, but even more food was stuck in his teeth. His breath smelled strongly of ale.

"'The Iron Pass—no, the whole Iron Forest—is haunted, Wilson,' he said, and I knew as he said it that he knew it. 'For thirty years of my life, I crossed that pass at least twice a year. So sixty times, least. Sixty, and over a dozen of those times I saw things . . . heard things. What kind of things? you might ask. The answer is . . . I still don't know.' His eyes misted over when he said this, and I could tell he was seeing them all over again. 'Mostly white, Wilson. Sometimes 'long the ground, sometimes through the air, floating 'mong the trees. It weren't until I'd crossed that pass maybe twenty times that I first noticed them. I had no reason to be worried.' He grinned cheerily at me, but all I saw was the meat stuck between his rotten teeth.

"''Most anyone traveling through the Iron Pass will tell you about the noises. The whispers. Very faint. So much that you wonder if you heard it at all. You wriggle your fingers in your ears to check they aren't ringing. That's the way folk are. Wanting to pass strange things off as a weariness of the mind.

"'In fact, first time I saw a glimpse of the white, I passed it off as just that, fatigue, and it weren't till another year or two that I saw it again. A sliver of white, as pure and evil as anything I've ever seen. I shouted out to it, but it was gone in a blink. Now any man who sees something unusual once is likely to pass it off, twice he thinks he's seeing things, thrice and he knows he's not mad—unless he is. But I knew I weren't a fool, and when I saw it that third time, I started asking questions.'

"Then old Barney Dentin told me about people he'd met, both sides of the pass. People'd seen or knew others who'd had similar experiences. He learned the story of the Massacre of the Pass that went back clear to two hundred years ago now. He told me about all of it."

"What massacre?" James asked.

Wilson looked genuinely surprised at James's question. "You a military man, and you ain't heard it? It goes way back, when Avalon was one country, before Pappalon and Greenhaven and all them other countries broke apart from it. Blithmore and Avalon had an argument over the sea trading. I can't remember the particulars now, but the king of Avalon got mad enough to send an army to work things out the old-fashioned way. He sent five hundred troops by boat and five hundred on foot. Those on foot were to go through the Iron Pass and head north, drawing away Blithmore's armies. They'd supposedly received a promise of alliance from Neverak, but that's not been proved. The way Barney told it, the five hundred men who arrived by boat, soon as they landed, Blithmore struck hard with an army of two thousand. The other army never made it through the forest, and no one ever saw any member of the army again. Blithmore and Avalon have never fought since."

"Weren't search parties sent after the army?" James asked.

"Of course, but they never found nothing worth reporting. No sign the army'd even been on the trail. Nothin'."

"And—and—and that's where we're headed?" Brandol stammered. "We're going to this same Iron Pass? There ain't two?"

"It's the very same one."

THIRTY-THREE

In the Night

Maggie was the only one of the group who seemed convinced by Wilson's story. Well, Brandol obviously was too, but Henry didn't count him because he was scared of everything lately. Isabelle usually dismissed anything supernatural, but now she appeared to be somewhere in between James and Ruther's utter rejection and Maggie's conviction. Henry also noticed that the more Wilson spoke, the more he addressed himself to Maggie and Brandol since they were the ones who seemed to believe him.

"How convenient that no traces of the army were found," Ruther remarked.

Wilson smiled at Ruther's reaction. "Say what you will, but it's all true. Barney carried around a little book about it, written by a Pappalonian historian. Everthing was accurate. When you take into account how many people have seen things or heard things since . . . and that army ain't the only death. There've been others. Small parties. A lone traveler here or there. Never seen nor heard from again."

Wilson paused as if to gauge his audience's reaction. "Well, I can see I ain't going to change your minds on this, and yet, it's worth thinking about."

"We appreciate you trying to warn us," Henry said.

"I'm off to bed now," Wilson said. "Do you still plan to stay through tomorrow and leave the day after?"

"Yes," Henry answered. "We're very grateful for your hospitality."

Wilson dismissed the compliment with a half wave of his hand. He glanced surreptitiously, but pointedly, at Ruther, reminding Henry to keep watch, and then retired. The six scuttled about the room, arranging their makeshift beds. The fire kept the room heated and filled with the rich scent of burning wood. Henry was quite aware of a deep feeling of contentment as he listened to his friends fall asleep one by one. Unlike them, however, sleep again eluded him. His mind raked over the stories Wilson had told. While it was true they hadn't deterred him from taking the Iron Pass, he could not dismiss them as easily as James or Ruther.

He tried to imagine a logical explanation for five hundred men disappearing at once, leaving no trace of their existence. If all the information Wilson had given them was truthful, where could they have gone? These questions spawned several others. Could spirits even touch or affect people? Why would they want to protect the Iron Forest—or Blithmore for that matter? Divining answers to these questions was like trying to pound a peg into a board using his forehead. He decided to speak to Isabelle about it when he had a chance.

When sleep finally seemed possible, a stirring came from across the room where Brandol and Ruther lay. Soft noises continued for several seconds, then turned into footsteps. The source of the sounds stopped at the front door. It was too dark for Henry to see anything properly. A small blast of cold air hit his face, chilling him. Then the door closed once more. Henry waited a few minutes before getting up, not wanting to alarm the person who'd left.

"Henry?" Maggie asked in a faint voice as he passed her.

"Go back to sleep. You're having a dream."

"Oh, right, never mind."

Henry peered out the door. The gray clouds that had closed over them two days ago had given way to a brilliantly starry night. Two full moons cast their white-blue light on the blanket of snow. When he saw no one, he slipped through the door and all but closed it behind him. A few minutes passed and the stable door opened. A horse exited, led by a cloaked figure. Holding the reins with one hand, the figure used the other hand to close the stable door firmly, then mounted the horse and slowly trotted off.

Quaking violently from the cold, Henry went back inside. He didn't need to sneak around the room to find out which friend had left. Nor did he need to follow the figure to find out what he was doing at this hour on such a cold night. The moonlight was enough, and the figure's outline was unmistakable.

Henry ran his fingers through his hair as he went back to his small bed of blankets. The cold followed him despite the closed door. He pulled the blankets back over himself, grateful for their warmth, grateful for the pillow's depth, grateful he was too tired for emotions.

The next morning, Henry went back to the woodshop with Wilson to work on both the wagon and a few other small projects. Wilson's sons and most of Henry's company helped as well. Ruther's attitude was more jovial than it had been in days. It helped that he once more had ale in his flask, which had, until that morning, been empty for the past several days. He sang, teased, and played word games all day. They all worked tirelessly, stopping only to eat. By evening, the carriage looked almost as good as the day Henry had built it.

James went hunting by himself and brought home several rabbits for dinner. Brandol, on the other hand, stayed in bed much of the day, complaining he wasn't feeling well. Becca, Maggie, and Isabelle prepared the rabbits for dinner. During the meal, the conversation stayed on the group's exodus, which would take place early the next morning. Wilson revealed several impressive maps he'd worked on over the years and reviewed them with Henry's company. He showed them the best routes to take between Washborough and Bookerton, and then between Bookerton and the pass. These paths, though further to the east than they had planned to travel, would keep them from bumping into almost anyone, especially soldiers. Ruther pointed out that it didn't matter since they had the writ of passage, but Wilson ignored his comments as he had done most of the day.

The discussion wound down as the maps were put away. Suddenly, Brandol stood up and cleared his throat, but his eyes stayed fixed on the table. "I—I have somethin' to say." The room fell silent. "I was just—just wondering if maybe I might," his eyes glanced from Henry to Isabelle and back to the table where they remained fixed once more, "if you'd consider, Mr. and Mrs. Wilson, me staying here. I work hard and ain't gonna be no trouble. I promise."

Brandol looked to be on the brink of tears, but he managed to hold his emotions in check. Wilson and Becca exchanged a surprised expression, and Henry saw Wilson give his wife a slight shake of the head. James regarded Brandol as though he'd fallen into a puddle of muck while wearing a clean uniform.

"I understand your fears, Brandol," Wilson said, placing a hand on the journeyman's shoulder. "You want to be out of this nightmare, but you have to keep going. It's not that I wouldn't mind having a helper 'round here. But it's too dangerous for me to let you stay. If you was to somehow get caught, I'd be in as much trouble as you." He patted Brandol's shoulder several times. "No hard feelings, I hope. Don't worry so much and you'll do fine. Ain't no one going to catch you on the paths I've showed you."

Brandol nodded and stammered out his thanks, and then the meeting was over. Not long afterward, Henry lay in bed listening as his friends fell asleep one by one, wondering what he would do if Ruther left again. Was it even his business if Ruther wanted to get out of the house? He still could not fathom the possibility that his friend would do anything to jeopardize the group. It seemed as likely as Isabelle running off with Brandol, or James telling a joke. There were certain things he knew, and one of them was that he could trust Ruther.

Small doubts crept in, however, when he again heard stirrings from where Ruther slept. This time, the dark figure moved slower and with more care than before. Henry stuffed his face into his pillow, determined to say nothing to stop his friend from leaving. When the door closed, Henry did not even bother looking up.

The next day started with a hearty breakfast. Blake and Lafe begged them not to go. Isabelle explained that they had to, and Henry and company were soon packed and ready to leave. Wilson stopped Ruther, Henry, and James on their way out of the stable.

"I ought to give you one last bit of advice regarding the Iron Forest, especially since most my advice previous weren't taken seriously. That was a mistake on my part because I do believe it's dangerous. So hear me now. When you reach the pass—and I hope and pray you will— follow these two rules of caution: Keep on the trail. And keep your weapons sheathed. If you do those two things, you should make it through untouched."

Ruther and James nodded affirmatively, but Henry could tell they didn't take Wilson's advice seriously. Henry waited until the others left and answered, "Thank you, Wilson. We'll give heed, be assured of that. Thank you for everything. Your generosity has been more than we could have hoped for."

"As I said when I first met you, any son of William Vestin is a friend of mine."

"My father would agree that you have more than repaid your friendship."

Wilson smiled again, a smile that could brighten a room. Their host stepped out of the way, and Henry nudged Quicken onward. When Henry looked back he could barely see the homestead, but Wilson still watched them with his hand shielding his eyes.

It was both a blessing and burden to be back on the trail south- ward. Perhaps they had grown too soft in their brief stay at Wilson's home, but Henry's mind and spirit were refreshed. The group as a whole seemed optimistic about their prospects, and Henry could not remember the last time Ruther and Maggie had gone so long without snapping at each other.

James decided it was best to follow Wilson's instructions, which they did for the next several days. The trails were sometimes difficult to find, but almost always provided plenty of cover and ease of travel. They got water from nearby streams, avoiding the Drewberry River altogether. The good fall weather had returned, the sun melting the snow and accompanying them throughout the day. It was not terribly warm, but with the absence of wind and snow their days were much more pleasant. Wilson had stocked them with enough grain and dried foods that they were able to travel almost three weeks without searching for a market, making better time than they had almost their entire journey, which had now lasted over nine weeks. In the three weeks from Wilson's home, Henry even invented several reasons why Ruther might have left twice during their stay.

Eventually, however, a stop in town became necessary. Their stores of food for both humans and horses were nearly depleted. This would be their last stop before Bookerton, barring any more bad weather. As Ruther was still unknown to the King's Guard and other soldiers, it was unanimously decided that he would take Ghost and a spare horse into Grubbingville for supplies. Their previous market forays had required two people, but James was confident that with the wild game he'd spotted in the area, they could supplement some supplies with fresh meat. The group discussed Ruther's strategy and gave him a list of supplies while Isabelle fetched the writ of passage and the needed gold from the carriage.

"Maybe I should also wear a disguise," Ruther suggested. "What do you think?"

"Not necessary," James answered. "Your fame is more of an asset than a hindrance, especially since you're not wanted."

A small flame of suspicion flared up in Henry. Did Ruther owe creditors in every town in Blithmore, or was he merely concerned for his safety?

"Henry," Isabelle called. "Henry, come here!"

Henry went over to the carriage where Isabelle stood, her head in the door, arms rummaging through several packs. Isabelle often used opportunities like this to sneak kisses when no one else could see.

"Yes?" He tried to conceal his smile and failed.

"I can't find it!" Isabelle was distraught, throwing things aside frantically. "The writ of passage!" Henry stopped smiling.

"Where was it last?"

"Here!" She pointed to a small, empty leather pouch.

"Don't worry. I'll help you find it."

He calmed her down and helped her look again. They thoroughly searched through pack after pack until Henry had the same panic as Isabelle. Once every pack had been investigated, he called the rest of the group over to assist. Every pack was searched twice. Everyone's pockets were checked twice, but it was no use.

The writ of passage was gone.

THIRTY-FOUR

The Missing Paper

It—it—it was here the day we—we—we left Wilson's house, Master Henry." Brandol's face was red and sweaty, and he wouldn't look at anyone. Isabelle had never seen him so upset or ashamed. Nor had his stuttering ever been so bad. "I swear in it! I—I—I held it on my hand!"

James shook his head in frustration. Henry had his back turned to his journeyman. Everyone wanted to scream at Brandol, but Isabelle knew it was no use pushing him anymore. The poor young man had vomited after they'd realized the writ of passage was missing. He had been in charge of making certain it was packed. It was his only responsibility. No one had thought it a difficult task for him since they rarely unpacked it. Now even Henry looked on the verge of raging at Brandol.

Isabelle took Henry aside to calm him down while James consoled Maggie, who had lost control after the last bag was searched for the second time. Isabelle had never seen Maggie so distraught. Ruther, however, seemed to take the situation in stride and began dressing himself in one of his costumes, then left without saying a word to anyone. She watched him ride toward Grubbingville with several empty packs and a second horse.

It took James and Isabelle an hour to get Maggie back in her right mind; meanwhile, Brandol cooked dinner. Isabelle guessed this was his attempt at making a gesture of peace, but she had a strong feeling that if someone did not help him with the meal, he might make things worse.

An hour later, Brandol finished preparing the food, but there was no sign of Ruther. Henry and James decided to wait for him to return before eating. Isabelle asked Henry to accompany her on a short walk while they waited. She held his hand and made small talk, but Henry was distant.

"Are you still thinking about the writ?" she asked.

Henry's face wore a strange expression as he stared at the ground and nodded. Something in his eyes told her it wasn't only the writ of passage bothering him. She responded by gripping his hand tighter. His gaze moved from the ground to the horizon, watching for Ruther's return. They sat together in silence on the top of a hill. Isabelle ran her fingers through Henry's hair—now much longer than it had been when they left Richterton—and wondered what he was thinking about and why he wouldn't tell her.

The concern on Henry's face only deepened when they returned to camp and learned Ruther hadn't returned. James suggested they eat before the food became too cold. No one argued. Isabelle sniffed the food before sampling it. It smelled good. She smiled proudly at Brandol, but he quickly looked away. As the meal went on and no one heard the sounds of an approaching gallop, a heavy mood settled over them.

When it came time to clean up, James and Henry excused themselves and wandered down a dirt trail in deep conversation. When Maggie suggested that she needed more water, Isabelle volunteered to fetch it. Taking two pails, she set off down the barren trail behind her brother and Henry. From between two thick trees, she spotted them. Henry was picking up stones and skipping them across the creek while James threw his knives at a tall oak. If they heard her approaching, they made no sign.

"What do you think the chances are that something happened to him?" James asked Henry. "I'm not suggesting he's been captured. Maybe lost, hurt, thrown from his horse, anything."

Isabelle couldn't see Henry's expression, but she heard the nervous tone in his voice. "How long do you want to wait before we go after him?"

"Is there something going on that you're not telling me?"

Henry shook his head.

"Something's different between you and Ruther," James said. "He may not know it yet, but if it concerns me or the safety of my sister, I should know."

"I understand," Henry said. "There's nothing going on."

Isabelle had the distinct impression Henry was lying.

"Have you ever noticed this scar on my scalp?" James asked, turning his head and parting his hair to reveal a four-inch-long jagged red line along the back of his skull. When Isabelle saw it, a jolt of sympathy shot through her.

"When—how did you get that?" Henry asked, trying to hide his revulsion with his hand.

"I was betrayed," James said. His face was grim and his tone bitter. Isabelle continued to stare at the grisly scar until James covered it with his hair again. "It cost me everything, including my place in the King's Guard. That is why I could not be reached by post when my mother passed away. You will not speak of this to Isabelle."

"I won't, if that's what you want."

"It is. I also want you to remember that if you ever think you know someone—*anyone*—so well that you would place your life in their hands . . . think about this scar first."

"Who betrayed you? How—"

"That is all I am going to say about it, Henry."

While Henry tried to figure out how to respond to James's warning, Isabelle quietly left the scene with her pails and filled them further downstream. Instead of returning to the camp, she sat on a fallen log near the streambank and let her thoughts wander. She wished Henry didn't have to bear so much responsibility. He was much happier as a master carpenter, filling orders and managing his business. Their predicament was her fault, not his. If she had stood up to her father and urged Henry to leave Richterton, they wouldn't be in this mess.

Don't live in the past, Isabelle, she told herself. At the same time, she heard James's advice to Henry repeating in her head. Think about this scar first. Living without an ability to trust sounded like a terrible way to live. James's bitterness reminded her of their father.

When she returned, she sat close to Henry at the fire. Her hand brushed his, though he never took it. His eyes stared into the dancing flames. Maggie kept herself busy with more cleaning, but she jumped at any small sound and constantly glanced toward the hills where Ruther had headed on his way to Grubbingville. Brandol helped her. By the light of the fire and the sun's last rays, he looked pale and sick. James sat stiffly, sharpening his knives with more concentration than usual. No one spoke, though the same fear weighed on everyone's thoughts. It was as if some unknown force prevented them from voicing their concerns about Ruther's safety. Finally, James got up to throw his knives again, though there was not much time before the sunlight would fail him. Isabelle found the sudden, repetitive noise of metal into wood an irritant, like Maggie persistently glaring at Brandol. Finally, when she could take no more, Isabelle stood up and went to Quicken. Henry followed her.

"I'll go after him," he told her in a whisper.

"I can't sit here any longer," she answered.

Henry tried to dissuade her until she stopped him. "I am riding with you, so accept that." Her lips pressed against his for a long second and then released him.

"As you wish," he said with a grunt as he mounted Quicken.

Isabelle saddled one of the carriage horses. The evening was a crisp, dry cold, the kind she found refreshing. Henry pushed Quicken at a good pace, and Isabelle kept up. The horses' hooves fell softly in the cushioning grass as they rode westward. They were still a mile and a half from the most western homes in Grubbingville when she saw a shadowy figure on the horizon.

"Over there," Henry said, pointing to the nearest trees. They slowed the horses' pace and waited in a spot where they would be obscured by tree trunks and low branches. Her heart beat insistently in her chest as she watched the figure approach on horseback.

It was Ruther. Isabelle could tell as soon as she saw the second horse laden with packs being led behind the rider. She smiled at Henry and saw that he was less than pleased to see his friend. Henry whistled the chirping signal only members of their party would recognize. Ruther immediately turned toward them, answering with two shrill whistles.

Isabelle left the shadow of the trees toward Ruther. Henry followed.

"Are you all right?" he asked Ruther. The question sounded brusque.

"Yeah," Ruther responded breathlessly and with a bit of a slur, "it wasn't fun, though."

"You were only supposed to be gone two hours. What kept you?"

"How long have I been?"

Henry shrugged. "Four, maybe five hours. How many mugs of ale did you drink, Ruther?"

Ruther hissed, swearing softly. The smell of drink was strong on his breath. "Should I have sipped water? Goat's milk? Would that make you happy? Sorry, friend, but at least a dozen guardsmen were in the town square, and I thought it best if I waited until they finished their business."

"You waited two hours for them to leave?" Henry's voice grew more strained.

"Better two hours of waiting than us all captured, yes? Why is that a problem, Henry? Should I not try to be safe?"

"It's not a problem." Henry's answer came as quick as a bowshot. "We were worried. All of us."

"You mean most of us."

"I said what I meant."

Ruther snorted.

Isabelle had never heard them speak to each other like this. "Let's go back to camp," she suggested as she prodded her horse to move. "They'll be wanting to see you, Ruther."

"Just a moment," Ruther said. "We've got more to discuss."

"What is it?" she and Henry asked simultaneously.

"I learned something in town that concerns us."

"Is it bad?" Henry asked.

"It's nothing resembling good. I stopped at an inn for the news, and I'm glad I did. One of the patrons told me the Emperor has become directly involved with the search for his would-be-assassins."

"How directly?"

"He's sent five hundred of his men—five hundred of his Elite Guard."

Isabelle suddenly wished she had not eaten so much dinner. Her stomach churned. "Five hundred?" she repeated.

"That's what I was told. Their sole purpose is to hunt for us. They've also declared you five to be Enemies of the King and put a much larger bounty on your heads."

"Lord Almighty help us," she whispered. "How can we survive?"

"It's not so terrible," Ruther said. "You're looking at this with only a negative eye."

An owl in one of the nearby trees hooted so loudly it startled all three of them. Isabelle found the source and then faced Ruther again.

"How else should we view this, Ruther?" Henry asked. "With optimism?"

"I'm not saying there's no need for concern or caution, only that things aren't impossible. The Neverak soldiers, they don't know Blithmore. They won't work well, if at all, with King Germaine's armies."

Henry shook his head and spurred Quicken away. "More troops looking for us is never a good thing."

"I didn't say it was, friend."

Isabelle and Ruther followed Henry at a trotting pace. All was silent but the muffled movement of the horses. Ruther finally spoke up, "I have something else I think we should discuss here in private."

Isabelle halted her horse and gave her full attention to Ruther. There was enough moonlight now that she could see his face. It was tired and worn. A thought even occurred to Isabelle that perhaps Ruther was thinner than when they first set out—not much, but a little.

"I think we need to consider the possibility that the writ of passage was stolen from us."

"Stolen?" Henry repeated. "By Wilson?"

"That's the most likely possibility. He was around the carriage often enough. It doesn't make sense for us to be angry at Brandol."

"I'm not angry at Brandol," Isabelle stated. "Henry hasn't said a cross word to him, either."

"By 'us' I meant Maggie and James, but it leads me to think what else Wilson may have done to sabotage us. Perhaps he's given us bad information about our route. Or worse yet, he may have set us up for an ambush."

"After taking us in?" Henry asked. "Giving us shelter and food? The ale has gone to your head."

"We were trapped there in the snow, but so was he! Now he knows where we're headed, when we expect to be there, and how many of us there are. I could go on. With our writ of passage gone, we've lost all protection."

"He knew we were stopping in Grubbingville," Isabelle cut in. "It would have been the perfect opportunity—"

"To send guardsmen after us?" Ruther cut in, reminding her that he had indeed seen the King's best men in Grubbingville.

Isabelle thought for a moment of everything that had taken place, every conversation they'd had with Wilson. She could tell Henry was thinking the same thing.

"No, Ruther," he said for her. "I trust Wilson. We must have misplaced it."

"Who would have misplaced it?" Ruther countered. "Brandol? The kid is more afraid of losing his life than anyone. He guarded it like a dog."

"But not Wilson," Isabelle said.

"Who, then? One of his children?"

"I don't know, but—"

"His wife?"

"We don't know, but we trust him!" Henry shouted.

Ruther jerked back as though Henry's words had burned him. "It was just an idea," he mumbled, then led Ghost and the pack horse past them.

Isabelle remembered what James had said to Henry earlier. Her brother was right. There was something deeper going on between these two friends.

The rest of the party was thrilled to see Ruther return. Maggie even smiled, a rare thing if Ruther was involved. That small act made Isabelle realize that things were not hopeless despite losing the writ of passage. They had enough food to last to Bookerton and, thanks to Wilson, a good knowledge of back trails that should keep them far from prying eyes. Over the following days, a sense of cautious optimism returned to the company. Henry was the exception, but despite Isabelle's pleas, he would not tell her what troubled him.

A chasm had grown between the two best friends. She saw it in their small talk, in the way Ruther looked at Henry with a sad smile, and in how he accepted Henry's decisions without debate or sarcastic remarks. It wasn't the Ruther she knew, yet for all the hurt it was causing them, Henry wouldn't talk about it.

They followed Wilson's route for two more weeks until they were near Bookerton. As Wilson had promised, the party encountered no trouble. It put to rest the argument between Ruther and Henry of whether or not Wilson could be trusted. What it did not put to rest was the question still on everyone's mind: where had the writ of passage gone?

THIRTY-FIVE

Tightening the Noose

One week after the meeting between General Attikus and the King of Blithmore, the general's carriage moved steadily southward toward New Germaine, a town in the center of Blithmore. This was where Attikus would have his headquarters, commanding his Elite Guard forces until he received information about where the objects of his search might be. Sitting across from him in the carriage were his two lieutenants, Wellick and Kressin.

Both men had begun their military service when Attikus had served as general under the former emperor, but most of their career advancement had been under General Derkop, and they had been involved in every decision executed under Derkop's leadership for the past several months. Attikus had come to learn fairly quickly that General Derkop would not have run an effective campaign in the search for the Emperor's enemies.

Not too far into their journey, Attikus grew weary of his new lieutenants' conversation, which mainly consisted of each trying to outdo the other with tales of bravado. It was time to give them their orders. "Lieutenant Wellick," he said, "you will take your half of the Elite Guard directly to the southeastern port cities and towns. You will coordinate those efforts with your captains. I know the leaders of your companies; there shouldn't be problems. On your way, every town, village, and community is to be addressed. Detailed descriptions and sketches of the criminals should be placed at every inn, marketplace, public house, church, and any other place where groups gather."

"Yes, General," came Wellick's sharp reply, still too formal for what the general was used to from his old lieutenants, but these men were still under the influence of the rumors about him. He wasn't amused by the way they watched him closely, trying to discover which, if any, of the rumors were true.

"You will do the same, Kressin, but your group will patrol the southwest. If they plan to leave the country, we want to be certain they have nowhere to go. You may send a small contingent out to watch the Iron Pass, but only if and when you receive my order to do so."

"Yes, General."

"I will remind you again, the Emperor wants both Isabelle and Henry alive. If they are killed, there will be very serious consequences for anyone involved—imprisonment or worse. The other criminals are under no such restriction. You may do with them as you will."

"General, may I have permission to speak?" Wellick asked.

"Yes."

"What is to be done if the King's soldiers find them before we do?"

"The Emperor has not answered that question yet. I suppose it will become a diplomatic matter at that point." Though Attikus spoke these words, he did not believe them. His suspicions were that the Emperor would go to great lengths to protect his investment and have revenge on his assailant. If the King's men were to succeed before his troops, the general was fairly certain diplomacy would be tossed aside. He preferred to not think about those aspects of the royalty he served; it made sleeping easier.

"General, will we receive further instructions when we accomplish our assignments?" Wellick asked.

"Sooner, most likely," Attikus answered.

That was another difference between Attikus and Derkop. Derkop rewarded his men too often with short periods of leave. Not Attikus. He demanded that his men always be doing something productive. Wellick, he guessed, would flourish under his leadership. Kressin, however . . . it remained to be seen. If he found Kressin needed replacing, Attikus already knew of three good men who could take his place. "With the number of rider stations we have established, you'll be able to reach me by post within two or three days."

The carriage slowed. A glance out the window told Attikus that they had arrived at their outpost in New Germaine. He nodded to his men. "You have your orders." They exited the carriage, and the general's lieutenants turned to face him. Both men saluted the general and repeated the motto, "For the glory of Neverak." Attikus returned their salute with vigor as the carriage rattled away. The Elite Guard companies were already in New Germaine, waiting to be put to use. Wellick, if anyone, would be successful in capturing the criminals. Attikus knew Blithmore extensively. If the criminals hadn't already found some hole to hide in forever, then they were headed south, most likely following the Drewberry River.

According to the reports of the King's Guard and his regular soldiers, several companies had been sent searching along the river. If his hunch was right, then it was only the fortune of the criminals or the blundering of King Germaine's army that had preserved them until now. His mind's eye stretched out, imagining himself to be one of the criminals, desperate and hunted, and it was with this pretense that he made his decisions. Where would they go? Would they, as he imagined, try to leave the country? If so, would they indeed leave by boat? None of the criminals held any real loyalty to the throne except the guardsman, James, yet the Emperor's spies said he had been dishonorably discharged from the King's service just weeks before the attack on the Emperor.

Their other options of emigration were northward into Neverak, heading west over the Great Mountains, southward by sea, or eastward through the Iron Pass into Pappalon. Going into Neverak or trying to cross the mountains so late in the year would be the equivalent of suicide. As for the pass, Attikus knew the stories and did not believe they would take such a risk. Certainly they would make for the southern shore and hire a boat. Though the Emperor had brought him into the hunt a few weeks late, Attikus still had time to beat them to the ports.

He remembered the first execution he had witnessed as a boy. He and his parents had lived in a hovel, cheek-by-jowl with the animals they raised to sell, mostly pigs. In Neverak, executions were special occasions, particularly in small villages, and everyone came to see them. The sentenced man, Keaton, had been the leader of a band of robbers whose swift demise came when they stole a crown jewel en route to the king of Avalon.

The Emperor released the might of Neverak to hunt down Keaton and his men. Their capture—and the Emperor's retribution—was swift. The Elite Guard spared Keaton only long enough to make a public statement to any others who might dare to defy the royal family. Attikus attended the execution with his mother and father, though he was too small to see above the backs and heads of the people in front of him. A strange scent permeated the air, and young Attikus recognized it as the fervor of the crowd around him. It was a rudimentary sensation—a salty, bitter flavor.

Pushing his way to the front of the crowd, Attikus watched as the executioner took a piece of rope, something so harmless and commonplace, and knotted it into a weapon. Its shape fascinated him. Children played games with ropes every day, and yet what he saw as a toy could be used to end a life. The rope ended in a simple circle, but that noose held all the power. It allowed that circle to shrink and shrink until the circle had fastened itself so tight around the victim that escape—and breathing—became impossible. From where he stood, Attikus could see the individual fibers of the noose quivering from the criminal's fear, then going still when Keaton the criminal lost his life.

The noose was a lesson he had never forgotten, but it was only one among the thousands of lessons he'd assimilated into his intellect. In his mind's eye, he saw Wellick marching his troops through Furnton, Dermatosh, Boggermon, Grubbingville, Strandling, Treebush, and finally Bookerton, and a dozen more smaller villages along the way. With every town they passed through, the noose grew tighter and tighter. He knew it was possible that he had been summoned into this affair too late—but that was unlikely. If the timetable he had set for Wellick and Kressin was kept, Wellick would be at Bookerton in three weeks' time, cutting off the criminals' chance of escape to the east. Then any chance of leaving to the south by port would be sealed off by Kressin.

"General," a voice called. Attikus recognized it as of one of his runners. "An urgent letter from Neverak. From the Emperor."

"I'll take it now, thank you," Attikus replied. The boy, no older than fifteen, handed it over, saluted like a man, and received the general's returning salute.

THIRTY-SIX
Disaster at Bookerton

Four miles northeast of Bookerton, in a wooded area that provided barely enough cover, Henry suggested to James they stop and hold council.

"We need some ideas for our strategy in Bookerton," Henry stated, "and I don't have any."

"What's wrong with me going in by myself again?" Ruther asked.

"It will look suspicious," James answered, "if you're going around with two horses loaded down with packs of food."

"Then Brandol and I can do what we did back in Fletchersville—with the nobleman and the squire."

"You'll be the nobleman?" Henry asked.

"Of course," Ruther said, "and Brandol can be my charming, boot-licking squire."

A sharp clatter startled everyone as Brandol threw down his dishes. "I ain't going to Bookerton! I won't do it. You ain't makin' me."

Maggie reached over and grabbed Brandol's arm. "Don't overreact. No one's making you do anything."

Ruther seemed on the verge of saying something rude to Brandol, so Henry interjected with a question. "Ruther, how many times have you performed in Bookerton?"

"I did two one-week stretches. The last was well over a year ago."

"You're no good, Ruther," James stated. "Someone is bound to recognize you."

"*I'm* not wanted. It doesn't matter if I'm recognized."

"You're not thinking like a soldier." James tapped his own head as he spoke. "Bookerton is a major stop for most travelers. There will be a lot of guardsmen and soldiers and possibly even Elite Guard with nothing to do except follow people who look suspicious. A storyteller from Richterton with three horses laden with supplies is suspicious enough to garner their attention."

"Ruther is the best chance we have," Isabelle said. "He's inventive enough to talk himself out of any situation, no matter how strange it may look. I think he's right—he should go."

Ruther gave a grateful nod to Isabelle, who smiled back at him.

Maggie spoke up next. "As much as I loathe the idea of putting my life in Ruther's hands, I don't see a better choice either."

"It's a bad idea to send him alone," James commented. Henry knew those words were meant for Brandol, even though James didn't address the journeyman directly. Brandol kept his gaze fixed on the ground. His face was white but his jaw set. The conversation paused as everyone pondered the same question: who would go with Ruther?

"I won't allow Isabelle or my sister to go," Henry finally said. To make certain Maggie or Isabelle weren't offended, he added, "Not because I think either of you are incapable, but because I want you safe."

"I must disqualify myself as well," James added, but he wouldn't look at anyone as he said it. "It's likely I could be recognized by someone I served with during . . ."

Ruther held out his fingers and began counting. "So that leaves us with—"

Henry threw a pebble at his friend. Despite all the awkward feelings between them recently, Ruther batted it down with a smile. "Like old times, friend." He winked roguishly. "Always getting into trouble."

"And always getting out of it," Henry answered with similar gusto, though he envied Ruther's reckless confidence. "I'll need a disguise, won't I?"

"My blond wig will work."

Isabelle started to object to this idea, but Henry begged her not to with a simple look. Her eyes communicated back to him her worries, and Henry silently told her he understood, but this had to be done.

"It'd be best to go first thing in the morning," James said, "when the market is busiest."

"We should have someone waiting nearby in case something happens," Maggie added.

"I agree. Who should it be?"

Again, everyone was thinking of the same person, and this time Brandol raised his hand, albeit reluctantly.

"Good," James said. "I'll be the second point of the relay."

"Glad that's all settled," Ruther declared. "We should go to bed. Big day tomorrow."

Soon, six ragged beds of blankets were laid around the campfire. Isabelle pulled hers close to Henry's and draped an arm over him. Without even thinking, Henry scooted himself closer to her, kissing her on the cheek.

"Are you worried?" she asked him.

"No," Henry lied. "I'm sure everything will be fine."

He didn't think she believed him. She gave him her best smile and whispered "I love you" in his ear.

"I love you more," he answered back, kissing her again, this time on the lips.

"All right, you two," Ruther called out from the opposite side of the fire, "go to sleep."

Henry didn't think sleep would come easily, but it did. Something about Isabelle's touch and her closeness soothed his mind. His sleep was deep and peaceful, only briefly troubled when he dreamed Ruther was leaving camp again. In his dream, he heard Ghost's soft gait as he bore Ruther away from camp, but Henry's mind was too content to be alarmed.

When he woke in the morning, he felt calm and optimistic. Ruther and James had already eaten. They woke Brandol, who decided to leave without breakfast. The morning was chilly, but they had traveled far enough south that the winter's bite had lost its teeth. The frost on the ground disappeared soon after the sun rose. Henry guessed they had four or five hours yet until noon. Each man rode on his own steed with Henry and Ruther bringing along the spares.

They left James at the edge of a cotton field two miles from Bookerton's markets. He had only his pack, his horse, and his sword. He waved to them as they rode away. "May the Lord of All Worlds grant you protection in the city," he called out.

Henry, Ruther, and Brandol rode on. They had no need to speak now. Everything had been discussed the previous night. The silence was uncomfortable, but Henry didn't break it. His mind was clear, strangely enough. He had expected to wake up anxious or frightened, but no matter how much he thought about the danger, that sense of calmness stayed with him.

Brandol, on the other hand, wasn't even paying attention to the road. His eyes roved over everything, and he constantly looked over his shoulder to see if they were being followed. Henry watched his journeyman with mixed emotions. Brandol would rove around the outskirts of the market as though he was searching for something, staying within distance of Ruther or Henry's call for help. If he heard it, Brandol was to ride to James. After leaving him to his post with words of encouragement, Ruther and Henry rode straightway into town. As they passed the houses and shops, Henry heard the locals speaking in their strong southern accents.

"Do you think they'll be suspicious of us?" he asked Ruther quietly.

"Nar, I 'ighly doort it," Ruther said in a near-perfect replication of the accent. "B'sides, they gert larts of viztors round 'ere, and you look mighty genteel in that big yella wig o' yours."

Henry chuckled and itched under the wig's lining. "I think it better if I refrain from speaking altogether."

"A wonderful suggestion, friend."

The markets were as James had said they would be: busy, even so close to winter. It was one of the great differences between Richterton and Bookerton. In Richterton, the great public markets were closed for almost four months out of the year. In Bookerton, they never closed.

Before entering the market, they dismounted and led their horses on foot, as riding was banned during the busy morning hours. From stand to stand, the streets were jammed with people. It was impossible to move without brushing into someone, and the crowds moved along slowly. Henry wanted to split up to cut the time it took by half, but Ruther insisted on staying together.

"I don't trust you to not give yourself away," he told Henry, still using his Bookerton accent.

They bought dried meat and fruit without incident. Ruther handled the transactions. As they made their way toward the herb stands, Henry's wig was pulled off by a passing woman carrying a large basket on her shoulder. He turned back to see his wig clinging to the brambles of the basket. The large woman didn't even notice it hanging there. Henry thought about stopping her when Ruther cut him off.

"Best to not make a scene."

At the grain stands, someone recognized Ruther. The merchant was a portly man with a good-natured face and no more than a dozen hairs left on his head. When he saw Ruther, his eyes lit up. In an accent so thick that Henry barely understood him, he said, "Now, aren't you that storyteller what 'oo came 'round nowt long ago?"

Ruther basked in the recognition. "Yes. Yes, I am."

The large merchant grabbed Ruther firmly by the hand and said, "Yes, you are! Richard, right?"

Ruther clapped his hands with a laugh. "Yep, that's it in one guess. Richard. What's your name, sir?"

"Willard."

"Good morning, Willard," Ruther said, shaking Willard's dusty hand heartily a second time. "I am in need of grain today."

"Just a moment," Willard said, then cupped his hands around his mouth and shouted, "Gaffen! Now—Gaffen! Come 'ere, Gaffen!"

Henry and Ruther turned to see who Gaffen could be. Toward them peered a tall, pale, and skinny man with a mop of gray-brown hair who'd been selling barley and oats two stands over. The customers to whom he'd been speaking had all turned around to see why Willard was yelling.

"Come 'ere, Gaffen!" Willard shouted.

Gaffen spoke a few more words to his customers and gestured for them to wait. Ruther turned back to Willard and said, "Oh no, that's fine. I actually don't have time—"

"Oh, Gaffen thort you were the best thing to 'appen to 'im since his wife left fer a sailor. He'll wanter meet you."

"Hmmm, I—uh—I might have a moment to spare." Ruther glanced back quickly at Henry, who closed his eyes in frustration.

Gaffen made his way through the crowd until he arrived at Willard's grain stand, pushing past Henry without a thought. Willard turned Gaffen to face Ruther.

"Remember this fella?" Willard said with a gigantic grin on his face. "Don't tell me you don't remember 'im!"

Gaffen's face instantly showed recognition. "The best storyteller in Blithmer! Would I ferget? Ferget Luther?" Gaffen grabbed Ruther's hand and shook it like a dusty rug. "I'm Gaffen. I sell raisins, oats, you name it . . . right o'er there."

"Er, no, Gaffen, it's Richard," Willard said with an embarrassed smile to Ruther.

Ruther patted Gaffen on the shoulder. "Don't fret, it's been over a year."

"You're back in town now, eh?" Gaffen asked. "Where will you be performing?"

"I won't be, unfortunately. I'm passing through on my way west."

Gaffen finally noticed the horses and packs Ruther had brought with him, then his eyes rested on Henry. "This fella with you, too?" he said, jerking a thumb into Henry's face.

"Uh, no," Ruther said. "Not really, I mean. He's pointing me to the places I can find the best grain for Ghost." He patted his horse's face affectionately.

"That's the finest compliment I've 'eard in a while, young man," Willard said to Henry with another extended hand. "What's your name?"

"Without any intentions of being rude in my haste," Ruther added, "I must be moving along. I have many miles and too few days ahead."

"O' course!" Willard said, now moving as though he were twenty years younger to satisfy Ruther's demands. Gaffen, meanwhile, continued to stare at Henry.

"So what is your name?" he asked.

Henry pulled out the first name that popped into his head. "Jennifer—no—Brad."

"Jennifer Nobrad?" Gaffen repeated.

"Ain't Jennifer a girl's name?" Willard asked.

Ruther spoke before Henry had a chance. "Jennifer is actually from up north. Up there, it's becoming very common for folks to name their boys with girls' names, and girls with boys' names."

"I always say them northerners are odd folk, don't I, Gaffen?"

"That you do," Gaffen responded, still looking at Henry, "but I swear there's something familiar aboort this one." The same thumb went back into Henry's face. More than anything, Henry hated being referred to as "this one" because the men adored Ruther. "You certain you and I ain't met b'fore?"

Henry nodded, looking to Ruther for help.

"So let me purchase that grain now," Ruther said with an enthusiastic clap. "If I don't get out of here soon, I'll be late meeting the man who'll be guiding me west."

Right when Gaffen was turning to head back to his oat, raisin, and you-name-it stand, six soldiers passed through the crowd no more than a dozen feet from Willard's grain stand. Panic stung Henry's chest, but he knew if he pretended that he belonged like anyone else, he'd be fine. He told himself a dozen times in two seconds not to look at them, to keep his attention on anything but the soldiers.

But he couldn't help himself, and Gaffen was quick to notice.

"Criminal!" Gaffen screamed over the din of the market. "Criminal 'ere!" His hand clamped on Henry's shirt.

Henry jerked himself free and stumbled backwards into one of the horses. Gaffen screamed again, louder than before, and the soldiers barked orders for the crowd to part for them. Henry picked himself up, and without bothering to look back at Ruther, he called out to Brandol, a short, loud, and distinctive whistle.

Confusion broke out in the marketplace. Between the yelling of the soldiers and the shouting of the crowd, Henry had no chance to collect his thoughts. Women scrambled to pull their children to safety while others hustled to make way before they were injured. Dozens of shoppers rushed over in Gaffen's direction to watch what promised to be an interesting scene. The six soldiers behind him were not guardsmen, but to Henry they were the difference between life and death.

Ten more soldiers turned a corner ahead of him. Behind him were still the six. Henry ducked between two stands: one selling onions, carrots, and potatoes, the other selling fish. The owner of the fish stand picked up a particularly large bass and swung it at Henry, catching him across the bridge of his nose and forehead. Henry took the full impact standing, but felt and heard something snap in his nose. His eyes watered. A smell of blood and fish mixed in his nostrils. The vendor swung again at the back of Henry's head, but Henry ducked it.

"This way," the vendor yelled. "Over 'ere!"

Henry ran between two houses, a tight space even for someone like himself. Something strange was happening. His vision began to narrow. A thick wetness covered his face, and Henry tasted blood, tears, and sweat combined with the slimy residue of the fish. His hands groped at the walls as blackness continued to envelop his vision like a swelling blot of ink. He knew he was not moving fast enough because he heard the soldiers coming into the small alley behind him.

Beyond the narrow alley, he thought he saw someone—Brandol?—on a horse, and he made the call again. Hands behind him tore at his shirt. He ran faster but stumbled again. A body fell against him. As hands scrabbled at him, tearing and yanking his clothes, blackness filled his vision, and his mind went out like a candle in a windstorm.

THIRTY-SEVEN
The King's Guard

Henry awoke briefly when the soldiers jerked him up by his arms. He must have muttered something they didn't like because a thump on the back of the head made him pass out again. He woke up not long after, and another blow to his head gave him the strange sensation that someone had thrown a potato at him. Not three minutes later, he was thrown into a chair, but in his state, every thought in his brain had to travel through miles of cobwebs. He mumbled to himself and tried to move, but his mind was too groggy to do much more. Then a bucketful of frigid water soaked his head.

Henry gasped. He sputtered. He even believed for a moment he had died. When he tried to open his eyes, he found himself unable to do so. Voices around him called for his attention.

"What's your name?" The shout belonged to a man, but it was high-pitched and whining.

Henry almost said, "Henry Vestin," without any hesitation, but he stopped himself. "Jennifer Nobrad," was his answer instead. He did not need his eyes to know that in the silence following his response, the soldiers in the room were exchanging looks of deep skepticism.

"Where are you from?"

"Richterton," he said, hoping one true answer would support the lie. Then he cried out, "What's happened to my nose? The pain is terrible."

296

"It's bleeding."

"It feels like it's on fire," Henry told them, not concealing his terror. He was not lying, either. Something horrible had happened to his nose.

"Do you recognize the name Henry Vestin?" the same grating voice asked.

"Of course!" Henry used his own anger and pain to fuel his lies. "Everyone knows that name. Why can't I open my eyes?"

"Are you him?"

"Am I Henry Vestin?" His own blood and spit almost choked him, and he coughed it up when he tried to fake a laugh. "My name is Jennifer! Why can't I open my eyes?"

"Your eyes are open."

Henry thought the man was lying to him until he tried blinking his eyes and found he could do it. He began to weep. "I can't see! What have you done to me? I can't see!" He tried standing up, but several hands forced him back into his chair where he continued to sob in fear. "What have you done?"

"Why are you in Bookerton?"

Henry was through answering their questions. He struggled once more to his feet. The blindness consumed every thought as he said, "I can still see. I can. I can see." He didn't believe it, but kept repeating it anyway. He needed to hear the words.

"Shut up!" someone snapped at him, striking him on the back of the head. Pain exploded across his face.

Henry's mumblings ended and he fell back onto the chair, quaking as he tried to quell his sobs.

"Who is traveling with you that can confirm your identity?" the soldier questioned. It seemed the more impatient he grew, the higher in pitch his voice became.

"No one," Henry forced himself to say. "I have no friends . . . very little family remaining. Please help me."

"How convenient." The voice sounded more sniveling than whining now. Henry could see this man's smile in his mind's eye as clearly as if he could actually see it. "How terribly convenient. A vagabond, traveling through Bookerton, with no one to claim him. Yet you have the arms of a man who works for a living." The man clasped Henry's hand, which he jerked away. "And your hands are rough. Perhaps like a carpenter's."

"I *am* a hard worker," Henry said, his voice thin and shaky. "I've worked many different jobs to earn my way south. Please . . ."

"Name one person you've worked for."

The first person whose name came into Henry's head was old Master Franklin, the silversmith next door to him in Richterton. "Master Matthew Franklin," he sputtered, praying no one would know to whom he was referring, "the silversmith in Grubbingville."

"Write that down," the man said. Henry heard for the first time the sound of a quill scratching paper, writing down every word spoken. "That will be investigated. You have a long journey ahead of you, *Jennifer*. I doubt that's your name, but it's what I'll call you for now."

"Where am I going?"

"To Richterton, for examination by the Royal Interrogator."

Henry sputtered even worse, feeling drops of blood and spit fly from his lips. What could he say? "You—you can't take me. I—I don't want to go! I'm not the man you want!"

"Shackle him," the man ordered in a voice so excited, so high that it barely registered.

The door slammed open and a pair of boots stomped into the room. "Who is in charge here?" a voice barked so loudly that it startled Henry. He imagined he could hear every head turning toward the man with the whining voice.

"I am, sir!" came a squeak.

"And who in Blithmore are you?"

"Under-Brigadier Ercumist, sir!"

"I know you are not a brigadier!" the new voice stormed. It astonished Henry that this man could bark so loudly without losing his voice. "Do you know *how* I know that?"

"No, sir."

"*Because a brigadier would have followed orders!*" the man bellowed so loudly that several people in the room jumped, including Henry.

"I have not disobeyed orders, sir," came a response so weak and high that Henry thought the name Jennifer might be attached to the wrong person.

"Are you not aware that the King's Guard was to be alerted immediately when one of the high-priority criminals were taken into custody?"

"Yes, sir!"

"Then why did I not receive word?"

"I sent word immediately to Lieutenant Wellick—"

"*Lieutenant?* We don't have *lieutenants* in Blithmore! Lieutenant Wellick is an officer of the Neverak Elite Guard!"

"Yes, sir, but—"

"And the soldiers of King Germaine do *not* take orders from the Elite Guard!"

Henry had temporarily slipped out of the insanity his blindness and the pain in his face had caused. He wondered how long this man could keep yelling. The new officer stood close, close enough that Henry got a whiff of his terrible breath.

"'In a time of joint cooperation—'" the under-brigadier squeaked.

"Don't you *dare* recite code to me!" the new man shouted. More stomping and swearing came, followed by a smack. The whining soldier yelped and hit the ground.

"I am the reigning officer from the King's Guard. You answer to me!"

"Yes, sir!"

"Has this man been interrogated?" the booming voice of the guardsman asked.

"Yes, sir!"

"What is his name?"

"Jennifer Nobrad, sir!" The under-brigadier's answer was followed by a brief commotion punctuated with yelps, grunts, enraged interjections, and vile curses: "Disgrace of a soldier! Jennifer is a woman's name! Never would have believed it! Not fit to wear the uniform of Blithmore!"

The under-brigadier whined for mercy, and when it finally came, he began to sob.

"Who is *second* in command here?" came the question.

Henry wondered if anyone would dare to volunteer.

"I am, sir," came a voice directly to Henry's right. It was much braver than Henry had expected.

"Name and rank."

"Captain Markel Steele."

"Captain Steele," the angry guardsman said, getting nearer to Henry. The guardsman's breath hovered around Henry's face, choking him. "Here are your orders: Clear out your men. Give word to Second Guard Hanson on the far west end of town to send a half-company of guardsmen to me. Write yourself a letter of promotion for me to sign, and as your first act of duty, demote Under-Brigadier Ercumist to stable duty at Germaine Castle. It's clear that he is unfit to oversee anything but horse droppings."

Henry heard no hesitation in Captain Steele's voice, only compliance. "Clear out," the new Under-Brigadier shouted with fresh vigor.

"And Steele . . ." the guardsman barked.

"Yes, sir?"

The guardsman now stood at Henry's feet, close enough for Henry to feel the man's breath on his nose and lips. The smell almost made him gag. "Hand me that horsewhip."

The hairs on the back of Henry's neck stood straight up at *horse-whip*. He again lost control of his emotions. The fear of being discovered, the blindness, the pain in his nose, the smell from the guardsman's mouth, the thought of being whipped—all of it came to a head and he broke down.

"Please . . . I don't want . . . I'm blind . . . don't whip . . ."

As he blubbered in terror, he heard the man walk away to receive the whip.

"Thank you, Steele. See that you follow your orders."

The brutal guardsman slammed the door shut. When Henry heard the first crack of the whip he lost all abandon and screamed. He screamed and screamed without realizing the whip had not hit him.

"Henry!" a voice hissed in his ear. "Henry, stop it!"

Henry's mind was so far along the path of madness that it took a hard shake from rough hands to call him to his senses.

"Shut up, Henry, don't you recognize me?"

Henry gasped for air. It was James. The brutal, barking, foul-breathed voice belonged to James. Henry's voice cracked as he cried out to his savior: "I'm blind, James! I'm blind! I can't see anything. Not light or dark."

"We can deal with that, Henry." James touched Henry's nose with his hands. "Your nose is probably going to be crooked for the rest of your life as well. We need to leave this place before more men come. Do you understand?"

Henry nodded. "How—how did you get your breath to stink like that?"

"A special powder made with rotten onions we use sometimes to make soldiers miserable." James pulled Henry to his feet, supporting him with an arm, and helped Henry take his first steps. Henry put most of his weight on James, trusting him to be his guide. Only a few steps outside the guardhouse, James ran into more trouble.

"We heard word one of the Richterton rebels was caught," another new voice said.

"It was a mistake. This is not the man we're searching for," James barked back, resuming the terrible voice Henry still did not recognize.

"Forgive me, sir," the same voice replied, "but this man matches the description and sketches we've been given by the King."

"What's your name, soldier?" James asked.

"Ranger Ryan Thompson," the young soldier replied.

James muttered something about insolent rangers, and Henry felt a jerk and a sudden heat in front of his face. The crackling of a lit torch filled his ears. "Does this help?" James shouted. "There's no reaction at all. This man is blind. He's been taken advantage of by your men."

"Yes, sir," Thompson said, "but we were sent here to inquire about you, too."

"What about me?"

"With all respect, sir, one of the Richterton rebels was a First Guardsman. James Oslan."

"I know his name!" James replied. "I'm not him."

"We require proof of that, sir."

James swore at Ranger Thompson. Henry couldn't imagine what Isabelle would have said if she heard the stream of curses flying from James's mouth. "This is insubordination. If you wish to request my commission papers, show me someone with the authority to do so."

"Yes, sir!" Thompson said. "Until then, it's been requested that we escort you to headquarters."

Henry heard the clopping of horses' hooves on the stone around the guardhouse. An old man's wheezing voice called out in a thick southern accent, "Excuse me, I've received word that First Guard Wilmore is here. May I speak to him?"

"Who are you?" Ranger Thompson asked.

"Friar Bentley," the old man croaked. "Is Wilmore here?"

Henry tried to follow all the voices with his head, but being unable to see made it utterly useless to do anything but stand and listen.

"I'm here," James answered.

"Ah, it 'tis you," came the response. Henry could hardly understand him through the ancient accent. "I didn't see you there, Wilmore. These eyes of mine used to see clear across the town, can you believe it? Now I can hardly see ten feet ahead—if I ride slowly."

"What's your business here, Friar?" Ranger Thompson asked.

"At the House of the Lord of All Worlds we take in the homeless, naked, and lame." The scent of ale was thick on the friar's breath. "Doesn't that man look lame to you? These eyes of mine have never seen lamer."

"I sent for the friar to have this man sheltered for the night," James said, still using his ask-me-no-questions voice.

A pause told Henry that Ranger Thompson was trying to decide what to do. Finally, the decision came. "Friar, you may escort this man to the church so long as you keep him there under close watch. We may summon him for further questioning. Newsome!"

"Yes, sir!" yet another soldier said with a snap. Henry hadn't even known he was there.

"Return to headquarters and find someone who can inquire about First Guard Wilmore. I will remain with him until you return."

"Yes, sir!" was followed by the sound of a horse departing at full speed.

"Leave now, Friar," Thompson ordered.

Henry felt James's and the friar's strong hands helping him onto the horse behind the friar.

"Wait a minute!" Ranger Thompson's command froze everyone.

"Yes?"

"What need does an old friar have of a sword?" Thompson's voice had become interrogating once more.

The old friar replied, "You need to read the Word more, young man. The good Lord of All Worlds once said, 'I did not come to bring peace, but a sword.'" Then Henry felt the old man move quickly—very quickly—and heard him unsheathe his sword. It cut through the air followed by what Henry could only guess was the sickening sound of the haft of the sword striking the soldier's head.

"And I am His disciple."

THIRTY-EIGHT

The Jeweler

Ruther let James lead the way back to camp. James took them on a long, tortuous route, stopping every few minutes to check for signs of being followed. Henry clung to Ruther as they rode. Ruther wanted to say something to comfort his friend, but didn't know what to say. He couldn't remember the last time he'd been so frightened or felt so guilty.

After Henry had been taken by the soldiers in the market, Ruther had finished purchasing the grain then headed back to camp as fast as he could manage all the horses. Brandol wasn't there, but James was in the carriage changing into his guardsman uniform.

"James won't speak to us," Maggie said. Tears streaked her face, and her cheeks bore imprints from her fingernails. "Please tell us what's going on!"

"Is Henry all right, Ruther?" Isabelle asked. "Where is he?"

"I'm sorry, but I don't have time to explain," Ruther told them as he opened the back compartment of the carriage, grabbed his monk's robe and sword, then closed it again. "Hurry, James!"

"Head back to the market," James barked back like he was a soldier giving orders. "Find Brandol and figure out where Henry has been taken. I'll meet you at the east end."

Ruther found Brandol, who had followed Henry to where he'd been taken, then returned to the spot where James had been stationed. After telling Brandol to head back to camp, Ruther met with James at the east end of the market. It was James who came up with the plan to rescue Henry and executed it with perfection. Ruther had to admit he was impressed with James's improvisation.

After two hours of riding and checking to be certain they weren't being followed, Ruther, Henry, and James approached the camp. James paused once more to survey the area for any pursuers. This time, he found one. Brandol, pale as the white horse he was riding, appeared not more than a stone's throw away. James cursed to himself, and Ruther knew why. Brandol was riding one of the carriage horses, which meant the horse was not harnessed to the carriage, which meant another delay before they could leave. And the last thing their party needed now was more delays.

Ruther whistled to Brandol, who turned and rode to them. His face was dirty, his eyes wide and still watery. "Everything's wrong," he muttered almost is if James and Ruther weren't there. "We're all going to die. We're all runts." When he saw Henry clutching Ruther's waist, he started to cry.

"Where have you been, Brandol?" James asked.

"Lost," he groaned. "I didn't know where to go after you said to go back, because I—I—I was scared! So scared! Master Henry, is you all right? I'm sorry! I was scared!"

After calming Brandol down, the four men returned to camp. Isabelle and Maggie came running when the men approached. Ruther had never seen Maggie so distraught. Her face, puffy and pale, revealed red eyes and deep worry lines carved into her skin. Her fingers pressed into her cheeks, and when she saw Henry behind Ruther she cried even harder.

James stopped Maggie and Isabelle from asking questions by commanding: "Talk later. We need to leave. Brandol, help Henry into the carriage while Ruther and I prepare the horses. Isabelle, you'll ride Quicken. Maggie, get on the carriage."

Fortunately for everyone, Maggie and Isabelle had shown excellent foresight by packing the new supplies into the carriage and readying the harnesses. Ruther helped Henry climb off the horse and into Brandol's arms. Maggie grabbed Henry's face and held him to her, but when she tried to ask Ruther what had happened, James interrupted.

"Later."

The moment Ruther and James finished securing the horses in their harnesses, the party began traveling east. The day had grown late, and while only two hours of sunlight remained, Ruther knew their trek would push on late into the night. He rode next to the carriage to be of some comfort to his friend, even if he could not be seen or heard by him. Up front, James spoke to Maggie and Isabelle.

"We—we—we ain't going to make it to no pass, Master Henry," Brandol told Henry inside the carriage. "They gonna hunt us down. We—we ain't gonna make it. They near got you in Bookerton, now they must know we're here. They'd've killed me if they caught me. They know where we are. I don't want ta die. Everything's so dark now. I—I don't want ta die."

Ruther listened for several minutes while the journeyman muttered on and on about being caught. Brandol's voice was quiet and high-pitched, not at all normal, but he never seemed bothered by Henry's lack of response. It reminded Ruther of men he'd seen caught cheating at dice and backed into a corner, desperate to say whatever it took to save their necks. He finally asked the journeyman to stop and allow Henry some rest.

Dropping back from the group, Ruther sighed as he thought about Brandol. The one person who had not wanted to be involved in Henry's dilemma had been named, along with his master, one of the most dangerous criminals in the country. What a lucrative tale *that* would make someday! Ruther wondered why he'd never spoken to Brandol about their identities being mistaken at the Glimmering

Fountain. Then again, Brandol had never brought it up with Ruther either.

James, Maggie, and Isabelle were deep in conversation as they rode side by side. Maggie asked Ruther to join their discussion. He urged Ghost forward until he was next to Isabelle.

"Is Henry really blind?" Maggie asked him.

"I don't know."

"What happened to his face?" Isabelle asked. "It's so swollen. Did the soldiers beat him?"

"I didn't see much," Ruther said. He reached for his flask of ale and took a long swig, feeling better instantly.

"But you rode with him."

"He didn't say much."

Ruther gave his version of what happened from when he, Henry, and Brandol had left James, carefully omitting the poor decisions he'd made which had led to Henry's capture. The ale helped him through his story, and the flask was empty by the time he reached the tale's end. Isabelle listened closely, her face almost as emotionless as James's. Her constant glances at the carriage betrayed her worry. Maggie, meanwhile, seemed unable to control herself. Several times while he spoke she covered her face, sniffing loudly. When Ruther finished, she whispered a word of gratitude and fell silent. Ruther did not reply. He deserved no gratitude.

The topic of conversation turned to the ramifications of Henry's injuries, and what the group would do if his blindness were permanent.

"He'll be fine," Isabelle said. "Henry's intelligent. He can adapt to anything. Give him enough time and you won't even know he's blind." The care Ruther heard in her voice made him feel small.

They continued east at the fastest pace they could manage. The night brought a chilling breeze with clear skies. They built no fire and carried no torches. The moons were large and low, giving enough light that they easily kept to the route Wilson had marked for them on their map. Only Maggie seemed to struggle keeping to the trails in the twilight. James asked her several times if she was getting too tired to drive, but she insisted she wasn't even sleepy.

Every half hour, Ruther or James rode off from the group to check for signs of being pursued. After several hours with no evidence of being followed, James and Ruther decided they were safe, at least for the night. Ruther thought it ironic that he had fought Henry about using Wilson's advice. If anything saved them now, it would be Wilson's map keeping them off the main roads.

Very late into the night, James brought the company to a halt. "We should take turns keeping watch. I'll do it tonight and then sleep in the carriage tomorrow. Isabelle has volunteered to take the second night. Brandol will take the third. Then Maggie, then Ruther. We'll rotate in that pattern until we reach the Iron Pass."

No one argued or debated his decision. They were too tired. Ruther fell asleep quickly despite the lumpiness of the ground and the wind blowing across his face. His dreams were filled with shadows and angry voices; when James woke him early in the morning, he felt like he hadn't slept at all.

Henry came out for breakfast with everyone else. He let Isabelle wash the blood off his face, which improved his appearance a great deal. The swelling around his eyes and nose had gone from a dull red to a dark purple and green, and his nose was slightly crooked. Isabelle sat on his left, and Ruther occupied the space to Henry's right. No one spoke, but Ruther noted that the others kept glancing at Henry. He knew what they were thinking. What would they do with a blinded leader? How could Henry manage a woodworking shop with no sight?

Ruther watched Henry pick the raisins out of his bowl for several seconds before he actually realized what Henry was doing. Then he began to laugh. It was a teeth-clenched snicker that turned into a full-bellied howl—one he desperately needed. The stares went from Henry to Ruther, who doubled over, clutching his stomach.

"What are you laughing at?" Maggie asked.

Ruther could only point at Henry, who now had the same case of the fits.

"What is so funny?" Maggie asked again.

Ruther didn't answer. Hysteria had overcome him.

"I can see!" Henry announced, holding up the raisins. "I can see. Not very well, but I can make out the shapes of the raisins in the bowl."

Isabelle shouted her joy and hugged Henry to the ground, kissing him furiously. When her lips gave him enough room, he yelled, "Careful, my nose still hurts!"

Ruther watched Maggie trying to decide between beating Henry to death and crying. She finally settled on stumbling over to the carriage under the pretense of searching for something. Isabelle almost had to be pried off Henry, and even James chuckled at them kissing each other. Henry had transformed a glum breakfast into a cheerful event, and cheer was something they all needed.

Over the next several days, cold winds blew in from the north. Henry's improving health and vision offset the worst of the wind's effects on the company's mood, but good fortune did not warm their skin as it did their hearts. As the party moved east into the foothills of the Iron Forest, a bitter wind crashed into them with full force. The company remained hopeful because beyond the foothills waited the pass.

James remained cautious as ever, assigning a watch both day and night. On Brandol's second night standing watch, Ruther approached the journeyman to see if he could take his place.

"Why would you want ta do that?" Brandol asked.

"I haven't been feeling well, and I could use a day of rest in the carriage."

Brandol made his skepticism known by the face he made, but still agreed to let Ruther keep watch.

It was a quiet night in the foothills. Ruther waited two hours after everyone went to bed before making his move. He'd intentionally tied Ghost with a weak knot so it took little effort to undo. He put several double crowns in his pocket along with a lumpy red cloth, grabbed his sword, and started off heading south. He rode quietly, so as to not wake anyone, but after putting distance between himself and the camp, he rode Ghost at a light gallop. A little voice in the back of his mind nagged him about leaving the group unguarded, but the chance of anything actually happening now was slim to none, despite James's belief.

He rode south for almost an hour to a small, sturdy village named Reddings. The homes and shops were sights he had not seen in over ten years, not since moving to Richterton with his dying uncle. As clusters of houses appeared, memories popped into Ruther's head, things he hadn't thought about since he'd left. Most of them were memories of his uncle; others were of friends he'd made or small adventures he had been a part of that now seemed trite.

He looked for one house in particular, the one he'd ridden all that way to visit. He didn't think twice about the unwelcome hour when he knocked four times with the palm of his hand.

He listened for movement, but heard nothing, so he knocked again, harder this time. A loud grumble came from upstairs along with the shuffling of feet and creaking boards. The glow of a lantern appeared under the door, first dim, then brighter.

"Who in the—" a rough voice with a faded Pappalonian accent shouted as the door jerked back and the lantern's brightness blinded Ruther. The owner of the house peered closer at the intruder's face. "By the devil himself. Ruther? *Ruther?* Is that really—?"

"Yes, it is."

"When did ya turn into a small whale?"

"What do you mean?"

The man poked Ruther square in the stomach. By nature, he spoke very quickly. "I mean you're fat. You're a pig with red hair. What do ya want?"

"Remember the favor you always told me you owed my uncle?"

"What about it? You're here to collect on it? At the most sun-forsaken hour of a frigid night? Are ya a fool? Of course ya are! Why do I even ask?"

"So you'll do it?"

"Do ya have money?"

"You owe my uncle the favor."

"If ya had come during the day, it would be free. In the middle of the night, the favor is me answering the door."

Ruther smiled and removed two double crowns from his pocket, though he still had more inside. The man scowled when he saw it.

"You're a miser. This better be an easy job."

From his other pocket, Ruther removed the red lumpy cloth and handed it to the man. "Please, Quincy, can you fix this?"

Quincy took the lump and unwrapped it. Maggie's necklace gleamed in the light of the lantern. He picked it up gingerly and examined it. "Who made this, may I ask?"

"I don't know," Ruther answered, impatient in the cold, "but I'm short on time."

"All right! All right! Go around back, and I'll let ya in."

Ruther followed Quincy's instructions, and the back door opened to him.

"I never thought I'd be seeing ya again, ya know? And I won't lie, it's good that I did."

"Thank you." Ruther couldn't help grinning. "It's been almost eleven years, hasn't it?"

Quincy grunted his affirmation as he busied himself building up the fire in the bellows. Ruther took a seat on a bench and watched the sturdy old man work in his small but tidy shop. It reminded him of the many hours he had sat in the same place doing the same thing as a lad. In those days, more often than not, a bowl of soup had rested in his hand, compliments of Quincy's wife. Each day Quincy would ask Ruther to make up a story and tell it. Then the jeweler would pick the tale apart after Ruther finished.

Quincy scanned his tools through weary eyes. His thin, gray hair was tousled in parts, flattened in others. "So what are ya doing here, boy?"

"It's a long story," Ruther replied.

Quincy chuckled at the remark. "So what are ya waiting for?"

"Can I trust you to keep a few secrets?"

Quincy glared at him as he began blowing air into the fire.

"Sorry," Ruther responded.

He missed having a bowl of soup in his hand as he told his story, but he wished even more that he had some ale. Quincy's wife was a fine cook, and Ruther's stomach grumbled. He started his tale by giving Quincy a brief history of his life in Richterton: how his uncle used his last connections to get Ruther a place as an apprentice with the late Mr. Vestin, his education there, the blunders that led to his being kicked out by Mrs. Vestin at age sixteen, and finally, his decision to become a traveling storyteller.

As Ruther spoke, Quincy worked on the necklace, fixing the broken links and adding touches here and there to make it look better than the day it had been cast. Ruther paused only when the jeweler would hold up his hand, staring angrily at a bit of gold. He would mutter to himself in frustration, then say, "Go on now, boy. Go on."

Ruther felt like he was ten again. The acrid smell of molten metal and the hissing sound of water meeting fire comforted him. The jeweler stopped him to ask questions every so often, just as he had when they were both over a decade younger.

"Hard to believe you got caught up in all this nonsense with the Emperor of Neverak."

"I know."

"It sounds to me like you've become a lot like your uncle whether ya wanted that or not."

Ruther frowned. "What? Why?"

"Don't act like a shocked woman, Ruther," the jeweler said. "Look at yourself: no wife, no job, I can tell ya drink too much because you're so fat, and I'll bet ya gamble, too. Probably up to your ears in debt."

"I'm *not* my uncle."

Quincy pointed his metal tongs at Ruther's gut. "Yes, ya are. Ya loved your uncle, didn't ya?"

"You know I did."

"Then, confound it all! Why would ya become him? That's the last thing he'd have wanted for ya."

"I'm not my uncle," Ruther repeated.

Quincy held up the necklace with all the love and tenderness a jeweler could show a string of gold. "Ya love her?"

"No," Ruther answered without hesitation.

"Then ya are your uncle," the jeweler told him, "because he couldn't love either."

"He loved me."

"He *liked* ya," Quincy said, still inspecting the necklace with eyes too old to be so keen. "Close as he could to loving ya, but he never did. He told me that once." His eyes slowly moved from the necklace to Ruther, whose face had fallen.

"I don't believe you, Quincy," Ruther said before thinking. It wasn't Quincy's place to say such things. "He—he told me he loved me." As he said it, he searched his memory for a specific instance when his uncle *had* told him that.

"Your uncle only loved two things, and ya know what they were because neither of them were named Ruther."

Ruther's chest heaved twice, and he stood up to calm himself. "I still don't believe you."

"Now don't go blowing your lid, Ruther," the jeweler said, almost amused. "Your necklace is done." Ruther moved to accept it, but the jeweler pulled it back. "Where in all of Atolas did ya get it?"

"It isn't mine."

"Then ask her where she got it from."

"It was her mother's."

Quincy gazed lovingly on it once more. "There must be some story behind this necklace, for I've seen very few that equal it. Can't you see how magnificent it is?"

Ruther looked at the necklace closer. Other than the gold, he did not see what made it so grand. "How much would you say it's worth?"

The jeweler pulled the chain away from Ruther with mock disdain. "I won't tell ya so as not to tempt ya."

Ruther made an impatient noise with his lips. "Really, Quincy, I wouldn't sell it!"

"I'll tell ya if ya tell me why ya want it fixed," the jeweler teased.

"All right. It's a parting gift." Ruther hated the guilt that stung his heart as he voiced his intentions aloud.

Quincy wrapped it gently in the red cloth and handed it back to Ruther with similar care. "Depends on where ya sold it. In the south, ya'd get four—maybe three or four hundred crowns for it. In the north, closer to Richterton, double or triple that."

Ruther wished now he hadn't asked its price. He *was* tempted. Did Maggie know this? Did she even have a hint of its value? The jeweler saw all this in his face and shook his head.

"You're a pathetic man, Ruther," he said. "I won't lie, I expected more of ya. I expected ya to use your gift to tell stories and change the world."

"I *do* tell stories," Ruther answered glumly.

"Then ya gamble and drink all your money away so nobody gives one lick about ya as a man. Ya got no credibility."

Ruther shook his head. "Thank you for the repair, Quincy. It will mean a lot to my fr—my friend's sister."

Quincy took Ruther's hand in his and kissed it with dry lips, a Pappalonian custom. "It was good to see ya, Ruther. Real good. How old are ya, boy?"

"Barely twenty-one."

Quincy nodded as though he'd known this all along. "Then you've got plenty of time to change."

Ruther gave the jeweler a small smile and pocketed the necklace in its cloth. "I don't know about that, Quincy. I don't know about that at all." It weighed heavier in his pocket than before, far more than the additional repairs could have added. When Quincy opened the door, Ruther saw a faint glow on the horizon and swore under his breath.

"I've been here far too long! I've got to go!" he ran for his horse and called out over his shoulder, "Thank you again!"

Quincy stood in the doorway waving at Ruther as he rode away. Ruther made the best time he could on his way back, but he knew he would be very lucky to find everyone still asleep when he returned, especially with James's cursed military habits. Exhausted and worried as he came to the hill nearest where his friends camped, Ruther steeled himself for the worst.

THIRTY-NINE
A General's Post

Three days after Henry's party escaped Bookerton, Attikus sat deep in council with his sub-lieutenants when his daily post arrived. Attikus followed the runner with his eyes as the young man passed the window and let himself inside the general's quarters. The boy held a small stack of papers and envelopes, most of which were reports from his various subordinates throughout the field, perhaps a personal note from a family member.

One in particular caught his attention: an envelope near the top bearing the royal Neverak seal. It was no great thing to receive parcels from the Emperor, but this one was different. It was in a black envelope with a red seal. Emperor Ivan had carried over the tradition from his father: a letter inside a black envelope with the red seal of the Emperor was to be read alone and burned immediately after the recipient finished reading it.

"Excuse me a moment," he said as he stood.

The other soldiers stood and saluted him as he left to return to his own quarters. Rather than returning the salute, he accepted his mail and left. This was the first black envelope he'd received since his reinstatement as general. He had received only two during his entire service to the old emperor.

He closed the door to the adjacent room and locked it. By the light of the fire in the fireplace, he checked the envelope for any signs of tampering. Satisfied everything was in order, he opened it:

> General Attikus,
>
> Your orders in regards to the "Richterton rebels" have changed. The Carpenter and the slave are still to be captured and delivered to the palace with no more harm than is necessary, particularly on the part of the slave. However, the rest of the party is to be allowed to escape, without exception, in order to preserve the illusion that the rebels remain at large.
>
> It is in the Empire's best interest that the Carpenter and slave are secured without the knowledge of the Blithmore army and royalty. Furthermore, no evidence should remain of their apprehension. Your orders are to remove any evidence of their capture at any reasonable cost.
>
> On a personal note, your youngest son recently received his commission in the Elite Guard. I do not doubt that your example will lead your son to a brilliant career in the service of Neverak. My blessings are upon you.
>
> > For the glory of Neverak,
> > Emperor Ivan Richter Krallick III

Attikus burned the letter the moment he finished reading it. The heat of the crackling fire that consumed the parchment was nothing compared to the furnace raging inside him. He wanted to scream the Emperor's name in conjunction with every curse he knew. The epistle had been an insult with every word, every sentence—a backhanded slap across his face that would be never be forgotten.

Did the Emperor think Attikus's loyalty needed to be anchored to Neverak by veiled threats against his children? Apparently. Furthermore, after years of impeccable service to his father and years of teaching and training Ivan in swordplay and the art of war, the Emperor rewarded the general with deceit.

The general's own mistakes also glared at him. He had ignored what he knew resided in the Emperor's heart simply because he had loved Ivan's father like a brother. He had gone against the quiet voice in the back of his mind warning him to not trust a man known to keep slaves and murder those who offended him. After a lifetime of military service, where insults and backstabbing were common as men climbed over one another to secure promotions and placements, Attikus was certainly familiar with this kind of behavior, but not from the man to whom he had pledged fealty under any circumstance.

He sat in his chair and gazed over a table strewn with maps laden with small lead figures that represented several hundred Elite Guard—his work. He wanted to wipe everything off and throw the table across the room, but he knew it would not improve his situation. Nor would it help to let bad thoughts stew. Then it occurred to him that he had not finished reading his post. He returned to the pile; those he deemed important he put in one stack, the rest in a second.

He read report after report from his lieutenants and sublieutenants explaining why they had no sign of the rebels. Each of these reports would be saved for future reference, although Attikus rarely referred to them. He possessed the ability to recall anything he read, and kept reports only for proof of the information he acted upon.

One of the last pieces of post was not a report, nor was it an arrogant betrayal from an emperor. In fact, he did not know *what* it was. At first glance, he suspected it to be a personal letter from his wife, but she did not use such crude parchment for her letters. On the front was scribbled:

to the leader of the armies

Whoever the writer was, he had scribbled this in haste, then folded the paper in half. The penmanship inside was no different:

we are going to iron pass. east Bookerton in hills. i have writ of passage. exchange this letter for freedom.

Beneath this cryptic message was only blank parchment, no name or insignia. Attikus added the letter to the stack of important documents, wondering how credible the information could be. After all, the Iron Pass was the place he least expected the criminals to go. No sooner had this thought crossed his mind than a knock came at the door. A rider of the Elite Guard waited outside bearing another letter.

"General," the soldier said in salute, "urgent news from Lieutenant Wellick."

Attikus accepted it with thanks and began reading. The report left him very upset. It detailed the capture of a man fitting the description of Henry Vestin by Blithmore soldiers, his release by a member of the King's Guard who did not exist, but fitted the description of the former–First Guardsman James Oslan. It revealed details of an assault on a soldier by a monk wearing a robe identical to the one Vestin had worn in the Glimmering Fountain.

Attikus wasted no time. He collected his papers and returned to the council. If he acted immediately, the criminals might be cut off. If Vestin's party reached the pass first, it would be impossible to take them at all.

He reentered the meeting to set forth a storm of action. First, he briefed his sub-lieutenants on the information, then he gave specific orders that two independent companies should go to the pass taking separate routes, one through the hills and one on the roads. Whichever reached the entrance to the pass first would set up a bivouac and scout, waiting for the other. Then, in private, he wrote a reply to Lieutenant Wellick, ordering him to assume command of the first company that arrived at the pass, repeating to him the same instructions he had received from the Emperor. Finally, Attikus sealed the orders, gave them to a waiting rider, and sent him away on the freshest and swiftest horse.

FORTY

The Theft

Less than an hour before Ruther rode back into camp from Quincy's shop, James roughly shook Henry awake. "Ruther's gone, Henry! Get up! Ruther's gone!"

Henry thought James had made some mistake. Night still covered the sky, with only the faintest glimmer of the rising sun. "Gone?" he repeated as he squinted his eyes to peer around the camp. "Where did he go?"

James's jaw was clenched, his eyes ablaze. "I don't know. Get up. I'll wake the others."

Henry slowly looked over to the horses. Ghost was not tied up with the rest. The old suspicions planted in his mind by Wilson then sown by Ruther's actions blossomed yet again. Henry headed straight to the carriage, determined to count the gold and see for himself what remained. James went back to waking up the rest of the travelers, starting with Isabelle.

Henry's vision, still not fully restored from the fish attack, was too cloudy to see well inside the carriage. He rummaged around for a few minutes, then called for help. Isabelle was the first to respond.

"What's the matter?" she asked sleepily. "Ruther wouldn't have left us, would he?"

"Can you find the gold for me?" he asked her.

"Why?"

"I want to count it."

The bags of gold were usually easy to locate. When she didn't find it right away, Henry started worrying.

"Henry, it isn't here! All the bags are gone!"

James cursed Ruther when he heard Isabelle. He grabbed his pack and mounted Sissy.

Henry ran over and held Sissy's harness. "Where are you going?"

"You know where," James answered, gripping the reins tighter.

"No!" Isabelle told him. "That's a foolish idea. We can't wait here for you."

"I know," James said, not looking back at his sister, "but my intentions have never been to follow you into Pappalon. Keep going until you reach the pass. I'll catch up to you after I find Ruther and the gold."

Henry wasn't surprised at James's pronouncement, but Maggie and Isabelle were appalled. Brandol seemed incapable of doing anything but standing in place and listening to the conversation with his mouth open. Again Henry was not surprised. Brandol's nerves had grown worse every day since they'd left Bookerton.

"Why aren't you coming with us?" Isabelle asked.

"I have my reasons. Finding Ruther adds one more to the list."

"You planned to leave us all this time?" Maggie asked. "You're a fugitive, James—you'll be killed."

Isabelle grabbed her brother's arm. "Why didn't you tell me this earlier?"

Maggie hushed them all. The other four voices quickly fell quiet. "Someone's coming." She pointed southward. James put his hand to the hilt of his sword. Isabelle grabbed the largest pan. Henry crept out over the crest of the hill and saw Ruther riding Ghost over the hills not far in the distance.

"It's him," Henry said.

They waited in silence for Ruther to ride into camp. James

unsheathed his sword, stabbed it into the ground, and yanked Ruther down from the horse hard onto the earth.

"James, no!" Henry shouted as he ran to Ruther. James shook Ruther like a rag doll, and twice slammed his fist into Ruther's face.

"You took our gold!" James cried. The voice of the brutal guard was back as James continued to jerk Ruther up and down. "Tell us where the gold is, you filthy thief!"

Henry tried to pull James off Ruther before he landed another crushing blow to Ruther's swelling face. Isabelle held onto Maggie's dress to stop her from joining James. Brandol sat in the dirt moaning, "Lord of All Worlds, help us! We're all dead!"

James shoved Henry onto his back, but it allowed Ruther to squirm his way out from underneath his attacker. When Ruther drew his sword and pointed it at James, Henry thought James was a dead man. Henry had seen Ruther in bad situations before, some of them even recently, but Ruther had never had such a fearsome look in his eyes, a feral expression of both terror and rage.

A large cooking pan sailed through the air and caught Ruther on the side of his head. He fell hard and hit the ground groaning. James pounced on him, wrested the sword away, and dragged him over to a fallen log. Ruther made no attempt to resist. His eyes were dull and unfocused.

Henry looked over at Isabelle, who had thrown the pan.

"I couldn't let him hurt James," she explained. "I thought—I thought—"

James rummaged through Ruther's pockets and pulled out several items, some of great interest to the group, others not: three double crowns and several pieces of lesser coinage, a small map, a feather pen and torn parchment, and a lumpy red cloth. Once satisfied Ruther's pockets were empty, James went to the fire Brandol had just built and removed the pot of water.

"Don't do that," Henry and Isabelle both shouted in protest, but before they could stop him, James threw the water in Ruther's face.

Ruther yelped and cursed several times at James while spitting water out of his mouth and coughing up the rest.

"Let's talk," James said. He squatted down in front of Ruther.

"Wait!" Henry said. "Let's all—"

"Stay out of this, Henry," James warned, still sounding like the man Henry had heard ordering soldiers around in Bookerton.

"You are not interrogating him," Henry said. "He came back. He deserves a chance to tell us his story."

"*Story*," James said as if Henry had uttered a vile word. He gestured angrily at Ruther. "What has he ever done but tell stories? I'm not going to let him be comfortable enough to tell another story."

"I won't let you hurt him."

"Neither will I, James," Isabelle said. "You're not that kind of person."

"I *am* that kind of person," James answered. "If that disappoints you then so be it, but I don't hear Maggie or Brandol disagreeing with me."

Henry looked at Maggie, but Maggie refused to meet his eyes. "Maggie . . ." he said softly, but she refused to look at him. "*Maggie!*"

"No, Henry!" she answered with a voice as loud and angry as his. "You think Ruther's your friend—you've always thought he's your friend, but look! Open your eyes! He is not!"

"He is," Henry said, "and so is James, and I will not watch my friends harm each other."

Maggie did not answer; James did not protest. Henry turned to Ruther now, his expression neither kind nor cold. "All right, Ruther, tell us everything."

The way Henry said that last word got Ruther's attention. Everyone stared down at him as he squirmed like a worm on a hook. His clothes were so disheveled he couldn't hold himself normally. His face had turned bright red with purple splotches and small scrapes, all testaments of the abuse he'd suffered. His eyes, normally bright and laughing, were now bloodshot and drooping. Despite everything Henry knew about Ruther, he didn't believe his friend could have stolen the gold. Maggie and James had to be wrong—they had to be.

"What do you want me to say?" Ruther asked in a scratchy voice.

"Tell us where you were and what you did," James ordered.

"I went to a jeweler," Ruther said, pointing wearily at the lump in the red cloth. Maggie finally recognized it and opened the cloth. She gasped when she saw her necklace and looked up at Ruther with a sick face.

"You were going to sell my mother's necklace?" she shouted. Her features twisted in rage and pain, and she whipped Ruther across the face with the gold chain, cutting a thin bloody line into his already bruised cheek. "My dead mother's necklace!"

She wept as she raised her hand again, but Isabelle grabbed it. Maggie tried to slap Isabelle, too, but missed. This seemed to give her some control over herself. Ruther cried out in protest during all of this, but Maggie's voice had more energy and drowned his out.

"I didn't!" he bellowed. Now he also wept. "I didn't! I didn't try to sell it. I fixed it. Lord Almighty, tell her. I paid a jeweler to fix your necklace!"

"Why are you lying?" James shouted in Ruther's face. He grabbed the necklace and held it in his fingers for Ruther to see he'd been caught.

Ruther shook his head and swallowed hard. "I fixed it. Look at it."

James held it high and let it dangle from his fingers so everyone could see that the necklace was anything but fixed.

"No—no—no," Ruther protested into his hands. "That can't be right!"

James stood and went to Henry. "You see what I'm saying? He will not tell the truth. He's incapable of it."

Henry pushed past James and sat by Ruther. "What was the jeweler's name, Ruther?"

"Quincy."

"Why would he fix something for you in the middle of the night?"

"He's an old friend of my uncle in Reddings," Ruther struggled to explain. "He owed my uncle a favor, so I collected on it. Henry, I'm telling the truth. Go speak to him if you wish. Go!"

"We don't have time to go," James argued. "He knows that."

"Why did you have some of the gold in your pocket if he owed you a favor?" Henry asked.

"It wasn't free, but it was cheaper than if anyone else had done it. The chain must have broken when James pulled me off the horse. It was in my pocket."

Ruther's voice was so pathetic and worn, Henry wondered if his friend was manipulating it for greater effect. He had seen him do it before, but never imagined Ruther's talents being used against him. Then again, he never imagined a scenario like this.

"Where is the gold, Ruther?" James asked.

"I don't know! I swear it!" Ruther kept repeating this until Henry cut him off:

"You've been stealing from me to pay off your debts all along."

Ruther shut up fast and stared at Henry. He stared straight into Henry's soul with large, haunted eyes. He reminded Henry of a captured rabbit. "If you knew, why didn't you say anything?"

"I didn't want to believe it." Henry spoke first to Ruther, then to everyone. "Wilson told me. Wilson told me about your debts, and I didn't want to believe him. He thought less of me for it. I thought less of myself, too, after I saw you leave for town while we stayed at his house."

Ruther's eyes did not deny it.

"You paid off debts in Washborough, Fenley, Grubbingville, and who knows where else. Even Bookerton?"

Again Ruther's expression confirmed it.

"How much did it cost you?"

Ruther swallowed again and spoke, his voice drier than ever. "Four hundred crowns . . . almost."

Isabelle began crying behind Henry. James, Maggie, and Brandol said nothing. Henry didn't know who to speak to now, so he stared at the ground and addressed everyone. "I'm sorry for saying nothing. I didn't want to—I don't know anymore, but I'm sorry. This is my fault too."

"No, it's not," James said. "Don't blame yourself for this filth."

Ruther pleaded his case once more. "I was going to pay it all back, Henry, I swear it. Not all of it came from the bag. I used the money we got from the soldiers after that performance, too. That was over forty crowns. They gave us a lot."

"Why pay off your debts?" Henry questioned. "We're leaving the country." Then he looked into his friend's face with utter disappointment as he divined Ruther's intent. His friend's exhausted stare dropped to his hands. "You weren't going to go into Pappalon—because you're not a wanted criminal like the rest of us."

"I was going to see you safely to the border. I was going to tell you about the money, that I'd pay you back. I was going to go back to Richterton and get the money from the sale of your house and shop and bring it to you! It wasn't supposed to come out this way."

"Ruther," Henry wanted to stop himself from saying the things on his mind, but could not find any other way to say it. "Ruther, that money was given to Isabelle by her mother. It was for us to start a new future. You are part of our future."

"So where's the rest of the money?" Maggie spat.

"I don't have it," Ruther said, matching Maggie's venom with his own. "I didn't take it. One of you did."

James barked a laugh. "How would you know that? You were gone all night."

Ruther looked at Henry while he addressed James. "A thief or a band of thieves wouldn't come out here randomly looking for a large chunk of gold, and what they would have taken would have been more like horses, swords, clothes. They would have killed the men and kept the *woman*."

Maggie ignored Ruther's insult and appealed to Henry. "He took the gold. I know it. I've never trusted him, Henry; you know that."

Henry dropped his voice low enough that Ruther would not hear. "He told us how much gold he's taken. Why would he lie about the rest?"

Maggie stared at Henry with an intense ferocity. "One reason for every piece of gold."

Henry shook his head. "I believe him."

Maggie slapped Henry so fast that it shocked more than hurt him. In fact, he felt no pain at all. Her eyes were full of tears again, and she held her own hand tenderly. "You're a fool! I've tolerated your bad decisions and imprudent trust, but I won't be led around by a fool any longer." She turned her back to him and went to James. "He knows where the money is. He wants to convince us it's not him so we turn on each other."

James nodded as he watched Ruther try to apologize to a still-tearful Isabelle. He retrieved his sword from the dirt and stood again in front of Ruther. In his other hand he held one of his small throwing knives. Henry had never appreciated until now how sharp James kept them. "Tell me where my mother's gold is, Ruther, or you're going to lose toes. Then fingers."

Ruther looked as though he wanted to make a joke, something to lighten the mood. He sputtered something, but Henry could not understand it.

In response, Henry drew his own sword. "You will not harm Ruther."

"That gold was not yours—"

"It wasn't yours either, James," Isabelle said. "Mother left it for me."

"If you're going to do nothing to reclaim it, then I will. I love you, Isabelle. You know that, but you are hopelessly naive. Between Henry's lack of spine and your naiveté, you've put yourselves and the rest of us into a bad situation that could have been avoided."

Henry steeled himself. "I will fight you, James. Will you harm me in order to harm Ruther?"

"What would you do, Henry?" James asked in a dangerously calm voice. "Would you let him go?"

"Yes."

"That's what he wants. That gold weighs too much to carry very far. It's here somewhere. Let him go, and when we're gone he'll come back here for the gold."

"Then so be it. Think of your father, James. This is something he would do. That's why Isabelle and I had to leave Richterton and why we're here now!"

"No," Maggie said, "Ruther is not going to deceive you again, Henry. I want you to see him for what he is!"

Henry's face turned red. Isabelle addressed Maggie for him. "How can you be so depraved? What is it about Ruther that you hate so much? He's been with me every step of the way, putting himself in danger as much as the rest of us. And he's complained no more or less than you, Maggie!"

Before Maggie could say anything, James broke in. "Henry, I respect you and have followed you for over twelve weeks, but that money is no longer yours and Isabelle's to speak for. All of us have invested blood and suffering in that money—in yours and Isabelle's happiness. I will not come all this way to see someone rob you or my sister of that, even if you would step aside and let it go."

"This is too far," Henry said, gesturing to James's knife.

"It's not your decision alone. We will put it to a vote."

FORTY-ONE

The Vote

N o," Isabelle said. Her face mirrored Henry's own revulsion at the suggestion. "I won't vote. Not on something like this."

"Yes, you will," James said.

"It doesn't matter what you vote," Henry told James. "I'll stop you."

"You'll lose," James said. "You know that. And when I render you unconscious, I'll escort my sister and yours away, and then Brandol and I will find the gold one way or another."

Henry went to Maggie. "Please, you can't support this."

Maggie would not look back at him. "My vote is for James."

Henry shook his head. His voice was thick as water. "You are not my sister."

"You are not my brother when you allow someone to betray you and still offer him a hand of friendship time and time again. Mother would be disgusted with you."

"I am not offering him friendship, but I won't submit him to James's methods."

James and Maggie and Isabelle stared now at Brandol, who had his head between his legs and his hands over his head. Henry felt fresh shame that his journeyman had been compelled to join them and now had to witness this brutal display of humanity.

"What is your vote, Brandol?" James asked.

Ruther began to shake, his face covered by his hands. Henry knew why. Brandol had disliked Ruther ever since being forced to play the part of the soldier in *A Soldier and His Lady.* Brandol had been humiliated in front of all those soldiers when his pants fell down to his ankles, but Ruther had made it worse by teasing him about it for days.

Henry spoke with great tenderness. "You don't have to say anything, Brandol. Please don't let them do this." Even as he spoke, he prepared himself to rush on James.

Everyone but Ruther had their eyes on Brandol, whose sniffling was the only sound in the camp besides the fire's sparse crackling. Brandol was watching a small beetle burrow into the dirt, and finally looked up. His eyes were red and swollen. He looked at James first, then at Henry, and finally at Ruther. Ruther kept his eyes on the ground, but Henry saw one of his hands closing around a handful of loose soil.

The journeyman's voice was barely audible, but the silence made him sound like a magistrate pronouncing a sentence. "I vote for Master Henry."

Ruther sobbed into one clean and one dirty hand. James dropped his sword. Maggie's face was stone. Isabelle rushed to Brandol and hugged him. Henry gave Ruther his hand, but Ruther shook his head and continued to sob. Henry gripped his friend's arm and pulled him up into a long embrace. Ruther's hot breath warmed Henry's shoulder in rapid puffs of air.

"I forgive you, Ruther," Henry whispered, "but you have to go now."

Ruther nodded and croaked an apology. Henry let go of all of the accusations and suspicions he had held. The man he held in his arms was once again his boyhood friend and the man who had saved his life three times. Once from a farmer's dragonox chasing them through a field, the second time in an inn where an emperor had tried to kidnap Isabelle, and last, with James at his side, when Henry had been blinded and cornered by the King's armies.

Henry slipped the coins that had been discarded back into Ruther's pocket. Ruther made no sign that he'd noticed it. "I love you, brother," Henry told him. "Thank you for everything. I wouldn't have made it this far without you."

Ruther nodded again and let go. He hugged Isabelle briefly and nodded to Brandol, who reacted by fixing his eyes on the digging beetle once more. After a glance at Maggie, Ruther grabbed his pack from the carriage. Henry noticed Ruther did not take his second pack, nor did he collect his costumes. Ruther never looked back after mounting Ghost, and after a few short minutes, even the rhythmic pounding of his horse's hooves could not be heard.

No one spoke. No one needed to. The band of friends, now one person too small, stood around not knowing exactly what to do. Henry sensed that his little group was now broken, but perhaps not shattered. As difficult as Ruther had been at times, over the last twelve weeks he'd become as important as anyone else.

"It's time to go," Isabelle said to no one in particular.

Still not speaking, they packed their belongings and mounted horses. The gold had mysteriously disappeared as abruptly as it had arrived. Henry saw no point in searching for it. He wouldn't know where to begin. His situation had turned precarious: emigrating to a new country with no money and no contacts.

It didn't matter, he told himself. All he cared about was Isabelle's safety. If Maggie, James, or Brandol wanted to be safe with them, so be it. If not, he would wish them well too.

The wind, which had chilled them for days, died down to a breeze. Henry wished it hadn't. He wished the wind would roar loudly enough to fill his ears, because the silence of his peers was unbearable. Even the biting cold would be fine because his body was already numb. The only comfort he found was when the Iron Forest appeared on the farthest horizon, rising above the hills to the east.

Maggie drove the carriage with only Brandol inside. James, Henry, and Isabelle led on their horses, and though they rode side by side, no one conversed. Henry sensed an invisible barrier between himself and James. After their last three months together, he thought he knew James, but now he realized he had no idea who the man riding with him truly was. The same concerns applied to Ruther. Had he really known his friend of over ten years?

He remembered the time James had shown him the horrid scar on his scalp and told Henry to trust no one. It troubled Henry that he might be so naive and not know it, always assuming that a person's best qualities defined him or her. The words Maggie and James had thrown at Henry and Isabelle cut deep. Had *all* these troubles been caused by his own foolishness? He thought of the hatred in Maggie's voice and James's willingness to do whatever it took to make certain Ruther told them the truth. He never wanted to become that cynical, but what if they were right?

They rode on after sundown, and Henry's thoughts ran in circles. He looked back often, telling himself he was only checking for signs of someone following them, perhaps even the thieves who had stolen their gold, but he really wanted to see his friend's face. Once when he looked back, he saw Maggie also facing in the opposite direction. At some point in the night they stopped and set up camp. They spoke little, only when necessary. Isabelle came and took Henry's hand, leading him away from camp. At first Henry thought she wanted to get away from the others, but something told him she needed his comfort, so he waited until they walked far enough away that no one could see them. Then he wrapped her in his arms and let her cry. It was all the speaking they needed.

The next day was the same except the wind blew harder through the valley again. Henry looked to the horizon less often, but he still wondered about his friend. The pass waited for them ahead, but no one mentioned it. Henry thought many times to ask James what he planned to do when they reached it, but every time he thought about asking, he remembered that James's answer would change nothing.

"Look," James said, pointing to the apex of the hill to their north.

On the hill's peak, a large black buck grazed nervously at stubbles of grass. The rhinelk raised its giant horned head abruptly as if it sensed Henry's stare, the horn on its snout pointed straight at Henry. Then it continued chewing while watching them, probably trying to decide if the strange creatures below posed a threat.

"I'd kill it for the meat if . . ." James did not finish the sentence, and Henry knew why. Ruther had taken his bow with him.

The long periods of silence nearly drove Henry mad. While Maggie and Brandol prepared another cold dinner, he took Isabelle by the hand and led her up a shallow hill where they could sit and watch the stars appear.

"Are we doing the right thing with Brandol?" Isabelle asked before he knew what he wanted to say.

"I don't know. I don't know anything anymore."

"He's terrified, Henry. I think he fears what lies ahead as much as what could be behind. What does he have to look forward to?"

"We won't be impoverished," Henry answered, "I promise you. Once we're established, I'll help him get his own feet set somewhere. I won't leave him with nothing."

"I know, but he has no family while everyone else does. I'm certain he feels lonely."

"He'll meet people—even a woman if he'd start talking more. I've known him for almost two years now; it's not as though we're strangers."

"Will James come with us?"

"I don't know. Sometimes I think he will, but—"

"Why would he go back? It's madness—it's as if he doesn't care that he could be killed."

"He must have some idea or he wouldn't—" Henry's words ended abruptly as he remembered the jagged scar on James's scalp that he had promised not to mention.

"What?" Isabelle asked.

"Nothing."

"Tell me."

"Maybe James doesn't really intend to clear his name. Maybe he has other plans."

"Such as?" Isabelle turned to Henry to ask.

"I don't know. Who could know what he's thinking?" Henry said this, but felt almost certain that James's reason must have something to do with that scar. He kissed Isabelle's forehead to make the thought of James and his scar go away. It was easier with her scent fresh in his lungs and her warm breath on his neck. Isabelle sighed happily and stroked Henry's hair and face.

"I want to tell you something else," she said, pulling him in for a kiss. "I am so proud of you for standing up for Ruther."

"Thank you," Henry said with a surge of emotion that forced him to swallow.

"That's why I want to marry you. You're a real hero."

He chuckled at her comment, but it was hollow. "A real hero? I don't even feel like a man, especially after what happened in Bookerton. I couldn't defend myself, and I wouldn't be able to defend you, either. It's shameful."

"No," she insisted. "You are a hero. You forgave Ruther for doing something terrible because you love him. Most people would feel only hate. You're better than that. You let your friendship guide your actions, and I approve, Henry. I love you."

Henry let out a bitter laugh. "I wish I believed in me as much as you do," he said, not feeling at all cheered. He suddenly missed his friend so much he ached from it. Then another question came to his mind, and he asked it before thinking. "Why do you think Brandol chose to let Ruther go?"

Isabelle pulled her head away from Henry's chest so she could look at him. "I feel like I know Brandol as well as anyone can. He's quiet, and when he talks it's always about something important to him."

"He hasn't ever liked Ruther," Henry stated.

"I know, but that doesn't mean he wants to see Ruther treated that way. I wouldn't want even my father to go through something like that."

"Not even a finger?" Henry asked, nudging her.

"Maybe a toe," Isabelle responded in the same playful tone. "No, not even that. Brandol is a good person, but he's very, very timid. I think—I think his parents made him that way."

"Why?"

"When I asked him about his mother and father, he told me he didn't want to speak about them. He said they didn't like him."

"When all this started back in Richterton, it was about us. You and me just trying to marry. Now it's so much bigger. It's about Maggie's future, James's, Brandol's . . . and even Ruther's still. It became about all of us."

"Because everyone invested themselves in us. In our future."

"I feel regret," Henry said, "not because of what we did, but because I think we've ruined people's lives. Destroyed friendships. I feel like it was almost selfish of us to involve them."

"I know how you feel." Isabelle leaned over and kissed his cheek. "I know exactly."

They heard James's whistle calling them to dinner. Henry felt only a little better as they walked back to camp. Maggie greeted him with a small smile of her own when he arrived. It was the first time they had looked at each other since Ruther left.

Emotions ran high that night as they prepared for sleep. The next day, barring any incident, they would reach the pass late in the afternoon. Henry was nervous and relieved, excited and sad, triumphant and even slightly defeated. Traveling from Richterton to the Iron Pass was an arduous task for anyone, but for Henry and his friends, it had been a tremendous feat.

It was Isabelle's turn to watch over the camp. Henry kept her company for a while before he retired. They chatted about their future, about getting married in Pappalon, and about setting up a new woodshop. When he awoke in the morning, she smiled at him sleepily, kissed him, and went into the carriage to rest.

No one wanted breakfast, not with the border so near, but they forced themselves to eat because they needed the energy. James and Henry struck camp with an excited Brandol helping. Henry had never seen his journeyman so giddy. He and James rode in front, Brandol riding the spare horse alongside the carriage.

The winds were determined to not let them go without a fight, whipping through the valleys and dips, sometimes swirling up clouds of dust, forcing them to squint or shield their eyes to see. They had a very brief lunch around noon and then pressed onward. Brandol asked to ride in the carriage with Isabelle to get some rest for his night watch. Henry knew the entrance to the pass couldn't be more than a few miles away, and he was glad they would reach it with plenty of sunlight remaining.

The endless expanse of the forest stood like an ocean of trees on the near horizon. The Iron Forest had received its name from trees covered with bark so hard that even saplings could not be cut down without great effort. These trees formed a forest so impenetrable that the only way through had been forged long, long ago and had become the fixed eastern border of Blithmore and Neverak and the western border of the countries of old Avalon on the other side.

Not long after lunch, when they were out of earshot of Maggie and Brandol, James struck up a conversation with Henry. "I won't be going through with you," he said over the wind's whining.

Henry didn't respond.

"I know that disappoints you, but I won't be much use to you once you leave Blithmore."

"It's Isabelle I'm concerned about," Henry said. "She wants you near. You're the last of her family, and this may well be goodbye forever."

"I know. I'll tell her once we reach the mouth of the pass."

Henry nodded, not bothering to hide his displeasure. First Ruther, now James.

"It was a difficult decision," James explained.

"That won't make it any easier for her."

James looked at Henry for a long moment and then shrugged. "She doesn't think the same of me since Ruther left."

"Each of us changes a little every day. Some days change us more than others. Out here, we've been pushed to our limits, and it'd be unfair of me to judge you when your emotions were at such an extreme."

James smiled as though he agreed with Henry. "Perhaps after I finish some things, I will come to join you."

"How will you follow us if we don't know where our journey ends?"

"It will be a challenge," James admitted.

Henry knew better. If James left, there would be no reunion of brother and sister.

"I—I never intended to do those things to Ruther, but I wanted him to believe I would even at the cost of you trying to stop me."

Henry didn't believe James. He'd heard the rage in his voice and seen what was in his eyes. Maybe he was wrong about James, but it didn't matter now, anyway.

"And Maggie?" he asked. "Did she know your true intentions?"

James looked away for a moment. "No, she didn't, but I don't want to part with you thinking ill of me."

"I don't, James. I bear no grudge."

"Thank you. I hold you in the highest regard. I couldn't think of a better man to marry my sister."

"Thank you." Henry hesitated before speaking what was on his mind, then decided that if he didn't say it now he'd probably never get a chance. "How did you get that scar, James? Is it why you refuse to leave Blithmore?"

James ran his fingers along his scalp as a dark expression covered his face. "I do not wish to speak of it."

Henry shook his head. James was a lost cause. "My apologies for asking."

"You don't need to apologize." James's expression was one of deep sorrow. "You are a far better man than I. You've proved that, and I think my mother would—" He stopped and his face turned pale. "Lord of All Worlds, help us. They're right there. On the hill!"

Henry turned to look up the north hill. Ten soldiers of the Emperor's Elite Guard rode toward them. Maggie screamed and spurred her horses on faster. Henry and James broke into a gallop. Shouts came from the top of the hill as their enemy urged their steeds onward.

"How far are we from the pass?" Henry yelled to James over the sound of the horses and the wind.

"Two miles at the most," James answered. "By the time they get down that hill, we'll be ahead of them, but not by much."

The Elite Guards blew their horns, though Henry could not imagine why. Did they expect his party to stop for them? When the horns continued, Henry realized what James must have already known. The horns called more soldiers. This was no accident. It was an ambush.

After only a quarter-mile, the Guards were no more than thirty yards behind them, well in range to use their arrows. Even with the swirling winds, nine arrows aimed from trained bowmen would soon find their mark. The tenth Elite Guard stayed on the peak of the north hill, blowing every ten seconds into his horn, an ensign for reinforcements.

"Lord of All Worlds, help us," James repeated.

Ahead, eight more soldiers rode directly toward them, coming down from the southern hills.

Nine behind them. One on the hill. Eight ahead. Eighteen in total. The hills on each side were too steep for the carriage to have a chance at climbing out of the valley.

"Would you still call Ruther your friend?" James asked him.

"What do we do?" Henry asked. "Surrender?"

"I brought a spare sword," James said, his brutal soldier voice returning. "It's in my pack. Give it to Isabelle. Remember what I taught you!"

The few lessons James had given Henry were suddenly a great blur in his mind.

"Tell Maggie and Brandol to grab whatever they can use as weapons. We'll need the horses if possible. Prepare yourself, Henry. I do not think we will see the sunset tonight."

FORTY-TWO

Battle at the Pass

J ames waited to hear Henry relay his orders to the others. The moment Maggie's carriage stopped, Brandol jumped out, screaming in terror. Isabelle exited moments later with James's spare sword and a heavy skillet for Maggie. Henry went to retrieve his sword from the rear compartment of the carriage. Satisfied Henry had carried out his orders, James rode toward the Elite. His seven years of experience in the King's Guard told him they would not survive the battle. Brandol, in his insanity, would die first, followed by Maggie and James. Henry and Isabelle would be captured and taken north. James's mindset was simple: kill as many of the Elite Guard as he could before dying.

Each time he entered the field of battle, James heard the voice of his training officer in his mind: "Why do you attack first, Oslan?"

"To reduce the number of enemies as soon as possible!" James's own voice shouted in response.

"Correct!"

The knives in James's belt jingled as he put Sissy into a gallop. He pulled the first one out when he was still forty yards away from the first guard. The throw felt perfect, and the guard did not expect it. The guard fell off his horse clutching his bleeding stomach.

The other guards broke rank. James drew his sword, as did the other seven guards in the front pack. James prepared himself for a soldier's death, one hand on his sword, the other gripping a throwing knife. His sword clashed against the blade of the closest guard and slid off without causing harm. He threw his knife at the second guard and missed. The third guard had a clear shot at his right side, but did not take it.

Once James had passed the group of guards, three of them turned to face him. The rest rode on toward the carriage. Now James understood. The guards' orders were to capture only Isabelle and Henry and harm no one else. James had been involved in several skirmishes during his service to the King, but never against anyone so foolish.

He drew another knife, but it nearly slipped from his fingers. Before he lost his grip, he did something he never thought he would: he used the same hip flick he'd observed Ruther perform in their contest. James had practiced it when Ruther wasn't watching and had developed a deadly aim. A second guard fell. It happened so quickly even James was surprised. Beyond the two remaining Elite Guards, James saw Henry, Isabelle, and Maggie fighting back thirteen more with swords and a skillet, and since it appeared that Isabelle possessed the most skill with a sword, James needed to reach them soon.

He charged Sissy into the last two guards. They met him with all the force they could, defended his blows, and drove him back. He charged a second time, and they pushed him back again. His next knife flick missed. He charged them a third time, this time expecting them to perform the same maneuvers. They did. He yanked Sissy's reins hard to the right and slashed with his sword at the right guard. The guard deflected it, but not well. As James passed, his sword struck either the shoulder or the neck of the guard. He did not turn to look, but hoped it was the neck.

The Elite Guard showed no desire to engage James one-on-one, and turned to the hills. James rode toward the carriage to help his friends. Brandol was hiding under the carriage holding something over his face. Maggie still had her skillet. Isabelle was fighting rather well, which James expected, since he had given her several lessons over the years. The one wounded guard was nearest to her. Henry slashed his sword back and forth wildly, ignoring everything James had taught him and endangering Maggie and Isabelle almost as much as the enemy.

The senior officer saw James approaching and the carnage he'd left behind and ordered his remaining men into two groups: five for James, and eight for the others. James recognized the look in these five men's eyes as they surveyed what he'd done to their comrades. They had the same love for each other that James had had for the men he'd served alongside. Orders or not, they were going to kill him.

James pulled a hard left this time, leading them away from his friends, who were now cut off from his help. He rode as far away as he dared, knowing that going too far would make them simply turn around and go back.

As he wheeled around, he threw another knife. It wasn't a perfect shot, but it struck the guard in a spot that, if he moved too much, would ensure his demise. The remaining guards began cursing and taunting James. He held the longest knife in his hand now, using it as a small dagger for emergency parries and quick slashes. The guards pressed him back further. James hacked at them viciously, using every last bit of wit he had to try and outmaneuver them. However, it was four on one, and even with two weapons he was no match for the guards.

He sliced at the leader, whose name he guessed from the shouts of other guards was Wellick. Wellick blocked him so well that James almost lost his sword. Instead he fell off Sissy, landing on his back.

"Level the field of battle!" James's training officer had shouted at him time and again.

James wasted no time following that advice with a knife throw into Wellick's horse's underbelly. Wellick barely avoided being crushed by his horse's fall. Another guard rushed James, swiping for his head. James used a maneuver taught to him by another one of his field officers. He parried the block close to the hilt, gripped the attacker's wrist with the left hand, and pulled hard. Now two guards were off their horses.

Wellick ordered his other men back to the carriage. James chanced a glance and saw three guards dragging Maggie off. Henry fought back two more guards, trying to make it to his sister while more guards chased Brandol, who now waved something in his hand as he ran up the hill. In the commotion, James could not see Isabelle.

Before he was able to spot her, Wellick and the second guard attacked. James yanked his last knife from the horse's flank to use again as a dagger. Wellick, who showed more skill of the two, was on James's left. James moved his sword to his left hand, but all he could do was parry and wait to make a brief attack.

The guard to his right was eager for a kill. If one of his strikes went wide, James might have enough time for another throw. Over Wellick's shoulder, James saw Henry take a nasty blow to the arm. Henry's sword fell from his hand, and Henry exposed his back to pick it up. James knew Henry was a dead man until the guard who made the strike jerked violently and then fell to the ground.

James parried several more attacks, but made only two of his own. Finally the guard on the right overreached for a kill shot. James flicked, too eager for the finish, and caught the man low. The injured guard thrust at James as he fell, cutting James's leg.

Wellick brought his sword down hard on James's blade, which was still supported by his left hand. James could not withstand the blow and lost his balance, falling down on the weak leg. Again he prepared himself for a good death—a soldier's death. Wellick put his foot down on James's throat, cutting off his air supply. James struggled mightily, grabbing the man's boot in a last-ditch effort to prevent him from crushing his neck.

"Today is not your day for death, Oslan," Wellick said. There was no contempt in his voice, only truth and a hint of respect. "But it will be if you don't tell me which one is Henry Vestin."

Spasms ripped through James's chest as he struggled for air. He looked into Wellick's eyes as he considered reaching for his sword, only inches from his body. He could never make it in time. Wellick knew this, too. James released his grip on Wellick's boot. His eyes scanned the remains of the battle going on behind Wellick. Another small company was coming down the hill to the south. James could not see anyone he knew. Then he saw Brandol. The journeyman ran faster than James would have guessed. The guards still had not caught him as he scampered up the hill waving around a paper. Not any paper, James realized, but the writ of passage. In a flash of insight, James realized Ruther had not betrayed them. Brandol was the thief. He'd hidden the writ of passage and stolen the gold, too.

Wellick shifted his weight slightly, which allowed James to see Henry lying on the ground, his body half under the carriage. What about Isabelle and Maggie? James still couldn't find them. His vision blurred. Wellick's foot was an anvil on James's neck, and James could do nothing now but point. Brandol and Henry looked remarkably alike. Wellick couldn't tell them apart and was afraid to bring back the wrong one.

"There," James hissed through his teeth.

Wellick followed his finger to the hill where Brandol was still running like a headless chicken. The paper in his hand had vanished.

"Him?" Wellick asked with obvious disbelief. The boot pressed even harder on James's neck, hard enough that James thought he might be crushed at any moment.

James jabbed his finger at Brandol frantically. His face boiled despite the cold wind that battered it.

Wellick put his hands to his mouth and called out, *"Henry!"*

It was a miracle. Brandol looked in Wellick's direction, slipped on a rock or a loose clump of dirt, and tumbled down to the guards.

Wellick's foot lifted from James's neck immediately, and he inhaled the most delicious air he'd ever breathed. Then he pulled his sword from the ground with his right hand as Wellick turned to watch his guards capture Brandol. James thrust his sword, making certain Wellick never made such a mistake again.

Four guards captured Brandol and hauled him off, thrashing and screaming like a wild animal. Henry still lay where he'd fallen. James was not certain if his friend was alive or dead. Maggie and Isabelle were nowhere to be seen. When James stood, a burning pain shot down his leg. He ignored the stinging and walked off to find his horse.

Sissy was eating grass fifty yards away. A whistle brought her back to him. He mounted her with a leap, his leg in agony, and rode back to the carriage. As he approached, he heard a screech far away, either Maggie or Isabelle. He turned Sissy to the north and directed her up the hill, trying to block out his worst fear. Even if these guards were under orders to not kill, there were other things they could do, particularly to the women. He spurred Sissy harder, willing her up the hill.

Several yells came from above the crest. One of them he was certain belonged to Isabelle.

"It's her! It's her!" a man yelled.

More shouts followed. James couldn't understand everything being said.

"Get the other!" cried another voice. "Get the uh—"

"Where's that coming from?"

"In the tree!"

"The tree!"

James could not tell what was happening. Halfway up the hill, Sissy's fatigue began to show. The hill's steepness wore at her.

"Come on, girl, don't give up on me!" he urged.

Sissy's pace continued to slow.

"Come on, Sissy!" he yelled.

"Fall back!" someone shouted. James recognized the tone of authority in the man's voice. "Fall back, Guards! Sound the horn!"

A trumpeting blast followed. Whoever blew the horn must have been nearby, because James's ears were assaulted by the noise. In his battle-weary state, the sound startled him enough to make him let go of the reins to cover his ears. Sissy reared back and bucked him off. It was only the second time in his life he'd ever been bucked, the other being the first time he'd ridden her. Sissy hated riders who showed fear.

For the second time that day, James hit the ground on his back. This time he rolled. End over end, he fell down the hillside. His fingers tried to rip into the cold earth and sparse grass, but he couldn't stop himself. James saw whirls of colors: brown, green, blue, gray. When he finally stopped rolling near the bottom of the hill, James saw Henry staring back at him. An eerie emptiness filled Henry's eyes. Faint screams floated down from the top of the hill.

"Isabelle!" James gasped. He tried to get up. He pushed himself halfway up into a seated position, but his body would not obey his mind any longer.

Maggie! Isabelle! He had to help. The world began to spin uncontrollably. He pushed against the world to make it stop, but it insisted on spinning. He fell for the third and final time onto his back. His head rolled to the side and again he stared at Henry, and those blank eyes looked back at him. He thought he saw Henry blink, but then he realized that it was he who had blinked, only he hadn't reopened his eyes. Another scream echoed in his head—this one very, very far away.

Was that his name he'd heard? Was it Isabelle pleading for him to help?

His body jerked as his indomitable will tried to force himself to get up, but nothing could make it go. His eyes refused to open. His leg burned, though the pain was distant now. A thick darkness formed in his mind, smothering out all possibility of thought and action.

FORTY-THREE

The Mistake

After leaving camp and his friends behind, Ruther rode south as long as he could last. All he thought about was the vote. He couldn't believe Brandol had voted with Henry. Ruther had ruthlessly tormented Brandol—all in good fun, of course, but Brandol had never taken it well. In the end, Brandol had proved to be the bigger man and had pulled Ruther's fat out of the fire. Such a turn of events made Ruther's stomach ill. Quincy had been right. He *had* become his uncle.

When he and Ghost could travel no further, they stopped to rest outside of Reddings. Ruther tied Ghost to the only tree around, pulled out the thickest blanket he had in his pack, found a little shade, and tried to sleep.

Every dream was a reminder of what had taken place at camp, magnified by his vivid imagination. It was not James holding him at bay with a sword, threatening to remove his fingers, it was a giant tree monster in a guardsman's uniform. The enormous beast clutched Ruther in his twisted branches. Its gaping mouth with jagged, yellow teeth of iron-like bark began chewing Ruther's fingers off one at a time.

Ruther gasped when he awoke, looked around, and then fell back asleep. Something sailed through the air at his head. This time it wasn't Isabelle's pan. Maggie had thrown a dead raven, its beak made from James's knives, and it stuck in the side of his head, causing him unbearable pain.

When he opened his eyes, he was still in pain. Tossing and turning, his head had rolled onto a small, pointed rock. He dug it out of the ground, threw it aside, and slept.

Henry embraced him, but whispered terrible oaths of vengeance upon Ruther in a hoarse, devilish voice. He promised to hunt Ruther and his posterity to the ends of Atolas and make them pay in flesh what Ruther had taken from him in gold. Ruther begged him to stop, but Henry swore the oath over and over again in a terrible chant.

Ruther awoke for the last time, screaming.

"Am I going mad?" he asked himself. It was the middle of the day, and sleep had forsaken him. He saw no point in staying by the tree. He packed away his blanket and moved on. He considered going back to Quincy's house. The jeweler might let him stay for a few days, but Ruther would have to endure more lectures. He didn't think he could stand that. He made up his mind to sleep in Reddings and then return to Bookerton and try to stir up some employment. If he was half as popular there as Gaffen and Willard had let on, he'd have no problem finding work.

The worn path he followed brought him to a rundown, one-room shanty about a mile west of Quincy's shop. Trees grew around all sides of the hovel, their branches invading the window holes. It was almost exactly as Ruther remembered it. He tied his horse to one of the trees and entered through the only door.

The unfettered wind had carried enough dirt and leaves inside to cover the floorboards. Ruther remembered how excited he had been when his uncle told him they would live in a home with wooden floors. Against the south wall was the fireplace where he had cooked on the days his uncle came home with food. On the days he hadn't, they'd played a game called *What would be fun to eat?* A few feet away from the fireplace was the spot where he had slept every night for three years. In the corner was where he'd kept his few belongings: a small wooden sword, two silver eagle feathers, and a spare set of worn clothes.

"I need a drink," he muttered.

Without another thought, he left the hovel and rode to a small inn. He had never been inside this inn before, though his uncle had frequented it. It was a small place with seating for only a dozen customers. Ruther had been inside similar inns all over Blithmore. There was nothing special about this one. The owner gave him a troubled look.

"Have I seen you before, young man?"

"No, because I've never been here before." Ruther's tone made it clear he didn't want conversation. He pulled a few of the smaller coins from his pocket. "Ale?"

The owner may not have recognized Ruther, but he recognized his money, and the ale came without another word. Ruther wasted no time draining the mug and refilling his flask. For more than a minute he did nothing but sit and stare into the empty vessel, his brain void of all thought. Things didn't seem so bad now. Ale always made life better. Ruther licked his lips and rubbed his eyes sleepily. He doubted the owner would mind if he napped. It was early enough in the day that he would have few customers, so Ruther put his arms up on the table and used them as a pillow.

This time, there were no nightmares.

When he awoke, he was back in his uncle's house, lying on the dirt-and-leaf-strewn floor with his head on a soft pile of leaves. He had no idea how he had gotten there. The fireplace had a blazing fire, and he was warm. That, at least, offered some relief to his confused state. He looked around for his traveling pack, but couldn't find it.

The crunching of leaves and twigs outside drew his attention to the door. Without fanfare, his uncle walked into the house. Ruther backed into the wall in shock. His uncle was tall and portly with red hair. Their features were incredibly similar, even down to the subtle coloring of their eyes. In fact, now that Ruther was grown, he would have sworn his uncle was his older twin.

"When did you get here, Ruther?" his uncle asked, not surprised at all to see him.

"I don't know," Ruther answered. He felt like a boy of nine or ten again, the same age he had been when his uncle died. "I woke up here, but I think I'm still dreaming. Watch."

Ruther slapped himself in the face but didn't feel a thing. "No pain."

"You're being silly," his uncle told him. "What are you doing in our old shack? I thought you were trying to be a hero with your friend, Henry."

His uncle's friendly tone hadn't changed a bit. He had never cursed at or hit Ruther when he came home drunk—he liked to philosophize. He would sit down and lecture Ruther on the principles of life, mythology, and religion. His favorite topic of discussion was the Path and how all things were governed by a magical power emanating from a central star made of a color called Lyrial. Some of Ruther's most memorable lessons had been late at night after his uncle staggered through the door with "a head full of ale," as he would say.

"That's not me," Ruther answered. "I'm not a hero."

His uncle sat down on a chair across the room, on the other side of the fire. Ruther had not noticed the chair earlier. "You're right, kiddo, you're not a hero. We're not a family of heroes. Was I ever a hero for you?"

Ruther had to think about it. "Yes, sometimes."

His uncle laughed. Ruther thought it sounded an awful lot like his own laugh. "No, I wasn't, kiddo. I ran up debts in every city that would let me and moved you around more times than I could count. I never even told you I loved you."

"But you still cared for me."

"Not very well. Best thing I ever did was take you to Richterton and introduce you to the Vestins. They gave you a good education, didn't they?"

"Henry's mom was a good teacher."

"Yeah, too bad they taught you things you were better off not knowing. Who have I always told you comes first in your life?"

"Me."

"Right. You're the most important person in your life. That means you take care of yourself first."

"I did—I do! You don't need to worry about me."

"Listen, kiddo. You need to remember this. People are going to try to tell you every day of your life that love conquers all, and all you need is love, and if you put the happiness of others before yourself you'll be happier. But here's the truth—"

"The people who do that wind up conquered, needy, and un-happy."

His uncle chuckled so hard his belly quivered. "You're a grown man now; I can see that. You don't need me anymore."

"It's still good to see you," Ruther said, remembering fondly their discussions that went late into the night.

"Good to be seen." Then the older man got up from the chair and walked out the door. Ruther thought perhaps his uncle might say more, especially since it was a dream. Perhaps he might tell Ruther that he loved him, but he didn't. He walked out the door without clos-ing it and was gone.

Back at the public house, the owner shook Ruther awake. "Look, pal, I don't mind if you drink, but if you want to sleep, you're going to need to buy a bed for the night."

"Please stop shouting," Ruther grumbled, even though he knew the owner had not raised his voice. Every bone in his body ached. His head swooned heavily on his neck. He had never been so miserable, and when he smelled himself he almost vomited. "How much is a room?"

"One silver crown per night."

"Is it clean?" was Ruther's next question. For some reason that seemed important.

"It will be for another silver."

Ruther let out a long sigh, reached into his pocket and put one of the double crowns he had received from Henry on the table. The owner picked it up and placed it in his own pocket, returning him change of three gold crowns and two more silvers. "Follow me, sir."

Ruther thought that the moment he got into the bed he would sleep for at least three days. He was wrong. It was a small, quaint room, clean and quiet . . . but it had been purchased with Henry's money.

Henry's money.

Now more than three months ago, when he and Henry had plotted ways to make certain Isabelle left The Glimmering Fountain safely, Ruther had known he had a big gamble facing him. His adventures would make a great story, a very lucrative story—if things ended well. He saw himself traveling Blithmore, dazzling and delighting hundreds and thousands of listeners. His adventure would make him rich . . . again, *if* he survived it. He saw himself living the life his uncle wanted to give him, had his uncle only been able to get ahead.

"Why *had* he never been able to get ahead?" a voice similar to Quincy's asked in his head. Ruther ignored the voice.

When they had been chased out of Richterton by the King's armies, he had known that the story could only get better from there. Of course, he'd believed at the time he had become a wanted man. Saving his own skin was motivation enough to leave with Henry and his little band of followers. Once they'd left Blithmore, Ruther would be free to tell his tales all over Atolas to any audience who spoke his language. Then something unexpected happened—he discovered he was *not* a wanted man. In a laughable turn of events, the King and Emperor were after Brandol—not Ruther, the talented and devious friend of Henry Vestin—but Brandol, his bumbling, mumbling journeyman.

The night Ruther had learned this information, he'd had great difficulty sleeping. He was free to leave, he realized, free to go and tell his stories. The only problem was that he had a reason to stay: the story was still a gold mine, and the longer Ruther risked his life learning—and being part of—the story, the more wealthy he'd become.

Yes, that's the reason you stayed, a voice like his uncle's said in his head. Not because Maggie was fun to tease. Not because Henry needed you, nor because you felt some unfounded loyalty to him. He's not your brother—he's your friend, and friends come and go.

You felt guilty taking that money from Henry, didn't you? Quincy's voice asked.

Yes. Sometimes awful guilt, but it went away when he remembered he had to look out for himself. He had to be his number-one priority, as he'd been taught. Henry had more gold than he needed. It wouldn't hurt to take a little to pay off debts as they traveled south. He told himself he would pay Henry back. Somehow. If he survived.

He tried to get to sleep in a bed paid for by Henry—a clean comfortable bed. Under the same stars, Henry would be sleeping on the cold earth with a blanket or two. Isabelle would hold him close since there would be no fire, and the warmth shared between the two of them would have to suffice no matter how hard the wind blew. And Ruther would lie here in his purchased bed, safe and well and warm.

He rolled onto his stomach, pressing his face into the pillow. "My uncle was right." He whispered the words so no one else could hear the shame in his voice. He closed his eyes and opened them again. "No, he was absolutely wrong."

The bag holding all his possessions tipped under its own weight and fell to the floor near the bed. Ruther rolled onto his back to stare at it. "They don't want me back."

He considered his own statement for several seconds, then answered. "I'll never know unless I try. Besides, I left my costumes with Henry. Those were expensive."

"James was going to cut off my fingers and toes," he argued back. "Why go—why?"

The question "Why?" lingered until he realized how simple the answer was: he wanted to. He wanted to go back and not be rejected. He would appeal to Henry; he would beg him if he had to. If he had to take off every last piece of clothing and stand naked in the wind on top of the carriage until they either knew his heart or let him die of cold, then he would do it.

Ruther stood up, but had to steady himself. "Whoa . . ." he said nervously as he swayed and watched the world spin around. Descending the stairs almost did him in, but clutching the wall at the last second saved him from breaking his neck.

The owner looked up the stairs, startled at the noise. "Are you all right, pal?"

"Yesh," Ruther slurred, trying not to vomit on the owner of this fine establishment. "I need you to give a message to Quincy."

"Quincy the jeweler?"

Ruther nodded because he knew it would be quicker than trying to say yes again.

"Tell him Ruther realized he was right. He was right."

"That's all? What kinda name's Ruther?"

Ruther simply nodded. If he did not get on his horse soon he was going to pass out. He lurched forward and grabbed the double crown out of the owner's pocket and returned him the change, scattering it across the table. The owner stared with more surprise than anger.

"And this isn't mine to give you . . . *sssssssooo* . . . I'm leaving."

FORTY-FOUR

Ruther's Rage

By the time Ruther set out, it was evening and growing colder every minute. He managed to ride into the night before exhaustion set in and he almost fell off Ghost. When he awoke and saw the sun's position in the sky, he knew he'd slept too long. At least twelve hours had passed, probably more. Cursing himself, he got up and moved on without delay. He chose to ride high in the hills, north of the party's trail, giving himself a better chance of finding them before they spotted him. The drawback was that from that vantage, he caught the full force of the wind relentlessly trying to push him south.

At one point during the day, Ruther thought he had caught back up, but it turned out to be a gang of rhinelk on the trail. They twitched as he rode by, ready to spring off if needed. Ruther left them alone and pushed onward. The forest loomed many miles ahead, like a massive city wall stretching out in both directions. After all his mocking of Wilson's Iron Forest tales, the thought of going in by himself made his hairs stand on end.

To make up for lost time, he rode late into the night. He knew James and Henry would be pushing their group late as well, so he kept going until he couldn't stay awake. When he awoke, he briefly lingered to gather edible mushrooms growing in the shade of two bent trees.

He rode hard the third day, stopping only to let Ghost rest and eat while he searched for more food growing wildly around him. He envied every bite of grass the horse chewed, but he let his hunger drive him to reach the others that much sooner. Even if they did turn him away again, naked and cold (he was determined to stand on the carriage naked if he must), they might at least give him some food.

He listened for the sound of horses or travelers but heard nothing. A way ahead of him stood a lone, knobbly tree towering above the hills. He thought about climbing it to give himself a better view of what lay ahead. He had not climbed a tree in many years. What if he fell? Ruther decided against it.

Then he heard a horn in the distance, coming from the general direction of the tree. Shouts followed. Ruther squinted, and then he saw them: Neverak guardsmen, just past the solitary tree, riding out of a small dip in the hills and down into the valley where the main road fed into the Iron Pass.

Ruther's first instinct was to flee. The urge was so strong that he pulled the reins of his horse before catching himself.

"What kind of friend *are* you?" he muttered in a strange but strong voice—a voice not similar to his uncle's at all.

After taking a long swig of ale from his flask to calm his nerves, he rode swiftly until he was a hundred yards from the tree and secured Ghost to a stake from his pack. As he ran for the tree, he refused to think about what he was doing, even as the Neverak horn blew again. Images of his dead body pierced with numerous wounds would not help keep his hands steady. He heard more shouting over the hill, but the crest blocked his view of the scene.

The tree was a large one, gray and twisted from too many bitter winds blowing as they were now. Yet the tree was a survivor, a trait Ruther hoped to share. The knobs grew out every few feet covered in tough, weather-worn bark, making the tree easy for him to climb. Its branches were thick and numerous. As Ruther climbed higher, the scene in the valley below unfolded itself to him, nearly making him lose his balance.

The first thing he saw was James riding straight at a group of guards as though he had a lance to knock them over, yet he carried nothing but a sword.

"The fool is going to kill himself!" Ruther said.

Near the carriage, Isabelle, Henry, and Maggie were fighting another small swarm of guards while Brandol hid under the carriage. Ruther continued to climb until he found a good spot where he could stand and brace himself. A sturdy branch grew out of the trunk and split into a V. He stood on the branch below and rested his back in the V's junction.

The battle had already changed dramatically. James fought several guards, and Brandol had appeared, waving what looked like a flag and running up into the hills like a scared dog as more guards chased after him.

Ruther drew his bow and nocked his first arrow. He knew he would miss his first shots until he got an idea of what the wind was like in the valley. The first arrow he directed at one of the guards chasing down Brandol, as they were the farthest away from everyone else. He did not want an errant shot hitting one of his friends. He released the string, which made a loud *twing*. The arrow flew wide, heading toward Brandol. Ruther held his breath as it missed.

His second shot was better, but not perfect. He aimed closer, this time at a guard attacking Isabelle. It hit him not square in the back, but slightly left of where he'd aimed. Isabelle looked as shocked as the guard.

Farther away, James had somehow survived his suicidal assault and now fought with two men on the ground. His three friends around the carriage, however, were badly outnumbered. Ruther had no idea how they'd managed to survive against so many Elite Guards.

Twing!

Ruther's third shot missed again. He had tried to adjust for the wind, but ended up missing wide left. He cursed at himself loudly, but the oath was drowned in a man's scream. Ruther looked back to the carriage and watched in horror as a guard removed his blade from Henry's limp shoulder and then raised his sword again to kill. Ruther shot at once and dropped the guard like a stone in a lake. Isabelle was completely overwhelmed. Ruther knew exactly why she hadn't been killed yet. These men were under orders to return the Emperor's precious cargo to him unharmed. He would have to worry about her later. Maggie had three guards chasing after her.

Ruther aimed with careful regard for the wind and injured one of them. The other got scared and thought twice about pursuing Maggie, who retreated up the hill. She seemed to have lost all her wits and ran blindly away—away from Ruther, away from everything. A cry pulled his attention back to Isabelle. She had been caught, and the guards were dragging her up the hill toward the tree.

Now Brandol was screaming, still waving that flag. Henry had fallen to the ground and was not moving. Ruther swore at himself as he tried to take out one of the men chasing Brandol but again barely missed his friend. The arrow tore Brandol's flag clean out of his grasp.

Ruther heard noises to the north. Another small company of guards was on its way. He cursed again and counted the men in the new company. Nine more. Ruther knew he had about thirty good arrows, and five more that he doubted would fly straight, if at all.

He took aim at one of the men carrying Isabelle. It was a dangerous shot. He could easily kill or seriously wound Isabelle. He aimed low.

Twing!

A primal cry informed Ruther where the arrow had hit. When he looked, he grimaced. "You probably didn't deserve children anyway, friend," he muttered.

The other guards were worried now. One of them bellowed,

"Move faster! Faster!" They carried Isabelle in a sort of trot. Ruther had to adjust his footing now for a better view, but the guards were close enough that he didn't have to worry much about wind.

Twing!

A second guard tripped, clutching his arm and shouting warnings. The other guards dropped Isabelle. Ruther was impressed with how quickly she collected her wits and ran toward the protection coming from the tree. The other three guards gave chase. One of them took an arrow to the chest. The other two ran for shelter among the new company now arriving.

Isabelle ran under Ruther's tree and continued west along the top of the hill. Ruther yelled at her to stop, but the wind dulled the sound of his voice. The guards from the north saw her, and three others rode up the hill from the south carrying something or someone, Ruther could not tell who or what. He watched Isabelle sprint away, but she had no chance of outrunning a horse. Ruther aimed for the guard in front of the northern company, but missed. The guard heard the whistle, however, and looked in Ruther's direction. Uncertain if he had been seen, he took aim again and knocked the guard off his horse with an arrow to the side.

Two other guards rode in from behind, and one of them scooped up Isabelle.

"Help!" she screamed. "James! Henry! Help!"

Ruther aimed again but hit the horse of the guard who was not carrying Isabelle. The horse stumbled but kept moving. The rider looked around for the source of the arrow. Ruther shot again, hitting the horse a second time. This time the horse fell with the rider trapped beneath. Isabelle's captor, on the other hand, was almost out of range.

"It's her! It's her!" the guard yelled to others in the company. "I've got her!"

Ruther guessed he had one good shot left before Isabelle's captor got away. He aimed carefully and said a silent prayer for the Lord of All Worlds to guide his hand. He let the bowstring go and watched the arrow fly. It sailed an inch over the shoulder of the rider. Ruther hurried to get another shot off, but it fell short.

"No!" he shouted at himself. "Isabelle!"

Isabelle continued to scream for help for as long as he could hear her. Unable to help her, Ruther looked around for the others. Maggie had run far to the east, but several soldiers saw her and went after her. Ruther caught the right leg of the first of these.

"Get the other!" shouted another guard, pointing at Maggie. "Get the—"

Ruther silenced him, too. It was much easier to hit targets on the hill crest, but more guards still chased after Maggie.

"Where's that coming from?" a nearby guard asked.

"In the tree!" came a response.

"Who is he?"

Someone shouted on the other side of the hill. It sounded like James, but Ruther couldn't see a face.

"It doesn't matter! We've got the carpenter and the girl. Fall back! Fall back, Guards! Sound the horn!" A horn blasted right under the tree, scaring Ruther so badly his foot slipped off the branch. He barely caught himself.

"Fall back!"

More than a dozen guards retreated, some on horseback, some on foot, and others being helped or carried away. Not in defeat, but victory. Ruther watched them go until he heard another cry—Maggie's.

The four guards still rode after her. Once they caught up to her, they dismounted and gave chase on foot. One of them tripped over nothing but air, his legs strangely bound together. No sooner had this happened than Maggie fell too, her legs collapsing underneath her.

Ruther knew what the soldiers intended to do when they caught her. Something inside him shattered, perhaps his sanity, because he could not explain nor remember climbing down the tree so quickly.

He did not get Ghost. Instead, he sprinted after the four guards. He could have run forever and ever if he needed. As he ran he pulled three arrows from his quiver and clenched two of them between his teeth. He wanted to yell with all the ferocity of a lion, but silence was better. So he let his primal rage reverberate around in his head until it strengthened his heart and stomach.

He saw the first of the soldiers over the next hill. They had all abandoned their horses. They shouted and cheered each other on, drowning out Maggie's pleas for mercy. Ruther chose the one nearest to her, the one standing over her.

"Hold her down!"

He released the string of the bow.

"Be still, you—"

The arrow caught him in the shoulder, twisting him around. Ruther aimed next at the guard to the right, but missed. His hands were shaking, not in fear, but from a black murderous wrath he'd never known. Two other guards turned toward him. One of them suddenly flew through the air toward and then past Ruther as though swept aside by a massive hand. Ruther couldn't explain what had just happened, and he didn't care to. It didn't matter. The guard to the left charged at Ruther. He was too close for Ruther to get another arrow ready. Ruther dropped the bow and drew his sword.

In swordplay, Ruther's skill did not compare to James's. He had been taught by his uncle to throw knives, but he didn't carry them in a belt as James did. Good throwing knives were expensive and hard to come by. As a youth, the bow and arrow had been his obsession. Swords had been almost an afterthought until he began traveling through the countryside for performances. He knew about the possibility of running into thieves, so he'd paid a swordmaster to give him several lessons. Though he had learned quickly and well, he was not a trained soldier, nor an Elite Guard.

But in Ruther's state of mind, none of that mattered.

He gripped his sword in both hands, slashing so violently that the guard nearly lost his grasp on his own blade. Ruther threw his shoulder into the guard, knocked him to the ground, and finished it by piercing the guard's heart. The third guard attacked viciously, but Ruther's insanity had not ended, nor had his bloodlust been satiated. He parried the attacks one after another. His mind had a clarity he had not experienced in some time. It almost seemed effortless to beat this man. They crossed swords at the chest, Ruther's foot kicked out fast and hard. The guard did not block in time. As he doubled over, Ruther slew him.

All that was left was the guard with the shoulder injury—the man who had intended to rob Maggie of her most precious possession. He lay on the ground, clutching his chest and moaning in pain. Ruther heard a wet, wheezing sound each time the man breathed. That was all he heard. Everything else blurred into the background.

Ruther advanced on him with a face of stone. His mind still hadn't recovered from the soul-piercing screams of Maggie and Isabelle. His sword was red and dripping to the hilt, but he did not bother with it. What happened when Ruther reached that last guard was never mentioned again. When he finished, and Maggie was safe, Ruther knelt down on the ground and wept as he raised his flask to his lips, hoping to drink the fresh memories into oblivion. The stench of the drink burned his nostrils. Rather than drink, he emptied the ale onto his sword, washing off the blood. Then he flung the flask away into the grass.

FORTY-FIVE

Picking Up the Pieces

Maggie's body quaked, and she was unable to clear her mind of the terror that had gripped her while the soldiers held her down. Ruther held her to his chest, and she clung to him. The grass around her was wet with blood. She noticed more on her dress and arms. It was so quiet now; the yelling had stopped, and all the other guards had left or been carried away.

When the trembling lessened, Ruther helped her to her feet. She stood weakly, leaning on him for several paces. "What happened to your strength?" he asked.

"My legs . . . they gave out. I'm so tired, Ruther."

"They took Isabelle and Henry," he said as they walked toward the carriage. In his voice, she heard the remnants of his rage.

Maggie breathed deeply, trying to gather her wits about her. Tears dripped down her face, and she wiped them away repeatedly. Her embarrassment at running from the battle burned in her chest. She had always seen herself as a woman of strength and courage, but not anymore.

"Oh no," Ruther exclaimed as he ran in front of Maggie over the edge of the hill and out of her sight.

Maggie followed as quickly as she could, but her legs felt like they'd been filled with water. Her arms were no different, but when she saw James's body at the bottom of the hill, dusty and bruised, her fatigue vanished. And when she saw Henry's body only yards away, an eerie numbness crept into her limbs.

"Henry!" she cried as she shook him. "Henry! Answer me, Henry!"

Henry did not answer her. His eyes had a glazed appearance and his chest rose and fell only faintly.

"He's badly hurt," Ruther said. "Look at his arm."

Blood drenched the shoulder of his shirt and ran down the left side of his face.

"What do we do?" Maggie asked.

"We need to get out of here as soon as possible," Ruther said. "They may come back."

"Why?"

"Because they think they have Henry, and they'll realize they don't soon enough."

"I don't understand."

"Neither do I. I'll put James and Henry into the carriage if you'll round up the horses."

"See to their wounds," Maggie said. Her voice had more force than she intended, but Ruther didn't seem to care.

She found Quicken and Sissy grazing in the valley. She walked them back to the carriage and kept searching. The others took more time. The spare horse had gone over the south hill, and Ghost was staked to the ground west of the tree. When she'd gathered them all, she watched from behind as Ruther tended to James and Henry's wounds.

"I—I thought they had taken him," she said with a shaky voice. "I heard them yelling—they said they got him."

"They thought they did," Ruther said and gave her a meaningful look. "Where's Brandol?"

No sooner had he asked the question then she understood his expression.

Her hand flew to her mouth. "No!"

"Yes, and if that's the case, we've got to move. It won't take long for Brandol to correct their mistake."

Maggie helped Ruther wash Henry's wound. The cut was deep, but not so bad that it couldn't be cleaned. In one of her packs she kept fresh bandages and healing herbs. Ruther crushed several of these and mixed them in cold water to form a paste that he spread in the wound. The source of the bleeding on Henry's head turned out to be from no more than a long, shallow cut. Henry was lucky. Once she knew he would be all right, her thoughts went back to Brandol and Isabelle.

"How are we going to rescue them?" she asked.

"What is this?" Ruther asked, holding up a brown pouch.

"Where did you find it?"

"Tucked inside his shirt," he said as he fumbled with it to get it open. "How come I've never seen this before?"

"Don't open it!" she said, startling Ruther.

He stared at the pouch inquisitively. She took it from him and put it back in Henry's shirt. "I've only seen it once before—I found it while playing under my father's bed. When I showed it to my father, he gave me the worst whipping of my life. Then he told me that I had no business looking in it."

Ruther didn't press the subject. Once they were satisfied with Henry's and James's condition, they closed the carriage door. Ruther seemed determined not to look directly at Maggie more than necessary, and she knew why.

"All right, then," he said, staring to the east and then back west. "We're leaving. Leaving Blithmore."

"Wait," Maggie said, "we can't leave. How are we going to help them?"

Ruther pointed northwest and asked, "Help them?" He shook his head. *"Them?"* When he turned back to face her, he still could not meet her gaze. "We're not."

"We can't abandon them," she argued.

"Do you have a brilliant plan to share with me? Do you know where they are or how we're going to leave your brother and James to sneak into a camp full of guards and free them? Do you know how to do all that?"

Maggie gasped for air, fighting away her emotions. "I don't know. I hoped you would."

"It's impossible, Maggie. If it weren't, I'd do something. We can't help them today, but we can help James and Henry. We can care for them, and together, the four of us, we can do something. We can figure something out once we're safe in Pappalon."

Maggie nodded and wiped her eyes. She wished he would look at her, but she was also glad he didn't.

"Sorry for yelling at you," he added as he climbed onto Ghost's saddle. When he was seated, he said, "No, I take that back. I'm not sorry. Why didn't you believe me, Maggie? You've known me more than ten years, and you thought I'd steal from you? Steal your necklace?"

Maggie had no answer. Now it was she who could not meet Ruther's eyes. "Do—do you have everything ready?"

"Yes."

"Then we should go."

They rode in silence toward the pass. Ruther and Ghost were ahead of her, probably so he would not have to look at her. She tried to imagine the day when she might return to Blithmore, but it didn't seem possible. It seemed she would be forever traveling from city to city, town to town, and country to country. She would become an eternal wanderer. The wind died down to a light breeze. Normally, she enjoyed its gentle coolness on her face, but nothing comforted her now.

Maggie had been a girl of about six when Ruther's uncle showed up on the Vestins' doorstep and begged Mr. Vestin to take him on as an apprentice. As any girl would have done when a gangly, red-haired boy with a southern accent moved in, she took a strong liking to him. Whenever Ruther's manners and bad habits set Mrs. Vestin on edge, she aired her frustrations to Maggie.

"That Ruther has a terrible influence on Henry, and if it weren't for simple charity . . ." she'd complain. Other times she would say, "Maggie, you deserve the best gentleman out there. If he's anything like Ruther, you run the other way."

For a while, her mother's nagging only made Maggie fancy Ruther more, but time took its toll. Maggie grew to see her mother's reasoning and eventually despised everything about Ruther, yet even Mrs. Vestin would have been appalled at how Maggie had cast her lot with James in the vote. She'd been absolutely certain Ruther had taken the gold, the same way she was certain he wasn't fit to be Henry's friend. She thought she had seen the last of him. Instead he had returned to save her life. No wonder Ruther didn't want to look at her. She didn't want to look at herself either.

They traveled the last miles to the Iron Forest without conversation. It had been weeks since Maggie had thought of the tales Wilson had told them. Too many other incidents had shoved any fears of the pass out of her mind. But now, as they reached the lone path cutting through the dark and eerie forest canopy, she recalled them vividly.

The entrance to the Iron Pass was not inviting. It reminded her of the eye of a needle. Low branches from tall trees hung over the path, which was darker and smaller than she had imagined. The dirt road was so narrow that no more than four men could walk side by side on it. The sparse grass of the valley floor ended in a perfect line where the dirt path began winding its way through the woods. Maggie thought this odd since the path was so rarely traveled.

"Don't draw your weapons, and don't leave the trail," she said, repeating the advice Wilson had given them. For all she knew, this could be the end of their journey. They might not live to see the other side of the forest. A whole army had disappeared inside the confines of this mysterious forest, yet she and Ruther were going to plunge in without hesitation. She envied Henry and James, but at the same time, she wished they were well enough to ride with them and protect her.

Ruther stopped at where the grass ended and the road began. "Are you ready?" When he spoke to her, he didn't look back. His voice carried none of its friendly familiarity.

Maggie was not ready. She was scared. She was ashamed. She was lonely.

Ruther turned around when she didn't answer. By then she had lost all control of her emotions. Her body convulsed but she did not hide her tears behind her hands. She felt strangely justified crying in front of Ruther because he'd done it in front of her not more than an hour before as he'd cleaned his sword. It had been an intimate moment, and now it was gone, replaced with bitterness and ill memories.

"Are you ready?" he repeated more gently.

Maggie wiped her eyes and nose again. Her skin was chapped and raw. "No." Her voice came out husky and hoarse. "I'm not."

"Why not?"

Her eyes met his for the first time since the vote on the hill. He looked away and then back again.

"Why not, Maggie?"

She wanted no sympathy, so she forced the tears to stop. Ruther continued to watch as she composed herself and sat up in the driver's seat. They needed bravery in the Iron Pass, not tears. It had to be now, or she would never do it.

"Ruther, I am—I am so very sorry. Will you please try to forgive me?"

FORTY-SIX

Torn Asunder

An Elite Guard carried Isabelle away from the battlefield, slinging her over his horse in front of his saddle, from which she watched the hills pass by much too quickly. As they rode, she kicked, punched, bit, and squirmed to free herself from his hands. She used all the strength she had, but no matter how desperately she fought, the guard's grip held strong.

When they arrived at the Elite Guards' camp, several men rushed forward to keep her from escaping. These men handled her as though she were a giant pail full of gold dust that might spill at any moment. The instant her feet touched the ground, she broke through their grip and ran. She made it perhaps five steps when massive hands grabbed her arms and pulled her back.

She screamed and fought, showing no restraint. Her throat burned, but she didn't care. She knew if her cries reached Henry, he would come and rescue her. It was impossible that these men could drag her away from everyone she knew and loved. She knew this as well as she knew her own name. These men would not make it out of the country with her, so she screamed anything that came to mind, and the guards let her.

They dragged her by her arms until they came to a cage. When she saw it, she protested, "No! Don't put me in there! I won't go in a cage!"

The men put her in anyway. As they did so, she realized how gently they handled her, as if they feared hurting her. She redoubled her efforts against them. If they were afraid to hurt her, it would not matter if she hurt them. She pulled at their hair, gouged their skin, and did anything else she could to make it difficult for them to close the cage door. Finally it shut with her inside, though it had taken more time than the guards wanted. She continued to scream, ignoring the fiery agony building in her throat.

Guardsmen inserted two large poles through the bars of the cage so it could be carried by four men.

"No, you won't!" Isabelle shouted at them. Then she laid on her back and kicked at the poles, spinning them so the men lost their grip. Several times they dropped the cage. The cage's bars slammed into her, bruising her, but she blocked the pain. All she had to do was delay them. The men were frustrated that they could do nothing to retaliate. Isabelle took no satisfaction in this; she only let their anger fuel her.

After one particularly nasty fall, she caught a glance at another cage being carried in similar fashion behind her. She could not see who was in it, but she already knew. They had Henry. The Emperor wanted her and him both. He had promised Henry he would kill him . . . or worse. She shouted his name again and again, but Henry didn't respond. How badly had they hurt him?

"Let us go!" she screamed at the guards. "We haven't done anything to anyone. I won't be a slave. The Emperor wants me for a slave. Let us go!"

Her protests fell on deaf ears. At the west end of the camp, three carriages waited. These three were of a different design than the carriage Henry had built. They were light, built for swift traveling on well-maintained roads, not paths. One carriage was open at the rear and waiting for her.

Isabelle begged her captors not to do this, not to steal her life away. She pleaded with them to think of their own daughters and wives. "What would you do if I were one of them?" she asked, but the doors shut on her and the carriage set off.

She continued to shout, though each time she spoke, her voice sounded more and more like an old woman's screech. Over and over again she begged the driver to release her, entreating upon every sympathy of a man's heart she could think of. Finally, after an unknown amount of time and pain, her voice failed and her tears fell silently.

Darkness fell, but the carriage did not stop until late at night. Isabelle refused to let her body rest. She could tell by the sounds when the horses and drivers were changed. The doors in the carriage's rear opened briefly only to let in a sack of water for her. Isabelle picked it up, examined it with her hands for anything useful, and then dashed it against the bars of the cage.

Her first night in the carriage was torture. The air was cold and her enclosure too small. Besides being unable to stand or stretch, her body ached for food, water, and sleep, but she denied herself all these things. When the sun rose, she tried her voice again, but found she was still unable to scream properly. This did not stop her from trying. Again her captors brought her water and food, and again she threw it back at them. While the guards cleaned the messes she made, she begged them to release her.

Her thoughts constantly went to Henry. The times the carriage stopped and the doors opened, she saw an identical carriage behind hers. Sometimes she called his name, but he never answered. Her silent prayers for help focused on him, beseeching the Lord of All Worlds to spare and heal Henry so they could escape together.

Isabelle's behavior remained the same. She rejected food, took little water, slept rarely, and screamed whenever she found strength. On the third day of her captivity, the doors were flung open, poles inserted into her cage, and she was carried out with the same extreme care. Isabelle cried out, but her voice was nothing more than a frog's croak, and her body was too weak to fight back.

She did not know where in Blithmore she was, but they took her into a large tent and set her down on the floor. A man in a highly decorated Neverak uniform waited for her. He appeared neither friendly nor antagonizing. He unlocked her cage and opened the door. Isabelle had the sense to know that she could try to escape, but her limbs had no strength. The guards removed her from the cage and sat her on a chair opposite this man. It sapped most of her energy just to sit upright and glare.

"You are excused," the man told the other soldiers. He was an older man, his brown and gray hair cut short, his face remarkably smooth. None of this impressed Isabelle. His deep, wood-brown eyes looked down on her with, she imagined, a sense of sadness. After the guards left the tent, the man in charge turned to her and said, "You are free to leave. Go."

He watched as she tried to stand, only to fall on her knees in front of him.

"You can't escape because you haven't eaten," he said. "If you don't start eating, you will die. What good will that do you?"

Isabelle shook her head imperceptibly and began to weakly sob.

"You would die rather than serve the Emperor. I understand."

"Help me, please," she whispered as loud as she could. Her eyes looked straight into the brown eyes of this somehow important man. For a moment he seemed affected by her pathetic state and sincere plea, but the sympathy quickly vanished, replaced with resolve.

"I can't do that, Isabelle." He spoke tenderly but with no smile on his face. "I can only ask you to eat. Take care of yourself so that Henry does not come to harm."

"The Emperor . . ." she tried to say, ". . . will kill him."

The man closed his eyes. "That may well be, but as long as you live, you have hope."

"Why?" she asked.

"No more discussion now, Isabelle." The man clapped his hands, and two soldiers outside the tent brought in a tray of food that looked and smelled exquisite. The man watched her emotionlessly. "Eat."

Isabelle swallowed a few bites and soon felt sick. She touched nothing else, but the man appeared satisfied. "From now on you will be allowed to walk around each time we stop the carriage. If you try to escape you will lose that privilege for the remainder of the day. If you do not eat your food, Henry will be lashed ten times for every meal you skip and twenty for every waterskin you break."

Tears threatened to fall again, though Isabelle did not want to cry any more in front of this man. His cruelty was the worst. He knew her situation perfectly, even sympathized with her, but did nothing to help. She was placed again in the cage with a new waterskin and taken back into the carriage. Then the journey continued.

For Henry's well-being, she ate. Every day, always at different times, she tried to escape. She never got more than a few feet except for once when the guard lost his grip on her arm and she stumbled over to Henry's cage. They tried to pull her away from it, but she gripped the bars tightly and shouted his name. To her great shock, the man who looked up at her wasn't Henry. It was Brandol. What she had wanted to say strangled in her throat as she stared at him. Apparently, the guards did not share the same reverence for Brandol's comfort as they did hers. His face was a bruised, swollen mess, covered in filth and dried blood. He sat up when she came to his cage, his fingers brushed hers, but he said nothing.

Brandol had betrayed Isabelle and her friends at the pass. She had recognized the writ of passage when he pulled it from his shirt and ran, waving it like a flag of surrender. During the battle, she hadn't had time to absorb the shock, nor had she thought much about it since. Looking at him now filled her with so much hate that she was ashamed of herself.

How had they mistaken Brandol for Henry? Hadn't Brandol told them who he was? Whatever the answer was, seeing Brandol caged made her feel stronger. Henry was free, probably somewhere on her trail, planning her escape.

Brandol looked at her with empty, blackened eyes and an expression that erased her hate and replaced it with pity. The exchange between them lasted only seconds, and then the guards ripped her away and locked her back in her own cage. After seeing Brandol, however, her imprisonment did not seem as terrible. Her heart was lighter; her discomfort decreased. She stopped trying to escape, and in her prayers she asked the Lord of All Worlds to help Henry find her and to ease Brandol's suffering.

Over the next days, as the carriages rolled north, Isabelle let her mind free her of the bars surrounding her. Instead of being locked in a small cell, she was back in Henry's house being tutored by Mrs. Vestin alongside Henry, James, Maggie, and Ruther in that small schoolroom where they had learned to read and write. Isabelle had written Henry her first note using words she'd been taught by his mother:

Dear Henry, you smell bad. Take a bath.

Her mind took her to the hill near the pond where she had hidden and watched Henry and Ruther skip rocks. She loved seeing Henry's face grow serious as he tried to beat Ruther's distances. She saw the same expression as he learned his father's craft at an astonishingly young age, becoming the youngest master of any trade in Richterton at eighteen.

Her mind took her home to the days when a mysterious admirer began putting fresh flowers on her doorstep each morning. Sometimes she found an accompanying note:

Isabelle, someone loves you and hopes to see you today.

The notes never bore a signature, but she had been certain they were from Henry. However, he tricked her by sending Ruther to put them on her doorstep, and it was Ruther she'd caught. Ruther tried to hide the truth from her, but she knew better. She ran over to Henry's house early that morning, only weeks before his father and mother passed away from illness. She stormed into the kitchen as if she was madder than a hive of bees and said, "Henry Vestin, if you don't kiss me right now, I'm—"

Before she finished her sentence, Henry did just that. Her lips tingled and her breath caught as he kissed her so fiercely they became one soul. At that moment her life was perfect. She knew then that if her existence was to have its greatest meaning, Henry Vestin must be included in it.

Her memories carried her far beyond the confines of the bumpy carriage and iron cage and back to Henry—not physically, but in every other way. As they traveled north, the air grew colder, and the guards gave Isabelle blankets and warmer clothes, but it was the thought of being reunited with Henry, someday, somehow, that got her through that awful journey inside a cage in which she could neither stretch nor stand.

Then one day the journey ended. The carriage came to a stop, as it had hundreds of times before, but this time she heard voices giving orders from a dozen directions at once. The poles were brought out and the doors thrown open, and before Isabelle had really awoken from her sleep, they lifted her and placed her on a horse-drawn cart.

She had crossed into the borders of Neverak at least a week before. Reckoning time was no longer easy. It had not been the grand change she expected. She saw more pine trees and less colorful vegetation. She heard only Neverak-accented voices. The style of homes and dresses were different, but Neverak still had grass and water and sky. The sun still rose and fell.

Then she saw Neverak Palace. It reminded her more of a towering cathedral than any castle. Demonic and angelic gargoyles decorated the exterior at almost every corner. The largest bells she had ever seen hung in the two-hundred-foot-tall bell tower. The castle had a wide moat surrounding it, certainly man-made. She had read of castles with moats but had never seen one. With a thundering boom that startled the horses, the drawbridge crashed down to the road, giving the guards access to the palace. As Isabelle's cage drew nearer, she noticed the stone of the palace was odd too. From a distance, it appeared brilliant white, but as she drew closer, the color dimmed until it was black as coal.

The main door opened, and several servants spilled out and down the steps to meet the guards and relieve them of their burdens. A second cart, similar to the one carrying Isabelle, pulled up alongside. In it sat Brandol. Isabelle had not seen him since trying to escape. He looked worse. His face was thin and white, which made the purple and blue bruises on his face, neck, and arms stand out. Dried blood covered half his face and matted his hair. Isabelle was not certain he noticed her. He seemed lost and empty.

The Elite Guard in charge beckoned to the Emperor's chamberlain, who stepped gingerly over to him. It was not the same soldier with brown eyes who had convinced her to eat again. Isabelle wondered where he had gone. The soldier told the chamberlain: "Give her a bath. Not him. Then both are to be taken to the Emperor immediately."

FORTY-SEVEN
The Journeyman's Journey

Brandol's journey differed from Isabelle's in almost every way. He did not bother with yelling. He knew no one would come for him. Why should they? When James had announced the arrival of the guards near the pass, something had happened to Brandol. It was as though a firebrand had pierced his brain, and every thought was consumed in the heat save one:

Get away!

Everything after that thought deteriorated to madness during the fight. Maggie had tried to give him a skillet, which was absurd. He had no idea how to use a sword—what could he do with a skillet? He remembered hiding for a while. As he hid, his fright built and built until he thought he was going to die. When he finally realized the guards could see him underneath the carriage, he ran again, this time for the hills. He waved the writ of passage so the guards would know it was he who had tipped them off, but someone snatched it from him. When someone shouted Master Henry's name, Brandol had made the worst mistake of his life: he turned to look. Then the soldiers snagged him and wrestled him to the ground.

He tried to explain that he wasn't Henry Vestin, but his stammering and stumbling prevented him from speaking clearly. When he finally managed to say something coherent, the guard smacked him. Hard. Brandol stopped talking after that. They put him in a cage like a dog where he suffered for hours listening to Isabelle's screaming. He thought he'd claw out his ears if she didn't stop. Her cries hurt worse than the pain of the bruises and other wounds the guards had given him, and yet she went on and on and on.

"You're weak, Brandol," his family had told him ever since he could remember, "and weak people don't survive in this world."

His mother and father had been right. He was weak. When he turned seven, his father made him tag along to the market to buy cucumbers. As Brandol rode on their horse, seated behind his father, he watched with envy as other children ran and played. Brandol was never allowed to play. Three boys chased each other out of a house; Brandol thought he recognized them. Behind the boys, several puppies tumbled out, barking in high-pitched bursts. Three of them were black, two were spotted, and one was almost completely white save for its ink-dipped tail; he was also smaller than the rest and had trouble keeping up with them.

Brandol's father pointed a heavy finger at the smallest. "See that?"

Brandol nodded against his father's back so his answer would be felt. He didn't speak if he could help it. He always said the wrong thing.

"That's a runt, Brandol. Like you. Sometimes runts die because they can't fight for their mama's milk. They're too weak—unless they learn to be strong." Then his father spat a great black wad into the street near the white puppy.

Brandol nodded again, watching the puppy closely. He wondered then, as a seven-year-old boy, how long he would live as a runt. His brothers, in a family not known for producing tall men, were all much larger than he. His only sister liked to wrestle him to the ground and tickle him until he wet himself.

His secret joy had been finding different colors with which to paint pictures. He found all sorts of wildflowers that he could crush to make paint. Once his father found him painting instead of working and whacked him with the painting, then made him paint himself for everyone else to laugh at. That was the day Brandol's stammering had begun.

At age ten, Brandol's father and mother took him aside and said he would not be able to work on the family farm. "You can't pull your weight here," they said. They knew of a carpenter in a nearby town that needed an apprentice, so he was sent there. After six years, the master he worked for was ready to give up on him and send him back to the family farm, now that he'd grown even taller than his brothers. Brandol didn't want to go back. That was when Master Henry had stepped in and offered to give Brandol his first post as a journeyman.

One of the conditions Master Henry had set was that Brandol had to learn to read and write. The journeyman never thought he would—or could—learn. To his astonishment, reading and writing were nothing like speaking, and he learned quickly.

Master Henry had shown faith in Brandol. He had said Brandol's work promised to be greater than anything he had seen. "If you'd only show more confidence in your work," Master Henry told him often, "many of the problems you run into would go away."

Brandol tried to be confident. His work did improve under Henry's hand, but then he got caught up in Master Henry's problems and lost faith in him.

The soldiers. The play. Ruther's blunder at the Friendly Fenley. Then they'd almost died in that blizzard in the forest. It was Master Henry's fault for listening to Ruther. Brandol knew it; so did everyone else. Yet, despite all the other small missteps, the turning point for Brandol had been hearing about the ghosts awaiting them at the Iron Pass. After that, the idea cemented itself in his mind that he if did not start looking out for himself, he would die with the group, either before they reached the pass or inside it. The same night that Wilson had told them about the Iron Pass, he'd heard Ruther leave the house and return without anyone knowing. So the next night, Brandol crept out to the carriage and hid the writ of passage in the deepest pocket of his traveling cloak. He thought that by hiding that important slip of paper, he would be able to seize an opportunity to sneak away from the group and use it to reestablish himself somewhere else.

He was wrong.

He had never been so terrified as when they went into Bookerton. Even keeping watch away from the danger had been bad enough. As soon as he alerted James to Master Henry's call, he knew he had to act. Doubling back into town, he sent a letter to whoever was in charge of the local military. It was a stupid thing to do, driven by his panic that they'd never reach the border without being caught. It forced him to make his boldest move.

He needed gold if he was going to start over. His friends had already bought all the supplies they needed to reach Pappalon. They would be safe. All Brandol needed was the opportunity, which Ruther again provided. When Ruther asked if they could switch their night watches, Brandol knew he intended to sneak out. His hands shook badly as he hefted all those bags of gold to the next hill and hid them in the bushes.

When it became clear they were going to reach the pass, Brandol's mistakes weighed on him like a stout beam across his shoulders. He wanted to tell Master Henry where to find the gold, but he feared what James would do to him. Perhaps he could run away? No, if he disappeared, James would hunt him down. So Brandol kept quiet and prayed his letter had been delivered too late.

It hadn't, of course. And because of that, he had endured three weeks of pain. The guards seemed to delight in his torment. All he knew was pain and fear. But the agony had purged some of the ugliness he felt inside at his actions. He deserved to hear Isabelle's screams. He accepted it all because he was a runt that was too weak to survive. Misery and pain kept his mind intact. Focusing on them barricaded his thoughts from what horrors awaited him in Neverak.

Twice he tried to tell the guards he wasn't Henry Vestin, but they abused him even more when he tried to speak. As they beat him, they called him a coward, and weak. To his mind, it was the same as *runt*.

He slept as much as he could. Between his injuries, the cold, and receiving so little to eat, he did not have the strength to stay awake for more than eight or nine fitful hours a day. His greatest surprise came when someone banged into his cage. He sat up only to see Isabelle staring at him. It took him a while to recognize her; she was so thin and filthy. Her eyes revealed so many emotions: relief that Henry wasn't in the cage, anger at Brandol's betrayal, fear, pain. Last, he saw sympathy in her eyes. Even after all he had done, she had sympathy for him, for Brandol the runt. He liked Isabelle. She had been very kind to him when they'd ridden together in the carriage.

"Oh, Lord Almighty," he cried out that night, "please fix this. I didn't understand. Please fix this."

If someone out there heard him, he didn't know. He'd never had a reason to believe in the Lord of All Worlds. Up until two years ago, no one but Master Henry had shown him kindness. Even the apprentices had teased him when Master Henry wasn't around. Yet Brandol had repaid Henry in the worst way possible. He spent many waking moments repeating this prayer. His first master had called it the Stupid Carpenter's Prayer: *please fix this for me*. It was all he could think to say.

One day, the guards allowed Brandol a short walk in the early morning, while it was still bitter cold. Though he had not kept count, he guessed it had been six or seven days since he'd last been let out of the cage. Isabelle was not in sight. They had never been let out at the same time.

The guards had chosen to stop at a group of stables where fresh horses waited to be harnessed. He tried to enjoy the sounds of animals and the feel of wind on his face, not knowing if he would ever experience these things again. The scent of hay and pine was strong.

It reminded him of working in Master Henry's shop, and those memories were good and worth clinging to. He heard a bark and saw a dog poking around one of the stables, sniffing around for mice. The dog had an all-white coat and an ink-dipped tail, but it was no runt. It had grown into a handsome beast with strong muscles. Perhaps the guards used it as a hunting dog. Brandol didn't know. He wondered if it were even real.

"See that?" he heard his father say to him again. "That's you, Brandol. A runt. Sometimes runts die because they can't fight for mama's milk. They're too weak, unless they learn to be strong."

Brandol hardly moved at all during that short walk. He watched the dog. The runt had grown to be mighty.

"What are you looking at?" a guard asked him, with a hard knock on the neck. The dog looked up at the soldier's voice, tilting his head and staring at them curiously. Brandol shook his head and let himself be taken back to the cage.

"Please, Lord of All Worlds, help me fix this," he pleaded as soon as the carriage doors shut him into darkness. "Help me find a way to fix this mess." And for the first time in a long time, Brandol smiled.

Strong winds blew fiercely cold around Neverak Palace. Brandol shivered as they brought his cage out of the carriage by means of the long poles. They dropped him haphazardly on the back of a cart and drove him across the moat. As they pulled into the courtyard, he saw Isabelle in a nearby cart, watching him with concern. He knew he must look terrible, because so did she. He didn't know of any part of his body that did not hurt.

He tried not to stare at the palace as his cage was carried off the cart and inside the great black doors. Its grandeur would only intimidate him, and he refused to be scared ever again. He saw torches and fireplaces almost everywhere, warming the air inside the palace walls. At the first fork, Isabelle's cage went left, and servants carried Brandol's straight ahead.

Again he tried not to think of what was to happen to him. The possibilities were so endless and he had no way to guess. He observed the portraits and art hanging on the walls. Many of them were former emperors and empresses, he supposed. Some were bright and lively, others much less so. After innumerable twists and turns, they stopped outside two massive wood and iron doors. As Brandol waited, he tried to hold the fragmented pieces of his sanity together by praying fervently. Finally the guards took him inside.

He had no doubt the throne room's grandeur was designed to intimidate visitors. Brandol thought it worked well. Everything was larger than life. Giant golden statues of past emperors lined walls that reached to the sky, ending in a brilliant white and gold ceiling. Plush black and red carpet led from the door to the throne.

With each step the servants took, Brandol could better see the Emperor sitting on his massive throne, adorned with so much gold and so many jewels that it was grander than anything else in the magnificently decorated room. The Emperor wore thick red and black garments, but he did not seem so unpleasant. The Emperor was a younger man, older certainly than James and Master Henry, but not by more than ten years, Brandol guessed. He smiled at Brandol as his cage drew near.

The Emperor stood as his servants put Brandol's cage down with more care than he'd been shown in weeks. Emperor Krallick held out his fingers to the nearest servant and was given black gloves, which he deftly pulled over his hands. Then he received from the same servant a handkerchief. Even at a distance, Brandol could smell the flowered scent of the white cloth. The Emperor held it to his nose as he approached.

"I promised you, didn't I?" he asked in a voice so serene that Brandol could not imagine the Emperor ever yelling.

Now was the moment Brandol had prepared himself for since

seeing the dog. Of all the things Ruther had taught him, one had stuck in Brandol's mind: "Never stop performing."

"You did," Brandol said. To his surprise, he did not stammer at all. He tried to make his voice strong like Master Henry's, but his body was so weak that his voice croaked.

"Why did you run?" the Emperor asked as if he truly did not know the answer. "You wasted other people's lives. Your sister, the guardsman, even your journeyman—they will all be caught and killed in time. Do you see your folly?"

Brandol said nothing.

"Of course you do, but you won't admit it. I understand this." The Emperor of Neverak seemed very genuine. He stepped closer to Brandol, clamping the handkerchief tightly over his nostrils. "Between the two of us, Carpenter, my respect for you has grown through all of this. Ultimately, you have done me a great favor."

Still uncertain how to respond, Brandol lowered his head. The Emperor watched him, and with every step closer he took, he pressed the handkerchief deeper into his nostrils.

"You talk so little. This wasn't so at the inn. Why the change?"

"I have nothing more to say." Brandol steeled his nerves, trying to be Master Henry in every possible way. He could not stop the trembling completely, but he did his best.

"Not yet, of course." The Emperor's voice sounded as soft as silk.

Brandol closed his eyes and asked the Lord of All Worlds again for help. He heard the echoes of footsteps approaching the hall from the same entrance the guards carrying him had used.

"Not yet," Emperor Krallick repeated. "At one time I swore to do terrible things to you, Carpenter, but I no longer feel that's needed."

"Why?" Brandol whispered.

"I realized that I would have done the same as you if our positions were reversed, and I now believe that I swore my oath in a vain temper. Even I make follies."

More servants came down the carpet carrying Isabelle to the throne. She had been quickly bathed, dressed in a robe, and placed in a new cage with new poles to support it. She looked healthy and clean.

"My dearest Isabelle," Emperor Krallick said with great delight. He walked to her cage, put his gloved hand through the bars, and took her hand in his. Isabelle withdrew back into her cage. The Emperor looked upon her with compassion. "All things in time, of course. The Carpenter and I were chatting while we awaited your arrival."

Brandol imagined that if he were Master Henry, he would be anxious at the sight of the woman he loved. He pushed his head into the bars of his cage. "Isabelle," he said in his hoarse voice, "I'm sorry. I'm so sorry!" He wanted to make certain she understood what he tried to do. "Please . . . forgive me."

The Emperor left Isabelle's cage and returned to Brandol's. "For what have you to apologize? You made the greatest sacrifice anyone can make for another person. You have no need to ask for forgiveness."

He ordered one of his servants to unlock Brandol's cage.

"Now we will see how you choose to die, Carpenter. Like a man or like a dog."

Brandol's trembling began again, and, for a moment, he thought he would not be able to stop himself from spilling out the truth and pleading for his life. Tears fell from his eyes. His chest heaved in great gasps. The cage opened and he stepped out. When he did so, the Emperor gave him a strange look—a suspicious look.

Brandol's heart froze. He had failed. Something had given him away. He shuffled on his bare feet, which the Emperor glanced at next. "For a moment, I was concerned," Emperor Krallick said. "You were taller in the inn, but, of course, you are now barefoot."

A servant entered the hall carrying the most beautiful sword

Brandol had ever seen. While he did not feel it an honor to perish by the blade, he stared at it with an odd fascination.

"This will be the means of your death in a few moments, Carpenter. Not many people know how they will die. Do you think it makes you fortunate or unfortunate?"

"Unfortunate," Brandol answered.

"Why?"

"Because of the future you take away from me and the woman I love." He looked in Isabelle's direction as he finished his sentence, but in his mind, he thanked the Lord he had said all those words without stammering or sounding like an imbecile.

"I take away nothing which is not mine."

Isabelle began to weep again. Brandol turned toward her. "She will always be mine."

"We shall see. You have done me a grand favor, Carpenter. One I wish to repay you for, in a way which I am able. Have you a request?"

Brandol's heart beat so rapidly he thought it might burst. This would be the one place to either seal in the Emperor's mind that he was Henry Vestin or bring it all to ruin. What would Master Henry ask for? "Please, Lord Almighty," he asked silently for the last time, "help me fix my mistakes."

He cleared his throat as best he could, but the words still came out with great effort. "A kiss."

The Emperor examined Brandol with great interest again, but Brandol did not sense any suspicion. Isabelle continued to cry in her cage, but the hall was quiet. A smile appeared on the Emperor's lips. "Yes, of course. That is appropriate. My servants will dismiss themselves now."

As the Emperor's command was obeyed, Brandol walked to Isabelle's cage awkwardly. He didn't know how she would react. He had never kissed a girl. Perhaps his mother had given him kisses when he was a baby, but he did not remember. He knelt on the floor, as tenderly as Master Henry would have done if he had been there. He placed his hand in the cage. Isabelle took it.

"I love you," he managed to say despite his weak voice. And in his heart, he felt real love for her.

"I love you, Henry. Thank you. Thank you for everything." They held hands for many seconds, and Brandol wept because he had never had a chance to experience something so wonderful as the love between Henry and Isabelle. He wept because he had never known the joy of someone touching him with such tenderness. And he wept when she pressed her lips firmly against his, grateful that he had been allowed one such moment in his life, when he saw who he was and liked what he saw.

"Thank you," she whispered again, holding his hands tightly in her own.

Her eyes locked with his, and Brandol knew she forgave him. He stood up on his own accord, like a man, and walked back to the Emperor. His knees hit the floor, and he bowed his head. The weariness and pain in his body was gone. He had been renewed.

"I do not kill you out of hate, Carpenter—you are a brave man. As such, were I to let you live, you would never rest until either I died or you had your love back safely. Isabelle is rightfully mine, and so I must protect what belongs to me."

The Emperor of Neverak and Brandol surveyed each other. As the Emperor watched him, he rubbed the scar on his neck where the blade of Henry's own sword had been pressed against him.

"You die well, Henry Vestin. You die well."

He raised his sword.

Brandol's lips pressed tightly together and whispered reverently, "Thank you, Lord, for helping me fix this." Then every color dissolved as the entire world transformed into something pure and beautifully white.

Epilogue

The sword came down and Brandol the journeyman perished under its weight. Isabelle cried out the name of her love, and her heart experienced real pain. The tears that fell were no less real than if Henry had died in front of her.

The Emperor cleaned the blade of the sword with his handkerchief and placed it back in its sheath. As he removed his gloves and dropped them with the handkerchief, his focus stayed on Isabelle. "For him, it is finished, but your new life begins today, and your cleansing begins now."

· · ·

Silence reigned when the old man stopped speaking. His voice had grown tired, and yet I had never heard a storyteller with such an ability to captivate an audience. Listening had been as natural as breathing, and my imprisonment had been a joy. The comfortable silence was broken as the crowd slowly realized that he had ended the story for the day. Whispers came first, as no one wanted to break the enchantment that had fallen over us. Even I, writing as furiously as I had, could not mistake the power in his ability to weave the tale.

Someone dared to raise his voice: "Keep going!"

Several others lifted their voices in agreement, though less rudely. The old man did not respond; instead, he stood and picked up his walking stick and supported himself on it, no longer using it lightly as he had when he arrived at the inn. The owner took the stage while the old man stepped away and slipped unobtrusively into the crowd.

"Now hear me, folks!" the owner said. "Hear me! The story is over, but it's going to pick up again tomorrow night. Come early for drinks and dinner to make certain you're not late."

"Why can't we have it now?" one asked. "I want to know—"

"Because I can't stand to have you in my tavern for that long."

A roaring of laughter accompanied the owner's comment, and that seemed to do the trick. Without further argument, dozens of bodies turned for the door and the joust began to see who could get out fastest.

I tried to keep my eye on the old man as he made his way through the throng; I wanted to speak to him—thank him—for the employment, but the sea of people made it impossible. His cloak looked like so many others. I could not give chase with my stacks of papers and ink bottles cluttering the table. I hastily gathered my things, looking up every few seconds to try and spot him through the masses. By the time I'd jostled my way through a sea of large and small bodies, he had disappeared.

Two quarter moons smiled down in the clear sky when I stepped out of the inn. When my feet touched the street, I turned all around, even jumping in place for a hint as to where he'd gone. I heard nothing, not even a tap of his stick. The old man had left as strangely as he'd arrived. Perhaps his enchantments extended beyond his ability to put an audience in a trance. My questions—pressing questions that only he could answer—would have to wait. I sighed in place as more patrons brushed past me, chattering about what was to come. They too would have to wait until tomorrow night. And if I wanted a good seat, I would have to arrive early.

Acknowledgments

I wrote this book in my first year of dental school. In fact, it almost got me kicked out because I was too busy writing instead of studying. That's when I learned that "the urge" is something a writer can't ignore. It's stronger than my potato chip addiction, stronger than my desire to play video games, and stronger than my need for sleep. In the end, that's how I did both dental school and writing. (Less sleep, not less chips—unfortunately.)

After *Psion Beta* and *Psion Gamma,* I started a few other projects, things I might someday get back to. I had an idea for a book about a dentist-turned-assassin, one about modern gladiator games, and another that's a sort of fantasy novel. But *Tale* is special. It's the first book idea I ever had, planted way back when I was eighteen and working for Feature Films for Families, selling movies over the phone. (For shame, I know!) Plotting out book details kept me going. I never thought I'd actually write the novel. And I didn't do it alone; I had lots of help and advice along the way. After all, this was only my third book.

I want to thank Raleigh Jones, Braden Atkins, Lewis and Natalie Gunther, Nancy Block, my father, my mother-in-law, and anyone else I may have forgotten for reading and offering criticism, praise, and enthusiasm. I owe great thanks to my workshoppers, who had lots of helpful criticisms and ideas: John Wilson, Britta Peterson, Dan Hill,

Natasha Watson, Kellie Buckner, Jana Jensen, Alyssa Harnagel, and Benjamin Van Tassell.

I also owe thanks to Britta Peterson, Adam Morris, Shannon Wilkinson, and Caity Jones for their early help. Thanks to their hard work and assistance, I was able to attract the attention of Shadow Mountain Publishing and receive my first book deal. For that deal, I'd like to thank Heidi Taylor, Chris Schoebinger, and especially Nada Midkiff, who pushed my book to them in the first place. Along with them, I owe many thanks to Brandon Dorman for a terrific cover and to Derk Koldewyn for his stellar editing.

In the end, this is a book about two things: love and adventure. And so I have three more people I want to specially thank. First are the father and mother of my ex-fiancée, who inspired one of the villains in this novel. Thank you, R. and K., for breaking us apart with your abnormal cruelty so I could meet the woman who discovered with me everything I know about love and adventure: my wife, Kat. After almost nine years of marriage, our relationship seems to get better and better.